Operation Pegasus
By

Robert Cubitt

Carter's Commandos – Book 7

© 2021

Having purchased this eBook from Amazon, it is for your personal use only. It may not be copied, reproduced, printed or used in any way, other than in its intended Kindle format.

Published by Selfishgenie Publishing of, Northamptonshire, England.

This novel is entirely a work of fiction. All the names characters, incidents, dialogue, events portrayed and opinions expressed in it are either purely the product of the author's imagination or they are used entirely fictitiously and not to be construed as real. Any resemblance to actual persons, living or dead, events or localities is entirely coincidental. Nothing is intended or should be interpreted as representing or expressing the views and policies of any department or agency of any government or other body.

All trademarks used are the property of their respective owners. All trademarks are recognised.

The right of Robert Cubitt to be identified as the author of this work has been asserted in accordance with sections 77 and 78 of the Copyright Designs and Patents Act 1988.

In memory of all the Commandos of World War II
and in memory of one commando in particular. The truth of what they did is often stranger than any fiction that can be written.

Contents

Foreword	9
1 - Back in Training	15
2 - D-Day	55
3 - The Merville Battery	107
4 - 84 Days	133
5 - Operation Blackcock	181
6 - Operation Widgeon	211
7 - From the Aller To The Baltic	237
Epilogue	279
Historical Notes	285
A Brief Account of the World War II Commandos	301
Further Reading	313
And Now	315

FOREWORD

I haven't included a Foreword in any of the previous Carter's Commandos novels, but I thought it necessary for this one.

The story of Operation Overlord, otherwise known as D-Day, is a familiar one, probably the most familiar of the War. This is not that story.

The reason for that is because 156,000 men landed on the beaches on D-Day and many thousands more arrived in the days that followed. Each of those men (and a few women) had a story of their own to tell and it is the stories of individuals, rather than of vast armies, that are the most interesting. D-Day may form the backdrop for the beginning of this book, but it goes on to cover far more.

The story moves on to the aftermath of D-Day. To watch documentaries on TV it would be easy to believe that D-Day was the end of the war. It may have been the beginning of the end, but the end took a long time to arrive. The war in Europe continued for another 336 days (a year all but 29 days) and far more men died during that period than died on D-Day itself. About 4,400 Allied soldiers, sailors and airmen died on D-Day, but 19,000 died during the Battle of the Bulge, five months later. And that was just one battle out of many.

The Germans didn't just give up and go home after D-Day, they fought for every inch of ground and they fought with tenacity and bravery. While we British may see this as a fight to defeat the Nazi scourge, for the average German soldier it was a fight to defend their homeland and we should not damn them for that. They fought on despite Hitler, not because of him. Yes, there were Nazi fanatics who fought on because of a belief in their cause, but by that stage of the war they were no longer the majority.

This book starts well before D-Day and continues to the end of the European war. It is told using some of the real-life stories of the men of 3 Commando, which I have taken and given my own treatment in order to provide a readable (I hope) drama based around my fictitious 15 Commando.

The British campaign to end the war in Europe can be broken down into three phases. Phase 1 was D-Day and the building of the beachhead that launched the phases that were to follow. Phase 2 was the breakout from the beachhead and the advance through France and Belgium, which came to an untimely end with the ill-fated Operation Market-Garden, the attempt to capture Arnhem bridge (a joint operation with American and Free Polish paratroops). That was compounded by the Battle of the Bulge, which was Hitler's last throw of the dice in the west. It was aimed at splitting the Americans from the British in Belgium and surrounding the British. The final phase was the ultimate crossing of the River Rhein and the advance through northern Germany until the Allies reached the Baltic Sea.

Note that in the previous paragraph I said 'the British campaign'. The Americans were doing their own thing, so to speak, through Southern Germany, aided by the Free French (Actually, by that time they should really be referred to just as 'the French'). The objective of the Americans wasn't the Baltic, it was Berlin. And, of course, we must also not ignore the part played in all this by the Russians who were advancing from the east.

Many engagements were fought during those three phases and I couldn't possibly cover them all in a single novel, so I'm not going to attempt it. But it is worth remembering that while I may concentrate on the activities of one army unit, there was a lot of fierce fighting going on elsewhere. I will make reference to it where it is relevant to the plot of this book, but my not referring to it doesn't mean that it was insignificant or unworthy of mention. Someone has to be the centre of attention in a novel and in the case of this novel, it is Carter.

There is a quote (I can't find a reliable citation for the originator) that says that war is 99% boredom punctuated by 1% sheer terror. I think I can safely assume that my readers aren't interested in the boredom part, so I have had to help the 1% of sheer terror along with some stories that are fictional or which took place elsewhere and which I have borrowed for this book. The Historical Notes at the end of the book separate fact from fiction. As always with stories about the commandos, some of the fact is more unbelievable than the fiction.

But much of the action takes place in locations other than Normandy and tells the stories that are little known, but without which the war could not have been won, or which would have delayed the winning of the war.

This book also tells a few stories that are oddities, such as the Roman Catholic padre who persuaded two German soldiers to surrender when he himself was their prisoner. Or perhaps you would be more interested in the fact that the commandos found themselves in the beer brewing business for a few days. I would be quite surprised if any reader, other than those with a connection to the commandos, have heard either story before.

I have no doubt that there are thousands, perhaps hundreds of thousands, of undiscovered stories such as these. I can only give you a taster within these covers, but it's more than you will get from your average TV documentary about D-Day.

Author's Note On The Language Used In This Book

This is a story about soldiers and to maintain authenticity the language used reflects that. There is a use of swear words of the strongest kind. It is not my intention to cause offence, but only to reflect the language that was and still is used by soldiers. Apart from the swearing there is other language used that may cause offence. I don't condone the use of that language, but it reflects the period in which the story is set. While we may live in more enlightened times and would never consider using such words, the 1940s were different and the language used is contemporary for the period. We cannot change the past, we can only change the present and the future and I'm glad that our language has changed and become more sensitive to the feelings of others, but we must never forget our past. We should, however, seek not to repeat it.

Abbreviations of rank used in this book (in descending order of seniority):

Army Ranks

Lt Col – Lieutenant Colonel (often referred to simply as Colonel by their own subordinates)
Maj – Major
Capt – Captain
Lt – Lieutenant
2Lt – Second Lieutenant
RSM – Regimental Sergeant Major (Warrant Office Class 1)
CSM – Company Sergeant major (Warrant Officer Class 2)
TSM – Troop Sergeant Major (Warrant Officer Class 2) as used by the commandos.
SMjr – Sergeant Major (generic)
CSgt – Colour Sergeant

SSgt – Staff Sergeant
Sgt - Sergeant
LSgt – Lance Sergeant; a Brigade of Guards rank, but sometimes used by the commandos instead of Corporal.
Cpl – Corporal
LCpl – Lance Corporal
Pvt – Private
Tpr – Trooper, a cavalry rank equivalent to Private but used by the commandos.

Cdo – the abbreviation used when naming a specific commando, eg 15 Cdo.

Royal Navy ranks

Lt Cdr – Lieutenant Commander, equivalent to a Major.
Lt – Lieutenant, equivalent to its Army counterpart
SLt – Sub Lieutenant – equivalent to a Second Lieutenant in the Army.
CPO – Chief Petty Officer – equivalent to Warrant Officer Second Class in the Army.

Other military terminology is explained within the text where the narrative allows, or is explained in footnotes.

1 – Back in Training

A flurry of snow greeted Carter as he left the shelter of the station's main entrance. Not serious snow; not the sort of snow he had seen recently in the Scottish Highlands, but enough to let the good citizens of Worthing know that they were still in the grip of winter.

The front of the town's station was busy with troops as they exited the building. NCO's shouted at soldiers, soldiers shouted to friends and lorries tooted to try and clear a path through the milling crowds of men that had just arrived off of trains. Soldiers clambered onto the backs of trucks while others were chivvied into ranks in readiness to march to closer destinations.

To one side Carter could see a Sergeant with a 15 Cdo flash on his shoulder, organising men into three ranks. They looked different from the other troops; were they more upright, more confident, more ready? Whatever it was, they were noticeable. Or was that just his imagination?

Carter wasn't going to interrupt the NCO's activities. He didn't need an officer interfering. Instead, he hefted his kitbag onto his shoulder and followed two other officers along the station's frontage to where a single taxi stood.

He had seen them on the train, so young they looked like they had borrowed their big brothers' uniforms. But officer candidates for the commandos were harder to come by these days, as were volunteers from the other ranks. It wasn't as if there was a shortage of men adventurous enough to apply, it was commanding officers discouraging them. It was easier to go into the recruit depots, the Young Soldiers battalions and officer training units and recruit them there, before the doors were slammed shut.

But it carried a penalty in a lack of experience. It was always better for a commando to have heard the sound of weapons fired in anger before he joined, so everyone would know he wouldn't funk[1] it the next time he heard the sound.

Carter's rail journey from Scotland was the one that most commandos would take when they left the training depot at Achnacarry to join their new units, at least until they got to the southern part of the country and had to diverge towards the various towns where the commandos were located. He had spotted these two at Glasgow Central Station and managed to avoid getting into the same carriage. If he wanted a peaceful journey and a couple of hours of sleep, it was best not to travel with hero worshipping subalterns who wanted to know how it felt to be in combat, or to hear the stories of how he had won his medals.

So Carter had slunk off to another carriage. He hadn't had a peaceful journey, however. The neighbouring compartment had been occupied by American officers who had just discovered the joys of Scotch whisky and had brought plenty of the product along with them for the journey.

But now, with only one taxi available, he would need to introduce himself.

"Joining 15Cdo?" he called at their backs. He knew they were, they couldn't be joining any other commando, not in Worthing. But it was a conversation starter.

They stopped and turned, spotted the crowns on his epaulettes and snapped to attention. Their hands were occupied by their luggage, as were Carter's, so they were unable to salute.

"Yes Sir!" One said crisply.

"Perhaps we should share this cab." He made it sound like a suggestion rather than an order.

"Of course, Sir." The other replied. "Our Pleasure." It probably was. As a Major, Carter was more likely to pay the fare.

Carter dropped his luggage and offered his hand. The two officers also dropped their luggage but threw up salutes before accepting the courtesy.

"Carter, 2IC."

"Holdsworth." The first replied."

"Marchant, Sir." The second added.

"Ah, yes. I was up at Achnacarry a couple of weeks ago and Col Vaughan[2] mentioned your names."

"Did he Sir?" Holdsworth blushed pink at the honour of being singled out. In fact, it had been Carter's mission, given to him by his CO Charlie Cousens, to interrupt his leave and travel to Achnacarry to identify likely candidates for the commando. He could have left the job to the Combined Operations staff officer responsible for personnel, but Cousens didn't like to leave things to chance. If he could give the man a list of names of men he wanted, there was a much better chance that he'd get the pick of the men that were available. Although it wasn't an approved practice, it had worked in the past and Carter could see that it had worked again on this occasion.

"Oh yes. Colonel Vaughan was most complementary about you. That's a big reputation to have to live up to though, so don't let the Colonel down by proving him wrong." Carter chuckled.

"We won't Sir."

"Good. Now, let's grab this taxi before another train arrives and some bloody Yank nicks it." Americans were always more popular passengers for taxi drivers because they could be persuaded to pay in dollars, which were more easily exchangeable for black market goods which had originated on American bases. The dollars would find their way back there and into the pockets of GI[3]s who would send them around the circuit again by buying things in their PX[4] to sell to the black marketeers.

The journey to the barracks took only a few minutes. It was late in the evening and there were few people around. At the main gate a commando sentry threw up a brisk salute after checking their identity documents, then directed them to the Officers' Mess

An aged civilian employee was roused from his doze behind the reception desk and handed them the keys to their rooms. Carter persuaded him to seek out some tea and sandwiches from the kitchens. A hubbub of noise came from the bar, but Carter wasn't yet ready to face his colleagues. After a journey that had lasted over twelve hours, but had felt like it was three times as long, he needed some sleep before he was ready to socialise. He would face his friends and colleagues best over breakfast, before he located his new office and set about getting the commando organised.

His leave hadn't been a great success. The tension between himself and his wife that had been present before his departure for Gibraltar, fifteen months earlier, was back. The freshly healed scar on his upper arm, a souvenir from the fighting at Termoli, hadn't helped to ease the tension.

While Carter had dismissed the scar as a mere scratch, Fiona had used the span of her hands to measure the distance to his heart. She had said nothing, but the fearful expression she had tried to hide spoke volumes.

"But it, missed. That's the important thing." He had tried to make light of it.

"It missed this time." She replied, turning over in bed so that her back was towards him. Later, in the darkness, he felt her body vibrating as she sobbed.

He had enjoyed seeing his twins, a boy and a girl, bouncing them on his knees until they got sick and then taking delight at changing their clothes. He even volunteered to change their nappies, a task that seemed to increase in frequency every day.

Seeing Carter so clearly enjoying being a father had been one of the few things that had brought a smile to Fiona's face. Cousens' request that he travel to Achnacarry and make forays into the Scottish garrisons to try to find new recruits, had caused an argument between them.

"You're supposed to be on leave!" Fiona had snapped. "Why can't they leave you alone for just a few weeks?"

"It goes with the territory, Darling. I'm not a junior officer anymore. I have responsibilities." Carter had tried to placate her. "We lost a lot of men in the Med and they have to be replaced. The CO just wants to make sure we get the best men available." On the morning he had left to take the train north, she had turned her back in a silence frostier than the ground beneath his feet.

At the garrisons and barracks his reception had been even colder than at home. Commanding officers were fed up losing their best men to the commandos. The only place he was made welcome was at the recruit training depots. They were sausage machines, taking in civilians and churning out soldiers with the basic skills necessary to keep themselves alive while fighting the enemy. Where their charges went after they left the depots was of little interest to the commandants, so it might as well be to the commandos as anyone.

At Achnacarry it had been different. Vaughan had welcomed him home like a long-lost son and had wined and dined him, while pumping him for news about his experiences and the welfare of other former students. He was also keen to find out what alterations to the training might be made to help improve the commandos' performance.

"To tell you the truth," Carter had replied, "most of what you teach is good. What is sometimes a problem is whether a soldier really has what it takes to be a commando in the first place. Up here you can weed out the weaklings and those without the drive and determination that is needed. But until they've heard bullets fired, we can't know if they're going to fight or flee. Nowadays so few of the volunteers have experienced real combat."

"Is it much of a problem?" Vaughan had asked.

"Not a major one. At least, not so far. But we had an officer recently who let us down a bit. It was when we were cut off behind enemy lines …."

"The River Gabriel operation." Vaughan had interrupted.

"You've heard the story?"

"Some of it. I'd like to hear more if you have the time to tell it. You had to disperse and make your own way back to the Allied lines, if what we've heard is correct."

"It is. Well, the CO … he was still the 2IC then … rounded up a few of the men and was set on ambushing German traffic on the road from the bridge. One of the junior officers, I won't name him as he's not here to defend himself, wasn't keen on the idea at all. He just wanted to get back to the Allied lines as quickly as possible.[5] The

CO wasn't best pleased with the example he was setting. He didn't think he was being aggressive enough."

"I can imagine that. Charlie Cousens always was a bit of a fire brand if I recall correctly. So, what do you think we should be doing here at Achnacarry?"

"I'm not sure what can be done. I don't think there is a way to test a man's bravery in battle. Up here you make things as real as they can be, but at the back of the mind we always knew that you weren't really trying to kill us. Unlike the enemy, who are always trying to kill us. It is that final step that is the one some men can't make."

"Perhaps there is a way of helping. I was at a meeting at the War Office recently and over lunch there was some discussion about selection procedures for officers. It seems that some of the boffins, psychiatrists or whatever, think that they can devise tests that will assess genuine leadership potential. As you know, at present if a man comes from the right family or went to the right school, he can pretty much walk in as an officer. But, as we know, some of them aren't that great and some of the men who get promoted from the ranks do just as well, if not better."

Carter knew that Vaughan had risen from the ranks, whereas he himself had just come from the right family and done well at school. But the point was valid. There was good and bad in both systems of selection.

"Well, anything that can be done to weed out any weak links before they get to the commando would be welcomed."

"I'll look into that a bit more. There may be something we can do.[6] What happened to the officer that earned Charlie Cousens' disapproval."

"Charlie, sorry, the CO, made sure he was posted out. I think he's counting paperclips at a supply depot in Cairo now. He's still nominally a commando, but those in the know will make sure he never gets into the front line in a commando unit again." Carter knew it was probably worse than that for the man. Once he'd been given the mark of Cain from a commando unit, it was unlikely he'd ever be promoted again.

As before, Fiona had thawed a little by the time Carter's leave came to an end, but she would never be happy while he was a commando and he would never be happy being anything else. At least, not while the war was still going on. He hoped, for the sake of his marriage, that it would be over soon.

[1] In 1944 the word 'funk', as in 'to be in a funk' meant to be frightened. To be extremely frightened would be 'to be in a blue funk'. It started out in the 14th century as a German word, *fonke*, meaning spark, migrated somehow to mean ill-humour or depression and from that it appeared in Scotland and Northern Ireland in the 1740s as a term meaning fear. How the term became associated with music isn't known, but that started in the USA, as a racial slur referring to body odour. This probably evolved from a French word meaning smoke, as applied to smoked cheese. Some American refer to food with a suspicious taste as being funky. Its musical links started to appear during the Jazz age, meaning a song that was earthy or deeply felt.

[2] When Achnacarry was established as the primary training establishment for the commandos, in March 1942, Lt Colonel Charles Vaughan was appointed as its commandant, having served in both 4 and 7 Cdos. He had risen from the enlisted ranks of the Buffs (East Kent) Regiment to reach this senior position and was something of a legend amongst the commandos. He appears in cameo form in Book 1 of this series, Operation Absolom.

[3] GI – General Issue. The description given to items of military uniform and equipment that were standard issue to all new recruits and conscripts into the US army. The term became attached to the soldiers themselves, replacing "Dough Boys", a term that went all the way back to the Continental Army of the American Revolution. That had become a nickname because pipeclay had been used to keep the white piping on soldier's uniforms pristine and when it got wet it turned into a doughy blob. The replacement of pipe clay with

specialist products (Blanco (meaning white) in the British army) made the term obsolete, to be replaced by GI.

[4] PX – Post exchange, a shop providing American soldiers with everything from chocolate bars to hi-fi equipment. They were established on most American bases and still exist today. They accept only dollars in payment and the goods are cheap because they are sold at American prices and, outside of the USA, are free of both American and local taxes. The ability of American GIs to offer British girls presents of nylon stockings, perfume and cigarettes was one of the reasons their presence was resented by British men, spawning the slur "overpaid, oversexed and over here." It was forbidden to sell products bought in the PX to the British, but the prohibition was hard to enforce, which led to a healthy black market.

[5] This a conflation of a couple of true stories. Peter Young was the 2IC at the time and his accounts can be read in his book (see "Further Reading").

[6] Selection and training procedures for both officer candidates and for special forces now contain a high level of psychological testing for suitability. It is no longer possible to become an officer just because you went to the "right" school or just because a relative had once been an officer (though it probably still helps). The author of this book came from a humble (though military) background and worked his way through the ranks to pass the selection process and become an officer.

* * *

As Carter came out of the dining room after breakfast, he bumped into the CO in full marching order.
"I didn't know there was an exercise planned for this morning." Carter said. He had planned on getting to grips with compiling a training programme for the commando.

"No one knows yet. My little surprise for the men." It was the first day that everyone from the commando was back from leave and they were usually quite relaxed affairs, as everyone sought to settle into new accommodation and establish some sort of order in the barracks.

"I'd better go and get ready then." Carter turned to leave.

"No, that's OK, Steven. I want you to concentrate on compiling the training programme. We have no idea what's in store for us yet, so concentrate on the three Fs."

If you didn't know what your mission was to be, the three Fs provided a basis for any training plan: fitness, fieldcraft and fighting skills. They were the three things the commandos always needed.

"What we do know," The CO continued, "is that whatever we are asked to do, we'll have to travel by sea to do it, so set up contacts with Combined Ops for the use of landing craft. When we go ashore, I want the men to be able to do it in their sleep. We can refine the training once we know more. I'm going to a briefing later in the week which might tell us something."

Carter doubted it. It was still only January. The invasion wouldn't take place in winter or even early Spring. Carter thought May at the earliest, with June more likely. Late enough for the weather to have improved but early enough to get a solid campaign in before the next winter set in.

That being the case, only the high-level objectives would have been settled so far. Probably the location of the landing beaches and the major objectives to be captured on the first day. The allocation of units to tasks wouldn't happen until they had all been put under the microscope to see which divisions were best prepared and ready to do whatever was needed. Competition to be part of the first wave ashore would be high. Not from the men, obviously, but from the senior officers, who would see participation as an opportunity to stake their claim for promotion.

Making sure 15 Cdo was ready for anything was Carter's job and he was determined they wouldn't be found wanting.

To hell with promotion, thought Carter, the better prepared the men are, the more likely it is that they'll survive.

* * *

The Military Police corporal handed Carter his identity documents back and pointed him in the direction he needed to go. "Through the double doors, Sir. The Brigadier is at the far end, beneath the big map."

Vernon was now formally a brigadier and in command of 5th Special Service Brigade. The commandos didn't like the name, the initials having unpleasant connotations considering their use by the Germans. Representation had been made to Combined Operations to have it changed to 'Commando Brigade', but so far without any success.

The brigadier rose to his feet and stretched out a hand to be shaken. Carter stamped to a halt, saluted and took the proffered hand. "Take a seat, make yourself comfortable." The brigadier told him. "I've ordered coffee. We get it from the Americans, so it's good quality."

Carter wondered why Vernon was rolling out the red carpet. Normally on a visit to Brigade HQ, Carter was given over sweetened tea and, if he was lucky, a couple of biscuits. He recalled Paddy O'Driscoll's observation that when the Army start being nice to you, it's time to start worrying.

"How are things going down in Worthing?" The Brigadier asked.

Small talk, Carter noted. The Brigadier knew exactly how things were going. He had visited the commando only the previous week and observed them making a beach landing followed by an assault on Arundel Castle, several miles inland. He had been quite complimentary about the exercise.

"Pretty well, Sir. We're rather hoping to undertake some opposed landings, if we can find a unit willing to act as enemy for us."

Vernon let out a laugh. "Good luck with that. They don't like your men beating them up when they come ashore."

"We'll promise to play nice." Carter grinned, still wondering what the summons to HQ was about. He knew that Charlie Cousens had already been there that day, but there was no sign of him in the Operations Room.

Around and behind him there was the muted buzz of men going about their duties. A million things needed to be done before the invasion could take place and the men in this room were just a handful of the ones that were responsible for making sure that they were completed on time. He knew many of the faces; experienced commandos who knew just what was needed to mount a successful operation. They would be cutting no corners and fighting for every scrap of equipment that the units needed to achieve their objectives, whatever they were.

On which note … "Any news on what our role is to be yet, Sir?"

"All in good time, Steven. It's still months away. The daffs have hardly started blooming yet. Ah, you're wondering why I've called you in."

"If it's not for …." Even in this room he felt unsure if he should use the word 'invasion' No one seemed to use it, just in case it was overheard. "… whatever is to come, then it must be for something else. Have you got an op for us? A raid perhaps?"

"No. We're not risking units such as yours for pinpricks in the enemy's skin. We've got other units for that, who won't be going ashore on the big day. No, I've got some other news for you. Good and bad, I'm afraid. Which do you want first?"

This wasn't the first time that Vernon had said those words to him. The last time was to hand him his Major's crowns. Was that what this was all about. Was he going to get posted and the bad news was that someone else would be getting his place in 15 Cdo?

"Bad news first, if you don't mind, Sir. Get it out of the way." He pasted an expectant smile on his face, but behind his lips his teeth were gritted.

"Charlie Cousens is being posted to my staff. In fact, he's already upstairs being briefed on his duties."

In the great scheme of things that wasn't really bad news, in Carter's opinion. He liked Charlie Cousens and so did the men. He was a good CO and to lose him would be a shame. But the worse news was probably who would replace him. A new boy coming in from outside the commando wouldn't know their style, the way they operated, the way they did things. It could be disruptive and they didn't need that right now. But Carter was expected to say something; he could see that from the expectant look on Vernon's face.

"We're going to miss him, Sir." Carter admitted, truthfully. "He's been a good CO. We thought it was hard enough when you went, but he'll be just as hard to replace. Do we know who will take over the commando?"

"We do, Steven. I had it confirmed this morning." A small smile played around Vernon's lips. Carter realised that he was playing some sort of game. Teasing him. "Come on, Steven. Haven't you guessed yet? I haven't called you up here just to tell you something that Charlie Cousens could tell you when he got back to Worthing tonight."

Carter was still at a loss. He was missing something, he knew. No, maybe not missing something. His brain was trying to avoid something. That was different.

"It's you, Steven. You're taking over command of Fifteen."

* * *

There was something not … Carter struggled to put his finger on the right word. 'Not quite right' made it sound like he was visibly at odds with the world. 'Unlikeable' suggested a snap judgment. Apart from saying 'Good morning, Sir.' The man hadn't even spoken yet.

But there was definitely something that was setting Carter's teeth on edge.

It wasn't the fact that the man was wearing his Number 2 Dress uniform, complete with Sam Brown belt and shiny leather holster for his revolver. He had come from an environment where such attire was normal. It wasn't the fact that his peaked cap still bore the red band of a staff officer, matched by the tabs on the collar of his jacket. His cap badge, for a regiment that had been founded during the English Civil War and had fought in every war since, was shining brass, as were the miniature versions on his jacket lapels, but that wasn't it either. The commandos blackened all their brass work so that it didn't shine in the dark, but again for a staff officer, shiny brass was nothing unusual. Then it hit Carter.

The left breast of his uniform jacket was devoid of medal ribbons. The man was a Major in the commandos, but Carter couldn't think of a single officer of Captain rank or higher that didn't sport a medal ribbon of some sort. The commandos attracted Military Crosses and Distinguish Service Orders the way a magnet attracted iron filings. And there were no campaign medals either. OK, he had only just received his Africa and Italy Stars, but this officer didn't even have those.

In physical appearance, the man was unremarkable: medium height, medium build, a face that was neither handsome nor ugly, but sporting the sort of thin, matinee idol moustache that Carter had always disliked. Perhaps that was what was setting his teeth on edge.

"Take a seat, Howard." Carter said, pointing to a chair in the corner of the office that his new officer could fetch for himself.

Things had moved quickly since Carter's meeting with the Brigadier the previous day. Cousens had returned from HQ in time to be the guest of honour at his own farewell party. His and that of Andrew Fraser. The Scotsman was going to HQ as well, as one of Vernon's new staff officers. Molly Brown was taking over as 15 Cdo's QM, with a promotion to go with it. Carter had just seen Cousens out of the gate, with most of the commando cheering him along, when the new man had arrived.

Opening up the posting notice, Carter read the name again. Major Howard Ramsey; posted to 15 Cdo as Second in Command with effect from that day's date.

"So, tell me about yourself. When did you join up?"

The man's face broke into a smile of pride. "The day after war was declared. My father contacted his old CO, who now commands the old man's regiment and asked if he could give me a place. He agreed, so that was that."

It would be wrong to condemn Ramsey for using that bit of influence. It would make Carter a hypocrite. His own father had done the same for him when he had volunteered for service. Not that it had done him any favours. He and his CO had never got on and the need to escape was one of the things that had prompted Carter to volunteer for the commandos.

"By the time I'd finished OCTU[1,] the 1st Battalion was already in France with the expeditionary force, so I was posted to the 3rd Battalion, who were TA. When it looked like Italy was going to enter the war we were sent to Egypt. I'm afraid I was getting a bit bored out there, so when a signal came around asking for volunteers for special duties, unspecified, I threw my hat into the ring. Next thing I know I'm back in Blighty as a junior officer in 1 Cdo."

Carter did some quick mental arithmetic. Italy had entered the war on the Axis side[2] at around the same time as the Dunkirk evacuation and fighting started in Libya and Egypt only days later. But the commandos hadn't started to form until later in the month. Which meant ... What precisely? Had Ramsey volunteered in order to avoid the fighting in Libya or Abyssinia[3], which was a worrying thought, or had he heard that there was more adventure to be had by volunteering? 1 Cdo had formed on 13th June by merging two existing units, so the recruiting signals must have gone out after that. Something to think about, at least.

"As you know," Ramsey continued, unaware of the thoughts racing through Carter's brain. "No 1 was disbanded[4] a few weeks later so I found myself on the train to Manchester to join No 2 instead, to be told I was going to train to be a parachutist. That was fine, but before I got to do my first jump, I was sent up to Inveraray. They'd just started to undertake formalised commando training there. That was before Achnacarry opened, of course. So I stayed there for a while, then I was posted to Northern Ireland as a Troop

Commander with 19 Cdo. I stayed with them for a bit, then went to Combined Ops as a junior staff officer, then to the War Office as a specialist advisor on commando operations. That's where I was when I was told I was being promoted and posted here."

Forcing his jaw to stay shut when all it wanted to do was drop open, Carter realised that although Ramsey had been a commando for almost four years, he had probably never actually seen combat.

"Just out of curiosity, what did you do before the war?" Carter kept his tone light, trying not to betray his suspicions.

"I was an accountant, studying for my Charter examinations."

The penny dropped. Probably a good administrator, so when those skills were needed, he was the right man for the job. Being a good administrator would help him as Carter's 2IC, that was for sure. But when they went ashore in France, assuming it wasn't Belgium instead as some rumours suggested, Carter would need fighting men and leaders, not pen pushers.

"What raids did you go on?" Carter suspected he knew the answer but had to give the man the benefit of the doubt.

"None actually, Sir." His face fell into a frown, realising this exposed his lack of combat experience. "When I was in Northern Ireland we were supposed to go on a raid into Norway. We got as far as the Shetland Isles when our landing ship developed engine trouble, so the Op was cancelled. Then when I was in London, at the War Office, I was supposed to go on a raid to France with 18 Cdo. I came down to the coast and did all the training and everything. On the day before the Op I popped back to London for the afternoon and on the way back my train got held up by an unexploded Jerry bomb next to the railway line. By the time I got back to the docks the landing ship had set off. It was the damnedest bad luck."

But he shouldn't have been in London the afternoon before an Op anyway. Carter knew that and Ramsey should have as well. "What did you go to London for?" Again, the tone was light.

A smile, almost a leer, spread across Ramsey's face. "I went to see a girl. A right corker. The ladies love a commando and, for a change, I was wearing my green beret. She practically fell into my arms."

So, Ramsey had put his sex life before his duty, had he? Carter started to appreciate that his instincts had been warning him about this man since the moment he had stepped into his office. But don't judge too soon, he warned himself. He'd done some pretty stupid things himself in his time. But then again, he was now a Lieutenant Colonel at the age of twenty five, whereas Ramsey was at least five years his senior, had been in both the army and the commandos for longer and had only just managed to clamber up to the rank of Major and even that seemed to be based on time served, not on merit.

Never judge a book by its cover, he reminded himself. There might be more to Ramsey than what met the eye. Carter could only hope.

"OK, well, thank you for that. Most informative. First of all, I'd better tell you a bit about how we work in Fifteen. Every commando unit has its own personality and we pride ourselves on being reasonably relaxed. The only time we have parades is to hand out medals or to honour visiting dignitaries, for a start.

We treat the men with respect. We rely on each other and the man you berate today for not calling you 'Sir' may be the man who saves your life tomorrow, so think on that when you are dealing with disciplinary issues. We're part of the Army and we never forget it, but we trust our men and a sign of that trust is to let them think for themselves. If the men don't live up to expectations, we get rid of them back to whence they came and that is sufficient deterrent for most of them. I'll do as much with an officer that doesn't step up to the mark as well." Carter let the threat hang in the air for a moment before continuing.

"In terms of dress, you are a bit out of step with us ..." He put up his hand to forestall the protest that Ramsey was about to make "... That isn't a criticism, but what is good for Horse Guards isn't necessarily good for here. We wear battledress all the time, even when we visit Brigade. If anyone wants to you to dress more formally, they'll let you know. We never wear peaked caps, even with our No 2 Dress. Only the green beret. That is a hard and fast rule. If the King himself were to pay us a call, we'd parade wearing our berets. It's a badge of honour, not just something to attract the ladies." Ramsey at least had the decency to blush. "We also blacken all our brass work; badges, buckles, webbing, rifle slings, the lot. We don't want Jerry seeing anything glinting in the sunlight when we're trying to sneak up on him.

Your main responsibilities will be the training programme and everything related to it: finding the training areas, organising transport, landing craft etc. It's a pretty basic plan at the moment, because we don't know what our objectives will be. As we find out more, I will expect you to refine the programme to tailor it to the mission. Think you can manage that?"

"I'm sure that won't challenge me too much, Sir."

Carter didn't like the way he was so dismissive of his role. Carter knew just how complicated the delivery of the training plan could get at times. But he let it pass.

"As well as delivering the training plan, you will also have to participate in it. You will have a role to play when we go ashore and you will have to be ready to fulfil it. If it comes to a choice between doing the training or doing the admin, there is no choice. You do the training. Understood?"

"Understood, Sir."

"Now, I'm a little concerned that you haven't seen any action yet, so I'm going to make arrangements for that to change. I'll contact Combined Ops and arrange for you to go along on a couple of raids as an observer." Carter knew there was no such thing during a raid. You were either a fighting commando or you were left behind in barracks. But it provided an excuse for Ramsey to be on the raid, without disclosing that he needed the experience.

"Speaking of which, there will be no trips to London unless you are on leave or you've been summoned there. I'm not passing judgement on the way you run your social life, but the way travel is disrupted by the Jerry bombers I can't risk you being stuck on a train when you're needed here, or you're supposed to be participating on a raid. Do I make myself clear?"

"That seems rather harsh, Sir. I mean, a trip to the big city cheers a chap up …"

"When I start sloping off having fun, you can do the same." Carter made sure his voice carried the appropriate degree of threat. "If you don't like my rules, you are free to ask for a transfer to another unit."

"N … No, of course, Sir. Understood."

Carter smiled inwardly. To apply for a transfer would not give out the right messages. Carter was pretty sure Ramsey's new rank was only temporary, to be confirmed after a period of probation and a satisfactory report from his CO; from himself. Ramsey wouldn't want to lose that nice shiny new crown on his shoulder. He probably thought it impressed the ladies.

"Finally, we pride ourselves on being the fittest soldiers in the British army. That means all the way from me down to the newest recruit. No officer in this unit is ever the last man to finish an exercise. The only acceptable excuse for doing so is death and I do mean the officer's death, not someone else's. What is your fitness like after sitting around Whitehall for the last few months?"

"Not bad, Sir. I do regular exercise. I play a lot of squash and tennis as well. Got to maintain standards and all that."

Carter doubted the statement. There was more than a hint of a paunch on the man and Carter was sure that he could see paler cloth along the side seams of the man's jacket, where it had been let out an inch. There were also signs of strain on the buttons. "Well, we'll find out tomorrow morning. 6 Troop are doing a ten-mile speed march and you can join them." He was sure he saw Ramsey go several shades paler at this news. Carter stifled a smile. "Oh six hundred start, from the main gate. I suggest you take the opportunity to meet the men today. If you collapse halfway, they're the ones that will have to get you back here."

[1] OCTU - Officer Cadet Training Unit. Officer recruits spent several weeks learning military and leadership skills before transferring to a specialist unit for further training in the specific role for the job they would do (artillery, engineering, signals etc). Course lengths varied as training needs were re-evaluated as the war progressed. In 1939 the duration was as little as 8 weeks for an infantry officer but by 1943 had gone up to 15 weeks as specialist infantry training was added to the basic course. Different from the Royal Military College Sandhurst, which trained officers for a career in the Army and whose courses were too long to meet the wartime demands for new officers. Its peacetime training role was suspended and Sandhurst first of all became an OCTU, then a specialist training establishment for officers of the Royal Armoured Corps.

[2] Italy declared war on Britain on 10th June 1940. The British evacuation of Dunkirk had been completed on 4th June.

[3] Abyssinia is now called by its older Ancient Greek name of Ethiopia, however, it is still sometimes referred to by its other name. Ethiopia is more used by the Coptic Christian communities, while Abyssinia is more Muslim in nature.

[4] It is unclear why 1 Cdo was disbanded, but it probably amounted to political wrangling over who should have operational command over them. They became No 1 Special Service Battalion and weren't under the control of Combined Operations (established in June 1940 under Admiral of the Fleet Sir Roger Keyes, succeeded in March 1942 by Commodore Lord Louis Mountbatten). They were soon disbanded. 1 Cdo was re-established in March 1941.

* * *

There weren't many rules for the speed marches. The troop had to stick to the prescribed route, they had to be in full fighting order, including carrying one hundred rounds of ammunition, they had to finish together, even if it meant carrying a man and the clock didn't stop until the last man crossed the finish line. The target pace was ten-minute miles, but a troop that didn't improve on that could expect some degree of censure from their Troop Commander. Course lengths varied from a relatively unchallenging five miles to the seventeen-mile torture of the final march at Achnacarry. Commando units rarely felt it necessary to repeat that distance, but fifteen-mile marches weren't unheard of.

All the commandos hated them, but the only way to avoid doing more of them was to beat the target time.

The march was conducted at a cross between a fast march and a run. Generally the running was downhill or on the flat, while the men lent forward, put their backs into it and made the best pace they could up the slopes of the Sussex Downs.

Carter leant over the shoulder of the Sergeant that was the designated timekeeper for this particular march. It wasn't that no-one trusted the commandos to report their correct time, it was just easier for someone from a different troop to take on the task. It also helped to engender competition if everyone knew the times achieved by the other troops. Already Carter had promised crates of beer for the troop with the fastest average time over a set series of marches.

In the distance he could make out the troop struggling up the final hill towards the barracks. Local children ran alongside, cheering the men on or shouting casual insults, whichever took their fancy. Each section took turns to lead for a set distance, then dropped to the rear to allow the next section to set the pace for the next leg.

The troop appeared to be in good order, no sign of them straggling along the road. That was always a good sign. In front, as he should be, was Stefan Podborsky, who had taken over from Molly Brown as the troop commander. Marchant, one of the new officers, had replaced him as the subaltern[1] in charge of one half of the troop. Carter couldn't make out Ramsey. He was probably towards the back. There was no problem with that, at least for this march. When the commando as a whole did a speed march, which they did from time to time, Carter would expect him to be up at the front, running right on his own heels.

About a hundred yards from the gates, Podborsky brought the men to a halt and harried them into three ranks. He must have seen Carter hovering and decided to put on a show. It would cost him time, but he had a minute or so to play with so Carter permitted him the small vanity. All the troop commanders liked to show off from time to time.

Even from that distance Carter could hear the orders being shouted. "By the left, quick march!" The men stepped out smartly. After six paces another order was shouted. "Into double time, double …. march!" The men broke into the trot of one hundred and eighty paces per minute that fit soldiers could maintain for quite some distance. Making the final hundred yards to the gate would be no problem for the commandos, tired as they undoubtedly were.

The troop doubled through the gate and Podborsky brought them to a smart parade ground halt, turned them into line abreast, marched to the centre of the front rank and a threw up a parade ground salute for Carter's benefit.

"Very good, Captain Podborsky." Carter made sure his voice could be heard above the panting of the men. "That was an impressive time. Something for 3 Troop to think about." They were current leaders in the speed marching contest. "You may dismiss your …" Carter stopped speaking as he caught sight of Ramsey, hovering near what had been the rear of the column of troops and was now the right hand end of the front rank.

"Major Ramsey. A word, if you please."

Ransey made a half turn to the right to break ranks and marched stiffly across to stand in front of Carter. His salute was a little sloppy, but Carter could forgive that considering what he had been through during the previous couple of hours. His chest was heaving still, though most of the troops had caught their breath. He was also coated in sweat, despite the chill of the early March day. But that wasn't what had attracted Carter's attention.

As Ramsey saluted, Carter lowered his voice so no one but the 2IC would hear. "Would you care to describe what the men of 6 Troop are wearing, Major." Ramsey should have noted the use of his rank. Its formality should have warned him that his CO wasn't pleased about something.

"They're in battledress, Sir. The normal …."

"I'm aware of what is normal attire for a speed march, thank you Major. Which is why I am asking the question. What else are they wearing?"

"Fighting order, Sir." It was the name used for the assembly of webbing and kit that the men would carry if they were conducting a patrol or advancing to make contact with the enemy.

"And what are they carrying?"

By this point Ramsey must have been starting to get suspicious about the questions. He turned around to look at the troops still standing at attention in their ranks, as though he needed to check before he gave his answer. Each man had a Short Magazine Lee Enfield (SMLE) rifle held in his right hand, the butt resting on the ground, snuggly against the toe of his right boot. Even the officers.

"Er … Erm."

"Spit it out man!" Carter barked, loud enough for the soldiers at the far end of the troop to hear.

"They're carrying rifles, Sir."

"And ammunition?"

"I don't know about …."

"Captain Podborsky." Carter addressed the troop commander directly. "Are your men carrying ammunition."

"Yes, Sir!" The Polish exile barked back. "The ammunition was issued when the troop paraded this morning, Sir."

"Thank you, Captain." Carter retuned his baleful stare to Ramsey, lowering his voice again.

"Would you mind explaining to me, Major, why you are not carrying your webbing, neither are you carrying a rifle. You aren't even wearing a side arm."

"I didn't think …"

"What didn't you think?" Carter growled at his subordinate.

Ramsey gaze darted back and forth as though he was looking for an escape route. Perhaps he was. "I didn't think that a senior officer would have to carry so much, Sir."

"So, when we invade France and you go ashore, tell me: who is going to be carrying your kit?"

"I don't know, Sir. My batman I guess."

"The only person in this commando who has a batman is me, Major." In fact, Carter hadn't yet selected a man to undertake that duty, nor was he in any hurry to do so. "And I can assure you that on the day we land in France, he will not be carrying my kit. What about your weapon? Don't you intend killing any Jerries?"

"Surely, I'll be with our HQ troop, Sir. I probably won't need to get involved in the fighting. I'll have my pistol …"

"Ramsey. Stop talking." Carter growled.

Carter surveyed the front rank of soldiers, looking for a familiar face. "Tpr Pengelly." Most of the men were struggling to keep a straight face by now; none more so than Pengelly.

Pengelly took two smart steps forward. "Sir!"

"Tpr Pengelly, when the commando went ashore in Italy, at Termoli, where was the HQ troop?"

"There weren't one Sir. They'd been split up into the rifle troops."

"And where was I when we went ashore?" Carter asked.

"You were with our troop, Sir."

"Thank you. And when we went ashore to capture the bridge over the river Gabriel. Where was the HQ troop then?"

"Same, Sir. In the rifle troops."

"And where was the 2IC then? Where was Maj Cousens?"

"He was leading the second wave ashore Sir. He was right in front of me when we left the landing craft."

"Thank you, Pengelly. Return to your place.

"Are you starting to get the message now, Major?" Carter was standing so close to the man that their noses were practically touching. Carter could smell his sweat and, by now, not all of it was being caused by his physical exertions.

"I think so, Sir."

"Good. Now, tomorrow morning at 0600 hrs, 1 Troop are scheduled to do this same speed march. I have just decided that I will join them. I have also decided that you will also join them."

Two speed marches in two days was a significant challenge for any commando. It would be more so for the less fit Ramsey.

"Yes, Sir." He said the words though gritted teeth.

"And may I assure you, Maj Ramsey, that if you don't finish ahead of me, you will be on the next train out of here. And you won't go back to a cushy billet[2] in the War Office. You will go to Burma, where I understand it is hot and they have diseases that soldiers can't even imagine. I believe that is where your old battalion is currently serving, is it not?"

"Yes, it is Sir."

"I thought so. The last news I read from there suggested things aren't going too well for the 14th Army. Maybe your old battalion needs the assistance of a fully trained commando Major."

Before the man had time to answer, Carter turned away. Grins of delight vanished off the faces of the sixty men of 6 Troop, to be replaced by the commandos' normal look of steely eyed determination.

"Thank you, Captain Podborsky. Your men did well. It is a shame that they were set such a bad example. You may dismiss."

[1] Subaltern – an officer of Second Lieutenant or Lieutenant rank. In use in the British army from as far back as 1680. From the Latin sub, meaning under and alternus, meaning everyone. A subaltern is literally under, or inferior, to everyone else.

[2] Cushy billet – a soft posting or easy assignment. From the Hindi word *Khush*, meaning healthy or happy and the French *bilet*. Cushy could also descend from late 19th century Scottish and Northumbrian slang for a soft or useless person. A billet was a short length of flat

wood which the quartermaster would hang on the doorway of a house which he had commandeered for the accommodation of soldiers. The billet was annotated in chalk with the number of soldiers that were to live there. The practice dates all the way back to medieval times. If the house's occupants were lucky, they would get paid for the privilege but usually only if the army was in friendly territory. In modern usage a billet is any accommodation assigned to a soldier.

* * *

Back in his office Carter was surprised to find Prof Green laying a buff folder in the middle of his desk. As he wasn't wearing his beret the sergeant had obviously not been sent on some errand.

"What are you doing here, Sgt Green." Out of the line, Carter always made sure to behave more formerly with his subordinates, even one like Green who had shared so many adventures with him.

"The RSM thought that HQ Troop needed an NCO to keep things organised, now that it's expanded so much." Carter couldn't argue that the headquarters was bigger these days. When he had joined the commando in 1941 it had been the CO, his clerk, the 2IC, the QM, the Padre, the Medical Officer, the QM's assistant, a couple of RP[1]s and the RSM[2].

Now the HQ Troop had over thirty men in it, from clerks to signallers, to mechanics. But, as the point had been so forcefully made to Ramsey, when they went ashore, they did so as fighting commandos.

"I wonder where the RSM got such an idea." Carter said dryly. "I hope you aren't angling for a promotion to Staff Sergeant." Such a post would normally be held by the more senior rank.

"Never crossed my mind, Sir." Green grinned.

"And I suppose O'Driscoll is my new company clerk."

"Heaven forbid, Sir. O'Driscoll is a man of many talents but being company clerk is probably not one of them. No, he's your new driver."

Carter shook his head in wonder at the amount of manipulation that must have gone in to secure such a job. Driving the CO was prestigious post. "And Glass?" Carter knew that Glass wouldn't be far away, though as a corporal it would be harder to find him a job in the headquarters.

"He's looking after the Registry."

"Since when have we had a Registry?" Carter's mouth opened wide with shock.

"Since this morning. Sir."

"Do we have enough files that need looking after to warrant such a post?"

"As the NCO in charge of the commando's HQ, I am anticipating future demands upon the unit, Sir." Green was struggling to keep a straight face. "We're doing far more paperwork these days and someone has to make sure it doesn't all get lost. And some of it is classified as well, so we have to be doubly careful it doesn't go astray."

That was true enough, Carter had to concede. When they started to get information in on their objectives it would have to be kept under lock and key.

"Well, you can tell the corporal in charge of the Registry that I'm in need of a cup of tea."

"Right here, Sir." Glass appeared in the doorway suspiciously quickly, a steaming china mug in one hand and a plate of biscuits in the other. He marched across the room, placed both objects on the desk in front of Carter, one on each side of the buff folder, then stepped back, standing to attention.

"Since when have we had biscuits?" Carter asked. He had never seen such luxury on the desks of any of his predecessors. The best he had ever seen was a couple of hard tack biscuits taken from a field ration pack.

"Since the same time as we got a Registry, Sir". Glass said with a grin.

Perhaps the manoeuvring of the three of his oldest comrades wasn't so terrible, after all, Carter conceded.

"Make sure Major Ramsey doesn't find out about them." Carter said through a mouthful of custard cream.

[1] RP – Regimental police. Nothing to do with the Royal Military Police. They are drawn from the within the unit and maintain discipline on behalf of the RSM. They could be thought of as a type of Special Constable. Often chosen for their size rather than their intellect.

[2] RSM – Regimental Sergeant Major. The senior most NCO in a unit, responsible for organising duty rosters, maintaining discipline and the organisation of ceremonial occasions. It is considered to be the pinnacle of a soldier's career to be appointed to the post. Even being selected to become an officer can't compare to becoming the RSM.

* * *

A cold wind whipped in from the English Channel, but Carter didn't feel it. His mind was distracted as he gazed through the dawn light towards the mouth of the estuary.

This nervousness wasn't a feeling Carter was used to. It was usually someone else standing on a cold quayside waiting for news. But the Brigadier had been quite explicit in his instructions. "Under no circumstances are you to go on this raid, Steven." He had said, stabbing his finger into the map that showed where it would take place. "If I know you, you wouldn't stop until you got to Paris. Besides, it would be unfair on the officer leading it to have to babysit a Lieutenant Colonel."

"But Ramsey's going." Carter objected.

"Yes and I'm far from happy about that. But I take your point about his operational experience, so I'm allowing it. But only because of that. You don't have that excuse."

So Carter paced up and down the quay at Seaford, waiting for the raid to return. Ramsey had appeared to be nervous, but that was hardly surprising. Carter had been nervous on his first raid, just over three years earlier. That had been a full-scale operation, the whole commando with additional troops attached from other units, the RAF above, a Royal Navy cruiser offshore and four destroyers offering close support.

This was very different. Just ten men under the command of a Lieutenant, travelling on board a Motor Torpedo Boat. It was supposed to plant in the enemy's mind the idea that the invasion, when it came, would be across the Pas de Calais. By sending what appeared to be a reconnaissance team ashore to grab a couple of prisoners, the Germans might be persuaded. On the other hand, they had been fooled before and might not be so easily duped this time. It was just one in a series of raids that had been planned with the same purpose in mind. Ramsey was scheduled to go on another one the following month.

He could see Brigadier Vernon's point. Already he knew enough about the invasion to be of use to the Germans if he were to be captured. None of the commandos who were due to go ashore on the day of the landings was allowed out onto the sea for any reason other than practice landings on friendly beaches and there was always a warship loitering off the coast, ready to fend off any E-Boats rash enough to approach the shore. They just couldn't take the risk of soldiers, even commandos, revealing information by accident if they were captured.

The Germans didn't have to beat information out of prisoners. Sometimes all they had to do was chat to them and offer them a cup of something hot to drink. He had seen it done with captured Germans who had started out by insisting that all they would provide was their service number, rank and name, in accordance with the Geneva Convention.

The technique was simple enough. Examine the prisoner's possessions to see what information could be gleaned from them and use it to gain the prisoner's trust, or at least dilute their distrust. There were usually letters or photos, which always provided a starting point for a conversation. Offer the prisoner a cigarette, make a few jokes, let the prisoner talk about home and hearth. Then ask about how things were on the other side of the Channel. What was the food like, did they get to meet any pretty French girls, how were they treated by their officers? Very often the prisoner answered questions that he hadn't even been asked, just because he was being treated well.

It helped to have two prisoners, who could be kept in different rooms and interrogated separately. That way the interrogator could pretend to know more than he did, using titbits gleaned from one prisoner to feed into the conversation with the other. If the prisoner thought that the other man was giving away things, he had no reason to keep his own mouth shut and the information began to flow more freely

Over a period of a few hours a picture could be built up, a bit like doing a jigsaw puzzle. Over days the missing bits could be discovered and inserted. A casual word about an ammunition depot might well result in a high flying Spitfire being sent across the channel to take photographs, to confirm what was said and that would provide further leverage for use against the prisoner.

It was remarkable how subtle the technique was and it never once required the interrogator to threaten violence or raise his voice. All it required was patience, a supply of decent coffee (the Germans loved coffee, which was almost totally unavailable to them) and some cigarettes.

But patience wasn't something that Carter had a lot of, particularly when he was waiting for news of a raid. Had they made it ashore? Had they succeeded in their mission? Were they on their way back? There was no way of knowing. All he could do was pace

He had heard a pair of fighters cross the coast just before first light. That was the aerial escort sent to rendezvous with them and protect them against vengeful enemy fighters. Not that there were many of those these days. The RAF and the United States Army Air Corps dominated the skies over both France and the English Channel. The only aircraft the Germans sent up now were night fighters and bombers and even the bombers only flew at night.

But commando raids had been attacked on their homeward journey before; Carter knew that from bitter personal experience. So the pair of fighters had been sent to cover the MTB on its homeward journey. Carter wondered what they might be. Spitfires seemed the most likely choice, but the RAF were flying American P-51 Mustangs[1] now, as well. Carter had never seen one, but he might this morning.

O'Driscoll arrived at his elbow and offered him a mug of tea. It looked strong enough to stand a spoon up in it.

"Where did you get that at this time of day?" Carter asked, blowing across the top of the cup before attempting a sip.

"Early morning caff over that way." O'Driscoll nodded his head towards a point further along the quayside. "I can get you a sandwich if you want. I think I smelt bacon frying."

Carter's mouth watered, but at the same time his stomach rebelled. His nervousness wouldn't allow him to eat right now.

"Not for me thanks. But don't let me stop you."

"I already have, Sorr." O'Driscoll grinned. "Be careful with that mug. The owner made me leave a two bob[2] deposit for it. Bloody cheek."

Carter wasn't interested in any usury being practised by local café owners, but he appreciated the tea.

Ramsey's performance had improved in the weeks running up to the raid. The second speed march had seen the two of them arriving at the armoury to draw rifles from a sleepy armourer, before moving to the magazine, some distance away, to draw the requisite hundred rounds of ammunition, carefully counting each clip of five rounds, checking to make sure each clip was complete and stowing them in their pouches.

Despite the amount of ammunition that a commando expended in daily practice, each round had to be fully accounted for and it wasn't unknown for an armourer to cover losses, or even his own theft, by issuing a soldier with fewer rounds than he had asked for, getting a signature for the full amount, then blaming the soldier for the loss when he returned the rounds later in the day. It was unlikely that the man would try the trick on him, but Carter wasn't taking any chances.

Unsurprisingly, Ramsey had been even more exhausted, so the pace was slower this time, but Carter could see that the man was making an effort to keep up. As they approached the barrack gates Carter dropped back to run alongside him, then, as they passed through, Carter made sure that he was one pace behind him so that he didn't have to carry out his threat to dismiss Ramsey from the commando. The lesson had been learnt, that was the important thing.

The time was a slow one, barely achieving the maximum allowed, but Carter took the blame for that on himself and promised the troop it wouldn't count for the contest. None of them believed for a second that he was to blame for the slow time, but they appreciated the gesture. On the other hand, it meant that the troop would now have to do an additional march to provide a qualifying time. Carter told Ramsey to substitute a ten-mile run for one of the longer ones they'd have to do later, so that they wouldn't suffer just because he'd had to teach his subordinate a lesson in leadership.

"You did well enough, but you need to be fitter to keep up on operations. Go and see the PTI[3] and do an hour of instruction with him each day. If he doesn't think you're fit enough, you won't go on any raids and if you don't go on raids, you won't go with us on the big day. We can't afford to carry passengers." 'The big day' was now the euphemism being used for the invasion of France.

Ramsey had dutifully obeyed and Carter noted, from the reports submitted by the PTI, that his fitness levels had improved steadily. His paunch soon disappeared and he took part in more speed marches without having to be prompted by Carter.

When Carter received approval from Brigade for Ramsey to go on this raid, he allowed him to join 21 Cdo, who were mounting the Op, to train with the men who would go ashore. Their CO gave the final nod of approval for Ramsey to go with the raiding party.

Which was why Carter was now standing on the quayside, shivering and wondering if his 2IC had survived.

"Is that the escort?" O'Driscoll peered into the growing dawn light, pointing out towards the horizon. Carter fumbled for his binoculars, his haste making him clumsy. Into view sprang a pair of Spitfires, flying lazy circles above something beneath them on the surface. The MTB, assuming it was what they were escorting, was still invisible, below the horizon.

Carter could have calculated how far away they were if he'd had his slide rule, but he didn't. The aircraft were just beneath the cloud base, which was at about two thousand feet. All he needed was the approximate angle of elevation of the aircraft above the horizon and it was simple trigonometry after that. He wished he'd gone up to stand on the cliffs on the far side of the town, where the extra height would have given him a better view, but it was too late now. By the time he got up there, even in the Jeep with O'Driscoll driving in his customary mad fashion, the MTB would be in sight from the quayside anyway.

"No sign of enemy fighters." Carter declared. "That's something, anyway."

"They're too short of dem to go slamming stable doors after the horse has bolted, Sorr. They daren't risk getting fighters shot down just because they got banjaxed[4] again."

Carter wished that had been the case back in 1942, when his friend Huelen had been killed commanding the MTB that they'd been coming home in after just such a raid. If they'd been that short of aircraft back then, Huelen might still be alive. Carter pushed the thought from his head. No point in worrying about what might have been. Huelen was dead, that was all there was too it.

Carter's arms were starting to tire from holding the binoculars to his eyes, but he was loathe to lower them. Not that seeing the MTB would answer any of his questions. The boat might be fine, but it could be carrying a cargo of dead men, or even no commandos at all if they had been captured.

One of the Spitfires broke off from the pair and dived towards the sea, disappearing over the horizon. What was that about? Carter wondered. Unlikely to be a fighter plane, it would be flying too low.

An E-Boat perhaps. Maybe sent from Boulogne to try to intercept the MTB. E-Boats were a bit faster, so even though the MTB had a head start it would eventually be overhauled.

A minute dragged by, then another. Finally, the Spitfire reappeared above the horizon again, soaring skywards to disappear into the clouds before reappearing behind its partner and taking station once more. Whatever the threat had been, it was passed and there was still something down on the surface that needed an escort.

A dot appeared at the distant edge of the sea, then disappeared and emerged again several times as it dipped and rose on the waves. At last, it resolved itself into the front view a boat, a white bone of foam in its mouth as it drove through the water at maximum speed.

"I can see it, Paddy." Carter commented.

"They're expected that's for sure." Came a reply. Carter looked around to see what he meant. Driving down the sloping road that led to the quayside was a small convoy of vehicles. In the lead were two military ambulances, followed by a Military Police Jeep. Were the ambulances just precautionary, or did someone know something? None of the occupants got out of the vehicles after they drew to a stop. Was that because of the cold? Or were they just reluctant to make small talk with a Lieutenant Colonel.

There were no Royal Navy vehicles present, Carter could see. If the MTB's crew had suffered casualties, a senior officer from its flotilla would surely have come to greet them and take a report before the details of the incident were forgotten. A 3 Ton truck rumbled down the road and drew up at the rear of the group of vehicles. That would be to take the commandos back to their barracks. Behind that was a Jeep. Carter could see the face of Lt Col Morgan, the CO of 21 Cdo, come to welcome his men back.

He wasn't reluctant to climb out of his vehicle. He strode across to greet Carter, his hand extended to be shaken.

"Couldn't stay away, eh Steven?" Morgan grinned.

"No …. Malcolm." Carter had almost called him Sir, forgetting that they were now of equal rank. It was the hardest thing he had found about getting promoted, the change in status between him and other officers. Majors now called him Sir and he called Lieutenant Colonels by their first names.[5] "You got here quickly."

"Watching from up there." Morgan pointed to the cliffs. "I must have picked the boat out about ten minutes before you."

"Were this lot with you?" Carter nodded towards the other vehicle.

"Not the lorry. He was parked up the road a bit and saw me coming down the hill. But the others must have got a message from somewhere. Maybe the Coastguard, or maybe from whoever runs the Navy in this part of the world. The MTB will have radioed ahead."

The Navy used a lot of VHF radio to communicate between ships and also, when they were close enough inshore, between them and the shore. It could only communicate on 'line of sight', but if the receivers were on top of the cliffs, they would be able to pick up signals from much further out at sea. But when they left Hardelot, their target, they would have been much further east along the Channel, where the gap between England and France was much narrower. On a clear day you could see the opposite shore from the cliffs above Folkstone. From Dover you see France from the harbour wall.

Although the German High Command thought they had built an impregnable defensive wall from Denmark to the Atlantic Ocean, in places it was still no more than a tangle of barbed wire. The beach at Hardelot was one of those places. There were hardened strong points: pill boxes and artillery emplacements, but in between there were plenty of places where the defences were less than adequate. To make matters worse, many of the strong points weren't routinely manned. Troops would occupy them only if an alarm was raised from one of the positions that was manned. It was like trying to prevent water running through a colander by putting your fingers over the holes. It wasn't the first time the commandos had raided in that area and, Carter was sure, it wouldn't be the last.

Anxiety finally got the better of Carter. He crossed over to the leading ambulance and tapped on the passenger side window. An

Army medic wound it down and a cloud of cigarette smoke emerged, causing Carter to cough and pull his face away.

"Have you heard anything about casualties?" Carter asked, wafting the smoke away with his hand.

"No, Sir. We were at the local TA barracks, waiting to be told what to do when we got a call to come here for the RV. We've been there on standby for this all night."

"Is it normal for you to be here, even if there are no casualties?"

"We've never had a time when there weren't casualties, Sir. After Dieppe we were back and forth between here and Brighton all day, there were so many injured."

Being one of those casualties himself, Carter hadn't known about that until he woke up, but the stories had emerged over time. The raids on Dieppe and Honfluer had been a bloodbath, mainly for the Canadians, who had made up the largest part of the raiding forces, but also for the commandos.

"OK, thank you." Carter went back to stand with Morgan as the window was wound up again to keep the heat in the ambulance's cab. Carter noticed that O'Driscoll had disappeared, along with the mug that had held Carter's tea. Gone to reclaim his deposit, Carter assumed.

The MTB was much larger now, clearly identifiable for what it was. It looked like a fighting vessel, the torpedo tubes in the bow making black holes like a predator's eyes. Above and behind those sat a 6 pounder gun. Behind that was the squat superstructure, giving the craft the lowest possible profile, so it might not be seen until it was too late for its prey to evade it.

Another mile, Carter guessed, before the power to the engines was reduced and it started to slow down to make a more sedate approach into the harbour.

Behind them people started to gather along the wall that separated the harbour from the seafront. Idle curiosity mixed with a ghoulish desire to see if there were any dead bodies, Carter guessed. It was a small town and not much happened here. The only reason that the MTB was here was because it was easier to bring it to 21 Cdo than it was to take 21 Cdo to the boat. Seaford had its own naval residents, steam gun boats, but they weren't present, presumably away carrying out coastal patrols or escorting merchant shipping.

The boat entered the river through the pair of breakwaters, headed upstream for a few yards past the quayside, then turned back to have its bows pointed towards the sea once more. Huelen had explained that they tried to moor that way whenever possible so they could make a quicker exit if it was necessary.

There was no sign of any damage to the MTB, which was a positive. If they had been targeted by shore-based artillery there might be some sign, even if it was only a broken bridge window. The protective cover was still on the mouth of the barrel of the 6 pounder and the Oerlikons behind the superstructure were also covered, suggesting the boat hadn't had to deal with any attacks.

The bad news came when the boat was securely tied up and the gangway had been run ashore to bridge the gap between the quay and the boat's main deck.

The first casualty to be led out had his head bandaged so much that it was difficult to make out his face at all. His battledress was shredded, but Carter could just about make out corporal's stripes. So, not Ramsey. He was helped ashore by naval ratings, who returned below decks. When they came back, they were carrying a Robinson stretcher between them. The soldier had one hand free of the stretcher's tight embrace and was holding a cigarette. Between the sections of the stretcher Carter could make out bandages on both legs.

The two casualties were loaded carefully into the ambulances, which sped off, the clattering of their bells sending the gulls skywards, shrieking in protest. Next ashore were two German prisoners. They were in shirt sleeves, probably how they were dressed when they were caught. They cast morose looks around them but there was no fighting spirit. Two commandos followed them, their bayoneted rifles at the ready. At the top of the gangway the two military policemen placed handcuffs on their wrists and prodded them towards their Jeep, where the handcuffs were removed from one wrist before being attached to the frame that supported the canvass tilt of the vehicle.

Only then did the rest of the commandos appear from below decks and head towards the gangway. At the rear was Lt Freeman, who had led the raid, and Howard Ramsey.

Carter searched the faces of the men as they stepped off the gangway, looking for one in particular. There he was, second man from the rear of the file.

"LCpl Garraway. Good to see you again." Carter made a show of greeting the man who, until a few weeks earlier, had been in 15 Cdo. He led him along the quay a few yards, out of earshot of the others.

"How did he do?"

"Pretty well, actually Sir. When we stumbled into the mine field ... that was when we got the casualties, it was Maj Ramsey that led us out again. Lt Freeman was at the front, right behind the injured men, so he couldn't do anything. Then, when we were out, he helped the Lieutenant to get the causalities clear so we could patch them up."

A minefield. So that was how the casualties had been caused. They weren't always marked on the seaward side. "Didn't the mine going off raise the alarm?

"You'd have thought it would, but it didn't. Maybe they go off a lot. There were signs the dunes have been used for sheep pasture. If they tread on a mine it's just the same as a person doing it. Anyway, we took the casualties back to the beach and the Navy took care of them, while we carried on with the raid. Found the two prisoners sitting in a wooden hut, playing cards. Came along like lambs, so they did. So, we planted a few booby traps, cut some telephone cables and went back to the beach."

"And Maj Ramsey played a full part in the riad?"

"Lt Freeman gave all the orders, but Maj Ramsey seemed to be enjoying the whole thing. Kept asking where the Jerries were so he could take a few pots at them." Ramsey had taken a Tommy gun with him and seemed keen to use it.

"Well, thank you, Garraway. I'll let you get back to your mates. I'm sure you're tired.

"I am that, thank you Sir."

Ramsey was waiting at the foot of the gangway for him. "Checking up on me, Sir?" Ramsey said, a slight sneer in his voice.

"Yes, as it happens, Major. Just wanted a trooper's take on how you did. You'll be pleased to know he was quite impressed."

Ramsey seemed taken aback by the honest answer.

"I'll get a copy of Lt Freeman's report, of course, but if the men think you did well, it speaks volumes. Now, can I offer you a lift back to Worthing?"

"Actually, Lt Freeman has invited me to breakfast with him and his men. I think it may involve a little bit more than bacon and eggs."

"I think it probably will. That's OK, I don't expect you to undertake any duties after a night like you've had. I'll send my Jeep to pick you up in a couple of hours.

Carter watched as the man strolled towards the truck and climbed into the back. He could have pulled rank to take the favoured seat up next to the driver, but he left that to Freeman as one of the privileges of being the raid's leader.

After a faltering start, Carter wasn't too proud to concede that Ramsey was coming along nicely.

[1] The North American Aviation P-51 Mustang first entered RAF service in 1942. Although American manufactured, the aircraft was designed to meet a British specification. The early marks were fitted with an Allison engine which had a severe power drop off above 15,000 ft, making it unsuitable for use as a fighter. Instead they were used as an army co-operation aircraft, carrying out ground attack sorties. Later marks were fitted with a Packard built Merlin engine (manufactured under licence from Rolls-Royce), making it suitable for high altitude operations so it could be used as a fighter. They carried out hundreds of sweeps across France ahead of D-Day. They also proved quite effective against V-1 flying bombs, shooting down 232 of them (the record of 638 was set by the Hawker Tempest).

[2] Two Bob – two shillings, ten pence in today's coinage but worth a lot more back then. Two bob would have been enough for an evening at the cinema with a fish supper on the way home.

[3] PTI = Physical training instructor. Formed in 1860, the Army Physical Training Corps (it wasn't granted the title 'Royal' until 13th November 2010) provided instructors for units in the British army to raise the standard of fitness amongst soldiers. Although PTIs are still found in gymnasiums on garrisons and recruit training depots, nowadays their focus is mainly on physiotherapy, rehabilitation and remedial fitness training. At unit level, ordinary soldiers are provided with specialist training to allow them to run day-to-day fitness training sessions.

[4] Banjaxed = Irish slang for being beaten up, broken or injured.

[5] By tradition, junior officers up to and including Captain are permitted to address each other by their first names, even if they are of unequal rank. Above that rank, all officers address their superiors as "Sir". Also by tradition, a junior officer entering a colleague's office will salute him, even if he is of a more junior or of equal rank. It is a mark of respect for his authority within his own area of command.

2 – D-Day

The briefing room at Brigade HQ was already quite crowded when Carter, Ramsey and Brown arrived and took their seats in the middle of a row. Carter recognised De Freitas, the CO of 16 Cdo and Strong from 17 Cdo. He nodded a greeting to Tom Prothero of 49 (RM) Cdo, who he'd last seen in the transit camp in Bari the previous November.

There were others in the room he knew either because their paths had crossed in this very building, or because they'd served in 15 Cdo. Others were strangers dressed in khaki, navy blue and the paler blue of the RAF. There was even a civilian.

A sergeant stood at ease in front of an easel, on which a large flat rectangular object was covered by a sheet. No one needed to be told it was a map. With all the COs of all the commandos in the Brigade present, Carter knew this must be what they had been waiting for. This was when they would find out where they were going, when they were going and what their objectives would be when they got there.

A Colonel, the brigade's Chief of Staff, entered the room. "No room to stand, gentlemen, so when I call you to attention, please remain seated."[1]

The door at the back of the room opened again and the Colonel gave the command. The sound of chairs moving as bodies straightened made a rumble on the plain wooden floor.

"As you were, gentlemen." Brigadier Vernon intoned as he marched briskly to the front. It was enough for him that the gesture had been made. "No doubt you have all worked out why you are here, so I won't keep you in suspense any longer." He removed his beret and handed it to the sergeant, before placing a folder of papers onto the lectern that stood alongside the covered map board. "I must, however, issue clear orders as to secrecy. What you are about to hear must remain within these four walls. You will be provided with maps of your objectives that have all the names removed to prevent easy identification of the locations. You will use those for briefing your troops until you move into a secure area just before D-Day. Only then can you reveal the exact locations and timings.

D-Day, by the way, is the name being used to indicate the day of the landings, with H-Hour being the exact time the first troops will hit the beaches. As we don't want the exact dates to be revealed, you will refer to all dates as either D-Day plus one, plus two etc, for the days after we land, or D-Day minus for the days before we land. The same applies to H-Hour and the hours before and after. Now, gentlemen, for the big reveal."

The sergeant had returned to his post after hanging the Brigadier's beret on a peg. Vernon nodded and he pulled the covering sheet off the board to reveal a map of Northern France that stretched from Dieppe in the east to St Malo in the west. The coastline was divided into sections by coloured tapes, with white paper labels pinned onto the map to identify them.

"This, gentlemen, is Operation Overlord, the code name for the invasion of France. That name must also never be uttered outside of this room, not even after you arrive in your secure areas. It may only be used publicly after we have landed.

The operation requires a landing on five beaches on the Normandy coast. From east to west these are code named Sword …" Vernon picked up a long wooden pointer and placed the tip between the eastern most pair of taped lines on the map. "… Juno …" his pointer moved along one section "… and Gold. Those three are the British beaches, though it will be mainly Canadian troops landing on Juno. These two …" he pointed to the two areas that were furthest west, separated from the British beaches and from each other. "… are the American beaches, which are called Omaha and Utah. Once ashore the Americans will attempt to link up their beaches and also to link up with the right flank of Gold Beach at the same times as the British on Gold Beach attempt to link up with them. You can see from the position of Utah Beach, on the Cherbourg peninsula, that in the days following the landings there will be a major attempt to cut off and then capture the port of Cherbourg itself. The ability to use proper port facilities for re-supply is critical to the success of the operation."

He paused and turned to face the room directly again. "But you probably aren't too interested in what the Yanks are doing. You want to know what is in store for you.

Over the last few weeks, you have all been badgering my staff officers, suggesting what sort of targets you think the commandos should be used against. Gun batteries, bridges, strong points etc. You all made it quite clear you expected to go ashore before the main landings and do what you do best ... landing under the cover of darkness. All of your suggestions were relayed to the planners for Overlord and I have to say they received them very politely, before completely ignoring them."

Half the occupants of the room laughed, thinking a joke had been made, while the other half gasped with shock. Whatever their objectives were to be, they weren't what the officers had expected. Whispered conversations broke out around the room and Vernon had to hold up his hand up to restore order.

"I know how you are feeling, gentlemen, because I have already been through this with the planners myself, to no avail. But don't worry. You aren't being side-lined. Your missions will be just as challenging as you would expect for commando units, even if they are somewhat unusual.

What may surprise you even more is that you won't even be the first troops to land." That brought another outbreak of whispering, which Vernon had to silence. "Come now, gentlemen. If you keep breaking out into private conversations, we'll still be here after D-Day has come and gone." That brought a laugh, but it also stopped the conversations.

"5th Commando Brigade, as I insist on calling it, will go ashore on Sword Beach. 3rd Infantry Division will go ashore first, at H-Hour and you will follow one hour later. By then the beach will be secure and you will pass through the first wave to move on to your assigned objectives, which are different for each commando. Next map please, Sergeant."

The Sergeant removed the first map board to reveal a second one behind. This was a much larger scale one of the coast between a town at the eastern end and a smaller conurbation, a village Carter assumed, to the west.

"The whole of Sword Beach is about six miles long, with the town of Ouistreham at the eastern end and St Aubin Sur Mer at the western end, where it butts up against Juno beach. It has been sub divided into four sections. From west to east these are Oboe, Peter, Queen and Roger, which keeps things nice and simple if you know your alphabet. Each beach is then divided into two, red and white. Basically each beach has been allocated to one battalion of infantry from the assault brigades. Our brigade will go ashore at the eastern end."

Carter glanced at Ramsey, sitting at his side. The man was scribbling away in his notebook. Carter hoped he didn't have any essential personal information in it, because when they left the briefing that little book would become an official secret and would have to be locked up in the commando's new registry.

"I'll be giving detailed briefs to each commando in turn, after lunch, but for now I'll keep things broad brush, so to speak.

16 Cdo will land in the middle of Roger beach and, after clearing the beach you will move into Ouistreham itself and will seize German command and control facilities within the town. They've been identified from the number of aerials mounted on the roof. The infantry will be tied up clearing the defences along the sea front, so someone needs to prevent the Germans organising a local response and that is your task. You will have a troop of Free French commandos with you and it will be their honour to take the objective. It is your job to get them there so that they can have the honour in the first place. I'll get on to what happens after that later in the day.

Now, to 15 and 17. You are undertaking what has been called Operation Pegasus. During the night of D-Day minus one, the 6th Airborne Division will be landing here …" he used his pointer to indicate a point some distance inland. ".. astride the Orne River and the Orne Canal, which run parallel to each other at that point. Their task is to capture the two road bridges ..."

Oh no, not another fucking bridge, thought Carter. But he kept his face impassive.

"... that cross the river and the canal there. Those bridges will be vital to get forces onto the other side to secure the left flank of the beachhead. We don't want to have to wait while engineers construct replacements, because that will give the Jerries time to build up a defensive force that will be a real bugger to shift. Besides, we can't have the paras left high and dry on the far bank without any way of relieving them.

Carter raised his hand and he received a nod of assent from Vernon, allowing him to speak. "Why not just land on the other side of the river, Sir? Then we can send troops down both banks at the same time."

"Thank you, Steven. That was suggested, but it was decided not to do that. The river estuary on the eastern side of Ouistreham forms a natural barrier to protect the left flank of the landing beaches. If we go in on the far side, we'll have to use a bigger force because it will have to have more protection on its flanks. Once you are across the bridges, you will become the left flank for the whole invasion. But I'm getting ahead of myself.

15 Cdo will land on Queen Red beach and 17 Cdo will land on Queen White. It will be the job of both commandos to get from the beaches to relieve the paras and their friends in the air landing brigade[2]"

Carter saw a smug look spread across Ramsey's face. He deserved his moment of triumph. He had come up with a new training exercise that involved the commando embarking on landing craft, making a landing on the beach near Littlehampton, advancing inland to 'attack' Arundel railway station, cross the river Arun – always without using the perfectly good bridge that the town boasted and then assault Arundel Castle. It wasn't too dissimilar to the task they had been given. Had Ramsey had some inkling of this? He had friends here, made during his time at Combined Ops.

Carter returned his attention to the briefing.

"17 Cdo will remain on the western bank of the river to guard against a counter-attack from that side while 15 Cdo will cross over and move to establish a defensive perimeter on the eastern side. No doubt the paras will be very pleased to see you both by then. The distance you will have to travel is about six miles and you can expect to be under enemy fire all the way. According to the timetable, from the time the landing crafts' ramps drop you will have two hours to get to your objective."

Two hours to cover six miles was nothing for a commando, even carrying full kit and extra ammunition, which they would certainly be doing. Carter knew that. But to do it while fighting an enemy intent on stopping them was another matter. He could see now why the commandos had been given the job. They were probably the only troops who could be guaranteed to keep moving forward or die in the attempt.

"Now that I've got you worried, Steven …" had Carter let it show on his face? "… I can tell you that we will be issuing both commandos with folding bicycles[3] so that they can move quicker."

Carter had to react quickly to stop his jaw dropping. Bicycles? And how could they return fire at the enemy while pedalling and trying to maintain their balance? He shrugged mentally. Something for him and his officers to try to work out in the weeks ahead.

After detailing 49 Cdo's objective, which was to cover 17 Cdo's right flank and escort the Brigade HQ to the bridges, Vernon opened up the floor for questions.

"When is it going to happen, Sir" Tom Prothero asked.

"I'm afraid I'm not at liberty to reveal that yet. Just keep up with your training programmes and you will be given more briefings as each phase of the assembly is about to happen. However, those sailors amongst you, of which I know there are a few, can probably work out some likely dates from the tide tables."

[1] This is an official drill move. When at attention while seated, a soldier will sit up straight and look directly ahead. His hands will be

clenched into fists and rest on the knees, fingers and thumbs downward. His knees will be together, as will his feet.

[2] An air landing brigade wasn't made up of paratroops, they were light infantry who were flown to their objectives in gliders, which then landed (more like a barely controlled crash) as close to their objectives as possible. In the case of the Orne Bridges it was the 2nd Battalion Oxfordshire and Buckinghamshire Light Infantry, of 6th Airlanding Brigade, 6th Airborne Division, that actually captured the bridges. A quick way to pick a fight with a paratrooper is to point out that their regiment didn't actually capture Pegasus Bridge (as it became known) it was the infantry.

[3] Bicycles had been used to improve the mobility of infantry since before the First World War. The US Army's 25th Infantry Bicycle Corps was established in the 1890s and the Swiss Army were still training with bicycles in 2001. The British army had established a Cycle Corps as part of the Territorial Army (Britain's part-time reserves) in 1908, formed around cycle clubs. They never went into action on their bicycles, most of the corps didn't even go to France during World War I and they were disbanded in 1920. It was the Italians who were the first to try using folding bicycles for their paratroops. As Britain didn't have any paratroops until 1942, no one had considered such an innovation for the British army. In 1942 BSA (Birmingham Small Arms, who also made motorcycles) designed a folding bicycle that was hinged in the middle of its frame and secured with butterfly nuts. 60,000 were manufactured and some can still be seen in cycling and military museums. They weighed 23.5 lbs (nearly 11 kg). These were the type of bicycle issued to the commandos.

* * *

Standing on the jetty, Carter thought it might be possible to walk all the way to France just by jumping from the deck of one landing craft to the next. They blocked the river's estuary and stretched away into Southampton Water as far as the eye could see. He cast his eye towards the sky. Low cloud scudded across, causing him to frown.

The unseasonal weather had already caused the invasion to be delayed by twenty-four hours. If they didn't go today, the tides would be wrong and they'd have to wait at least two more weeks until they shifted around by another twelve hours.

It wasn't rain that was the problem, it was the wind. It whipped the seas up, threatening to flood the smaller landing craft and creating waves that would prevent a safe landing. Landing craft that needed to return to the ships to collect more troops, might be left stranded, high and dry on the beaches. Carter had personal experience of such an event.

He thought back over their weeks of training, wondering if there was anything they had missed; anything they could have practised more. They had gone to Dorling, north west of Fort William in Scotland, where they practiced their landings, each of them followed by forced marches of distances up to ten miles, with a fight at the end with a unit from the local garrison. With only blank ammunition and pyrotechnics, it wasn't possible to assess who was the winner of each encounter, but Carter was satisfied with his men's tactical performances.

Then each troop had been sent in turn to Limehouse in London, close to the docks, where a square mile of bombed out streets and factories had been set aside for urban warfare training. Some of the men from London had managed to get home to see their families for an evening, but no more. It wasn't fair to the soldiers from further afield if they were allowed proper leave.

There had been a parade of 5th Commando Brigade, in Hove, at which Montgomery himself took the salute and inspected the troops, recognising Carter form their one meeting in Sicily and greeting him by name, much to Carter's pleasure. Various other generals came to watch the commandos going through their paces to satisfy themselves that they were up to the task they had been given.

They crossed each hurdle with flying colours.

He heard movement behind him and saw Prof Green, also looking out across the mass of craft.

"Not watching the match?" Carter asked. To pass the time before boarding, 15 Cdo had challenged 16 Cdo to a football match in the muddy field opposite the Rising Sun pub. All the pubs in the village had been ordered to shut. There was going to be enough seasickness without aggravating the problem with alcohol.

"No. We're getting stuffed, so I decided not to bother. Thought I'd take a walk. Nice not to be hemmed in by Yank guards." For the previous three weeks the commandos had been enclosed in a tented camp on Southampton common, run by the Americans. While it had allowed them such luxuries as American rations, film shows, chocolate and Coca Cola from the PX, it had severely restricted their movements. Carter had allowed his troop commanders to organise 'bicycle training' rides around the local area, but they had been infrequent, fitted in between the endless briefings that hammered home the same message time and time again: no matter what, you must get to the bridges.

"What's the name of this place again?" Green surveyed the small village that sat on the estuary of the River Hamble.

"Warsash." Carter replied.

"Never heard of it."

"I dare say they've never heard of you, either, Prof. Popular with the yachting fraternity, I understand."

"You wouldn't get a rowing boat in here right now, never mind a yacht."

Nodding his head, Carter agreed. The great fleet of landing craft took up every inch of available space along the shore and extended out into the channel in rows that were moored to each other. Not only were 5th Commando Brigade boarding here, but so were 6 Brigade and several other units that were to form part of the second wave of landing troops. The first wave were using the smaller LC(A)s, with the ramps on the front that dropped down. They were too small to risk the crossing by themselves and would be carried on landing ships.

Feet thudded on the jetty and Carter saw a Royal Navy Commander approaching, a Petty Officer behind him carrying a clipboard. Green snapped to attention. Carter saluted, a courtesy between equals.

"We're going to start boarding in a few minutes, so I'm going to have to ask you to vacate the area." The Commander said.

"As that will include me, I'd better go and retrieve my kit." Carter said with a smile. There was a strict order for boarding on which they had all been briefed and Carter knew that even if they started immediately, it would be an hour at least before he led his men onto the gangplanks that linked the big LC(I)s together.

In the end it turned out that Carter was wrong. It took considerably longer than an hour to load the first commando, which happened to be 16. From where the men sat on the rain-soaked turf of a field, it wasn't possible to identify the source of the delay. Perhaps some troops were slow to move, or the rain slicked gangplanks were proving treacherous underfoot. Whatever it was, it was making the loading slower

Carter didn't mind too much. It was better for his men to sit out here, under the grey skies, than to be battened down below the decks of the LC(I)s. They were primitive affairs, built with only short-term occupation in mind. His men had experienced journeys in them far longer than their designers had ever envisaged, but that was the army for you; and the Navy for that matter. You used the tools you had at hand, not the ones you wished you had available.

He sent a runner to see if he could identify the source of the delay, but the man returned, having been sent back by the Regulator[1] guarding the gate. Carter considered going himself and pulling rank, but it would have been unfair on the rating. He was just following the orders he had been given and it wouldn't speed the process up to know. It was just one of life's petty frustrations, to be endured not enjoyed.

At last a whistle blast sounded from the gate and the commandos rose stiffly to their feet, gathering up webbing, weapons, stores and bicycles. Some of the smaller men were almost doubled over under the weight of their loads and even the larger ones had to lean into the weight to maintain their balance. They were in full marching order, carrying all they would need to keep them alive for several days.

Carter had told the troop commanders that, given the distance from the beaches they were venturing, they couldn't guarantee any form of re-supply. All it needed was for one determined German unit to get between them and the beaches and they could be cut off for days. The more seasoned members of the commando nodded sagely. It had happened to them in Sicily and Italy, so it could happen again in Normandy. Nothing could be assumed, every possible eventuality had to be planned for.

They trudged across the road, past the closed down pub and onto the jetty, their feet creating a staccato tattoo. Heads peered out of upstairs windows and children peeked out of the hedgerows where they had taken refuge, lest they be sent home by the patrolling MPs and Regulators.

Carter bent into the slope of a gangplank, turning right at the top, not needing to follow the outstretched arm of the naval rating stationed there to point the way. The first thing Carter had done when the trucks had deposited them in the village was to check out the three LC(I)s that had been allocated to his commando. Their numbers and positions in the fleet were etched into his brain. Three craft forward, four to the left. It was like playing a game of 'battleships' when he was a child. Only these boats were real.

16 Commando, who were ahead of them, were four craft forward and four to the left. In front of them was the Brigade HQ along with two troops from Four Nine Commando, though only the marines had boarded. The HQ personnel weren't even in Warsash, as far as Carter knew. A cynical corner of his brain wondered if they had found a nice restaurant in Southampton in which to take refuge until sailing time.

The men filed through the hatches to take their places below decks, but Carter headed aft towards the small bridge structure. He dumped his equipment on the deck in front, keeping only his Tommy gun with him. There might be no enemy threat in this backwater, but Carter would have felt naked if he had been unarmed.

At the top of the ladder, he was greeted by the craft's skipper, a Lieutenant wearing the wavey gold bands of the Royal Naval Reserve, who saluted. "Welcome aboard, Sir."

"Thank you, Lieutenant. I'd appreciate it if that could be the last time you or any of your men salute on this little voyage. I'd hate to be stood at the top of the landing ramp, being seen off like nobility, just as a Jerry sniper is trying to work who the most valuable target might be."

"As you wish, Sir. You think we might be within range of snipers when we beach?"

"A skilled sniper can kill at five hundred yards nine shots out of ten. At a thousand yards he'll probably make a hit every third or fourth shot. If the Yorkshire Snappers[2] don't make the progress that is anticipated for them, the Jerries will not only be within sniper range, they'll be within range of a well-aimed pistol. It might be an idea to remind your ratings of that."

"Yes, Sir."

"Now, will it be OK for me to remain up here while we leave port?" There was a small wardroom below decks, set aside for officers, but Carter didn't really want to use it. Most of the officers would probably stay with their men and those few that might use it could do without Carter being a witness to their nervousness. Carter also wouldn't want his officers to see his own nerves. Later, once they were out at sea, Carter would go below decks and have a chat with the men, moving from group to group. He had given his 'Cry God for Harry, England and St George'[3] speech that morning, before they had left the tented camp. The men wouldn't expect another speech now, which was good because he hated giving them.

He could see that the naval officer wanted to raise some objection but was reluctant to do so given Carter's rank. "If you could remain at the rear, out of the way, then I see no problem Sir."

"I'll stay out of your way." Carter's HQ troop had been disbanded, returning to their own troops until he set up a regular HQ once more. It would be some time coming, Carter thought. The briefing had said they would be in the line for up to a week. On every other operation where they had been given an indefinite timescale, they had always remained where they were for much longer than expected.

Carter had often been told that being in command was often the loneliest place to be. The men had each other, as did the junior officers. Even the 2IC and the QM could get together for a natter if they wanted to, but he was a man apart. In the Royal Navy the Captain of the ship wasn't even allowed into the Wardroom unless invited by its members. It was almost like being a vampire, he thought; only able to cross a threshold by invitation. So, better to stay here, where men were doing their jobs and he could hear their muttered conversations. He might still be alone but at least it wouldn't feel like it quite so much.

At the wheel stood the Cox'n, to his left stood a rating to operate the levers that connected to the throttles down in the engine room. Carter could feel the vibration of the twin diesels below decks. The Lieutenant stood to one side, naval binoculars hanging from a strap around his neck, looking out over the bows, waiting for the craft ahead of them to clear so that he could slip their moorings and follow them. At the front was a tug that would guide them along the crowded waterway and out into the open sea. It would also take any craft in tow that broke down. They needed every man, so leaving a hundred and twenty commandos bobbing about in the English Channel couldn't be permitted.

At eighteen-thirty hours precisely a signal rocket soared skywards, presumably from the tug, exactly as planned. They were off and Operation Pegasus, the advance to the Orne bridges, had officially started.

The ride was smooth enough to start with, along Southampton Water and out into The Solent. It was only when they had cleared the sheltering bulk of the Isle of Wight that the seas started to get really heavy. Carter's stomach lurched in protest in sympathy with the movement of the boat, but he knew it would be worse for the men, cooped up down below without an horizon on which to keep their eyes fixed. The worst sufferers would set off those with marginally stronger stomachs, in a chain reaction that would only be resisted by those most hardened sailors in the commando.

One of the gangway doors flew open and a soldier dashed across the deck to hang his head over the side railing. He was only the first. One after the other they came. They shouldn't really be above decks – a precaution against strafing attacks from the air – but it was better than them being sick down below. The air would be bad enough without the additional stench.

Some men chose the wrong railing to bend over and ended up having their own vomit thrown back at them by the wind. Clamping their hands over their mouths, they hurried to the other side to rectify the situation.

Carter tried to avoid upsetting his own stomach further, by taking in the view. In the early June evening he had plenty of light to see by. The brigade's landing craft sailed in rows of three, leaving sea room on either side for other ships. They would move into line abreast only when they started their final run into shore. In the distance Carter could make out the destroyer escorts, ready to chase away any German craft that was foolish enough to leave port.

The briefings had spoken a lot about 'element of surprise' and 'deception operations'[4] but Carter knew it would be impossible to keep a fleet of this size hidden. The capital ships, which would bombard the landing grounds, were still tied up in port. Their greater speed meant they wouldn't leave until almost midnight.

Above their heads wave after wave of bombers headed south, dropping a deadly cargo on rail heads and roads, barracks and artillery positions. Above the bombers flights of fighters circled, held back by the slower aircraft below. Later would come the transport planes with their paratroops and towing the gliders that would take the airborne infantry to their destinations.

As darkness fell, late in the evening, it left Carter with no excuse for staying above decks. He bowed to the inevitable and headed down to the wardroom. Dropping his kit in the corner, he greeted

Molly Brown. He had a pencil poised over a crossword. There was also the medical officer, a pink faced graduate who had come straight in from Achnacarry, where he had undergone a greatly reduced version of the commando training course. He was pretending to be reading a paperback novel. Carter was grateful to have him, wet behind the ears as he may be. On previous operations he knew that men who might have survived had died because of a lack of qualified medical help. The padre wasn't there, he noted. No doubt sitting in a quiet corner somewhere, providing spiritual sustenance for nervous soldiers. Again, the padre was a new addition to the commando.

"Where's everyone else?" Carter asked, knowing the answer already.

"With their troops. Going over the briefing one last time or just chatting and drinking tea." Brown replied.

"OK, I'm going to have a wander round below decks as well. Let them know the CO cares about them enough to want to see them even though they stink of vomit."

Brown gave a chuckle. "I think they know that already, Sir."

"Never hurts to give them a reminder."

There was a short gangway leading to a connecting door to the cavernous space where the troops were sitting in rows on the hard metal deck, their equipment piled around them. Carter caught the glint of a hip flask being hastily concealed as a sharp-eyed trooper spotted his arrival. He pretended he hadn't noticed. It wouldn't be the only one and if that was what a man needed to get him through the night, who was he to criticise? In fact, he wished he'd had the same foresight. His batman, Tpr Gordon, had offered to pack him a 'bottle of something' as he had referred to it, but Carter had declined. It wasn't that he didn't want a drink, it was more that if he started drinking, he might not stop. On his decisions men's lives depended and he didn't want his brain dulled by whisky, even the fine bottle of Jura single malt that Gordon had found from somewhere.

In the low-intensity lighting, he picked out the troops' officers squatting amongst their NCOs, poring over maps, discussing the plans in low voices. Along the rows, soldiers played cards, read paperback novels, comics and old newspapers or chatted to their mates in low voices. The more obsessive men were checking their kit; they would do it more than once before the morning even though they had done it before. Others were asleep, or at least pretending to be. At the far end, where the bow of the craft was, a hatch showed a brighter patch of light from the tiny galley.

Even from the rear of the room Carter could smell food cooking. It would be doing nothing to help the men suffering from seasickness. The men would be fed a hot meal at midnight then given sandwiches about an hour before they were due to land. All the men hoped they would be bacon sandwiches, but Carter knew they were more likely to be bully beef or sardines. The hatch had a broad shelf that was formed when the hinged upper half of the door was lowered and on that the navy cook had set an urn of hot water, so the men could make themselves brews throughout the night. The Navy hadn't thought of that; Carter had come up with it during one of the briefings. He'd tried to get a 'tot' issued as well, but the Navy had made no promises.

Moving along the lines, Carter waved the men back as they tried to stand up, instead squatting down beside them, holding short conversations, telling the same jokes over and over, offering the same words of encouragement. Despite their sickness they were all in good spirits, or they were hiding their nervousness well.

As he was returning to the rear again, after having spoken to the final group of men, he bumped into the padre.

"How are the men, Humphrey?"

"As you'd expect, Sir, nervous and wanting to hear comforting words. But the remarkable thing is, not one of them said he was afraid of dying. They only wanted reassurance that they'd go to heaven if they did."

"And did you reassure them?"

The padre offered a small smile. "If I didn't believe that myself, then I couldn't be here telling the men that I do. What about you, Sir? Anything you'd like to get off your chest?" Although 15 Cdo's padre was Church of England, the Catholics still went to him for confession; at least, those that hadn't managed to get to a Catholic priest before they had left Southampton.

"No, I think I'll save my sins for God to hear for himself." Carter hadn't been much of a believer before the war and, having seen first-hand what God's creations were capable of doing to each other, he was even less of a believer now.

"God knows what's in your heart, Sir. You don't have to worry on that score." After they had entered the short gangway that led to the wardroom, the padre pulled a hip flask from inside his battledress blouse. "Care for a drop?" he asked as he unscrewed the top.

"Really padre?"

"It's not just the troops who get nervous, Sir. It's my first time in combat and I don't even have a gun with which to shoot back."

"Would you use one if you were allowed it?"

"No, but it might help me feel braver to have it."

"Bravery comes from here." Carter tapped the padre's chest with one hand as he took the flask with the other. "A gun doesn't make you brave. It just gives you something to hold onto while you feel afraid."

Raising the flask to his lips, Carter took a generous mouthful, bracing himself for the burn of spirit. Instead he got a cloyingly sweet taste.

"Good God… Sorry padre … what the Devil's that?"

The padre chuckled. "I had better hope the Devil has nothing to do with it. It's communion wine. I have to say, not the best vintage but the ladies of my former parish seemed to like it."

"With respect, padre, they can have it." Carter slapped the man on the back. "Come on, let's try to get some rest. We're going to need it."

[1] The Royal Navy Regulating Branch was their equivalent to the Regimental Police (not to be confused with the Royal Military Police) and were under the authority of the Master at Arms, the senior most Warrant Officer aboard a ship (equivalent to the RSM). Their duties included maintaining order aboard ship, but also mounting patrols on shore to deal with unruly sailors on shore leave. Since 2007 they have been known as the Royal Navy Police, absorbing both the Regulating Branch and the Royal Marines Police.

[2] One of two nicknames for the East Yorkshire Regiment, the other being The Poona Guards. (Poona is the British name a city in northern India, now reverted to its original name of Pune). The origin of "snappers" is because they ran out of ammunition during the American War of Independence, but their officer ordered them to continue firing their muskets, the flints making a snapping sound on the empty pans. Although the weapons didn't fire, the enemy withdrew thinking they were still firing. Their official nickname was The Yorkshire Warriors.

[3] Henry V Act 3 Scene 1, Henry's speech before Harfluer that starts "Once more into the breach, dear friends, once more."

[4] Operation Fortitude was the Allied deception operation to convince the Germans that the Allies were going to land anywhere other than Normandy. Fortitude North suggested an invasion of Norway, but the far bigger Fortitude South was aimed at convincing the Germans that the invasion would be across the Straits of Dover to land between Calais and Dunkirk. When real tanks moved out of their parks they were replaced by rubber or wood/canvas dummies (a tactic that had been used with some success before the Battle of El Alamein) and an entire American Army group (First US Army Group or FUSAG), supposedly located in Kent and East Sussex, was created out of fresh air by moving vehicles and men around, switching unit identity badges, and sending out large numbers of radio signals from non-existent units. To give the deception greater

credence, "command" of FUSAG was given to General George Patton, who was still in disgrace, having struck two soldiers who were in hospital in Cyprus, suffering from shell shock – what we would now call PTSD. The Germans couldn't envisage the invasion taking place without America's greatest (in their view) living general being in command. The author's mother was a military telephonist at Dover Castle in the spring of 1944 and, such was the amount of telephone traffic she was handling from these fake units, that she became convinced that she was sitting in the middle of the invasions' assembly area, not nearly 100 miles away from it. As well as those operations, on the night before D-Day the Allies dropped hundreds of dummy paratroops (called Ruperts) over northern France and the RAF jammed German radar by dropping "Window", metal foil strips that confused radar signals by giving thousands of returns, meaning that radar operators couldn't tell which were real aircraft and which were the metal strips. The diversion was successful and Hitler concentrated most of his armoured units in the Pas De Calais area. Even after the invasion he continued to believe that the Normandy landings were just a diversion and kept his armoured divisions in place for several more days. It was probably the biggest error of the war as it allowed time for the Allies to consolidate their beachhead in Normandy.

* * *

There was an almost constant whoosh of shells passing over the landing craft, travelling in both directions. The naval rating standing by the winch that controlled the landing ramps, kept ducking in fear.

"Don't worry lad." A commando shouted from the side railing. "The ones you hear are the ones that will miss you. You'll never hear the one that hits you!" The rating remained un-reassured and showed his opinion of the advice with a two fingered salute.

Carter had come up on deck as they had passed through the line of cruisers that were sending volley after volley of heavy artillery shells towards shore targets. A pall of smoke hung over the beach, though what might be burning couldn't be established. The fusillade had started before dawn, targeting the forward defensive positions before moving southwards to batter targets further inland.

The next line of ships was made up with the destroyers and corvettes that had escorted the first attacking wave to Normandy, adding the weight of their smaller guns to the attack. Carter picked out an abandoned landing craft, still afloat but half full of water, probably hit as it returned to the landing ships that were further out at sea, behind the heavy cruisers.

But the traffic wasn't all one way. Great gouts of water flew skywards as the shore batteries attempted to sink the escort ships, the landing craft and the tugs. The cruisers were too far from shore to be threatened.

As Carter watched, a destroyer split in half, no longer able to stay in one piece after having been hit.[1] He hoped that the survivors had got off, but there seemed to be a lack of lifeboats in the water nearby. There was nothing he could do though. Rescuing sailors was a job for someone else. He had a lot more men than a destroyer's crew depending on him right now.

Carter was now standing on the port side gangway, just behind the hinges that connected it to the ramp that would be dropped down when they struck the beach. There was still some time before that would happen, but Carter wanted the men to see that he was ready and would be the first one of 15 Cdo to land in France. Carter had already arranged with the landing craft's captain that he should pull ahead of the other craft being used by the commando, so that none of his other officers could claim the honour of beings first ashore.

Shells started to erupt in the sea closer to them as an enemy artillery spotter picked out the new, and quite large targets that were closing with the shore. A shell hit the landing craft to Carter's right and it slowed visibly. A hit to the engine room, he surmised. But it was still underway. Judging by the distance, the troops on board would make it to shore.

Away to Carter's left he could see the row of craft carrying 16 Cdo into Roger Beach. They were almost there, having started out that few minutes earlier than Carter's flotilla.

"Begging your pardon, Sir." A voice shouted in Carter's ear, struggling to make itself heard above the explosions that were now erupting all around them. Water cascaded over the side, soaking Carter and all those close to him with chilly seawater. That was a close one, he thought, as he shook water from his eyes.

"Yes, what is it?" Carter shouted back at the Leading Seaman[2] who was standing on the main deck.

"Skipper's compliments, Sir, but he says we're running five minutes ahead of schedule and wants to know if we should slow down."

And make themselves an easier target to hit, thought Carter. Not bloody likely. "Please tell the skipper that I think we will be forgiven if we arrive at our destination a little before the allotted time. Continue the run into shore as planned."[3]

The seaman grinned and hurried away, the same thought about being a target having perhaps crossed his own mind.

Behind Carter, 1 Troop were arranged in single file, spilling back onto the main deck and into the doorway that led below decks. On the other side of the craft, 3 Troop were lined up behind Molly Brown. As soon as the ramps dropped, the two officers would sprint down the ramp into the water and then wade ashore onto French soil. Given the burdens they were carrying, 'sprint' might be a bit ambitious, but they would certainly run. The longer they were standing high on the front of the landing craft, the more likely they would be hit by a sniper or a machine gun, if any were still in range.

How far now? Two hundred yards, perhaps. The boat had slowed but was still moving at a fast walking pace. Bullets started to smack into the hull and crack above Carter's head. He didn't think they were aimed shots, probably the defenders firing on the assault troops and their bullets just continuing out to sea until they either hit something or gravity dragged them down into the water. If they were aimed shots more would be hitting the bows of the boat.

But it made Carter feel vulnerable. He had absolutely no cover where he was. Even Ronnie Pickering, standing behind him, had Carter's body and equipment to protect him. Carter gulped as a bullet pinged off the hull close to his foot.

The landing craft's tannoy crackled into life. "Brace for landing" the command was given, before being repeated. Carter took a firm hold of the railing on either side of him. Slow as it was moving, when the craft came to a stop the heavily laden bodies of the commandos would try to keep moving forward. On the small assault boats, Carter had been crushed by the men behind him on more than one occasion, as they pressed him against the ramp at the front.

The boat juddered to a halt and Carter had to tighten his grip to stop himself falling. If he did, he would doubtless roll down the ramp and land face down in the water to be trampled by the men behind. They had almost had a man drown when it had happened during one of their training exercises.

There was a split second's delay and then the ramp beneath Carter's feet was tilting downwards. Carter was moving before the far end hit the water with a splash that threw water sideways. No time to be tentative, he reminded himself. Keep moving or Ronnie Pickering will be using you as a duckboard to keep his feet dry.

The wood of the ramp was replaced by sand which shifted under Carter's feet. He looked up. They seemed to be quite a long way from shore still; further than he had expected.

He waded through water up to his thighs, then the ground under him seemed to disappear. So sudden was the change that Carter sank beneath the waves under the combined weight of his body and his kit.

Surely it wasn't all going to end like this? Drowning on a beach, in sight of land. No, it couldn't. He wouldn't let it.

He struck downwards with his feet, feeling them hit the ground and propelling him upwards again. His head cleared the water, his feet still in contact with the ground, at least they were until a wave rolled past him, submerging him again. He toyed with the idea of making himself lighter by dropping his bicycle. But no, that would

be too embarrassing. He couldn't be the only soldier to get ashore without a bike.

But he was five feet ten tall. Many of his men were much shorter. They would struggle more. At least they had their buddy system, where they worked in pairs, inseparable in almost all respects. They'd help each other.

Right here, right now, survival was the only option, a part of his brain told him. They had been warned of the possibility. The shores of Normandy weren't flat. The coast was littered with sandbanks that were hidden by the tide. Just his luck for their craft to have hit one of those.

He struggled forward, his head half the time under water and half the time above it, until he reached the ground that sloped gently upwards to where the waves broke. First his nose stayed clear, then his chin, then he found he was forcing his way through water that reached only his chest, then his waist and finally it was below his knees and he was able to run the final few yards to dry ground.

Ahead of him was the line of sand dunes that separated the beach from the road that they must cross. Bullets snapped above his head, but the dunes provided some protection, provided the Germans didn't get machine guns on top of them.

He passed a soldier laying on his stomach, seemingly unharmed, But Carter knew he was dead. No man lay with his face buried in the sand in that way if he was alive. He saw a group of soldiers lying behind a dune, one wearing the red cross armband of a medic. He angled his way across to them.

They were suffering from various wounds. The medic was attempting to staunch a nasty gash in a soldier's leg. Others already wore bandages.

"How far ahead is your unit?" he demanded.

"Fifty yards, maybe." The medic replied.

"Is that all? You're supposed to be three hundred yards inland by now."

"Well, Sir, mebbe tha should tell t'Jerries that. They're the ones that's pinnin' us down."

"Sorry, of course." Carter knew he shouldn't berate the medic. He was only doing his job and it was his officers that were responsible for keeping the advance moving. Fifty yards. That was about the distance to the road.

Carter clambered to his feet and headed around the dune, where 1 Troop were filing past. They were all soaked from head to foot, just like him. He noticed one or two had already lost their bicycles. It would a be a long walk to the bridges for them.

He found the infantry using the bank on which the road ran to provide them with cover. They were laying alongside it, firing to their left. He found a corporal, the only man of rank visible, and lowered himself down beside him. The commandos were kneeling behind the soldiers, waiting for instructions. Ronnie Pickering came to join him.

"What's the hold up, Corporal?" Carter demanded as he crawled up the parapet formed by the road.

"Jerry's got machine guns in them 'ouses, Sir." The soldier replied, pointing. As if to back up the soldier, a stream of machine gun fire swept along the road in front of them, sending stone chips flying. Everyone ducked, including Carter. He could see the houses, the nearest suburb of the town of Ouistreham.

"Is anyone doing anything about them?"

"No idea, Sir. That's Roger Beach, not ours. The Old Dozen[4] are over there."

Carter was about to berate the man, intending to point out that it was his unit that was being pinned down, so it should be his unit that should be doing something about it. But, again, it wasn't his fault. It was his officers that should be taking action. Instead, he asked "Where's your platoon commander?"

"Copped a bullet coming ashore." The man said.

"Your company commander?"

"Somewhere along there." he pointed to his left, further along the line. Carter couldn't spare the time to search him out.

Instead he turned to Pickering. "OK, let's get your men across the road. Maybe we'll find cover there. At least we'll draw fire off this position and maybe they can advance."

Pickering waved his men forward, spreading them out to lie between the infantrymen. "Now!" he shouted, jumping to his feet and sprinting forward. The road wasn't wide, just enough room for two cars to pass each other, but the crossing gave enough time for the German machine guns to fire on them. Carter heard a man fall close by, then he was sliding down the bank on the other side. He landed at the bottom with a squelch. The field was marshy, he could see and in places there were pools of water that had formed. Even tanks might get bogged down in that sort of mud and Carter wondered if the fields had been flooded as a defensive measure.[5]

Pickering was directing his men as they slid down the bank, forming a line that faced the edge of the town. The only cover was the tussocky grass and the occasional sodden hollow. Being wet already, the men didn't mind taking refuge in those. Their bicycles were left at the foot of the slope so as not to hamper them. Bren guns began to fire towards the town.

The Germans were obliging Carter by firing on the men still crossing the road. It was possible that in their low-lying field they might even be out of sight of the German positions.

"I'll see what sort of support I can get you." Carter said, turning and hurrying along the edge of the causeway formed by the road. He had gone several yards before he realised his was still dragging his bicycle with him. He dropped it and moved on. It was pretty unlikely that anyone would steal it.

Soldiers from 3 Troop had followed the example of 1 Troop and were crossing the road and throwing themselves down the slope into the field. Carter picked out one of the section commanders, Norton. A new boy but a bit of a firebrand, if his performance in training was anything to go by.

Carter tapped him on his shoulder to attract his attention. "Where's James?" He asked, wanting to know where the troop commander, James Mackie, was.

"Getting a wound dressed. Nothing serious. He'll be here soon."

Speaking of James, Carter wondered where his radio operator was. He hoped he was OK, but more than that he needed him. Without a radio it was going to be hard work keeping track of his command. But first things first.

"OK, send a runner back to find 2 Troop. I want a Vickers to go and help out 1 Troop, along there." Something slapped into the mud not far from his feet. Looking with horror, Carter realised it was a mortar bomb. The soft mud had prevented the detonator from firing. If it had, he and Norton would now be dead.

"It must have come from that orchard." Norton said, pointing. To the right of the houses that concealed the machine guns, Carter picked out the trees. The Calvados region of Normandy was famed for its apples, Carter recalled. He opened his map case and identified the feature. "OK, Give the runner this." Carter scribbled some numbers onto a page of his note book, tore it out and handed it to Norton. "Tell the runner to give it to an officer or an NCO from the mortar section. That's their target. Have you got a radio?"

"Not yet."

If most of the commandos were heavily burdened, it was even worse for the radio operators. No wonder they were slow getting across the road. "OK, you'll have to use runners, but for now you're going to be the forward observer for the mortar team. OK?"

"No problem, Sir."

"It's OK, you can call me Lucky until we're back in barracks again. Pretty much everyone does. Now, do you understand what you have to do, Phillip?

"Vickers to 1 Troop, mortar to fire on the orchard and I'm the observer for now."

"Good. But keep your men moving forward. 1 Troop will provide covering fire."

"No problem. I'll stick a rocket up their arses."

Carter gave him a slap on the shoulder and hurried on. More commandos were hurling themselves down the bank from the road. Apart from the bottoms of their trousers, Carter noticed they were almost completely dry. Lucky them. That was 4 Troop, the next landing craft in the flotilla to the one he had been in and the one that had also carried the Heavy Weapons Troop; 2 Troop.

Ernie Barraclough spotted him and waited for him to reach him. "You look like a drowned rat, Sir, but one that's been dipped in sugar."

Carter took a look at his uniform and saw how much sand was sticking to it. "A bit like one of those doughnuts the Americans like so much." Carter said with a chuckle.

"Precisely, why can't they just put good old jam in them?"

"A topic for another conversation, I think Ernie. Keep your men moving forward but be aware that there's Jerry machine guns and mortars over to the left. I'm trying to get them neutralised, but it might take a while."

Which reminded Carter that his Vickers and mortars may be able to kill gun crews, but they couldn't silence a machine gun or a mortar that way alone. The dead crews could and would be replaced. He had to get infantry into those houses to prevent their use by the enemy.

He slithered his way back up the bank and sprinted across the road, stone chips flying around his feet as the sprinted back across the road. Throwing himself down the other side he landed heavily, rolling over to find himself looking into the bemused face a young Lieutenant. Not one of his officers, so he must be one of the Snappers.

"Ah, an officer at last. Look, my men are directing fire on the machine guns that are to the left. I want your men to use the covering fire to attack the houses and take them."

"But that's Roger Beach, Sir. Nothing to do with us."

"I don't give a flying fuck whose beach it is, Lieutenant," Carter snarled. "My men are being prevented from advancing because of those positions and if you, or someone in your battalion, doesn't do something soon, thousands of paratroops are going to die." It was probably an exaggeration, but he thought the circumstances warranted it. "If we don't get moving soon, then someone is going to face a court martial. Do you want it to be you?"

"N ... No, Sir."

It was the curse of the infantry, one evident in the previous war as well, that they were very heavily dependent on orders from above. If you obeyed orders then you couldn't be blamed for what happened, but if you took the initiative you also took the blame if things went wrong. It discouraged freedom of thought and action.

"Right, Sir, then you, Sir," Carter prodded him in the chest, "had better make sure that someone gets my orders and damned soon." Carter couldn't order a battalion commander to do anything, but he could make his feeling felt. Any decent CO would use the covering fire to advance anyway, but if he didn't know what the commandos were doing, he might not even realise that the covering fire was being provided.

He didn't wait for a reply, he just made the sprint back across the road to try to find the rest of his command. 5 Troop were arriving where he expected them, but there was no sign of any troops advancing beyond them.

"Where's 6 Troop, he asked the nearest trooper." 5 and 6 troops had been sharing a landing craft.

"Shell exploded on their side of the boat, Sir. It was carnage."

Carter hurried on, looking for Jeremy Groves, the troop commander. He found him directing the fire from a Bren gun towards the far edge of the field, where the ground rose again to provide the bank for the road in the distance. The road his commando had to reach so they could proceed to the bridges.

"Where's Maj Ramsey?" Carter asked. He was in command of the half commando on the right-hand side of the beach and had travelled with 5 and 6 troops.

"No idea, Sir. Last I saw of him he was at the front of 6 Troop at the top of the Elsie's[7] ramp. I think I saw him helping a wounded man away to get him treated."

"Send a runner back to find him. He's to leave casualty clearance to the Navy and get across here. Have you any idea what's in front of you right now?"

"We're getting some machine gun fire from over there." He pointed in the direction where the Bren gun was aiming. "Not too bad, but there's mortars being used too. Luckily not many are exploding, thanks to the mud."

"OK, when the runner has found Ramsey, send him to 2 Troop to get the second Vickers up here. Use it to give you covering fire as you move forward. If you want counter-mortar fire as well, feel free to send fire orders back."

"OK, No problem. Where will you be if anyone asks?"

"I'll be at the front of the advance to the bridge, where I belong."

Carter ran as quickly as he could back to collect his bike, finding it exactly where he had left it. He hefted it in his left hand, held his Tommy gun in his right, and was just about to head off to join 3 Troop when a commando slid down the bank and lay still. A Vickers gun rolled out of his hands. Seemingly without a thought, Carter picked the weapon up and sprinted towards one of the pools of water, diving into it and sliding to a stop on the far edge. He had the gun, but it was useless without its tripod and ammunition. There was a splash and another trooper landed beside him and set about erecting the tripod. "Better let me 'ave that, Sir." The trooper held his hands out to take the gun from Carter. A third trooper splashed into the hollow and was opening an ammunition box before the water had stopped streaming from his face.

The tripod bearer opened fire with the Vickers, shooting at the twinkling lights in the windows that showed where the German machine guns were. There was no shortage of targets. The Germans had always favoured the machine gun when it came to defence.

"We're going to run out of ammunition pretty quickly if we don't get a third man for the crew." The replacement gunner shouted above the noise of his weapon.

Carter took the hint and went off to find some ammunition carriers. As the men had disembarked from the landing craft they had deposited their burdens of machine gun ammunition and mortar bombs on the sand to be collected by 2 Troop as they needed them. But that depended on there being men available to go and collect them.

Raising his head Carter looked for the nearest members of 1 Troop. There, two of them in the skimpy cover provided by a grass tussocks. He scampered across to them. "You two, you're not doing much right now. I want you to keep feeding the Vickers with ammo. Got it."

"No problem Lucky." One of them grinned at him. Carter didn't waste any more time and went back to collect his bicycle again.

He wasn't as heavily burdened as the troopers, so he caught up with the men of 3 Troop quite quickly. They were stretched out in a ragged line abreast, moving steadily across the marshy land. Occasional bursts of machine gun fire cracked over their heads, but it soon became apparent that the machine gunners were concentrating on anyone who tried to cross the road, rather than the men who were crossing the open fields. Mortar bombs continued to splash around them and the occasional one went off when it hit something more solid beneath the mud, but the mud acted as a cushion, absorbing the blast and preventing shrapnel from flying about. If the Germans had flooded the fields, it was working against them now, not for them.

The aerial photographs had shown that the fields were drained by a latticework of ditches and streams, these would now be full and if they had overtopped to form lakes, they provided traps for the unwary.

But the mud also clung to Carter's boots, dragging him down and slowing his pace. Each step was a struggle and he blessed the foresight that had prompted him to organise games of rugby on Worthing beach. The loose shingle had almost the same effect as the mud, strengthening the leg muscles. Carter doubted he'd have made it this far without that conditioning of his body. But the men had cursed him at the time, because it had been hard work and painful when they had been tackled to the ground.

A man went down to Carter's right, cursing and rolling in the mud in pain. More shots cracked past Carter, sweeping along the line of advancing commandos. Diving for cover Carter crawled forward until he reached the bank on top of which the road ran. He risked peeping over the top, seeing the twinkling of a muzzle flash from a row of poplar trees. It must have only just been positioned, because the British troops would have been visible for quite a distance.

"Bren gun!" Carter called, hoping one was nearby. Two troopers crawled forward to lie alongside him.

"Half right; four hundred; tall trees, machine gun at the base." He issued the firing orders.

"Seen!" the gunner replied, unfolding the bipod of his weapon and easing it over the top of the bank.

"Fire when ready. Keep firing …" But the rest of what he was going to say was drowned out by the hammering of the weapon.

The machine gun replied, sending stone chips flying off the road and forcing Carter to duck. The Bren gun fell silent and the loader switched magazines, thinking that was the problem. It took some seconds for him to realise that the gunner no longer had a face.

"Take over!" Carter commanded, dragging the dead gunner to one side before switching to the far side of the weapon to replace the loader and get the gun back into action once more. The hammering restarted but stopped almost at once, the gun's hammer falling on the empty chamber with a click. With practiced ease the replacement gunner removed the empty mag, allowing Carter to slide a new one into place and the gun started firing again.

An NCO had hustled men forward to line the bank and rifles joined in the firing, then a second Bren gun. After a few minutes of intense firing the machine gun fell silent, but it wouldn't remain so.

"Get moving." Carter yelled. "Get on the road before they replace the gun crew." Carter waved his hand, pointing along the road to the southwest.

Men started to gather their burdens together, then unfolded their bikes and secured the frames, turning an inconvenient lump of baggage into a usable form of transport. Carter picked James Mackie out of the crowd. "Keep your men moving, Jimmy. I'll keep this gun here until 4 Troop arrive, then send it along the road after you."

The officer acknowledged him with a wave then started waving men forward, encouraging them and berating them in equal quantities. Carter checked his watch. Oh eight twenty, give or take a minute. At least twenty minutes behind schedule. But if the Germans weren't blocking the road ahead of them, they could still get to the bridges on time. That was the blessing of the bikes. But if the Germans had worked out what they were up to ….

He dismissed the thought. It was defeatist. His men would get through. He smiled in realisation that his command was probably the furthest forward out of all the British troops to have landed that morning. That by itself was an achievement. If they had landed in the first wave, as they had wanted to, they would probably have been able to use the element of surprise to get to the bridges before the Germans had a chance to get organised. Now, however, the enemy was flooding north to try to push the Allies back into the sea before they could even dry their boots. They might get to the bridges on time, but would they be able to stay there?

Carter pushed his thoughts to one side. He had the much more immediate problem of keeping his troops moving.

4 Troop were in the distance, but if they went up onto the road where they were, they'd have to cross in front of the Bren gun. He stopped a trooper who was just about to mount his bicycle. "Nip down to 4 Troop and pass a message asking for Capt Barraclough to join me here. Then get on your way to the bridge."

The cyclist turned his machine around and headed off along the road. He was back only moments later. Carter tapped the Bren gunner on the shoulder. "Hold your fire till this bloke is past."

"On his way!" Carter just about heard the call as the cyclist whizzed past. Perhaps whizzed was a bit strong, Carter considered. More like trundled.

Ernie Barraclough arrived a few minutes later.

"I need one of your Bren guns here, to replace this chap, then bring your troop along the bank so they pass behind him. Pass the word to 5 and 6 troops to do the same. Also pass the word to Maj Ramsey that he is to form a rear-guard from what's left of 6 Troop. He can take men from 5 Troop as well if he needs to. They're to cover our backs all the way to the bridge."

"Isn't that 17 Cdo's job, Lucky?"

"We have no idea where 17 Cdo is right now, so until they show their faces, we're going to have to cover our own backs. Ramsey will know what to do if they turn up. Now, I've been here acting as a loader for too long. I want to get to the bridge with 3 Troop, they're the ones up front right now. So get that Bren gun over here so I can get moving."

The nearest section of 4 Troop were only twenty yards away and they had a Bren gun on the nearer flank. Barraclough gave a whistle to attract their attention and signalled for them to come over.

Carter addressed the loader. "Good job there. Sorry about your mate."

"We took bets on which one of us would cop it first." The trooper replied with a grimace. "Looks like I'll be the one collecting."

"Have you been together as a team for long?"

"Since Sicily. That's when we both joined the commando. He came in from No 6 and I came straight from Achnacarry."

"I know it's tough, but it's what we do. Will you be OK?"

"Yeah, I'll be fine. But any Jerry that crosses my sights is going to regret it."

"You go ahead of me down the road. If you need to use the gun before we get to the bridge, I'll be your loader."

"Well, Sir, you're a bit slow on the magazine changes, but you'll do." The soldier grinned.

"Cheeky bastard. Now get moving."

The man retrieved his bicycle from where he had dropped it and started putting it together. Carter did the same, then picked up the satchel of Bren gun magazines and slung it around his neck. Being the loader was probably about the best contribution he could make, now that the majority of the commando were on the road or about to get on it. But it was still the best part of six miles to the bridges. He may need to make some more tough decisions before they got there.

As the man peddled away, Carter realised he hadn't even asked him his name, or that of his dead gunner. The latter he'd find out when he received the casualty reports, but he really should know the loader's name. Had he been rude? Or was his mind too focused on other things? Whichever it was, it was something he had to rectify as quickly as possible.

Giving a butterfly nut a final turn, screwing it so tight it hurt his fingers, he pushed the bicycle up the slope and onto the road. Slinging his Tommy gun across his shoulder, he pushed off against the ground and started to peddle after the Bren gunner.

[1] This was the Free Norwegian Navy ship, HNoMS Svenner, the only ship to be sunk by German naval action on D Day. She was torpedoed by German T Boats operating out of Le Havre. Thirty two Norwegian crew and one Briton were killed and one hundred and eighty five were rescued, fifteen of whom were wounded. The ship's anchor was recovered from the wreck in 2003 and now stands as the "Svenner Memorial" on Sword Beach at Hermanville-Sur-Mer.

[2] Leading Seaman – the equivalent to a corporal in the army and the RAF.

[3] This conversation did actually take place, though it was face-to-face between Peter Young (see Further Reading) and the landing craft's skipper.

[4] Nickname of the Suffolk Regiment, taken from their original designation of the 12th Regiment of Foot.

[5] At Ypres in 1914, the British Expeditionary Force was in danger of being cut off from the sea by the rapid German advance. A fisherman in Nieuwpoort (Belgium) suggested that the authorities open the sluice gates of the River Ijser at high tide, allowing the sea

in to flood the low-lying ground between Nieuwpoort and Ypres, some 20 miles away inland. The tactic was successful and the German advance was stopped. The downside of the tactic was that it prevented the ground around Ypres from draining properly, creating the infamous mud that blighted the British trenches for the rest of the war. The Germans didn't have the same problem because they occupied the higher ground.

[6] Slang for LC(I), landing craft infantry. They had a carrying capacity of 180 men, but many of them on D-Day carried fewer in order to provide more space below decks.

* * *

Carter was almost there when something jerked on his handlebars, destabilising the bike and sending him crashing to the ground. Had he hit something lying in the road? He hadn't seen any stones or other debris. As if in answer, a burst of machine gun fire splattered the road around him. He dragged himself down the bank and then reached back to grab the rear wheel of the bike and drag the machine towards him.

He at once saw the problem. A Bullet had smashed one of the spokes of the front wheel. A lucky shot for him, as it could have hit him in the leg. But the bike was of no further use. The crash had bent the wheel, jamming it in the front forks.

"In here mate." A shout came from his right and an arm waved. Carter needed no second bidding.

It was a well dug position, almost circular with the soil piled up to create a wall around it. Must have taken all night to dig, Carter thought. Cut into the forward parapet was a V shaped notch with a Bren gun barrel poking through it. The gunner and loader lying side by side.

"Bastard's been tryin' to get I for a woile!" The loader said. "Oh, sorry, Din't see thee were an officer." He had a strong rural accent.

Explained by the shoulder flash of the Oxfordshire and Buckinghamshire Light Infantry.

"Don't worry about it. I don't like people calling me by my rank when I'm in the field anyway. Now, where is that MG?"

"Crawl up 'ere an tek a look along the barrel of my little girl 'ere." The gunner said, indicating the V shape at the front of the position. Carter did as he was told. "Now, th'see that white building? Ee's in one o' them upper windows."

"What is that building?"

"Map sez it's a maternity 'ome, but we saw nuns running from it a bit back, so it's probably a convent too."

"Can you get him?"

"That's what we bin tryin' to do since daylight. No luck so far."

"Don't you have any snipers?"

"None close enough to 'ere us 'ollerin'."

"I might be able to help." Carter raised his head. "15 Cdo. Any snipers here?"

"I saw Rawlings arrive a minute or so back." An anonymous voice replied.

"See if you can find him and send him to me."

"Who shall I say wants 'im?"

"Don't you recognise your own CO's voice?"

"Sorry, Lucky. Now you come to mention it I do."

"Did 'ee just call you Lucky?" The loader asked.

"Yes. I was given the nickname after I got stuck in Norway and had to steal an E-Boat to get back home, back in 41. So I've been called Lucky by the men since. Only when we're in action, of course."

The loader and the gunner exchanged looks that suggested the commandos weren't quite normal, which was probably justified. Nothing the commandos had done was normal, since the day Carter had joined them.

A soldier slithered over the rear wall of the dugout. "Ah, Rawlings. Got a little job for you. There's a Jerry MG targeting this stretch of road and shooting at our men as they arrive. Think you can deal with him?"

"Where abouts?"

"Take a look." Carter crawled backwards from his vantage point, leaving it clear for Rawlings to replace him. The gunner pointed out the right window for him.

"Range 'bout five 'undred yards boy moy reckonin'" he told Rawlings.

"Looks about right." Rawlings adjusted the sights on his rifle, unfolding the adjustable 'leaf' sight to replace the 'battle' sight that was fixed at 300 yards. He made some minor adjustments for range, then settled the rifle's barrel alongside that of the Bren gun.

"No problem for me, Lucky, but might take me a couple of shots." He plucked some grass and tossed it into the air, watching which way the wind blew it. Slightly in Rawlings' face, Carter thought, but not much. It would hardly deflect his shots.

"If you don' moin my sayin' Lucky …" he paused to see if he would be reprimanded for his informality. "'Tis getting' a bit crowded in 'ere."

Carter took the hint. "Is there another position nearby, I'd like to be able to see my men coming along the road."

"T'other side of the road, bout twenty yards. Couple of our mates is in it."

"Good luck Rawlings. Thanks chaps." Carter bid the two light infantrymen farewell, jumped to his feet, hurdled the parapet and sprinted for the far side of the road.

"Nice bloke." One of them said.

"The best." Rawlings said, before holding his breath and squeezing the trigger of his rifle. But Carter was already too far away to hear anything other than the crack as the weapon fired.

Pursued by machine gun bullets, he dived headfirst into the dugout that he had been directed to. "Sorry chaps, mind if I join you?"

"Mak' y'sel' at 'ome. boy." One of the dugout's occupants said, without taking his eyes off the section of field he had been assigned to cover. Bodies in *Feldgrau* littered the fields, evidence of the Germans' previous attempts to reclaim the bridge.

"Any Jerries out that way?" Carter enquired.

"Not close enough to get at. Seen the odd one in the distance, but 'tis all."

"Well, 17 Cdo will be heading that way soon, they'll clear them out."

"'Bout time an' all." The man said, looking pointedly at his wristwatch.

Carter checked his own. Nine forty five. Allow ten minutes for the time he'd spent in the other dugout and it meant he'd arrived at the bridge five minutes behind schedule. Some of his men would have been there earlier than that, but not by much. He'd closed the gap on the leaders quite considerably on the cycle ride there. But to the airborne troops who had spent most of the night under German attack, the wait would have been hellish.

A helmeted head rose above the rear parapet of the position. "I was told you were here, Lucky. What do we do now?"

"Are you at your objective yet?" Carter asked by way of reply.

"Well, we're still on the wrong bank of the canal … and then there's the river...."

"In that case, get on your bikes. If you go flat out you'll probably make it." Carter hoped he was right, but if the commandos stopped to think about it, they might not try to cross at all.

"'Course. Stupid of me to ask." The head ducked back out of sight as the embarrassed man crawled back to wherever he had been taking cover.

"Better warn 'im 'bout the sniper. 'ees got the centre of the bridge zeroed in."

Carter raised himself above the parapet and shouted "Sniper" at the man, but it was already too late. Five troopers were mounting their bicycles and peddling like mad for the bridge, about fifty yards behind Carter's position. From the top of the metal superstructure hung a maroon coloured flag with the emblem of a flying horse emblazoned on it in pale blue. The horse was being ridden by a spear wielding figure.

It was an ugly looking bridge, in Carter's opinion. It was over-engineered compared to others of a similar span. In order to let barges underneath, it was a drawbridge and the French engineers had just copied the designs of the original drawbridges, installed in castles.

Where Tower Bridge in London used counterbalances that were filled with water to raise the bridge and then emptied to lower it again, this used heavy chains to lift the span. It meant a large winch house had to be provided and that had been built at the top of the superstructure, across the approach road. There was nothing elegant about the design at all. He supposed that one day, someone would rip it down and start again.

The cyclists sped across in single file and had almost reached the far side when the middle one pitched off his bike and slid along the road's surface until he crashed into the side railings. His bike slid to a stop right next to him. But the others were across and continued along the straight road to where Carter could see the second bridge in the middle distance.

Rawlings' rifle fired again and then a third time. There was a triumphant shout from the other side of the road. "Keep your eye on that window until further notice." Carter shouted across.

Carter checked his watch again. He needed another officer here, or perhaps a warrant officer, so that he could cross the bridge himself to take the lead on the other side, but at the same time leave someone to keep the commandos moving.

He raised his head again, looking for a likely candidate. Along the road he could see plenty of cyclists, but they were still distant. The rest of 3 Troop no doubt. It was inevitable that they should become fragment as the Germans sought to intercept them. The road passed through three hamlets on its way to the bridges, Colleville-Montogmery, Saint-Aubin-d'Arquenay and Benouville, where the maternity home stood. All of them offered cover for a counter-attack, though he had spotted patrols of paratroops intent on preventing that. A few had stopped to wave at the commandos or send up a jeer as a token of their long-standing rivalries.

Out of the corner of his eye Carter spotted a hunched figure running towards him. The angle of his shoulders made it possible to see his rank badges; a lieutenant colonel, probably the CO of the Ox and Bucks.

He scrambled into the dugout. "I was told we had a high-ranking visitor." He smiled, offering his hands. "Mallinder; Ox and Bucks".

Carter shook his hand, feeling the peculiarity of the situation. Pleasantries more at home in a country house drawing room being exchanged in the middle of a battle.

"Carter, 15 Cdo."

"I say, I think we've met before. Now. Let me think …"

Carter studied the man's face. Yes, there was a vague familiarity, but no more than that.

"Got it." Mallinder cried out, slapping his thigh. "Sicily. Me and a few on my men were being held as prisoners in a farm and your lot came and recued us. Well, you attacked the farm and we happened to be inside."

"Torre Cuba. Yes, I remember. You'd been in a glider that had crashed nearby and the Italians took you prisoner. My God. The last time I saw you was heading off into the hills to find the rest of your lot. Did you succeed?"

"Oh yes. It took a day and a half of wandering around in the hills, but we found them eventually."

Carter refrained from reminding him that he probably would have found them sooner if he had taken his suggestion at the time and returned to the beach with the Italian PoWs and made inquiries at XIII Corps HQ. Instead he said "All's well that ends well, eh. So, what sort of night have you had?"

"Mixed bag. My glider came down miles away, so I had quite a hike to get here. Fortunately, some of the men were a lot closer and captured the bridge before the Jerries even knew we were here. They've counter-attacked on a couple of occasions, as you can see." He nodded in the direction of the scattered German bodies. "You made good time to get here. We couldn't be sure the Jerries wouldn't work out the plan and get between you and us."

"I must say we expected more resistance." Carter admitted. "What we have met seemed to be piecemeal and uncoordinated. An MG here, a mortar team there, a foot patrol. Mercifully no armour."

"No, that's all well inland, out of range of the ships' guns. No doubt they'll get organised eventually and then we'll know about it."

"What about him?" Carter nodded towards a *kubelwagen* that was canted off the road halfway between the dugout and the bridge. It was a burnt out shell, with a body leaning against the front wheel, its upper half burnt to a crisp but its lower half hardly injured.

"I have a theory about him. I think he was off seeing his mistress in Caen. When the balloon went up came screaming across the bridge, trying to get back to his unit, not knowing we were even here. One of my men lobbed a grenade into it which went off and started a fire on the backseat. Chummy here got out, only to be hit by half a dozen rifle bullets. Which was probably a blessing when you look at what happened to him when the car's fuel tank went up."

"Am I on the right road for the River Orne/" James Mackie's cheery call attracted Carter's attention.

"Jimmy, good man, you've made it. I want you to take charge here and keep the men moving across the bridge. Be careful though, there's sniper got it zeroed in. We've lost one man already."

"I'll see what I can do about that." Mallinder offered. "I wasn't too bothered by him while he was concentrating on the bridge, but I can see he'll be a bit inconvenient now."

"Thanks. I've got to move forward and reach our objective. We've been ordered to move north as far as Amfreville."

"OK, well 9 Para are holding the ground between here and there. But the Jerries are still in control of the Merville battery to the north and they won't want you going that way, so expect some resistance."

"OK, thanks for the warning." He turned back to address Mackie again. "If you see my radio operator, James, send him up to me. I feel slightly hamstrung not being able to communicate with you all. But for the record, the plan stays the same. Cross the river and the canal and then turn north to get to Amfreville. Tell the troop commanders to try and get a bit organised before they advance. They can't be effective split up as they are. We aren't under so much time pressure now, so we can pause for a little while to re-group. When Maj Ramsey gets here with the rear-guard, he can wait for 17 Cdo to arrive, then cross and come up to join us."

"So, you're leaving us on our own again." Mallinder said, jokingly Carter hoped.

"You seemed to have managed OK so far without us. Keep your hand on your wallet when 17 Cdo arrives though." It was an almost obligatory slur against a rival unit.

They shook hands again and Carter headed off towards the bridge, now on foot thanks to the damage inflicted on his bike. He crouched low and scuttled across, resting behind some of the larger bridge components when his legs muscles shrieked their protest. A bullet did spang off metal work, so he had been spotted by the sniper, but the bridge provided plenty of cover providing he kept low enough.

On the far side of the bridge he moved through some more defensive positions manned by the light infantry and headed for the second bridge. That was crossed without incident and he turned north, jogging steadily, his breathing a little heavier than normal because of his heavy pack. It was like being out on a solo speed march.

From his right came the occasional crackle of small arms fire, the crump of a mortar or the crack of a grenade. 9 Para, he presumed, holding the left flank against the Germans along the line of the direct road to Amfreville; the road that ran straight from the end of the river bridge. It was why he had directed the commando along this route. The alternative would have taken his men close to the front line. No point in exposing them to danger earlier than need be.

After a few minutes a group of cycling commandos caught up with him.

"Fancy some company, Lucky?"

"Normally I would be delighted to share your company, Phillip. But today I have pressing business, so I'll thank you to relinquish your bike, so that I can catch up with the leading troops."

The young Lieutenant's face fell, knowing he'd now have to walk the rest of the way. "What about my men?" He protested, thinking he was playing a trump card. "I won't be able to keep up with them."

"They'll be safe enough with me, won't you lads?" He surveyed the faces of the grinning men, taking a small pleasure at their officer's discomfort.

"'Course we will Lucky. Blokes around you have a habit of surviving." One of them spoke for all.

It wasn't true, Carter knew better than anyone, but he didn't want to damage morale by pointing out the number of commandos that had died by his side.

"There you are, Phillip, nothing to worry about. And I'm sure you can find another bike somewhere.".

With that he eased the handlebars out of the officer's hands and mounted up. "Wagons, roll!" he imitated the wagon masters of the American westerns that they had seen on the silver screen provided by their hosts at Southampton.[2]

He set off at breakneck speed, relying on the troopers to keep up with him. Having small groups of men isolated wasn't the best way to fight a war. It only needed a medium sized German patrol to spot them and they would be chewed up like dog food. He caught up with the group of four survivors that had been first across the bridge, lying alongside the road at a place called Le Haute Ecarde, where there was a right turn heading up a gentle slope to the village of Amfreville that sat astride a ridge running north to south.

The men had their rifles in front of them, as though taking aim but Carter noticed they'd fixed bayonets.

"What were you about to do?" he asked.

"I thought I saw some Jerries moving about on the edge of the village, so we were going to creep forward and take a dekko."[4] The man who answered was the one who had led the first little group of cyclists across the bridge.

"OK, but four of you are too small a group. I'll lead a recce patrol of …" he counted the number of men who had followed him; eleven of them. "… eight men. That's you four and you, you, you and you." He picked out a Bren gunner and his loader plus two more men. "The rest of you set up a defence here and when others arrive, stretch them along the road facing the village. Whoever's in charge, tell them to wait for us to come back or until I signal that it's safe to come up the hill."

At that moment a howling noise started, like a cow bellowing in pain. A series of explosions erupted in the field in front of them.

"What the fuck was that?" a soldier blurted.

"A Moaning-Minnie[5], at a guess." One of his mates replied.

Carter had to chuckle. He wondered where the nickname for the *Nebelwerfer* had come from.

But that was a question for another day. Right now he had to try and find a safe route that would get him closer to Amfreville.

To his left the road continued northwards towards the coast, straddled by half a dozen houses. They were deserted, the occupants having fled before the fighting got close. Or perhaps they were hiding in their cellars waiting for it all to end. But beyond the houses a hedge ran along the side of a field and beyond that were more houses and more fields. If they kept low, the commandos might be able to make it into the outskirts of Amfreville undetected. It was the only option. The road that took the direct route was too exposed. A German MG positioned at the top end of it could keep them pinned down all day.

"Drop your big packs." He ordered the chosen men. "They're too bulky. Make sure you've got plenty of ammunition and grenades in your pouches though. Oh, and put your helmets on." He looked pointedly at a trooper who was wearing his green beret, despite Carter having prohibited it in his final briefing to the commando before they left Southampton. The trooper blushed and snatched at the offending headgear, replacing it with his Brodie.[5]

Leaving final instructions for what the rear party should do if he failed to make it back within a couple of hours, he led his patrol through the village, dodging from cover to cover until they reached the far end. There was a short open stretch between the vegetable garden of the last house and the hedge that ran eastwards. Crossing to the far side of the road so they could drop down the bank and remain hidden, they moved forward at a crouch until they had the hedge between them and any watchers in Amfreville.

Peering across the road, the only part of the objective he could now see was the squat tower of its ancient church. It provided the ideal location for an artillery observer, as the crash of another volley of *Neberwerfer* rockets testified.

But that meant that the observer would have his eyes on the fall of shot, not on the ground to the north of Le Haute Ecarde. "Now!" Carter shouted, leading the men across the road in a dash. They dived for cover behind the hedge and stopped to catch their breath. Carter did a headcount. All present and correct. If they had been seen they would soon know about it.

The hedge stood at least six feet high and it had been a long time since it had last been trimmed, so it was also quite thick, providing good cover. But Carter had been on enough patrols to know that no cover was perfect, so he was cautious as he led the men up the slope. They reached the end of the field and found a gap in the bottom corner, perhaps created by animals forcing a way through. Too small for a cow or a sheep to pass through, but his men were able to force a passage by crawling on their bellies.

It took them about half an hour to reach the edge of Amfreville, marked by the rear garden of a small cottage. It was overgrown, suggesting that whoever the owner was, the cottage hadn't been lived in for a while. The Germans had cleared a lot of the population out of the coastal areas in 1940 and placed heavy restrictions on the movements of those left behind. Many of the French had decided life would be more pleasant elsewhere and had gone to stay with relatives further inland, if they had any. With the invasion anticipated, it is possible that more of the population may have been moved. The occupiers wouldn't want their supply routes blocked by refugees from the fighting that would follow any landings.

Finding a gap in the fence, Carter surveyed the rear of the house, looking for signs that it was being used as a defensive position. There were no sandbags at the doors or windows and all the glass was intact. That was a good sign. Soldiers always smashed windows so that explosions wouldn't send glass flying around like airborne bayonets. He raised his eyes and examined the roof. No sign of any missing tiles either, so no one had manufactured loopholes through which to fire weapons.

He checked the neighbouring houses in the same way. Nothing. Satisfied that they could move forward without being spotted, he pushed the fence to find out how strong it was. It wobbled under his touch. He signalled to one of the men to put his weight on it and it folded flat to the ground with only slight crackles from the wood; most of it seemed to be rotten. He waved the men through before putting his boots on top of it to allow the last man to follow. When he stepped into the garden the fence remained flat.

The men had split into two groups, each moving to one of the rear corners of the building. Another low moan came as more *Nebelwerfer* rockets passed over the village to crash at the bottom of the hill. A machine gun added its chatter to the symphony of sound.

During one of the briefings, the Brigadier had told the assembled officers that the Germans were short of many commodities. But the one thing they were never short of was machine guns, Carter thought. Since the trenches of the First World War, the German defensive doctrine said that the infantry should dominate the battlefield with the weapons. It had worked in defence, but in attack they were much less useful. They were heavy to carry and, being belt fed, it required more men to carry the spare ammunition. They also went through bullets at an alarming rate, which then tied down more men to bring fresh supplies from the rear. No wonder the Germans had invested so heavily in mechanisation to support their *Blitzkrieg* strategy. But now they were short of fuel and the infantry had to march whenever possible and how they must be cursing all those machine guns.

As Carter had suspected, the MG seemed to be firing from where the road from Le Haute Ecarde entered the village. The Germans must suspect an attack from that direction was imminent. Which meant that all eyes would be looking down the hill to where more and more of 3 Troop must be arriving.

Which meant they weren't looking in his direction.

Keeping the cottage between himself and the machine gun, Carter skirted it so that he could look out onto the road. A lorry trundled past carrying a section of men. It stopped in a square about a hundred yards away. Roads ran in from three sides. The one nearest came in from Merville to the north, he recalled, before continuing south to the Orne river crossing. At the far end of the third road was 3 Troop.

The soldiers tumbled out of the back of the lorry and an officer hurried them into positions facing the threat. So far as he could see, there were no pre-prepared defences, so the men would have to take cover wherever they could find it. probably inside houses. His thinking was confirmed as he heard the sound of glass being smashed.

But it wasn't a large force. There had been eight men in the back of the truck, plus an officer and the driver. Two men manning the machine gun and an artillery observer in the church tower, probably. But the MG crew wouldn't have been alone. They were probably part of a patrol sent forward to see what was happening and which had now been reinforced. So, let's say another six men, perhaps. It wasn't a strong force to hold a village this size.

And, most importantly, they didn't know that there were now nine commandos in the village.

Leaving a man at the front corner of the cottage to keep watch, Carter withdrew the remainder back into the garden.

"I think we can take this village." He gave a determined look to back up his words. "The enemy are all facing down the hill. If we work our way long the street, from house to house, we can get behind them. By the time they find out we're here, it will be too late."

The commandos returned his steady stare. If they doubted the wisdom of his proposal, they kept it to themselves.

Silence is assent, he thought, so he carried on outlining his plan. "We'll cross the road and get behind the houses on the other side. They'll provide concealment as we head towards the town square. Once we get there, we split; four men in each direction. Take one house between two on either side of the road and clear it. They won't have enough men to occupy more than two houses. Continue out the back door into the garden and clear that as well."

"What about you, Lucky? Who are you going with?" Was the man looking for a talisman? Perhaps, but Carter had to disappoint him.

"I'm going along the road to find the machine gun and silence it. Then we can signal the rest of the troop forward."

The *Nebelwerfer* fired again. Oh yes, mustn't forget the artillery observer in the church tower, either. But he could wait until the village was theirs.

It was a gamble, of course, Carter knew that. But for 3 Troop to fight their way up that slope, gentle as it was, against a machine gun and riflemen firing from cover, would be bound to cause casualties. On the other hand, there were nine good soldiers already inside the village and the enemy didn't even know they were there. It was worth taking the risk.

He concluded the briefing. "Next time that Moaning Minnie fires, you four …" Carter indicated the four men he meant, "… get across the square as fast as you can. If there is an observer in the church tower, he'll have his eyes on the fall of shot, so he probably won't see you. When you see me break cover, you all sprint for your two houses and clear them. Understood?"

Their grim faces nodded in assent. They moved along the backs of the houses until they were almost in the square. A fountain dominated the centre, water sloshing into it. The mains supply must still be intact, Carter thought. That will please the men, being able to make tea and even have a quick wash when the village was in their hands.

They heard the rising howl of the rockets soaring over the roofs and the four men detailed for the furthest houses dashed into the open, heading for the far side of the small square. It was the work of moments. They disappeared into the shadows of a shop doorway. Carter allowed a minute's pause to see if they had been detected. If they had, soldiers would be sent to cover the doorways of the houses. But no. They were still an unknown presence. Carter's hopes rose. The element of surprise was so valuable in these situations.

"Ready chaps." He whispered to the men clustered behind him. He braced himself, then sprang forward into the square, heading diagonally for the entrance to the road that led south. Above the hammering of his heart he could hear the thud of boots of the men following. Out of the corner of his eye he could also see the men of the far side of the square rushing forward.

As Carter entered the narrow street, he heard boots crashing against doors. A grenade went off, the normal preliminary to a house clearance. Throw in a grenade, let it explode, stunning or killing any occupants, then follow up with rifle and bayonet.

But Carter had his own job to do.

Ahead of him, about ten yards down the slope and to the left of the road, was a hastily constructed machine gun nest. Soil had been heaped up but old bricks, logs and other solid waste had been used to raise the front parapet and offer more protection. Within it lay a gunner and his loader, the barrel of the MG-42 projecting over the front lip with the bipod resting on the outer edge. The hammering of their own weapon prevented the gun's crew from hearing the grenades going off just a few yards away. Carter wasted no time. He raised his Tommy gun and emptied it into the backs of the two soldiers, raking the weapon from left to right. The gun stopped firing and the crew lay still.

A bullet cracked close to Carter's head. He had gone too far forward and was in the line of fire from the rear windows of the cottage. He pulled back, only to find himself running into a German soldier who was trying to escape through a side window. Carter didn't know who was more surprised, himself or the Jerry.

But Carter was the first to recover his composure. His Tommy gun was empty, but it was still a usable weapon. He swung it from left to right, the wooden butt of the weapon catching the German full on the chin. His head snapped back and his rifle dropped from his fingers to clatter on the road. Carter withdrew the weapon and hammered it back into the German's face once more, turning his nose into a bloody mess. The soldier slumped over the sill of the window, unconscious.

Carter kicked his rifle away and leant over the inert body. One of the commandos swung his weapon upwards, just avoiding shooting Carter, then turned away and ran through the door into the next room. two shots rang out and the shout "clear" reached Carter's ears.

The soldier ducked his head back through the door. "Nearly got yer fuckin' 'ed shot off, Lucky." He grinned, before disappearing once again.

More shots rang out, then silence fell. Carter could hardly believe it. They'd got away with it. He ventured forward a few yards and peered down the hill. The danger now was being shot at by his own men, who were still firing up the hill.

Carter returned to the window, grabbed handful of curtain and gave it a firm yank. Moving forward once again he started waving his make-shift flag back and forward. The firing from the bottom of the hill stopped. A figure stood up and Carter waved him forward. He walked forward a few yards, wondering if it was some sort of trap. Others rose from their hiding places and followed him.

Another salvo from the Moaning Minnie sent them diving for cover once again, but when the echoes of the explosions died away, they formed up along both sides of the road and made their way up the hill at a steady jog. As they reached him, Carter waved away their calls of congratulation and split them into groups of four, dispersing them across the village to carry out a search for any enemy soldiers that might be hiding. One man he sent back to the bottom of the hill to wait for the men arriving from the bridge, directing them upwards at best speed.

They had the village, but now they had to hold it.

[1] Carter was right; the bridge is still there but has been relocated to the grounds of the Pegasus Bridge Museum. The canal was opened in 1857 to provide a navigable commercial route from Caen to the Orne estuary at Ouistreham, the Orne river having started to silt up. It was wider and deeper than a British canal because it was designed for barges rather than narrow boats. That also meant that the bridge that spanned it had to be capable of being raised to allow the barges to pass beneath. The city of Caen has been important since the 10th century and was the seat of government for Duke William (the Conqueror), so the building of the canal was significant in it maintaining its prominence in later centuries. The Pegasus Bridge Museum is a regular stopping off place for visitors undertaking the battlefield tours of Normandy. A new drawbridge of more modern design replaced the original in 1994. The canal is now used mainly for leisure traffic. A new road, the N814, now crosses both the canal and the River Orne, just north of Caen.

[2] The Americans provided a cinema in the assembly area camp at Southampton, showing the latest releases from Hollywood long before they were available in British civilian cinemas. It was reported that one American Sergeant had been heard commenting "When I get home, my kids will say to me 'What did you do in the Great War[3], Daddy?' And all I'll be able to say is 'I showed *Claudia* (what we would call a romcom, released in 1943) to a bunch of goddam British boys waiting to go over on D-Day'". Stan Scott, Peter Young and John Durnford-Slater (see Further Reading) all claim to be the ones who heard the remark, so either the American said it frequently, or the story went around the camp to be claimed by all of them. Another quote from Stan Scott relates to a similar lament by an American GI who was tasked with looking after the latrines.

[3] By this time the British were referring to the First World War as 'The Great War'(we still do), but the Americans appear to have been using the term to refer to the Second World War.

[4] Dekko (sometimes spelt decco) – from the Hindi word "*dekna*", meaning to have a look. No doubt brought into the army by British soldiers stationed in India and then travelling back to the UK with them. Nowadays British soldiers refer to such reconnaissance as 'taking a sneaky peak'.

[5] The *Nebelwerfer* wasn't a single weapon, but a family of them. They started out as a type of mortar used for providing a smoke screen (*Nebel* is German for fog). It fired a rocket rather than a bomb, the thinner skin of which permitted a larger capacity of explosives, gas or liquid. Impressed by the Russian Katyushka multi-barrel rocket system, versions of which are still in use in various Middle Eastern wars, the Germans started to introduce their own multi-barrelled weapons from 1942 onwards. At different times the Germans used rockets that varied in diameter from 8 cm to 30cm, with launchers of up to 20 tubes. They were mounted on both tracked and wheeled vehicles. Having to reload multiple launch tubes provided a much slower rate of fire, however. The nickname 'Moaning-Minnie' goes back to 1847 when a French officer by the name of Claude Étienne Minié introduced a soft lead bullet that distorted when it was fired, producing a whirring sound that attracted the first use of the nickname. It was applied again during the First World War for a type of German trench mortar called a *Minenwerfer,* which was shorted to Minnie by the British and Americans.

[5] The Brodie helmet was named after its designer, John Leopold Brodie and was introduced into the British army in September 1915. Apart from a few minor modifications, it remained in service until 1944, when the Mk III "turtle" helmet (named because of its turtle shell like shape) started to be introduced.

3 - The Merville Battery

Commandos continued to trickle into the village from the bridge, in groups of anywhere between two and a dozen men. The troops were mixed together, 3 Tp in the majority at first, but then 4 and 5 Tps interspersed with them.

Ernie Barraclough arrived with a handful of men and Carter set him the task of getting them organised and allocating defensive sectors: 3 Tp in the centre, 4 Tp to the north side of the village and 5 Tp to the south. A couple of self-propelled guns added their weight to the Moaning Minnie, targeting the village itself now that it was apparent that it was no longer in German hands.

The artillery spotter had been rooted out of the church tower but had managed to get a final message out before smashing his radio set. He now sat under armed guard alongside the fountain in the centre of the square along with two other prisoners. The spotter was an NCO but the others were teenagers in uniform more than they were soldiers. Children sent to do a man's job. When the first artillery shell exploded, Carter sent the prisoners back down to the La Haute Ecard road junction, so they wouldn't be killed by their own side.

The simplest way for Carter to protect his men from the artillery was to move them away from the target. As the SP guns began the process of reducing a quite pretty village to a heap of untidy rubble, the commandos dug in on the forward slope of the hill, well clear of the houses.

Along with Barraclough had come his radio operator, much to Carter's relief. With the radio he was able to make contact with Ramsey, who had finally arrived at the bridge to take control of the troops that were still flowing in along the road from the landing beaches.

"Lion," Carter addressed Ramsey using his callsign, "I want you to gather the men into groups of at least three sections before allowing them to move forward. I want the first group to continue along the road to the west of Peregrine ..." That was the codeword for the village of Amfreville, which Carter had on a list of such words scrawled on a sheet of government issue Izal toilet paper. It was an innovation suggested by one the newer officers in his command. The thin filmy paper was easy to burn or even chew up and swallow if there was any risk of its possessor being taken prisoner. As a child, the officer had used the technique to pass illicit messages in class while at school. "They're to sweep north and take up positions on that flank. The next group are to do the same to the south. Be careful of friendly forces on that side." Having struggled through from the beaches, it would be tragic if the commandos were to be killed by accident by a trigger-happy paratrooper defending the approach to the bridge.

"What news have to you Wolf 1, 2 and 6?" Carter asked. The six troops all had the callsign of Wolf while he, Carter, was Tiger.

"I have radio contact with Wolf 1. They have finally finished clearing the outskirts of Harrier ..." the codeword for Ouistreham, "And are heading south following the canal. The ground is pretty boggy so they are making slow progress, but once they can get on the road they'll speed up. Wolf 2 are starting to arrive, but they're being slowed by their heavy loads."

Carter had always known that would be the case. All his plans had been based on the heavy weapons troop not being available for some while. A thought occurred to him.

"Get the PIAT teams to leave their weapons and ammunition with you and spread the load from the mortars and Vickers teams amongst the extra men. It should allow them to speed up. I need them here with me at the double." There was no sign of any German armour in the area, so they could manage without the PIATs for the moment. Their gunners and loaders would be of more use carrying mortar bombs and machinegun ammunition.

A counterattack had to be in the offing now that the commandos were in possession of the high ground dominating one of the major approach routes to the bridges. If the Germans hoped to recapture them, they would have to secure their flanks first, which meant evicting him and his men from Amfreville. Mortars and machine guns would make the Germans' task that much harder, so it was vital to get those weapons in position before too much more time passed.

"What of Wolf 6?"

"They were pretty badly mauled. I'm afraid Stefan didn't make it and neither did his number two. They were caught in the middle of the shell blast. Fortunately, young Marchant was bringing up the rear, so I've left him in command for the moment. They lost about a quarter of their men."

That was fifteen out of a troop of sixty. They would still be an effective fighting force once they reached the bridge.

"Any idea where they are now?"

"They can't be far away, I think. Being last to come ashore, the worst of the fighting on their line of advance is over. I expect them any moment now."

"OK. Tell them to dig in on the west side of the ridge. They can cover the back door and also act as my reserve. What about the rest of the brigade?

"Seventeen have cleared Hawk (Benouville) and are moving south to link up with the paratroops there. One of the men reported seeing Monarch sitting in a field having a picknick about halfway between Hawk and Falcon (Saint-Auban-d'Arquenay)."

Carter had to chuckle. That would be typical Vernon, putting on a show for the troops.

"Having said that, there's a body of troops coming towards us now that might well be Monarch's HQ and its escort." The escort were drawn from 49 Cdo, the Marines, who were covering the western flank of the brigade. Their arrival would complete the circle around the two bridges and secure them until 3 Division had advanced through towards their final objective, the city of Caen. Given the time of day, it was unlikely they would achieve that now. The Germans had the best part of the day to establish defences around the city in anticipation of the attack. But it would mean that the commando brigade and the airborne division would no longer be isolated and they could also be re-supplied from the beaches. The paratroops in particular must be starting to run low on ammunition.

"OK, when Monarch arrives …" Carter said, using Vernon's callsign, "let them know where I am and what radio channel I'm using. When the last of our men reach the bridges, round them up and move forward with them." That would be the men who had lost their bikes or who had been wounded but who were still fit enough to fight. "Steer clear of the village itself as it's under artillery fire."

Carter brought the radio call to an end, happy now that he knew where most of his men were. 3 and 6 troops had suffered the most. 6 Tp because of the artillery strike on their landing craft and 3 Tp because they had spearheaded the advance to the bridges and been involved in the most intense of the fighting.

Carter moved to a better vantage point and surveyed the terrain to the east. To his right was the imposing bulk of the Chateau d'Amfreville, the 15th century mansion that had been the home to the lords of the manor since the 12th century, or so Carter had been informed during their briefing sessions. At the moment, however, it provided a good position in which to site machine guns to pin down his men while a counterattack on the village was mounted. It lay about two hundred yards down the slope in front of his positions.

Ideally, he would incorporate the chateau's bulk into his defences, but it would almost double the size of his perimeter and even with the whole commando present, it would stretch them too far. It would be inevitable that gaps would exist that would allow them to be outflanked, especially at night.

Carter went in search of an NCO.

"Sgt Hammond." He found 3 Tp's sergeant berating a soldier for not digging his slit trench deep enough. Carter had to shout to make himself heard above the crash of the artillery shells on the top of the hill.

"Yes, Sir."

"I need you to take two sections and hold onto that big house for us. Do you think you can do that?"

Hammond looked towards the chateau. "Nice place. I've always fancied living in a castle. Shouldn't be a problem."

"Don't let the men inside the building itself. It's too obvious a target for artillery. Dig in around the perimeter and make sure that the Jerries don't get in there. But pull out if they threaten to overwhelm you. No point in letting yourselves be taken prisoner." Or getting yourselves killed, he didn't add.

Sending two sections down the hill would weaken his defences, so he'd have to pull men in from 4 and 5 troops on the flanks. They were desperately thin on the ground. If the Germans worked that out and attacked before the rest of the commando arrived, they would lose the village and control of the northern approach to the bridge.

Carter raised his binoculars again and scanned the distant tree line. That marked the line of the road from Caen to the coast. Somewhere there would be the two SP guns that were firing on them, along with the Moaning Minnie. And between them and the nearest hedge would be whatever infantry the Germans had at their disposal.

It was typical Normandy farmland. Directly to his front was a cabbage field, separated from its neighbours to the sides and behind by high hedges. Beyond the chateau was an orchard. If Carter wanted to capture the building, that would be side from which he would approach. It also happened to be the side closest to the Germans. He hoped he could get a mortar sited soon, because the orchard would be its target, denying its protection to the Germans if they wanted to capture the chateau.

"James!" Carter shouted, summoning 3 Tp's commander. He had spotted him arriving, so he must be somewhere close by. He was probably scouring the hillside looking for Carter himself.

The shout was passed from man to man until eventually the captain located Carter crouching behind the cover of a garden wall. "Lucky. I was wondering where you were."

Carter brought him up to date with his deployment of their defences and pointed out his arcs of fire.[1] "Have any of your men still got two inch mortars?"

"I haven't had a chance to find out yet, but they should have."

"OK, make sure they're ready to fire on the orchard on the far side of the chateau. If the Germans attempt to take it, that's probably the route they'll choose. Sgt Hammond has two sections of men concealed in there."

"Ah, so that's where Wally is. I was starting to wonder."

"Sorry James, but with you still not here, I had to look after your troop."

"Yes, sorry about that, I got stuck in Saint-Auban-d'Arquenay, dealing with a rather stubborn Jerry MG."

"No need to apologise. Things got rather fragmented coming from the beaches. Half the commando still isn't here yet."

"Good job Jerry doesn't know that." Mackie echoed Carter's own thoughts on the situation.

"Good job indeed. Anyway, carry on getting your men dug in. I think the Jerries will attack before too long, otherwise they'll miss their chance."

[1] In defensive positions, each soldier is allocated an 'arc of fire'; two points in front and to either side of him, between which he is responsible for maintaining a watch and providing weapons coverage. The intention is that each soldier's arc of fire will overlap with that of his neighbours, providing an unbroken line of defence along the front and to the flanks of their positions. If the arcs of fire are properly calculated, a position in which a soldier has to stop firing for any reason will still be covered by the arcs of fire of the positions on either side. Only if two adjacent positions were to be lost would gaps start to appear in the defences.

* * *

It was another hour before the enemy did finally make their move. Almost the full commando was now arraigned around the village, dug into the slopes of the gentle ridge. The first clue that something was happening was an increase in the rate of fire from the artillery.

Not the Moaning Minnie; its rate of fire was governed by the speed at which the rocket tubes could be filled. But the SP guns, which had been firing a round each every few minutes, doubled their rate of fire. Carter scanned the fields and was just in time to see a line of Germans soldiers break cover and sprint towards the orchard on the far side of the chateau.

"James!" Carter yelled at the top of his voice. "Get your mortars working now."

They had done a muster and two 2 inch mortar tubes had made it from the beach along with twenty bombs. It wasn't much, but it would have to do. Smoke erupted as the Germans used their own mortars to conceal the movement of the troops. But the presence of the smoke itself betrayed their intentions. Carter was sure they were in about platoon strength, probably twenty four infantry with machine guns. His two sections, if they were complete, numbered sixteen, so the numbers favoured the defences, so long as they were able to concentrate their firepower.

Mortar bombs started to fall amongst the apple trees as the commandos fired. The small, two pound bombs wouldn't have the devastating effect of the larger ten pound missiles of the 3 inch mortars. The shrapnel from those could cut through branches. But they would serve to slow the Germans down and perhaps force them out of the trees and into the open.

A Bren started to bark from near the chateau, indicating that the defenders were aware of the threat. Rifles cracked as well, keeping up a rapid rate of fire that was so intense the rifles were sometimes mistaken for automatic weapons.

Another mortar struck and a German soldier appeared at the side of the orchard nearest to his defences, trying to get out of the danger zone. One of the Bren gunners in front of Carter spotted him and loosed a couple of short bursts in his direction. It forced the soldier to dive for cover.

Realising the chateau was defended, the Germans tried to find a way around it, but if they exposed themselves on either side they came within sight of the defences on the upper slopes. They had no choice but to try a frontal assault using the orchard route and braving the explosions of the mortar bombs.

Carter felt the thud of a body landing behind the wall alongside him. "Where do you want my guns, Lucky?"

Carter turned to see the bulky form of Giles Gulliver attempting to squeeze himself in the narrow space behind the bit of ruined wall. Well, that was something. The heavy weapons troop had arrived at last.

"Two things, Giles. I want mortar bombs dropping into the orchard behind the chateau. Can you see it." Gulliver nodded his head in assent. "Then I want a Vickers gun enfilading the right hand side of the building to prevent the Jerries from getting around that side. There're windows there and if they start climbing through they'll be able to come at our boys from behind."

"OK. Got it. What about the second mortar and the second Vickers?"

"Get the Vickers out on the left flank, ready to tackle the main body of the German attack. They'll be coming soon, I think. Get the mortar set up so it can fire along a wide arc, depending on where the Jerries make their main thrust."

"Got it." Gulliver went into a crouching run and headed for the cluster of men nearer the top of the hill. Carter cursed. They were a tempting target if the Germans had an artillery spotter that could see them. That was bad fieldcraft and if the men survived he'd be having words with the officers and NCOs about letting the men bunch up like that.

It was a natural thing to do of course. The men felt that there was safety in numbers and, being the heavy weapons troop, they would want to stay close together to make it easier to assemble their weapons and keep up a good rate of fire. But it made the enemy's work much easier. A single artillery shell could take out the lot of them.

Gulliver must have seen the danger as well, because he heard an angry shout and the cluster of men scattered, diving for cover. The officer's imposing bulk intimidated lesser men and Carter wouldn't want to be on the wrong side of his wrath, that was for sure.

But, for reasons best known to themselves, the Germans were concentrating their fire on the village, which was now little more than a heap of rubble interspersed with some fires where there was still something combustible to feed the flames.

Surely their spotters must have been able to see the commandos digging in outside the village? It's pretty much impossible to dig a slit trench and hide at the same time. But perhaps the artillery was firing blind. The guns could be up to five thousand yards away and still be within range and if they were firing only on the basis of a map reference, they may have no idea that the commandos were outside the village's perimeter. The buildings were a natural source of cover and it was far easier to use them than to dig holes in the ground.

Which was exactly why Carter had ordered his men to dig holes in the ground. Try not to do what the enemy wants you to do; try to do what he doesn't want you to do. It was a basic lesson in tactics.

The firing in the area around the chateau had lessened. Carter raised his binoculars once more to try to work out what that meant. He had heard the first crump of a heavy mortar bomb exploding, then a second. He watched as the Germans started to withdraw back across the fields on the far side.

Gulliver must have seen them as well, because mortar bombs started to fall behind the retreating Germans, forcing them to abandon caution and sprint for the relative safety of the far side of the field.

But it didn't stop the attack. The German commander must have heard the same reduction in noise and interpreted it as his men having won the skirmish and taken control of the chateau. The hedge on the far side the cabbage field seemed to come alive as German soldiers rose from cover and started to slog their way through the mud and the brassicas.

Carter's defences stayed silent. They had used this tactic before to devastating effect in Italy. The advancing enemy interprets the lack of fire as a lack of an enemy. Then, when they get to within a hundred yards, the entire defensive line erupts in fire from automatic weapons, rifles, mortars and grenades. The impact in terms of casualties is high, but almost as bad is the effect it has on the enemy's morale. To see so many comrades fall in one go turns the bravest soldier into one who is terrified. The attack is halted in its tracks and the enemy starts to waver as their resolve crumbles under the onslaught.

Only commandos have the discipline to hold their fire for so long. Ordinary infantry aren't well enough trained. They get nervous when the enemy gets too close. Perhaps Carter was doing them an injustice, he thought, as he kept his eyes on the Germans' progress from his vantage point. Perhaps they could hold their fire for long enough, but no one had thought of doing it. The normal doctrine for defence was to try to keep the enemy as far from your positions as possible; it wasn't to give him a free pass to get so close you could smell his breath.

Fred Chalk would be the one to give the signal. He was in the middle of 3 Troop, taking temporary command of one half of the troop. They had lost two of their officers, their troop sergeant major and their other sergeant in the advance from the beach. To lose so many senior ranks wasn't unusual in the commandos. The leaders were always at the forefront of any attack. Altogether they had been reduced from sixty to just forty men, sixteen of whom were now isolated in the chateau.

Carter could almost feel the tension emanating from the commandos. He was thirty feet from the nearest slit trench, but the strain of staying hidden and silent seemed to roll across the French countryside like a fog. A rifle sling rattled as a soldier shifted to hold his weapon more firmly against his shoulder. Pebbles pattered to the bottom of a trench as someone moved a foot. Carter felt the tendons on his neck stiffen like iron bars under the strain.

Surely the Germans must have spotted the earthworks by now? Even the best camouflaged position can't stand up to really close scrutiny. A soldier carrying an MP-40 machine pistol paused, seeming to bend over to peer forward and get a closer look. An NCO or an officer, Carter assumed. Had he spotted something? The domed shape of a steel helmet perhaps? Or perhaps the barrel of a rifle projecting above a parapet, its hard edges standing out from the softer shapes provided by nature? But he stepped forward again, satisfied that there was nothing amiss. His eyes were now fixed on a point above Carter's head, which meant that he was looking at the buildings on the nearest edge of the village.

The artillery bombardment had stopped, the gunners making sure that they weren't endangering their own advancing troops. The silence was almost eerie, until there was the distant rattle of a machine gun somewhere to the south. It suggested that this was a co-ordinated attack, not focusing on Amfreville by itself, but on the whole eastern bank of the River Orne.

Carter watched a machine gun crew move to the side, creating an angle that would allow them to fire ahead of their own men, into the ruins of the village. Carter knew that a commando would be licking his lips as he settled his sights on the gunner. The commandos hated machine guns and always prioritised their crews for attention when they got the chance.

There were two men in each slit trench, so no doubt his partner would be lining up on the machine gun's loader at the same time.

The near silence was broken suddenly, almost without warning as a Very pistol cracked, sending a flare fizzing upwards. It didn't have time to burst in the sky before the commandos were firing. Brens rattled and rifles crackled. The Vickers gun kept up a rapid stream of fire, traversing along the line of advancing German troops. Men either fell or dived for cover amongst the cabbages before they could be hit. For many it was already too late. Carter saw the German machine gun standing almost upright, where its barrel had pitched into soft ground, like a javelin landing. As he watched, gravity asserted its dominance and the weapon slowly tilted to one side and fell over. The gunner lay out of sight amongst the bulbous heads of the cabbages.

How many Germans fell dead in that first salvo of small arms fire couldn't be established, but there were some still alive. Grey coloured helmets bobbed amongst the cabbages, looking for targets that could be shot at. Others seemed to be crawling away, back towards the hedges at the far end of the field. The attack had broken down; only firm leadership could set it back on track.

A man stood up, sweeping an MP 40 machine pistol from left to right, raking the commando positions, shouting orders and encouragement to his men. Carter had to admire his bravery. Half a dozen rifles cracked and the man fell. It was the last straw for the attacking troops. Crawling or running hunched over, zig-zagging and sprinting, they ran for the imagined safety of the hedges. The Vickers machine gun pursued them, sending more of them thumping to the ground.

Carter had estimated the strength of the attackers as being at least two companies, perhaps two hundred and fifty men. He doubted half of them made it back unscathed. It wasn't long before a white flag appeared and a soldier came forward to request a temporary truce while the Germans gathered up their dead and wounded. Carter agreed. To refuse would antagonise the Germans and there was little point in doing that. The war was far from over and his own men might one day need similar sympathetic treatment.

In the meantime, Carter used the brief lull to re-organise his defence. 6 Tp were sent forward to garrison the chateau, while the two sections that had been there were withdrawn back to the main positions. They had lost one man dead and two wounded in the firefight. Wally Hammond, the sergeant, had a field dressing wound around his head, his green beret perched on top. Despite his protests that he was alright, Carter sent him back to the bridges, where the paratroops had established a dressing station.

A sigh of relief broke from Tpr James as he slid his radio set from his shoulders and rested it on the ground behind the wall from where Carter was commanding the defence. "Maj Ramsey's compliments, Lucky, but he says he's finished with me now."

"Nice to see you, James. Have yourself a brew, then see if you can contact Brigade on that thing."

James had a small pack strapped to his chest, all he could accommodate along with the bulk of his radio set. He opened it up and sorted through it until he found the block of tea mixed with dried milk and sugar. He crumbled it into his mess tin and slopped some water onto it. Carter hated the stuff, regarding it as being no more like tea than sawdust. He always swapped his for oxo cubes or coffee powder. The foul tasing brew had recently replaced the loose tea in their ration packs and many of the commandos were grumbling about the lack of quality. And if you didn't like sugar in your tea, you had no option but to drink it anyway.

"I was in contact with them when we were at the bridge, Lucky. I was able to listen in on the exchanges." James busied himself with lighting his hexamine stove to boil up his brew.

"Were you able to work out how things were going?"

"Everyone was reporting their objectives met. I can tell you that much. No one mentioned casualties though."

No, that news could wait for the end of the day, when roll calls had been held and runners sent to check the dressing stations to see who had turned up there. It might take days to track down all the wounded, as they were scattered between the beaches and their present positions. As far as Carter knew, his command had suffered about ten percent losses. It was about what they had planned on; not that it would be a comfort to grieving relatives back home, when they got the news.

* * *

"We've been handed a bit of a sticky one." Carter told the assembled officers and NCOs of 4 and 5 troops. "About a mile north of us is the Merville Battery. As you may recall, Brigadier Vernon was very keen for that to be the major objective for our brigade, but was overruled, so we landed on the main beaches instead. The RAF were allocated the task of taking out the battery with bombs. Well, they dropped several tons of explosives, but failed to silence it. So, 9 Para were given the job of capturing it just before dawn this morning, so it wouldn't threaten the landings. After a bit of a scrap, they managed it."

Late in the afternoon more airborne troops had arrived, some in gliders but others dropping in by parachute. It was a dangerous thing to do during daylight and not all of them made it safely to the ground. But enough did for 17 Cdo to be relieved of their duties to the south west of the Orne bridges and head north east to start to join the brigade together once again. They replaced 15 Cdo around Amfreville, which allowed Carter to withdraw his men to rest close to the newly established Brigade HQ, which was using a farmhouse on the banks of the river. It was there he had been briefed on this latest mission.

"Unfortunately, 9 Para didn't have any explosives with which to destroy the guns, then they were withdrawn south of here to prevent the Germans recapturing the bridges before we arrived. Now, it appears, the Germans have got the battery back in operation and are shelling the beaches, much to 3 Division's discomfort. We've been given the job of going up there and evicting the Jerries once again. So, I need 4 Tp to mount the attack and 5 Tp to back them up."

"Who's going to command the attack?" Ramsey asked. Carter couldn't tell if he was keen to lead it himself or was more interested in being told that he hadn't been given the job.

"I'm going to lead it, with Ernie as my 2IC. The commando is officially in reserve but may have to move at a moment's notice so I want you, Howard, to remain in command here in case you're needed."

"Aren't you taking a bit of a risk leading this yourself, Lucky?" Ernie Barraclough asked. From their study of the aerial photographs of the battery it was pretty obvious that it was easy to defend.

"Whoever commands this is taking a risk and I'm not going to ask someone else to place themselves in danger on my behalf." The firm tone of Carter's voice warned anyone against trying to dissuade him.

"Now, Four-Nine are going to pass through soon, on their way to capture Franceville Plage, which will extend our front line all the way to the sea. But they can't risk that while the battery is still in operation, so we have to capture it before they can move further north. The aim is for both us and Four-Nine to go in at about the same time." He produced a sketch map from his pocket and unfolded it on the ground. The men squeezed in tight to try to make out the detail.

"Not an ideal briefing room." Carter quipped. "But it will have to do. Now, the battery faces due north, so we can attack it from the rear. The main entrance is on the east side, connecting it to the road that leads to the village of Le Home Merville on the coast. That's where Four-Nine have got to reach. To do so they would have to cross right in front of the guns.

So, we're going to advance past the northern end of Amfreville and approach from the south, which should be the least defended approach. I'll go forward with a couple of sections to do a recce, but I suspect that we'll go straight in over the back fence. We know from 9 Para's experiences this morning that there is a minefield on the eastern side, protecting an approach from the road and another on the western side, protecting the other flank. Across the front of the battery is an anti-tank ditch. The slope of it is too severe for us to attack from that side, not that we would want to.

But as far as we can establish, the rear approach is clear of mines. What I plan on doing is moving 5 Tp into a position where they can fire into the battery from the side, while 4 Tp advance from the rear." Carter paused, saving the worst news till last. "Now, we know from aerial photographs that the guns are housed in concrete bunkers, with more bunkers behind to store their ammunition. The barracks are also encased in concrete. The whole complex is connected together with concrete lined trenches with firing points set into them. There are more tunnels below ground so they can keep the guns in operation even during an air raid. So, it will be a messy old affair trying to get inside and get at the Jerries. But they can't fire their rifles from inside the block houses, so they'll have to come above ground to do that. We'll use 2 inch mortars to soften them up and keep their heads down as we go in for the attack. Once inside, its bayonets and Tommy guns to clear the way into the bunkers."

"How do we destroy the guns once we're in?" Ernie asked.

"Well, I asked for explosives from the brigade engineers, but they don't appear to have any and we can't afford to wait until some are found. So, we're going to have to do our best to wreck them with trenching tools. It won't be easy, I know." They had faced a similar problem when they had attacked the Goering battery at Honfleur in 1942 and their explosives had failed to arrive with them.

"Well, gentlemen. That's all I can tell you until I've had a look at the battery, so get your men ready to move out." He looked at his watch. "We leave at seventeen thirty hours and I'd like to launch our assault by nineteen hundred at the latest." The long June evening meant that the fighting day was extended significantly. Tired men would be even more tired by the time they returned to their starting point.

* * *

Carter raised his binoculars and watched 5 Tp creeping into position on the east side of the battery, using the cover of the roadside hedge. They were a little further back than he would have liked, which meant a loss of accuracy for the rifles, but the Brens would be able to cope. But he couldn't allow them any closer because they were almost bound to be detected in the open ground and that would put the enemy on his guard.

The defences had been much as he had briefed his men. Sentries paced up and down within the twin banks of barbed wire entanglements that protected the battery. Holes gaped where the paratroops had forced an entry earlier in the day, but new coils were spread across some of them. Along the trenches, Carter had made out soldiers carrying ammunition from the bunkers to the guns, followed moments later by the crash as the weapons fired.

They weren't the largest artillery pieces, considering the job they were expected to do; First World War vintage 10 cm guns built by Skoda in Czechoslovakia. But the fact that they were old didn't mean they couldn't pack a punch, so they had to be dealt with. They had a range of about five miles, which covered most of Sword Beach and a good deal of the shipping lying off the coast.

The intelligence reports said that the artillery unit that manned the battery was made up of youths and old men, but Carter had stopped relying on reports like that after his experiences in Italy. He preferred to rely on his own eyes to assess the enemy these days. Besides, even youths and old men could mount a stout defence from behind concrete barriers.

The movement to the east had stopped, which meant that 5 Tp were in position. Carter checked his watch: close to nineteen hundred hours, as he had planned.

A crump echoed across the landscape and Carter was able to see the small volcano of earth that a 2 inch mortar bomb had sent up. It was followed by the rattle of a Bren gun. It was as though someone had kicked over an ants' nest within the battery. Soldiers started spilling out of doorways and running along the concrete lined trenches only to be turned around and sent back again by an officer or NCO. Two streams met in the middle of one trench, with neither knowing whether they should try to keep going forward or to turn back again. A mortar bomb, exploding on the trench's parapet, settled the matter and the soldiers ran in opposite directions to get clear of the target area.

The contradictory movements of the German troops had made it difficult for him to count, but he estimated at least a platoon strength, plus the gunners and loaders, as well as any that might have been slower to react. Half a company of men, perhaps; around fifty to sixty.

And if his commandos had to winkle them out of the bunkers it would be a deadly game. Speed and aggression would win the day. Glancing at his men, lying in cover to either side of him, he saw their jaws set in determination as they gripped their bayonet tipped rifles.

He raised his whistle to his lips and blew one long blast. The note had barely sounded when the first men were on their feet and sprinting forward.

The small arms fire from the hedge intensified into one continuous crackle of reports as the men of 5 Tp tried to keep the enemy's heads down. But it was ineffective against the fixed firing points with their overhead protection. An MG 42 started up, accompanied by another and commandos started to fall.

Two hundred yards to go to the wire. Perhaps forty seconds of exposure for the men. How many would he lose before they got there? Carter heard the whip-snap of bullets passing his head and he instinctively ducked, but he stayed on his feet. If he went to ground, his men would likely follow. They had to keep going or they would get caught in the open with no cover. The whole area had been cleared to create a killing zone and the Germans were keen to make sure that the terrain lived up to its name.

But the disadvantage of fixed firing points was they limited the ability of weapons to traverse a wide arc. With a hundred yards to go Carter realised that one of the machine guns was no longer inflicting casualties. The men on his left were advancing almost unchallenged as the Germans were unable to bring the machine gun on that side to bear.

"Right hand flank, move to your left! Carter bellowed, doing his best to make himself heard above the racket. The man nearest to him relayed the order then moved across in front of Carter. He had to take care he didn't close up the formation too much, or they'd make a perfect target for a mortar. He felt sure the Jerries must have one there, even if they did, they hadn't yet fired it.

All of a sudden the wire was directly in front of him. They hadn't had time to get any Bangalore Torpedoes, so they would have to deal with it the other way. The first commando to reach the coils threw himself forward, flattening the coil to the ground. The man behind him ran straight along his back and jumped over his head, now within the confines of the battery.

As chance would have it, they'd reached one of the places where the paras had breached the wire that morning and only a single coil had been replaced. The third man fell dead as he tried to cross the barrier, but the fourth made it through. Carter dropped to one knee, looking for the marksman that had fired the shot. There, a rifle barrel poking above the parapet of a trench. He saw it move, levelling off as the man holding it rose to take another shot. As his head cleared the concrete Carter fired his Tommy gun and the head disappeared again. He doubted he'd hit the man, but it was probably enough to keep his head down.

More men had flung themselves onto the wire and now commandos were streaming into the battery. Not all of them made it. Carter saw one writhing in agony, clutching his thigh as blood spurted in a fountain.

Carter sprinted forward, felt the softness of a man's body under his feet as he crossed the wire, then he threw himself down beside the casualty. He pressed his hands hard against the wound, doing his best to stem the flow. "Tourniquet!" He gasped. The man fumbled in the breast pocket of his battledress blouse and came out with a bootlace. The experienced men always carried spares. Half sitting, the man started to tie it around his thigh above the wound. He had almost completed the task when he fell backwards. Shocked, Carter let go of the man's leg. The man was dead, his eyes staring silently skywards. A gaping hole, a bullet's exit wound, had taken away one side of his head.

In frustration Carter emptied his \Tommy gun towards the German positions, only stopping when the weapon stopped firing through lack of ammunition.

It was a good job it had, because a commando ran straight across Carter's firing line. He couldn't have avoided hitting one of his own men.

That's what anger does for you, he reminded himself. You have to stay cool, Steven, he told himself. Anger and frustration will get you and your men killed.

His men were in the trenches now and the Germans were retreating towards their bunkers, stopping at every corner to fire on the commandos. Grenades were thrown, the splinters ricocheting off the concrete walls to create a deadly metal storm. The commandos ran along the tops of thr trenches, firing down at any Germans who wasn't retreating quickly enough.

5 Tp would now be skirting the minefield and advancing towards the main gate of the battery, coming to the aid of their comrades, adding their numbers to the assault. The Germans would try to halt them there. But the gate's defences weren't strong enough.to stop a determined enemy.

With steel doors being slammed in their faces, the commandos were venting their frustration by hammering on them with the butts of their rifles. They had the battery, but they didn't control it. From within the bunkers the Germans could still keep the guns firing.

And all they had to do was wait for their own forces to come and take the battery back. Carter was under no illusion about that. He was at least a mile in front of his own lines and it wouldn't take much to surround them.

But with the defenders beneath ground, his men were free to move around above. Carter found an NCO.

"I need a dozen men to come with me. Make sure they have a couple of coils of rope with them. Get the rest in firing positions to cover the bunker doors. Shoot any Jerry that tries to come out. If a door gets jammed open, get men inside and start to clear a way through. Make sure everyone knows to head for the guns, but keep your backs covered."

"OK, Lucky." The Sergeant nodded his head and went off to start finding the men Carter had asked for. It came as no surprise that the first three to arrive were Green, Glass and O'Driscoll. The Irishman had half his ear missing and blood streaming down his neck.

"Get a dressing on that, Paddy." Carter instructed.

"There'll be time …"

"That's an order, Trooper." Carter barked, in no mood for the Irishman's bravado.

"I'm a Lance Corporal now." O'Driscoll grumped as he searched his pockets for a field dressing.

"You'll be a dead Lance Corporal if that wound gets infected." Carter snapped back. "Give him a hand, Danny. We'll be moving out as soon as I get enough men and I'm not waiting for anyone."

Glass gave a cheerful smile, took the dressing from O'Driscoll's hand and started to wrap it around his friend's head.

Once Carter had his dozen men, he led them over the parapet and up the sloping earth covered banks onto the concrete roof of one of the bunkers that housed the battery's guns. Its position dictated that it was the one that would be firing on the beaches, rather than out to sea. Dotted about were the U shaped ventilators that provided fresh air to the gunner within, or extracted the smoke from the discharge of the guns.

Gathering the men around him so that he didn't have to raise his voice and risk the men within the bunker hearing him, Carter gave them a rapid briefing.

"We're going to abseil down the face and start lobbing grenades in through the firing ports. I'll be on one rope and you, Curry, will be on the other. I need you two, he pointed out two heavyset commandos, "to anchor the ropes up here. Once the grenades have gone off, Curry, swing yourself into the port and get inside, kill anyone not already dead. The rest of you will follow. You'll know we're inside when the ropes go slack.

"Either that, or you're dead at the bottom of that tank trap." A wag at the back replied.

"In which case, the next two still follow and try to do what we didn't." Carter said back, not engaging in the banter.

"Shouldn't you let someone else go, Lucky?" Green was the only man senior enough to challenge the CO. "I'll go instead."

"No, Prof. This is my show, so I'm the one who'll take the risk. If I don't make it, you're the new CO of 15 Cdo." He grinned at him. They had both seen Ernie Barraclough fall as they had rushed the battery and there had been no sign of him in the trenches, so Carter had no idea who actually might be the ranking officer if he died.

"Any questions?" In the absence of a reply, he continued.

"Right! Get that rope uncoiled and let's go."

Carter slung his Tommy gun at his back and filled his pockets with grenades. He walked forwards to the front of the blockhouse. To his left lay the town of Ouistreham, but to the front the English Channel spread itself in a sheet of twinkling blue in scattered patches of June sunshine. From horizon to horizon shipping bustled about, maintaining the impetus of the landings. Carter would have liked to have taken a few moments to enjoy the show, but there was no time.

In the distance, battleships and cruisers fired their heavy guns before disappearing into a fog of their own making. They should have been pounding this battery into dust, but the commandos had been given the job of capturing it instead. Vernon had shrugged his shoulders when Carter had suggested the Navy take on the job. "We've been given our orders, Steven." Was all he would say.

Lying on his stomach he shuffled forward until he could see over the front edge of the bunker. He would need to make sure they dropped to either side of the gun port or they would be an easy target for anyone inside. They would also need to be level with it to make sure they could lob the grenades through.

The front of the bunker formed a shallow V shape, with a wide arcing bulge in the centre. That must be an overhang, protecting the guns from above, Carter thought. He'd wished he been able to carry out a reconnaissance from the front so he could see what it looked like, but the need for haste had prevented that. So, if he lowered himself down on the flat face to the left of the arc, he must be able to see into the firing aperture. And, similarly, Curry would be able to see in from the other side.

He stood up and returned to the men, who were watching Garvey and Moran, the two heavyset commandos, tying the rope off around their shoulders. Carter wished the bunkers had been grass topped, so that the men could dig the heels of their boots in. Concrete wasn't the best surface on which to maintain a foothold. At least their boots were rubber soled, rather than the leather and hobnails of regular army boots.

Positioning the two anchor-men where he wanted them, Carter passed the rope between his legs, around the front of his body and over his left shoulder, around his back and under his right armpit, so he was holding the loose end of the rope in his right hand. All the commandos had been trained to do this and Carter had done it many times, though it still gave him the willies to step out over the edge of a cliff.

He knew that by wrapping his arms across his body the friction of the rope would stop him falling, but he never quite had the faith in the method that many climbers had. Perhaps that was why he was still alive and so many climbers weren't. But this was going to be particularly tricky. Not only did he have to stop himself from falling, but he had to hold his position one handed while he wrestled the pin out a hand grenade with the other.

If it wasn't for that damned anti-tank ditch they could have crept around the sides of the bunker and done the job from ground level. But the ditch was twelve feet deep if it was an inch and, once in it, they'd never be able to climb out with the Germans lobbing grenades down on their heads from the gun port.

OK, the fall probably wouldn't kill him if the rope slipped, but it would break bones and that meant he would become a liability to his men. He pushed the thought from his mind and backed towards the edge of the bunker. His men watched, their faces a mix of anxiety and admiration. He waited until Curry was in position, then stepped backwards, allowing the rope to slip slowly through his fingers as he walked his way backwards down the sheer front face of the bunker. Looking over his left shoulder he could see the barrel of the gun projecting forwards. Every foot he went his view improved. He had thought the gun would be mounted inside the bunker itself, but it appeared to be inside some sort of metal turret perched in a wide opening in the face of the bunker. Through the gap in the sides and above, the darkness of the interior could be seen.

Carter brought himself to a stop by crossing his arms. Making a loop in the free end of the rope, he pushed it under his webbing belt, then tightened it into a slip knot, locking himself into position. He pulled a grenade from his pocket. He had already straightened the split pin that secured the safety arm, so that it would be easier to pull out one handed. He hooked the index finger of his right hand through the metal loop, pulled firmly with his left hand and threw the grenade across the roof of the gun's turret. If it bounced the wrong way it would fall into the ditch below him and shrapnel would fly up at him. There would be an irony; being killed by his own grenade.

But the grenade didn't bounce the wrong way. It clattered across the top of the turret and disappeared inside. Curry's grenade did the same. Carter tried to flatten himself against the concrete face of the bunker to avoid the blast. It echoed off the concrete and he felt a draft of air waft past his left side as first one grenade, then the other, exploded.

That was that, then. He grabbed the rope with his right hand and eased his weight from it so that he could pull the slip knot free. He had to be quick or any living Germans inside would take the opportunity to exact revenge on him from within. He felt horribly exposed now that they had announced their presence in such an explosive manner.

He lowered himself to ground level as quickly as he dared, then swung himself into the mouth if the gun emplacement, letting the rope run free as he did so. His shoulder jarred painfully against the turret as he landed and struggled to drag his Tommy gun round in front of him.

The gap between the turret and the wall wasn't large, but he was able to squeeze his way thought it. Bursting out the other side he started firing spraying bullets from left to right. But there was no answering fire. Two bodies lay in bloody pools, exposed flesh and clothing ripped to shreds by grenade fragments   Another man lay on his back, rocking back and forth as he clutched at his eyes, screaming in pain. Carter nodded at Curry to search to the right while he went to the left. Metal doors secured the rear of the bunker. Carter went to them and swung the locking bars aside, pushing it open. A shot smashed into the metal an inch from his face and he reeled backwards.

"It's me! Carter!" He yelled at the trigger-happy commando who had fired. It was his own fault; the soldier was just following the orders Carter himself had issued.

Men rushed forward along the trench and started to fill the room. Carter directed them into the tunnels that led off on either side, connecting this bunker to the others and to the ammunition stores.

It wasn't long before the sound of shots being fired echoed through them. Some of the Germans were resisting. The blank concrete walls of the tunnels would offer no refuge if the Germans thought to set up machine guns at their end.

It took another hour to clear all the tunnels. In the meantime, commandos had set-to with whatever tools they had available to put the guns out of action. They hacked at elevation and azimuth adjustment wheels, hammered at breach blocks and jammed hinges and axles, but they knew that whatever they did would only put the guns out of action for a while. Armourers would be able to return them to service given time and Carter didn't have enough men to garrison the battery and prevent the Germans re-occupying it.

The Germans attempted a counterattack and fierce fight ensued, but the commandos were able to beat them off. After a platoon of the enemy stumbled into the Germans' own minefield they withdrew to wait and see what the commandos would do. Carter had no intention of allowing his men to become trapped in the concrete killing ground of the bunkers' defences. So far from their own front line it would be too easy for the Germans to surround them and Four-Nine Cdo were too far off to the north to be able to help.

He had fulfilled his mission at considerable cost to his unit. It was up to 3 Div how they put the battery out of action permanently, because his priority was still the defence of the Orne bridges.

As the sun started to sink towards the western horizon, Carter led his men out of the battery. 4 Tp had lost all its officers and another six men killed. Twice as many were injured, with several being carried on stretchers that had been found in the German storerooms.

5 Tp had lost two men and one officer. Fighting a rear-guard action, the commando lost more men to the harrying attacks of the Germans with 4 Tp suffering particularly badly, with several men becoming separated and being taken prisoner.

But the biggest loss to Carter was Ernie Barraclough, the ever-cheerful Italian speaker who had been his close friend and companion since before they had left for Africa.

4 - 84 Days

Looking out from under the fly leaf of the canvass covering of the HQ dugout, Carter was greeted by a steady drizzle. After the brief break in the weather that had allowed D-Day to take place, the rain and winds had returned. A storm had ravaged the coast and it was rumoured that the temporary harbour at Arromanches, on Gold Beach, had been damaged, slowing the arrival of much needed supplies. Instead of using the large landing ships, which needed a port, stores were being brought in from England by smaller landing craft and deposited straight onto the beaches.

It meant that some sectors had stuff they didn't need but were short of stuff they did, while others had an embarrassment of riches. The Ordnance Corps were doing their best to sort it out, but some opportunist quartermasters were sending beach parties back and taking what they could. The Corps Commander had threatened dire punishments for anyone caught doing it, but it did little to stop the practice.

After delaying the movement of armoured units from the Pas de Calais, even Hitler allowed himself to be convinced that the Normandy landings were the real thing and not just a ruse. As expected, on the third day after the landings, the Germans counterattacked in strength, attempting to throw the British back into the sea.

The brigade had been re-organised into a defensive line running north west to south east, on the ridge on the northern side of Amfreville, known as Le Plein. 15 Cdo were sandwiched between 16 and 17 Cdos, with four-nine at the north westerly end. 9th Btn the Parachute Regiment were to the south of 17 Cdo, along with the rest of 6th Airborne Division. The new layout had brought the Chateau Amfreville within the British lines and the orchard now formed part of 15 Cdo's defensive positions. Carter couldn't allow the chateau itself to be occupied as it was one of the main targets for the German artillery, who seemed to take great delight in knocking chunks off it with their guns.

The Germans came in strength, supported by SP guns, armoured cars and tanks. But they had delayed too long and the commandos, though seriously understrength, were well dug in and had held them off. It wasn't that they were better equipped or better positioned, because they weren't. It was just that they refused to contemplate being moved off ground they had already shed so much blood to take.

The fighting continued for five days, until the Germans finally decided that they weren't going to shift the commandos. By that time the men were hungry, having had to make two days rations stretch to five because what resupply there was had concentrated on providing ammunition.

After the intense fighting the Germans withdrew to lick their wounds, retaliating the only way they could, with artillery fire, Morning and evening the "daily hate", as it was called, rained down on the brigade's lines and all the commandos could do was huddle at the bottom of their slit trenches and wait for it to end.

The positions started to take on a permanent air, with salvaged wood being used to support roofs made of ponchos, tarpaulins or bits of tentage, whatever could be found to keep out the rain. One end of a slit trench was left open to the sky to allow the two occupants to fight, the other end was used for sleeping and cooking, which was done in turns. The men grumbled about the weather, but that was quite normal. For a soldier the weather is the one thing no one minds them grumbling about because no one can control it.

The 2IC had wanted to put up tents for the men to sleep in, but Carter had vetoed the idea. A tent made an obvious target for artillery. The trenches were much smaller targets so were less likely to be targeted by anything larger than a mortar.

The commandos had been told they would stay in the line for a week, but it was already the third week after D-Day and there was no sign of them leaving. The battle to drive deeper into France was raging between Caen and Cherbourg peninsula, with the Allies struggling to move forward and the Germans unable to push them back.

"We're raiders, Sir." Carter had objected at the daily briefing, when the brigade's senior officers had been told that they would be remaining where they were for a while longer. "We're not suited to being line troops."

"So, we shall raid." Vernon had said firmly. "Major General Gale[1] has made it clear that we should make life as uncomfortable as possible for the Germans in our sector. Hit them hard and hit them often, is what he has said. Don't let them eat, sleep or go to the toilet without worrying whether a commando is going to pop up and send them to meet their maker."

The assembled officers mumbled their approval. If they couldn't do what they had been trained for and raid from the sea, at least they could take the fight to the enemy on land.

Carter issued his orders accordingly. Reconnaissance patrols were to be sent out each day to try to identify suitable targets. To support them there would be mortar observation posts positioned forward of the lines where they could remain in visual contact. Once a target had been identified, troop commanders were to put forward plans to attack them with fighting patrols under cover of darkness. The first priority was to take prisoners who could provide intelligence on the enemy's dispositions and intentions, the second priority was to degrade the enemy's ability to fight, in whatever way possible.

In some cases it was a simple matter of killing the enemy wherever they were found, but in others it was better to carry out acts of sabotage: cutting telephone lines, blowing craters in roads, blowing up artillery pieces, transport and stores. The only things that were off limits were bridges. The British would need those when the breakout came. It was, however, permissible to cut the detonator wires to those bridges that already had explosives attached, in the hope that the enemy might not notice.

Besides, finding that commandos had managed to get behind their lines to cut the wires and then get out again undetected, would be more worrying for the Germans than actually blowing the bridges.

No man was excused from participating in the patrols. Even the medical orderlies were expected to remove their red cross armbands and take part. Even the padre took part, though he went unarmed. The medical officer was exempt. If he became a casualty, it would take time to replace him and Carter didn't want to jeopardise the ability to save the lives of wounded men.

The same applied to the OPs. Officers had to take their turn going forward before dawn and sitting out the long summer days waiting for darkness to fall once more so they could withdraw. Carter made sure he took his turn, though his name was often left off the rota. He also took part in the patrols, especially the riskier ones.

A few replacements arrived from the training school at Achnacarry, though not enough to fill the gaps left by the D-Day casualties and those that followed in the immediate aftermath.

Most of the trainees going through the depot were Royal Marines. The stream of volunteers for the Army commandos had almost dried up as commanding officers hung on to their men in preparation for D-Day. Once the port facilities had been established the beach parties, made up of inexperienced soldiers straight from the recruit training depots, were used to fill the gaps in the ranks, but from a commando point of view they were almost useless.

The trained men didn't like having these untrained conscripts foisted on them and considered them to be a liability. The first time they had experienced the daily hate, several had broken down in tears, never having experienced concentrated artillery fire before. Carter withdrew them from the fighting trenches and used them for menial tasks, fetching and carrying for the commando.

He didn't like doing it as it was damaging to the men's morale, but to leave them where they were would have been even more cruel. It also kept the trained men where they would be most useful.

A few of the replacements begged to be allowed to fight and Carter set up training cadres behind their positions, with NCOs doing their best to instil some commando field craft into them. Some became good enough to man listening posts at night and take their place in defensive positions, but none were good enough to take part in the nightly patrols, where a single foot out of place could herald disaster.

Sniper teams were also sent forward. They were highly skilled and the tally of hits unofficially chalked on the commando's HQ wall told a lethal tale. Rumour had it that there was a pool running on which troop scored the most hits before they were withdrawn from the line.

6 Tp had discovered the hiding place for the Chateau's wine cellar, but the men were dismissive of wine. Most of the bottles were smashed as the commandos sampled them and then gave their judgment of what they called "poncey French piss". The 2IC found out what was happening and managed to salvage a few bottles, but most of it ended up being soaked up by the very soil that had grown the grapes from which it had been made. It was rumoured that the 2IC had broken down in tears when he had seen the labels and vintages on some of the broken bottles.

In the same half buried building a barrel of cider stood, a product for which the Calvados region was rightly famed. This was more to the commandos' tastes and they left a mess tin on the top of the barrel, so that any patrol passing close enough could dip into the stocks and refresh themselves. Carter allowed his officers to turn a blind eye on the drinking providing none of the men became the worse for wear. The men understood the boundaries and made sure no one abused them.

Carter's Jeep had arrived from the beach with the rest of their equipment when it was discharged from a landing craft. Somehow the QM had managed to persuade the REME[2] mobile workshop to fit an M2 Browning heavy machine gun onto a swivel on the back of the vehicle. It's point five oh calibre ammunition was a welcome addition to the commando's firepower and it had got more than one patrol out of trouble by being driven forward and taking the enemy in the flank as they had tried to ambush the returning troops.

The RSM also took great delight in finding hiding places for it where it would suddenly appear to attack German patrols, before beating a hasty retreat back to the British lines.

When not used for that, Carter would send small parties of men back to the beaches, ostensibly to pick up stores but in reality to let them bath in the sea. They had been promised a proper rest area before long, equipped with showers, a laundry and a cinema, but so far it hadn't appeared.

And so a routine was established, with the commandos harassing the enemy by night and the enemy trying to retaliate by day.

[1] Maj Gen Richard Gale was the commanding officer of 6th Airborne Division, which had captured the Orne bridges before dawn on D-Day. After the commandos arrived at the bridges on D-Day, they were attached to the division. Like the commandos, the airborne troops had expected to be withdrawn shortly after the landings, but the need to reinforce the British lines elsewhere meant that an infantry division couldn't be spared to protect the army's left flank and so 6th Airborne remained in situ until after the breakout operation began in August.

[2] Royal Electrical and Mechanical Engineers, the corps of the British army responsible for the maintenance of its vehicles. Established in October 1942 when it was discovered that Army units were having difficulty maintaining their vehicles using men drawn from within their own ranks. The increasing complexity of military vehicles also required improved professionalism for their maintenance. The corps drew its first recruits from the Royal Army Ordnance Corps, The Royal Army Service Corps, The Royal Engineers and Royal Signals, who had shouldered much of the maintenance burden up to that point. One of their most critical roles was the provision of mobile field workshops, close to the front line, so that fighting vehicles could be repaired and returned to battle as quickly as possible. Little known historical fact: In 1945 Maj Ivan Hirst and a team of men from the REME took over the Volkswagen works at Wolfsburg, Lower Saxony, and got it back into production making cars for the British and American armies. After leaving the

Army, Hirst stayed on and helped turn Volkswagen into one of Germany's most successful brands. The REME still exists today.

* * *

Silently, Carter led the men towards the Gonneville road, the line the Germans were using to mark their territory. The high hedges and deep drainage ditches formed a natural barrier which could be easily defended.

A recce patrol had spotted a group of soldiers digging a new trench just in front of the road, presumably to strengthen a weak point in the line. Carter was intent on raiding it. Experience had shown that once a position was raided, the Germans were reluctant to use it again. Perhaps their men were superstitious. Carter knew that it really spooked them to find that the men in a position were gone, as though spirited away during the night. Which, in a way, they had been. Collectively, the commandos had so far taken thirty prisoners that way.

Attached to the unit were two German speakers, Tpr Spencer and LCpl Ernest Langley. Neither were their real names. Langley was Ernst Langstein. He was Jewish and a native of Bavaria who had managed to escape the Nazis before the war. When war broke out he had volunteered for the British army and then for the commandos. Now he was part of 10 (Inter-Allied) Commando, the unit made up of men from a wide range of Nazi occupied countries. X Troop were the Germans speakers and most at risk, because they were either regarded by the Nazis as traitors, were Jewish, or both. Langley had been very successful at creeping close to German trenches and persuading his former countrymen to give themselves up.

Which was why he was with Carter that night.

The recce patrol had briefed them on the best route to take to approach the new trench without being detected. As usual it meant crawling along hedgerows and ditches, then creeping across the final stretch of open ground to reach the objective. That was the most dangerous part because if they were caught in the open, they would have no protective cover. It had been agreed that Langley would go forward on his own. He preferred it that way and it reduced the risk for the rest of the patrol. His fieldcraft was excellent, with the evidence of several similar raids on previous occasions to back him up.

Under the starlight they couldn't make out much of the trench. With trees and hedges behind it, it was like looking into a well in the middle of the night without a torch. But the recce patrol had estimated the distance to be about fifty yards from the end of the hedge. The vegetation had originally stretched all the way to the road but had been hacked down by the Germans to open up a field of fire. I'd have tripled that distance, Carter thought.

A parachute flare soared upwards and the Commandos lowered themselves to the ground. The pop of the flare gun and trail of sparks from the device gave a warning, unlike a trip flare, which just lit you up before you had time to do anything.

It was some distance away but would shed its light far enough to glint off metalwork; Not that the commandos were foolish enough to carry polished metal about their persons. But it only needed one shadow to be cast or one movement to be detected and the Germans would open fire.

The firing of flares at random intervals was routine for the Germans. They were scared of the commandos' ability to move through the night with ghostlike ease. The commandos themselves didn't fire those sorts of flares unless the enemy had actually been detected, so as not give away their positions. More than one German patrol had been greeted by the words "Evenin' Fritz" coming out of the darkness. It was usually the last sound they heard other than gunfire.

There was a visible hump where Langley had gone to ground, lying still. Carter could see him, but he knew where to look. The flare fizzled out and in its dying light the hump moved. Too soon, Carter thought. If he could see the movement then a sentry might as well. But Langley seemed to have got away with it. An uncharacteristic mistake, Carter thought. Perhaps Langley was in need of a rest. He seemed to be out most nights.

A machine gun rattled in the distance. At least a mile, Carter calculated. Probably a patrol from four-nine on the northern flank, or maybe a jittery sentry. It sounded like an MG-42, but it was hard to be certain at that range. But it would alert sleepy sentries, reminding them that there was a persistent danger when you were opposed by commandos.

Another flare fizzed skywards, closer this time. It bathed the area in light. Carter's men were still hunkered down under the hedge, but Langley was again caught in the open. His body was half raised as he eased himself forward on his knees and elbows. It had happened to them all during training, too slow to react. The standard drill was to freeze in position, as movement attracts the eye. Whether Langley panicked or whether his arms refused to support him any longer, he dropped to his stomach. But there was no doubt he had been seen.

An MG opened fire at close range. It had been set up to fire on a fixed line forward from the trench, but it was the work of a moment for the gunner to swing it in an arc towards Langley's prone body.

It took the twitch of an eyelid for Carter to react. If he wanted to save his man, Carter had to distract the gunner and anyone else in the trench.

"With me!" he yelled at the top of his voice, springing to his feet and sprinting forward. He fired his Tommy gun as he ran, spraying the trench.

More weapons fired from the German defences as the occupants realised how close the commandos had encroached. Someone was shouting "*Alarm!*" at the top of their voice, though it was being drowned out by the crash of weapons. Carter's boots thudded across the ground, closing the gap between himself and the enemy. More flares shot skywards and the area became as bright as day. He tripped, fell, rolled and was back on his feet almost without breaking his stride. But it had given time for another commando to pass him and take the lead. He was headed directly for the machine gun that was still being aimed at Langley. It was a fatal mistake for the gunner as the trooper took a flying leap, his bayonet tipped rifle stretched out ahead of him. He caught the gunner square in his side. The loader half rose to try to defend himself as Carter threw himself feet first into the trench. His boots hit him in the chest, driving him to the bottom. There was an explosive 'whoof' of air as the man's lungs emptied. Carter took half a pace backwards along the narrow confines of the trench, lowered the muzzle of his weapon and fired a short burst from his gun.

Rifles crackled from behind him as other members of the patrol engaged the other defensive positions. They would distract the Germans while Carter and his unidentified companion withdrew.

"Come on! We need to find Langley!" Carter pulled at the man's webbing to attract his attention. He clambered back over the lip of the trench and hurried in the direction he thought the exiled German might be.

One by one the flares blinked out, leaving the terrain in darkness. Carter's night vision was ruined, thanks to them, as would be that of all his men. But the darkness provided a refuge. "Withdraw!" Carter commanded. If he delayed, the Germans might send up more flares and his men would be caught in the open.

He tripped and fell and it took a moment to realise what he had tripped over. It was a body and it wasn't moving.

He cursed. "Are you there?" he half turned to address the trooper who had been in the trench with him."

"Aye, Lucky. Right here."

"Give me hand here. It's Langley. I think he's dead, but let's get him back so we can check him out properly."

They grabbed the fallen man's webbing and half carried, half dragged him back towards the hedge. They had just tumbled into its shadowy bulk when another flare popped in the sky.

They hunkered own.

"Number off." Carter hissed. Before they had left the safety of the British lines, the patrol had "numbered off", each man shouting his number aloud before his neighbour shouted the next.

"One." Carter hissed.

"Two, came a whisper from behind him.

"Three." Also behind him.

Then silence. "Who had been four?" Langley, yes, he'd been four, Carter was sure.

"Next." Carter instructed.

"Five."

The count continued until it reached twelve. All accounted for. "Anyone injured?" Carter asked

If they were minor injuries the commandos wouldn't mention them. They'd only tell him if they were unable to move.

As the flare died, Carter heard the sound of movement in front of them. Several bodies were in motion, he was sure. A counter-patrol, sent out to pursue him and his men, no doubt.

"Flare!" Carter instructed.

The man with the flare pistol obeyed the order and a red light appeared in the sky above them. At once the support party opened fire from a hundred yards behind them, raking the line of the Gonneville road. It would force the German patrol back into cover and allow him and his men to work their way back along the hedge to their rally point, where they would rest for a moment and take stock.

"OK, let's go." Carter gave the instruction in a voice loud enough to be heard above the crackle of rifles and Bren guns.

The trooper who had helped him carry Langley hoisted the man in a fireman's lift.

"Any sign of life?" Carter asked him as he passed.

"He's a gonner, Lucky, but I ain't leavin' 'im 'ere."

"Good man. Swap with one of the other's when you start feeling tired."

With the need for secrecy past, the journey to the rallying point[1] took them only a few minutes. In front of the Commando's position, about halfway between them and the German defensive line, stood Languemare Farm. By day the commandos sometimes used it as a mortar OP or as the jumping off point for a reconnaissance patrol, but at night it was used by the Germans as a forward listening post or a jumping off point for one of their own offensive patrols. Both sides knew of the arrangement and both sides tolerated it.

For the British it meant they didn't have to hunt too hard to find a couple of Germans to take as prisoners, while the Germans would always assume that there was a mortar OP within the shell damaged walls and keep their patrols well out of sight of it. If they did come under mortar fire, it was the first location they retaliated against, aiming their own mortars and heavy machine guns at it. Most of the time they were wrong, as the commandos moved their OPs around, but occasionally the unlucky occupants had to put up with a fire storm of ordnance.

It was inevitable that one day, two patrols would meet at the farm.

Carter's leading man kicked the front door of Languemare Farm wide and stepped through.

"Fuckin' 'ell." Carter heard him shout. "There's bleedin Jerries in 'ere."

He dived back through the door, landed in a heap then wriggled away from the opening just as an automatic weapon opened fire. By its rapid rate of fire Carter guessed it was an MP-40, better known as a 'Schmeiser'. So, an NCO or an officer, he thought. That probably meant a sizeable patrol, rather than just a night-time listening post

What was vital, now, was to react quicker than the enemy.

There was the flash of a grenade inside the building and a pair of commandos vaulted through a shattered window. Rifles cracked inside the house. Using the distraction, a pair of commandos snuck up on the other front window and threw a grenade inside, leaping over the sill almost before the shrapnel whizzed past their heads.

"With me!" Carter shouted, not knowing if anyone would hear him. He leapt to his feet and sprinted towards the farm's front door. The Germans realised the danger and hidden hands tried to swing the door shut before he got there. They almost made it as well. He threw his shoulder into the woodwork and felt the door move back a few inches. A gap wide enough for the muzzle of his Tommy gun opened up and he jammed the weapon into it, pulling the trigger as he did.

Using the butt for leverage and the door itself as a fulcrum, Carter heaved the weapon left and right, spraying bullets from side to side.

The weight on the door was released so suddenly that Carter fell inside, sprawling across the floor. His Tommy gun span from his grasp and skittered across the wooden floorboards. Carter instinctively rolled onto his back, scrabbling for his Webley revolver. In the flash of fire from neighbouring rooms, Carter made out the triumphant leer of a German soldier as he raised his bayonet tipped rifle to strike down into Carter's unprotected body.

Struggling to get purchase with his elbows, Carter tried to lever himself upwards and backwards at the same time. The German took a half step to follow him, then stabbed downwards.

Carter had anticipated the move and rolled away. The German tried to react, shifting his point of aim, but too late and the point of the bayonet slammed into the wood. The German heaved on it, trying to withdraw it from where it had stuck. Too late he saw the bulk of a commando barrel through the door, his own rifle extended, screaming his war-cry.

The German took the full brunt of the British bayonet in his chest; driven backwards, he slammed into the wall. The commando twisted his rifle in the text book approved manner, withdrew the bayonet from the man's body and slammed it into him a second time. This time when he withdrew it, the German slide to the floor and lay still.

Trying to stand up, Carter was about to thank the commando for saving his life, but he was too slow. The man had already sprinted along the short corridor to slam his way through a door towards the back of the house. He'd have to try to identify the man later.

Scurrying across the floor, Carter retrieved his Tommy gun and reloaded it. The firing inside the farmhouse was starting to diminish as the commandos cleared it, room by room.

When silence fell, Carter yelled at the top of his voice "Muster outside, then search the prisoners." He hoped that bit wasn't redundant and the commandos had actually taken prisoners, otherwise the whole patrol had been for nothing. Men with their blood up often fired first and accepted surrender only as an afterthought. The Geneva Convention had never taken that into account.

He stood in the hall as his men filed past him, German soldiers ahead of them, their hands on their heads, devoid of their weapons and helmets. A helmet made a useful weapon if not removed, as more than one soldier had discovered to his cost.

Carter spotted the insignia of an officer. That was good. Officers always provided better intelligence than the rank-and-file soldiers.

They waited for the support party to catch up with them, searching the prisoners and dressing wounds. Two of Carter's men had been injured, one by fragments from a German grenade when its dead owner dropped it; the other had taken a bayonet tip in the thigh. Neither man would die, but both would be out of action for some time as their wounds healed. They counted four Germans dead, three so severely wounded that they would probably die, two with lesser wounds and five uninjured prisoners.

Using the German's own rifles, the bolts removed to prevent them being fired, they fashioned make-shift stretchers. The uninjured Germans carried their own wounded comrades, with commandos making up the numbers. The commando with the thigh wound was also helped onto a make-shift stretcher, though he protested, claiming he could still walk. But Carter wasn't having any nonsense. Keeping the leg moving would cause it to bleed more and he had no intention of allowing the man to bleed to death on the journey back to the British lines.

The support party had the troop's radio with them, so Carter used it to request that field ambulances and military police be summoned from the rear to take both the injured and the prisoners. His own men he would see off personally before he allowed himself to sleep.

The adrenalin that had rushed through Carter's body as he had fought for his life, started to drain away, leaving him feeling more tired than he had ever imagined to be possible.

Well within range of the weaponry of 15 Cdo's front line, Carter sent up a green flare to let the sentry know that a friendly force was on their way in. They moved as quickly as their burdens would allow, which meant they crossed the lines ten minutes after they left the farm.

It took another hour for all the wounded and prisoner to be sent on their way. There was a pale line on the eastern horizon, indicating that dawn couldn't be far away. At the back of the HQ dugout, Carter threw himself to the ground to lie on the groundsheet that he used as his bed. He was asleep before he could take his boots off.

"Morning, Colonel". Was the next sound Carter heard as Gordon, his batman, gently shook his shoulder. "Brought you some tea, Sir."

"Is it time for stand-to?" Carter asked, sitting up and rubbing his eyes.

"Goodness me, stand-to was hours ago".

"Damn, why wasn't I woken?" He struggled to straighten up. His body felt like a herd of cows had trampled over him.

"2IC's orders, Sir." Gordon replied, calmly. "You weren't to be woken unless the Germans looked like breaking through the line. As they didn't attack, that didn't apply."

"I take it there was no 'morning hate', either then."

"Oh yes, Sir. Fourteen rounds in our section of the line this morning, and a salvo from a *nebelwerfer*. Jerry must be getting short of rockets, because there were only three of them."

Carter shook his head in puzzlement. He had actually slept through an artillery barrage. He wouldn't have thought such a thing possible for any man.

"OK, what about the Brigade briefing." It took place at seven each morning, after the commando had endured the morning hate and done a roll call and sick parade, so that the unit's effectiveness could be reported.

"2IC went in your place."

Carter pushed up the sleeve of his battledress blouse and checked his watch. Eleven o'clock. Well, a minute past. That must have been the time Gordon had been told to wake him. "I've got hot water on the go for you to shave." Gordon continued, turning to leave the dugout. "Oh, and a bit of a treat, I've managed to locate a couple of eggs. How do you want them? Fried or boiled?"

"Boiled." Carter said to Gordon's retreating back. Eggs; that would make a nice change.

[1] When a patrol sets out, locations along the way are designated "rally points". If a soldier becomes separated from the patrol, he heads for the nearest rally point and will be collected as the patrol returns to its own lines. If the patrol deliberately splits up, the place at which they will meet up again is referred to as an RV (rendezvous) point rather than as a rally point. There may be several rally points, but usually only one RV.

* * *

"The goulash cannon, Sir" Percy Lisle stuck his head around the end of the piece of tattered canvas that separated Carter's end of the dugout from the rest of it. It provided him with a combined working and sleeping area
"And good morning to you, Percy. What about the goulash cannon?" Carter looked up from the citation for meritorious service he was writing for Tpr Bendick, the man who had saved his life at Languemare Farm. Carter expected it to gain Bendick a Mention in Dispatches, at the very least.
"The men want to have a crack at it. It's driving them nuts, Sir."
Carter smiled. The goulash cannon, as it had been nicknamed, was a horse and cart that was used by the Germans to bring hot food to the front line. It arrived each evening after darkness had fallen. The smells from it were wafted across the front line when the wind was from the east, making the men's mouths water. Carter had to admit that the German food smelt a lot better than their own tinned rations. It was also guaranteed that a lot of German soldiers would be gathered in its vicinity as they ate their share of the food.
"The problem is, Percy. We never know where it's going to be." He liked Percy Lisle, he'd been posted in from 12 Cdo to replace Ernie Barraclough and had only been with the commando for a week. He reminded Carter of himself when he was younger.

Inwardly Carter groaned. Lisle was almost the same age as himself. It was just the amount of combat he had experienced that was making him feel so much older. In the past two and a half years he had experienced more than some men would experience in a lifetime of soldiering, even in wartime. But Lisle was keen and, according to Prof Green, who was now acting Troop Sergeant Major under Lisle's command, he was a good leader. He'd taken a patrol out only an hour after he'd arrived in their lines; "just to get to know the area." He'd said, though they came back with three prisoners and some captured documents, including a very detailed map of the German front line.

"But I think we do know where it's going to be." Lisle continued. "SMaj Green told me he's been tracking its location from reports from the forward listening posts. The Germans seem to have a pattern for it. On Monday it will be at such and such a location, Tuesday so-and-so, etc. It seems to be on a 12 day cycle. I checked his predictions for the past two nights and he was right on both occasions."

Trust Prof Green to apply some grey matter to a problem, Carter thought. But it piqued his interest. If they could attack the goulash cannon it would probably inflict heavy casualties, because of the way the soldiers hung around the area. And it would probably damage their morale as well because they would feel more vulnerable. The Germans would then be bound to move their feeding station further back from the front line, out of danger, which would mean either the soldiers having to walk further to be fed, or the food being delivered to them in containers and arriving cold.

"OK, where's it going to be tonight?"

Lisle spread a map out on Carter's desk. "According to the TSM, it should be here." He tapped a pencil mark on the map. "The crossroads where the Gonneville road and the road to Las Bas de Breville meet."

The Las Bas de Breville road ran down from the heights of Le Plein and formed the left flank of Carter's positions. On the other side of it, 16 Cdo's positions began.

"What's your plan?"

"I'll jam as many men as possible into your jeep, if you will allow me to borrow it, race down the road to the crossroads. The men jump out and open fire, while I use the heavy machine gun. Then we withdraw under covering fire from the mortars."

It was a simple plan and Carter liked simple plans; there was less to go wrong. Because of the time at which the goulash cannon arrived, it would be difficult to get a support party into position, but they might be able to use a diversion of some sort for that. Perhaps send out a recce patrol in the afternoon to take a look at a different section of the German lines, then drop off half of them on the way back, leaving them in hiding until later.

"OK, but one alteration. I'm coming with you."

Lisle's face fell. He had wanted to command the operation himself. Carter took pity on him. "It remains your Op, Percy. I'll just be there for the ride. In fact, I'll be the machine gunner, so you have the freedom to move around if need be."

Lisle's face lit up again. "Thank you, Sir. It will be our honour to have you with us."

"OK, let me know what time the briefing will be. And it's a risky one, so volunteers only."

Although all the men in the commando had to take their turn going out on patrol, something as dangerous as this was a job reserved for volunteers. There would be no shortage of them, however.

* * *

The sound of Carter's heart thumping almost drowned out his thoughts. It wasn't an unusual phenomenon for him. He often felt anxious before going into action. When he had asked the Medical Officer about it he had laughed. "You'd be a bloody strange person if you weren't a bit worried, Sir. Fear is nature's way of telling us not to do stupid things. Evolution gave us two responses to danger: fight or flight. To do either, you need to increase the amount of oxygen pumping through your muscles so that they can respond instantly when you make your decision. So that hammering heart you are worried about is as natural as breathing. Come back and see me if it starts happening when you're doing paperwork."

It had been reassuring at the time, but whenever it happened, Carter wondered if it was nature's way of making him run away from danger. Evolution had given him two options, the Doc had said. Up to now Carter had always chosen to fight, but would he always be able to do that? One of the instructors at Achnacarry had said that the only difference between a hero and a coward was that the coward responded to fear by running away from danger, while the hero responded to fear by running towards it.

Self-doubt wasn't good in a leader, Carter considered. If he doubted his ability to make decisions, he could put himself and his men in danger, by being too timorous. The commandos succeeded because they did the things the enemy didn't expect them to do; the things no sane person would do. It made them appear superhuman in the enemy's eyes. But the field hospital had too many of his men in its care for him to be in any doubt about how frail, in physical terms, his men were. And some of them were becoming frail in mental terms as well after being so long in combat.

The men did their best to hide it, but he had seen the tremors in the hands, the involuntary twitches and the stifled shouts of fear when shells exploded. Carter had been almost relieved when one of his officers, a youngster in 5 Tp who had only arrived with the commando just before D-Day, had received an injury bad enough to put him into hospital for a few days. He had been close to cracking, Carter was sure.

It wasn't that the man wasn't made of the right stuff. It was that he had twice been blown off his feet by artillery shells. Any man would be nervous of it happening again. The third time he might not be so lucky. The third time might be the last time. It wasn't only the field hospitals that were full. The temporary cemetery on the banks of the Orne held too many of his men and those were just the bodies of the ones who could be recovered. Many more lay in graves on the German side of the lines.

Taking a deep breath, Carter focused his mind on what he was about to do. The raiding party was assembling around the Jeep, in the shelter of a ruined barn, where the enemy's OPs, if they were still present, would be unable to see them. The sun was setting over the beaches behind them and that would help to dazzle anyone watching through binoculars. The support party had reported that they were in position, with the crossroads under observation.

It was standard practice to avoid crossroads, every soldier was taught that. It was the sort of feature that mortar officers and machine gunners aimed their weapons at. A soldier that forgot that lesson usually wasn't destined live long in this world.

The goulash cannon, therefore, wouldn't be parked right on the junction. It would probably be sited in the field beyond. That didn't matter. After weeks of artillery fire the hedges in that area were pretty shredded and didn't offer much cover. The crossroads also wasn't heavily defended, because of the attention of the mortars and machine guns. The defences were positioned further away, where they were in less danger but were still able to cover the approach route. Keeping those weapons quiet was the job of the support party. Carter had also arranged for a few mortar rounds to be sent in their direction, for good measure.

The shadows lengthened and the men climbed into the Jeep. By squeezing in tight they had managed to get eight in when they had tried it our straight after the briefing. There was the driver, who Carter was unsurprised to see was O'Driscoll; beside him was Danny Glass. Perched on the outside would be Percy Lisle, so he could be first into the fray.

Sandwiched into the back, sideways on, were two men to each side. Prof Green was one of them. He refused to be left behind, claiming that without his initiative in working out the pattern, there'd be no raid in the first place. Standing upright in the middle of the rear, clinging onto the machine gun's mounting, would be Carter.

The Americans referred to the Jeeps as "Purple Heart[1] wagons" because of the number of soldiers that were injured while travelling in them. Their low sides made it easy for a soldier to fall out on a tight bend or to be bounced out breasting a rise at speed. The vehicle also had no way of preventing the occupants from being crushed if it rolled over. The best a passenger could hope for was to be thrown clear; they'd probably suffer broken bones, but at least they'd live. Carter fervently hoped that no such accident would happen today. Just before they reached the crossroads there was a sharp left-hand bend followed by an equally sharp right. They were counting on the bends to conceal their approach from the Germans as they ate their meals, but they could also spill the commandos over the road, snapping bones like twigs.

Grabbing hold of the spare wheel to add some leverage, he hauled himself over the rear of the vehicle. Hands reached out to help, but he waved them away. Standing in the cargo space, his legs brushing the knees of the seated men, he grabbed hold of the machine gun's spade grips, trying to make it look as if he was unconcerned for his safety. But keen eyes would have spotted the whites of his knuckles, even in the darkness.

"Support party reports the goulash wagon approaching." James said, from his position beside the vehicle. There was no room for a radio and its operator in the already overcrowded Jeep, so he would be left behind. If the support party spotted trouble, they would fire red flares, but otherwise they would be driving into the unknown.

Heaving back on the cocking handle of the machine gun, he readied it to fire. Swinging the barrel from side to side he made sure that there was nothing interfering with the traversing action; he then did the same, testing the up and down action of the universal joint. They had one box of ammunition, hooked onto the side of the gun. That gave him one hundred rounds of ammo, enough for one fifteen second burst if he kept his thumb on the butterfly trigger set between the two handles. But by picking out targets and firing four or five round bursts, he could keep up a rate of fire for a couple of minutes. If they were at the crossroads for longer than that, they probably wouldn't get out alive. Even when surprised, well trained soldiers would recover their wits well before two minutes had expired. They had another box of ammunition wedged against the bulkhead that separated the front of the vehicle from the rear, but Carter knew there would be no time to reload.

"Ready when you are, Captain Lisle." Carter said. The officer squeezed himself in beside the front seat passenger and laid his Tommy gun across his knees.

"OK, O'Driscoll, let's see how well you can drive this thing." Lisle said, feigning calm.

Like a maniac, Carter thought, but the one thing that comforted him was that he could rely on the Irishman to keep a cool head if things got a bit sticky.

The vehicle lurched from its hiding place with a clash of gears, bumped onto the cobbled surface of the road, fishtailed as the wheels got a grip then they were barrelling down the hill. In his elevated position Carter felt like they were travelling at a hundred miles an hour, but he knew O'Driscoll had been briefed to drive at no faster than forty. Any faster would risk people being thrown out.

Carter felt his Tommy gun starting to slide around his body from where it had been hanging at his back and he let go with one hand to push it into place. Although he was the machine gunner, he had no desire to be left with only his Webley to defend himself with if they had to abandon the vehicle.

The jeep lurched on a bump in the road and Carter had to grab hold of the machine gun's grip again to prevent himself losing his balance. If he fell, his body weight alone would tip him over the vehicle's side or rear. Never had he felt quite so vulnerable, or so helpless.

"Bend ahead!" Lisle called out a warning. He had been counting the seconds since they had left the barn's cover, trying to keep track of distance. They daren't risk using lights, so there was no way of fixing their position.

O'Driscoll went down through the gears and started applying the brakes, peering ahead to try and see where the road started to deviate from its straight route. The windshield was folded flat to prevent flying glass from injuring anyone if the enemy started firing, which meant that O'Driscoll's eyes, just like Carter's, would be streaming tears caused by the wind. Carter made a mental note to ask the QM to try again to get them some motorcycle goggles. So far all requests had been refused on the grounds that they didn't have a motor cycle.

Above the sound of the engine and the wind, Carter heard the crump of mortar bombs landing as the Heavy Weapons troop targeted the defences to either side of the crossroads. To his right, Carter saw the twinkles of muzzle flashes as the support party also opened fire. Carter realised too late that he should have told Lisle to ask 16 Cdo to provide a similar party on the left-hand side. Something to be remembered for the future, if he had a future.

The jeep swayed to the left and Carter was almost thrown out, despite O'Driscoll having slowed down. Hands grabbed his thighs and pushed him back upright again. The second bend was less than fifty yards from the first. Carter braced his legs, ready for it this time.

With a screech of tyres, the Jeep swung around the last bend. Ahead of them Carter could see the beams of torches. From their height Carter guessed they were being used on the back of the cart to check on how much food was being ladled into each mess tin. Cigarette tips glowed as soldiers waited in line to be fed.

A well placed sniper would have a field day with so many targets offering themselves.

Carter pointed his machine gun in the general direction of the torch light and fired his first burst. A light spiralled upwards and then down to the ground, before the torch's bulb shattered. He must have hit someone, he registered at the back of his mind. Carter was thrown forward as the Jeep came to a screeching halt in the middle of the crossroads. His men spilled out onto the ground, sprinting away from the Jeep to give themselves space from which to fire. They all carried Thompsons, the best weapon for this sort of operation. They had also taped magazines topped to tail, so that they could remove the empty one, reverse their grip and slam the second one into the weapon in a fraction of the time it normally took to reload. It was a trick they had leant only recently, when a party of SAS troopers had visited them to take a closer look at the enemy positions in preparation for an operation of their own.

Steadying himself, Carter aimed his weapon again, towards where he had spotted the tail end of the queue. He raked the machine gun fire along the line. Men scattered belatedly, their minds finally warning that they were under attack. Some more alert Germans had started to return fire and bullets cracked around Carter's head and smacked into the Jeep's side. In front of him, O'Driscoll was changing the magazine on his Tommy gun prior to firing again. Grenades flew through the air to add to the carnage.

Above the hammering of the Tommy guns and the heavier thud of his own weapon, Carter heard the sound of a whistle. That was Percy Lisle, sounding the recall. They were about to leave. A shrieking sound rent the air and it took Carter a moment to realise it was a horse whinnying in agony. Carter fired towards the sound, hoping to put the animal out of its misery, but the scream continued, unearthly and horrifying. In the rush to get the operation ready, Carter had forgotten that the ghoulish cannon was horse drawn. Not that it would have made any difference. If you can kill men, you can kill horses too.

The closest bodies started to pile back into the Jeep. Carter panned his gun to the left, then started a slow traverse across an arc in front of him. Anyone in its path would be dead and it would allow his men to get back to the Jeep as the Germans kept their heads down to avoid being hit. The Jeep lurched backwards as O'Driscoll threw the vehicle into reverse, turned it in a tight circle, then changed into first gear to take them up the road, back the way they had come.

Lisle' right arm pointed skywards and there was the crack of a Very pistol firing, a single green flare. That would bring down mortar fire on the crossroads, preventing the enemy from setting off in pursuit. Not that they would catch the speeding Jeep, but they might intercept the support party as it withdrew.

As the Jeep exited the second bend O'Driscoll brought it to a stop and the commandos climbed out. The raid wasn't quite over for them. They would join the support party and provide additional covering fire for the withdrawal.

Before O'Driscoll could set off again, Carter stepped over the back of the passenger seat and lowered himself into it.

"Home, James, and don't spare the horses."[2] He grinned at his driver.

[1] The Purple Heart (originally the Badge of Military Merit) is an American medal awarded to all service personnel killed or injured while on active service as a direct consequence of enemy action. Approximately 2 million Purple Hearts have been awarded, of which 430,000 were posthumous. Three soldiers share the record of 10 for the number of Purple Hearts received. Charles D. Barger, who also won the Congressional Medal of Honour, the American equivalent to the Victoria Cross (World War 1); William G. "Bill" White, U.S. Army: (World War 2 and Korean War); Curry T. Haynes, U.S. Army (Vietnam War). There is no equivalent to the Purple Heart awarded in the British armed forces.

[2] The title of a comic Music Hall song released in 1933, recorded by Jay Wilbur and his Band, with vocals by Bertha Willmott. The phrase became popular slang for "let's go" or "hurry up," but said in a more friendly manner.

* * *

It wasn't just the enemy that killed Carter's men. A squadron of Martin Marauder light bombers unloaded their bombs over the commandos' front lines. One bomb killed a whole section of 1 Troop, landing squarely in the middle of their positions. An investigation was carried out but established very little except for the fact that nobody in 6th Airborne Division had requested an air attack, so what the American pilots thought they were attacking remained a mystery. No one had even been able to identify the squadron involved. Or, if they had, their identity was kept secret from the commando brigade.

On another occasion a returning patrol wandered too close to 17 Cdo's positions and blundered into a minefield. No one had thought to tell the neighbours it was there. One man was killed and another wounded before they could extricate themselves. The dead man was one of those who had been with the commando the longest.

Neither incident did much to boost the commando's morale. They needed a break, but Carter wasn't able to give them one. He did his best to get men out of the line for a few hours, but it was difficult. Officially they needed a reason to be away from the front line and he was hard pushed to come up with any. They no longer had the excuse of going to the beach to pick up supplies, because the logistics situation had improved and the RASC were starting to deliver to a drop location not far from the bridges.

It was bad enough having to write the letters to the grieving relatives to tell them that their son, or husband or sibling was dead, but to know their death was avoidable made it so much worse. Of course, he couldn't tell them that. They were told their loved one had died a hero's death in action. Carter hated having to lie like that about the circumstances.

His hand was shaking more often these days, he noticed. Sometimes he had to grip his pen so tightly that it hurt, just to make the tremors stop. He knew it was his nerves but knowing didn't help. Like his men, he needed a proper rest, but he couldn't get one either. Soon, he had been told. They'd be out of the line soon. But no one would commit to when.

At the beginning of August, replacements had finally arrived. Twenty eight men straight from the depot at Achnacarry, plus two officers, also straight from the depot. If they were committing men to his unit and the brigade in general, it meant they would be on the move soon. The replacements weren't enough to bring his commando up to full strength once again, but it was better than nothing.

The men seemed so young. Well, they were so young. They'd been recruited from the young soldiers' battalions, made up from youths who were too young for infantry service. Most had volunteered for the commandos to escape the tedium of their duties; guarding buildings, ports, stores depots and the like back home in England. They had been allowed into the commandos on the understanding that they wouldn't be sent to a combat unit until they were nineteen, in accordance with the rules that applied to all soldiers. The War Office had no intention of suffering the embarrassment they had during the First World War, when it turned out than boys as young as fourteen had died in the trenches. The public wouldn't stand for it again.

A third officer joined them, a more experienced man. He had escaped from a prisoner of war camp in Germany and made his way overland all the way to Gibraltar. The Free French had helped him in France and he'd received some reluctant help from the communists in Spain, but for most of his journey he'd had to rely on his own wits and resilience to keep him alive.

By rights he should have gone back to his original commando, but they were now in Burma and 5th Commando Brigade's needs were more pressing right then. Carter was glad to have him. Any man who had done what he did and lived to tell the tale was worth having.

Wasting no time, the new arrivals weren't even allowed time to unpack before they were sent out on patrol. It was vital that the new men experience combat as soon as possible, so that their NCOs could assess their capabilities. I fthey were given time to think about what might happen to them, as they witnessed other men becoming casualties, they might not be able to do their jobs. They'd all risen to the challenge though and Carter had given them each a personal pat on the back when they returned, dirty, a couple bruised and bloodstained, but all cheerful and in a hurry to tell of their experiences to their new comrades, who gave them tolerant smiles, nodded their heads and tried not to say 'Yeah, we've done that few times ourselves.'

As well as the arrival of the replacements, there was another sign that something was afoot. An intense battle was in progress around Caen[1], with the British gradually creeping into the suburbs of the ancient town. It hadn't fallen yet, but it wouldn't be long. With that strategic objective in Allied hands, they would be ready to break out at last.

On the reverse side of the ridge occupied by the commando brigade, an armoured regiment had set up camp out of sight of the enemy, occupying the lower ground between Amfreville and the River Orne. There were more than seventy Sherman tanks and their crews camped there, with a reconnaissance squadron of Daimler armoured cars as well.

"Are you in, Steven?" Carter's reverie was interrupted by the sound of Brigadier Vernon's voice, followed immediately by his head appearing around the sheet of canvas that cut his little corner off from the rest of the HQ dugout.

Carter made to get to his feet but Vernon waved him down again. There was too little room for the normal courtesies. "Still living in a hole in the ground, I see." He said with a cheery grin.

"I like to be close to the men, Sir." It was a poor reason. There were buildings close by where he could set up the commando's HQ in greater comfort, but while his men were living in slit trenches, there was no way Carter was going to allow himself to be seen to be living in luxury, even if it was only the luxury of having a shell-holed roof over his head.

"Well, you'll be out of here soon." Vernon leant forward conspiratorially. "Keep this under your hat, but the breakout starts in a couple of weeks, no more. Which is why I'm here today. Have you got a map handy?"

"Out here, Sir". Carter led the Brigadier back into the main part of the dugout, where a map was fixed to the dugout wall using bullets pushed through the paper and into the soil. On it were marked the positions of his own defences and those of the enemy's positions that were known, which was most of them. The reports from the recce patrols meant the map was up to date. Beneath the map lay of a box of matches and a small can of paraffin. If it looked like an enemy patrol was going to reach the dugout, whoever was on duty would douse the map with the paraffin and set fire to it, preventing the map from becoming an intelligence asset for the Germans.

Vernon peered at the map through the gloom. Carter picked up a torch from the clerk's table and offered it to his superior officer.

"Thank you, Steven." Vernon shone the torch onto the map, checked the grid line numbers and plotted the correct position from memory. "See there." He tapped the map. "That group of three buildings?"

"Yes, I've got them, Sir." They were about three hundred yards behind the front line. It was a bit further than the commando's patrols had ever ventured, but not by much. He had seen the cottages himself, from a distance.

"We sent a low-level reconnaissance aircraft over the whole front line yesterday. They brought back some really good pictures."

"Yes, my forward positions commented on it. It was so low they thought it was going to crash. It attracted a lot of Jerry ground fire."

"Well, he made it back safely, you can reassure your men. What one of the photos showed was that the middle cottage of that group of three has quite a lot of aerials strung around it. Enough to suggest that it's some sort of command post. It's too far forward to be a brigade HQ, but we suspect it may be a battalion or regimental HQ. If so, then it will house officers and we'd like to have a chat with one of them before the big day. Do you fancy setting up a meeting?"

Carter saw Vernon's right eyebrow raised, a sure sign he was making a joke.

"I'm sure I could arrange something, Sir. I take it the meeting would be at Brigade HQ."

"That's where you can bring him, or them. I'll pass them up to Division and their intelligence bods can do the interrogation. Our experience so far has been that once the Jerries are in the bag, they are happy enough to talk. Except for the SS, of course. They're fanatics. But the *Wehrmacht* are more pragmatic. Give them a packet of cigarettes and a cup of decent coffee and they'll chat for hours."

"I won't ask how soon you want this meeting. We'll go tonight."
"Good. And keep your diary clear for the 17th."

[1] Caen finally fell to the British on 6th August 1944. It was supposed to have been captured on D Day, 6th June.

* * *

Slipping his beret off his head and stuffing it inside his battledress bouse, Carter stood up. No challenge was shouted. The other men followed suit.

They didn't wear helmets when on patrol at night. There was too much risk of them hitting something and making a noise; a branch, a stone or even the barrel of their own weapon. Hearing, rather than sight, was the most acute sense at night.

Soon after they had started raiding, shortly after D-Day, they had discovered that once they were through the first line of the German defences, they could stand up and wander around almost at will. The Germans simply didn't think the commandos would be so bold. With no helmets to create an unfamiliar silhouette and their berets removed, the Germans assumed that anyone wandering around in plain sight must be a friend. At first it had baffled Carter and the other commanding officers, but then they had realised that the enemy was seeing what they expected to see. Anyone on their side of the defences must be a friend. It had cost them dearly, because it allowed the commandos to lay boobytraps and timed charges to destroy equipment.

When they had questioned prisoners, they had found that the Germans referred to them as 'ghost patrols', commandos so clever they could get in and out without being seen. But they were seen, on numerous occasions. They just weren't recognised for what they were.

Tpr Spencer, the second Germans speaker on loan from 10 (IA) Cdo, went with those sorts of patrols. If there was a challenge, or just a simple *'guten abend',* he would be the one to reply. On one occasion he had held a conversation with a German sentry for about ten minutes while the rest of the patrol slipped silently back through the lines. Then he had followed, using the excuse that he had to relieve another sentry in a forward listening post.

The three cottages sat beside the road to Le Bas De Breville, which Carter thought might mean 'Lower Breville'. They'd had to pass the crossroads where they had attacked the goulash cannon. The men formed up in single file along one side of the road, the barrels of their rifles pointing downwards so that the snub nose of the Lee Enfields didn't attract attention. The German 98k rifles had a longer length of barrel emerging from the wooden grip. It might take a sharp-eyed soldier to spot the difference in the dark, but Carter wasn't taking any chances. Rather than carry his Tommy gun, with its distinctive shape, he had opted to use a rifle himself that night.

"Smoke if you want to." Carter passed the word down the line. It was another bit of deception. The commandos never normally smoked while on duty and especially when out on patrol, but they knew the Germans lit up whenever they could within the apparent safety of their own positions. More than one commando sniper had claimed a night-time kill because of this recklessness.

As he led them off along the lane, he heard the sound of a match being struck and the shadow of a man briefly fell across the road, cast by the flaring light.

To avoid attracting too much attention, Carter had opted to bring only a single section, led by himself with one of the new officers as his 2IC. Pontin was his name. He was keen and Carter wanted to encourage him. The patrol was drawn from Pontin's troop, which meant, just for a change, Carter wasn't accompanied by the 'Three Stooges' as they were referred to by almost everyone except Carter. Green, Glass and O'Driscoll had protested about being left behind, but Carter let Pontin deal with them. It was beneath the dignity of a CO to be arguing with three ORs about such a matter.

As a recompense he had allowed 4 Troop to provide the support team, who were now lying out in the fields waiting to provide cover for the patrol as it withdrew, should they need it. The Three Stooges were with them as they were in that troop.

Ahead of them Carter could see the roofs of the cottages in the pale starlight. The Moon had yet to rise and give better illumination. The timing was deliberate. Carter didn't want enough light for their uniforms and webbing to be visible. Ideally, they would have started the raid an hour later, but that would have risked being seen under the moonlight.

He led the patrol along the road on the side furthest from the cottages, apparently ignoring them. But Carter was able to squint sideways to take in the buildings. There were gun pits dug at the corners of the nearest and furthest, with sandbags at the empty cottage windows. Precautions against attack, Carter new. It confirmed that the middle cottage was important. You didn't fortify buildings for the fun of it. But the defences were empty. As they passed the first one, two men dropped to the ground, rolling out of sight, any noise they might make covered by the unconcerned tramping of the rest of the patrol. The rest carried on as if nothing had happened.

Outside the front door of the middle cottage a sentry stood, relaxed, his rifle butt resting on the ground. Hs stiffened as the patrol approached.

"*Wie ghets?*" he asked, but he didn't sound alarmed; he didn't even lift his rifle to the ready position.

"*Guten abend.*" Spencer replied. "*Wir fahren nach Breville, um ein Glas Wein zu trinken*". It was their agreed cover story: off to Breville for a glass of wine. They'd heard from a prisoner that there was a cafe in Le Bas De Breville that was still open, serving wine to the Germans in the area; the only people allowed to move after curfew.

"*Habe eins für mich.*" The sentry replied, relaxing again. Spencer later told Carter he'd said: have one for me.

"*Na zicher.*" Spencer chuckled; of course.

They continued along the road for about a hundred yards until they were screened by a slight bend and hidden by the tall hedge, then Carter brought them to a halt. There was the possibility of there being another sentry at the rear door of the cottage, so Carter would have to split his small force, half going around the front and the other half to the rear.

They found a gap in the hedge and clambered through into a pasture on the far side. Slowly, carefully, they made their way back towards the cottages once more.

* * *

Back at the first cottage, the two men who had dropped from sight were crawling silently across the road, though the open gate and into the shadow of the cottage. There would be men asleep inside, they knew. Those defences would have to be manned instantly if the alarm was raised, so there would be no time to bring soldiers in from elsewhere. No doubt the same applied to the farther cottage. But the two men weren't interested in the slumbering defenders. They had a specific job to do.

Once they had gained the illusory refuge of the cottage's walls, one of them made his way to the end furthest from the sentry and around the back, while the one at the front crawled closer to the middle cottage. There had been a fence between the two at one time, but all that remained was some rusting metal posts and a few fragments of broken wire. The soldiers who manned these defences wouldn't want to go out onto the road to pass between one building and the other if they could make their way between the two gardens, so the fence had been cut.

Once in position, hidden by the middle cottage's corner, the soldier crouched and waited.

* * *

The light was getting brighter as it got closer to moonrise. It was noticeable the way it reflected off the rear of the whitewashed cottages. He would remain on that side, the most dangerous approach. He waved his hand to the left to send Pontin and the other three men to the left. The grass was long and in danger of making a swishing sound if they moved quickly, a breeze would have helped, shaking both grass and tree branches, but the weather was being uncooperative that night.

But they had trained for this, crawling through the cattle pastures of Scotland, the heather, the broom and the gorse. There was almost no terrain, short of tropical rainforest, that the commandos hadn't had to crawl across or through at some time. Even thick banks of nettles that left their skin looking like that of plague victims.

As he leant around the corner of the third cottage of the group, he could see the sentry at the rear door. He was nowhere near as alert looking as the one at the front of the building. His rifle lay propped against the wall and the man was similarly positioned, his head nodding until his chin touched his chest before snapping upwards again. Falling asleep on sentry duty could get you killed, Carter thought. He should know better than anyone. Tonight it would certainly have that outcome for the sentry, unless some mishap alerted him.

Carter crawled forward a few feet, then paused to see if the sentry had changed position. If his head turned towards him it meant that he had detected some slight sound. Or maybe it was just the sixth sense that experienced soldiers had. He knew that the battalion defending this section of the line had recently arrived and their unit history had included Russia, the harshest military training ground any soldier could experience.

But not all the soldiers in the unit had experienced that. Many experienced members of the unit remained in Russia, never to return home, which meant that a good proportion of the battalion were less experienced. Several prisoners taken recently had seemed so young they should probably have still been in school, or so Carter thought. Others were middle-aged men who should have been at home looking after their grandchildren. Germany was drawing on its last reserves on manpower, so the rumours said and the evidence of Carter's own eyes backed that up.

But even if half the men were too old, too young, or inexperienced, the other half weren't.

But the man was still facing forward, his head still jerking as he fought off sleep. Carter moved again, taking almost a minute to travel a distance of no more than a few paces.

Still no sign that the sentry knew of his presence.

At last Carter reached the corner of the cottage closest to the dozing man. There was now a gap of at least ten yards between there and the middle cottage. It was too wide for Carter to hope to cross it without raising the alarm. The dividing fence at the rear was in no better state of repair than the one at the front of the cottage, but it only needed one broken strand of wire to rattle for the sentry's head to snap up and turn in his direction.

Which was what Carter wanted right then.

"Psst" Carter hissed towards the man. At first there was no reaction. Carter reached around behind himself and drew his catapult from his belt. Feeling around in the overgrown flower bed that ran the length of the cottage's rear wall, he found a small stone. It would have to do. He raised the child's weapon and aimed it at the corner of the cottage. Releasing the elastic, he sent the pebble smacking into the side Wall, about six inches from the corner.

This time the sentry did react. He reached down and picked up his rifle, then turned towards the sound. But he didn't call out. He was suspicious, but not yet alarmed.

"Psst." Carter hissed again. The sentry straightened up to his full height and turned towards the sound, lifting his rifle so it was held in both hands, across his body. So, not an experienced soldier. A veteran would have pressed the butt of the rifle into his shoulder and pointed the muzzle towards the sound, ready to fire in an instant.

Carter picked up a handful of soil from the flower bed and threw it forward, into the gap between the two cottages. It made a pattering sound as it landed in the long grass. Carter could barely hear it himself. But the sentry reacted. At last he raised the butt of his rifle to his shoulder and stepped towards Carter.

That's it, my lad. Come and see what the noise is. Carter thought. Sounds like it might be a cat, doesn't it? Nothing to worry about really. You feel a little bit silly holding your rifle at the ready, it's such an insignificant little noise.

Carter spied movement behind the sentry as the man at the far corner stepped out. He had about five yards to cross without the sentry turning to see him. "Psst" Carter said again, keeping the soldier focused on him.

The commando must have trodden on something that made a noise, perhaps the solid surface of the rear doorstep of the cottage. It didn't matter, it was already too late for the sentry. As he started to turn to identify the new sound, the commando's arm snaked around his neck. The sentry's body arched towards Carter as his reflexes made him try to escape the dagger that was already sliding upwards under his ribs and towards his heart. The sentry let go of his rifle, which landed on the grass with a thump, grabbing at his assailant's arm but there was no removing the vice-like grip.

The soldier struggled and tried to cry out, but the commando's hand was firmly clamped across the sentry's mouth. The soldier went limp and his killer laid him gently on the ground.

Both Carter and the commando went still, waiting to see if any alarm had been raised. The loudest noise had been the rifle hitting the ground. It probably wouldn't be enough to wake anyone, but if there was anyone inside the cottage who was awake, they might have heard it.

Nothing. No cry of alarm, no shouts, no doors or windows opening. Just the sounds of the night. Carter raised his hand to beckon the three men who were behind him, still concealed by the corner of the cottage. He stood and walked carefully forward, his rifle held at his shoulder, ready to fire if an enemy appeared without warning. On the other side of the gap the commando who had killed the sentry had retrieved his rifle and was now waiting for Carter at the cottage's back door.

This was going to be the difficult part.

If this had just been a raid intent on causing mayhem, the commandos would have smashed the cottages windows, thrown grenades through and then barged their way into the building shooting at any target that presented itself. But tonight they wanted prisoners and they wanted prisoners who were capable of walking unaided back to the British lines. Which meant that subtlety was the order of the day and the commandos didn't do subtlety as well as they did mayhem.

The first thing to do was establish if they could gain entry quietly. If it had been a British defended cottage rather than a German one, the doors would have been locked, which meant that the sentry would have to knock on it and give a password before it would be opened.

But did the Germans do that? More importantly, did these particular Germans do that?

Carter took a tight hold of the doorknob and turned, leaning his shoulder against the door at the same time. He felt the grating of metal through his fingers, but the door didn't move. Perhaps a fraction more movement was necessary. He tried again, but the door refused to budge. He tried turning the knob the other way but got the same result.

Locked!

He gathered the four men around him. "Nothing else for it chaps. We go in hard and fast. Fix bayonets." Someone standing five feet away wouldn't have heard the breathed instruction.

They had decided not to fix bayonets earlier in case the Germans noticed. Troops heading off for a glass of wine would take their weapons, as good soldiers always did, but they wouldn't tip them with the wicked blades of bayonets, for fear of stabbing themselves or a comrade in the confined space of a café.

The metallic clatter of the metal being withdrawn from its sheath made Carter cringe. It was an unmistakeable and quite loud sound, even though the commandos kept the blades of the bayonets greased to reduce the friction. But their luck held. Still no sound of an alarm being raised. If there was another sentry posted inside the door, as

Carter would expect, he must have lost the battle with sleep that his comrade on the outside had been fighting.

Carter stood back from the door and motioned for the man behind him to move into his place. He raised his foot to mime a kicking action and the commando nodded his head. Carter took up the approved position for a bayonet charge, left knee braced to propel him forward, rifle extended in front of him with the bayonet tip hovering at chest height, the butt of the weapon held in a firm grip in his right hand.

He nodded his head. The designated man stepped in front of the door, raised his boot until it was level with the doorknob, then slammed it into the woodwork. The door crashed back on its hinges and the soldier stepped smartly to one side as Carter launched himself forward. The door bounced off the interior wall and swung back towards Carter, striking his left arm, but he just shrugged it off and continued his charge. Starting to rise from a chair halfway along the interior passage was the anticipated sentry, his mouth gaping open either in surprise or as he tried to shout something. It didn't make any difference. Carter's bayonet slammed into his chest, propelling him backwards and down towards the floor, the chair skittering along the passage to hit the front door beyond. Carter felt the rifle being dragged along with the man's body so he jammed his foot into the floor and the man's body slid off the end of the wicked weapon's blade. The body hit the floor with a thud and Carter stabbed down into it again, just to make sure. He felt the rasp of the blade as the man's sternum deflected it before the muzzle of the rifle stopped any further penetration. Giving the rifle a twist, Carter dragged the blade free.

A loud crash came from in front of him as the front door burst open, a commando barrelling through and almost impaling Carter. He just managed to turn it to one side and stagger to a stop. In the middle of the corridor, they looked around to see where the rest of the men were.

Behind Carter there was a door on either side, and behind the other intruder there was the same arrangements. A cottage with just four rooms, by the look of it; two at the front and another two at the rear. Commandos were already bursting through into the rooms. A light shone out from the one on the back left hand side. That must be the command post with the duty officer inside.

Shots rang out from within rooms. The rattle of an automatic weapon signalled that at least one German had been awake, then the lighter crack of pistol shots followed by answering bangs of Lee Enfields being discharged.

The firing ended, to be replaced by shouts, most of them in English. From one room Carter heard "Put your fuckin' hands up Fritz!" and from another "Stay where you are, you fuckin' kraut bastard."

But it wasn't the only source of shouting. More muffled cries of alarm were coming from outside and in German.

"Spencer!" Carter bawled.

"Ja ... I mean yes, Lucky."

"Get to the front door. Tell the Germans outside that if they try to come in, their pals in here will be killed."

It had been too much to hope that they'd get in and out of the German lines without detection. As soon as they'd had to break down the door Carter knew they'd wake up the sentries. Bluff would have to work for them now. That and the assumption that Carter's men were really the thugs and gangsters that Hitler had called them. The Germans already feared them, from the viciousness of the commandos' other raids into their lines, so the idea that they might shoot prisoners would be one that would be easy for the Germans to accept, even though Carter would rather die himself than actually carry out the threat.

"OK, Lucky." As the German headed towards the front entrance, Carter went into the brightly lit room at the rear. Inside he saw that it was laid out as a command post. Maps adorned the walls and three radios stood on a trestle table along one wall. A dead man, probably the radio operator, lay in a heap on the floor. The dials on two of the radios were lit up, indicating that they were in use, while the third, probably a spare, sat in darkness, the meters on the front with their needles pointing to zero.

So, it was a battalion HQ. One radio to communicate down the chain of command to companies and platoons and the other to communicate upwards and sideways to brigade level and neighbouring units. There were also field telephones with skeins of cable disappearing through the sandbagged window. It was probably those cables that had snagged the commando who had tackled the sentry outside the rear door.

Sitting in a chair in front of a desk was a German officer; a Major according to the rank badges on the epaulettes of his unbuttoned uniform jacket. His hands were above his head as he was threatened by the bayonet of the soldier who had been first into the room. A Walther P38 pistol lay at his feet, where he had dropped it. Probably the unit's second in command, taking the night shift, Carter thought.

The man's mouth dropped open as he saw Carter's rank badges. He obviously never expected to see such a senior officer so far behind his front line. Not one that wasn't a prisoner, anyway.

"*Sprechen Sie English?*" Carter asked.

"*Nein.*" The German said, shaking his head.

"Doesn't matter. Tie him up, Soames." Carter addressed the commando, then stood guard while the soldier carried out his orders.

"Take him into the front room." Carter ordered, stepping to one side. After they had gone, he searched the room, removing maps and other documents that might be of intelligence value and stuffing them into a canvass bag he had brought for the purpose. Satisfied that he had done all he could in the room, he stepped back into the narrow corridor.

"Smash those radios and the field telephones." Carter ordered a man standing in the narrow space. The sound of a rifle butt smashing glass and crunching metal was soon heard.

"All prisoners secure. One Lieutenant, the Major and two ORs. Two others dead and one wounded" Pontin reported. "One casualty on our side. Tpr Lofthouse took a bullet in the hand, but he's been patched up and will be OK."

"Well done. Get everyone ready to move. Leave the wounded Jerry behind. He'll just slow us down and his own side can take care of him." He stepped forward towards the front door. "What are the Jerries doing, Spencer?"

"Doing as they were told and standing back. They probably aren't bothered about the safety of the officers, but the ORs will be their mates."

"OK. Tell them that we're coming out and we're bringing the prisoners with us. Any attempt to stop us and we'll shoot the prisoners." It should be enough to deter any interference, but there was always the risk of some hothead acting on his own initiative. He hoped they wouldn't have to fight their way back to the lines. They were a good six hundred yards away and that was a long way to go with an enemy intent on stopping them. And even if they made it, that only put them in front of more weapons.

Carter formed the section into a loose circle around the prisoners, bayonets pointed threatening inwards. He placed himself at the back of the group, where he could keep an eye on the enemy soldiers. They were bound to follow. There were about a dozen of them, obviously the duty guard detail for the night. None of them seemed to be fully dressed, having been taken by surprise, but they were all armed. They would probably have been drawn from a reserve company, which would likely be camped close by. Had someone been sent to wake them? Or had no one thought to do that? Or had they heard the firing and were now assembling a patrol to come and investigate?

Carter pushed the questions from his mind. They would find out the answers only if they were intercepted and if they were, the plan remained the same: use the prisoners as hostages for the good behaviour of the defenders and, if that failed, try to fight their way through to the open ground in front of the enemy's defences.

The prisoners had their hands tied in front of them, making it easier for them to retain their balance as they walked, but they were also tied together with toggle ropes[1] and two of them were tied to the heaviest of the commandos, burly six footers. If they tried to run, they would have to drag their weight with them.

They made their way down the road as quickly as possible, not having to worry about concealment. As they approached the crossroads where the goulash cannon had been attacked, Pontin drew a very pistol from his belt and fired it, sending a green flare high into the night sky.

At once the support teams started firing on the defences to either side of the crossroads. It would keep the defenders' heads down and looking forwards, anticipating a commando assault at any moment.

A few seconds later, mortar bombs started to crump into the German positions, adding their weight to the encouragement for the Germans to sit at the bottom of the trenches and hope for the best.

But a body loomed out of the darkness of the hedge next to the crossroads. *"Halt!"* it commanded.

"Nicht scheissen." The German Major shouted, nervous that he might die at the hands of one of his own men. *"Lass uns durch oder sie bringen uns um."*

"What did he say, Spencer?" Carter asked.

"It's OK, Lucky. He gave orders to let us through." The commando replied.

The German soldier obediently stood to one side. Another thirty yards, that was all they needed. Above the sound of gunfire, Carter could hear the roar of an engine. He hoped it was what he thought it was and not a new threat. But as they reached the crossroads his Jeep careered along the road and came to a screeching halt.

"OK, get them in." Carter ordered. "Just the officers."

Standing in the rear of the Jeep a commando used the menacing barrel of the heavy calibre machine guns to threaten the soldiers that had followed them from the cottages. At last the officers were seperated from the junior ranks, loaded into the Jeep and tied into place. Carter used the time to move his men to the other side of the corssroads, a few yards further towards safety.

"OK. Go!" Carter shouted. At once the Jeep started to move, at the same time the heavy machine gun fired, creating confusion along the lane as the German soldiers dived for cover.

Carter's men dragged the remaining prisoners off the road and into the cover of the other side of the crossroads and out of sight.

Without waiting for an order, they started to sprint up the slope towards the British lines, the two remaining prisoners ensuring that the Germans didn't attempt to fire on them. The sound of the Jeep's engine dwindled, but Carter was able to track its progress from the receding sound. At least the high value prisoners would be delivered, even if the rest of the patrol didn't make it. But every yard they made was a yard closer to home. A parachute flare fizzed into the night sky, but all that did was cause the support team to intensify their fire. Under the flare's light the support team could see their own men now, which meant they could focus their efforts on providing close covering fire without fear of hitting the patrol.

Passing through a hedge, the raiding party were finally screened from the enemy and Carter brought them to halt to allow them to catch their breath.

"Well done men. Is everyone here?" He did a quck headcount. Nine men had gone in with him and nine men were now panting alongside him. The parchute flare fizzled out and darkness fell once more, but the support team kept firing, just in case.

[1] Each commando carried a six foot length of rope wrapped around his waist. On one end was a wooden toggle, like that of a duffle coat, and the other end formed a loop into which a toggle could fit to join two ropes together. At Achnacarry a rope bridge had been built across a river, made entirely from toggle ropes, and trainees were required to cross it as part of their commando training.

* * *

The grass beneath Carter's body was damp, but he was used to that. He raised his binoculars to his eyes and examined the slow flow of the River Seine as it passed by about a hundred yards in front of him. That was the next obstacle they had to overcome. As they advanced, they had heard the ripple of explosions as the Germans blew up the bridge they had hoped to capture.

It had taken from 17th August until the first week of September to cover the thirty four miles from Amfreville to Beuzeville, where the commando was now resting. It hadn't been their fault that progress was slow. Paratroops and airborne infantry had moved around behind them to attack the Merville battery once more and then advance along the coast. In their place to the south were line infantry battalions and the pace of 6th Airborne Division was being governed by the speed of that infantry.

If the division moved too quickly, they would leave their southern flank exposed and the Germans would drive a wedge between them and the troops to the south, isolating the division and probably chopping them up piecemeal.

So the commandos waited at the end of each day for the infantry to catch up with them and often had to withdraw to establish a continuous front line. If the enemy were counter-attacking at the same time, which they often were, it boosted their morale to see commandos withdrawing, even if it wasn't a consequence of their action.

The terrain they were crossing didn't lend itself to quick manoeuvring. Although it was typical Normandy farmland in many ways, it was crisscrossed by drainage ditches and minor rivers. The bridges that crossed each river and the broader ditches had to be taken intact or supplies of ammunition wouldn't be able to reach them. The failure to capture most of them meant that the pace of the advance was further slowed as they waited for engineers to come up and establish new bridges. The commandos shunned waiting and waded across whenever they could, but it often left them isolated, meaning another sodden crossing to get back to their own side again.

The first river had been La Divelle, a couple of miles in front of their own lines, then the Dives and a couple that barely merited the title of river. The most critical had been Le Ponte Eveque, across the

La Riviere Morte. The name meant the dead river and so it had proved for several commandos. Now it was to be the Seine.

To maintain their speed of advance, the commandos used the tactics that had proved so successful during their patrols. Once they had been given their objective for the next day, one or more troops would infiltrate the German lines and take up positions behind them. With the dawn there would be an artillery barrage then the rest of the commando would attack from the front, while the infiltrators popped up behind. With enemy on both sides of them the Germans either withdrew or surrendered, or both.

To overcome the problems of the destroyed bridges, Carter sent parties up and down stream to swim or wade across and get into position ready for the dawn attack. If the Germans had expected to be able to fend off the commandos by using the rivers as barriers, they had quickly found out that the commandos had other ideas. One by one the crossings fell with a minimal loss of life to the commandos. Sadly it wasn't a total lack of casualties and they had lost men to each assault. Carter hated to imagine what sort of casualty rate they might have suffered if they'd had to cross each river with a frontal assault.

Unfortunately, the infantry to their south weren't up to such bold tactics and had to fight their way through the Germans with sheer weight of numbers, supported by tanks. Carter and his men had barely seen a tank since they had left Amfreville. But Carter's success allowed troops to be transported north to cross the newly placed pontoons or Bailey bridges, before turning south again to secure their own crossing with flanking attacks on the Germans. If the commandos expected any thanks for their efforts, they were to be disappointed. Divisional and brigade commanders didn't like the lack of aggression from their own troops being so easily exposed. But they weren't bad troops, they just weren't as good as the commandos.

Turning and crawling backwards away from the river, Carter's three-man escort moved with him. Once they were out of range of

German snipers they rose to their feet and made their way back to where they had left the Jeep, hidden behind a small copse.

There they found Tpr James, the radio's headset clamped to his ears. It wouldn't do for the CO to go missing with no one available to raise the alarm.

"2IC's compliments, Sir. You're wanted at Brigade HQ."

"Better not keep the Brigadier waiting then. OK. Paddy, get her going."

The Irishman settled himself behind the steering wheel, hit ignition button and backed the jeep out of its cover and onto the road to Beuzeville, less than a mile behind them.

* * *

Beuzeville was a small place and the Germans hadn't put up a fight for it, so it was relatively undamaged, except for the Nazi propaganda posters and prohibition notices defacing the walls of the buildings. Those had now been defaced by the British soldiers who had marched through. The language used made Carter hope there were no English-speaking nuns in the town.

The reason the Germans hadn't put up a fight was the field hospital they had set up on the outskirts. It was still operating with its Germans doctors, orderlies and nurses, but now under the watchful eyes of the Royal Military Police. Some of its patients were commandos, men from Carter's own command and that of the rest of 5th Commando Brigade, with British medical staff working side by side with the Germans.

Small it may have been, but Beuzeville still had a Town Hall and that was where Vernon had established his HQ. Carter acknowledged the salute of the sentry, who had recognised him, and made his way into the Ops Room, where Vernon stood, studying a map.

He turned to greet Carter, a broad grin on his face.

Carter recognised the look. It was the same one he had worn the day he had told Carter he was taking command of 15 Cdo and the same one he had worn the day he had told them of the raid on the Gabriel Bridge in Sicily. Nothing could therefore be construed from it.

"Sorry to be so slow getting here" Carter apologised as he saluted. "I've been taking a look at the Seine. It's going to be a bugger to cross. Because it's tidal …"

"Not your problem, Steven." The Brigadier deflected his observation. "That won't be your next objective. I want you to take your men and turn north into Honfleur. It should be in our hands by now, but take care, just in case."

"What am I to do in Honfleur, Sir? If it's already been captured you don't need me and from there there's no way we can cross the Seine. Not unless …" The thought struck Carter that they might use landing craft to cross the estuary and land south of Le Havre, but it would be a tricky operation, with heavy artillery still positioned around the large French town.

"You seem to misunderstand me Steven, which is unlike you. You're not going to Honfleur to mount an operation. You're going there to wait for further orders. 15 Cdo are going home, Steven."

5 – Operation Blackcock

January 1945

Carter huddled closer to the fire, stretching his hands towards it to try to get some feeling into his numb fingers. Burma this was quite definitely not.

That was where he had been told they were going when he had visited the War Office for his first briefing after the commando had arrived back in the UK.

The men had dispersed, allowed to go home on much needed leave, but Carter had been called to London. It hadn't been all bad. His accumulated back pay had meant he could afford to bring Fiona down from Scotland and they had enjoyed a week together. Though he had spent his days in the many War Office outbuildings scattered around central London, Fiona had been able to while away the hours visiting those tourist attractions that were still open, or going shopping along Oxford and Regent streets.

The museums and art galleries were still shut, their exhibits shipped off to safety in remote parts of the country. The Tower of London was closed to visitors, in use as a military barracks and prison, but one of Carter's former comrades in 15 Cdo had been taken on as a Yeoman Warder after being invalided out of the Army and he had arranged a strictly-off-the-record visit for Fiona, where she had enjoyed a solo guided tour. About the only thing of note she hadn't seen was its most famous prisoner at the time, Hitler's former deputy Rudolf Hess.

She had also been able to attend some of the many daytime concerts that were organised to maintain the morale of the Londoners.

During the evenings they had dined at the best restaurants and seen several plays and shows. The commando badges on Carter's uniform had made sure that tables and tickets became available at a moment's notice. The lustre of the commandos lived on, even though they appeared in the press less frequently these days.

But that had come to an end, as all good things do. Carter had helped his tearful wife onto the night sleeper from Euston and stood on the platform, waving, until the train was out of sight. It was a role reversal, Fiona having waved him away so many times before.

Then Carter had hurried off to Lewes in East Sussex to get the barracks sorted out for the return of his men and establish the training centre in the overgrown garden of a country house that was supposed to be similar to the sort of jungle they would encounter in Burma. Carter didn't believe it and neither did his men. And the instructors who arrived, sun bronzed and straight off the ship from India, said as much.

While the garden could represent the thick vegetation of a jungle, it could never replicate the heat, humidity, mud, insects and disease of the real thing.

"Why don't you just send us out to do the training in place, in the real jungle?" Carter had asked. "There must be places in Assam that would provide more realism than East Sussex."

The lack of reply suggested that the Colonel giving him his briefing hadn't thought of that. But Carter now knew he was wrong in that assumption.

The presence of his unit here, in the small Dutch town of Linne on the southern bank of the River Meuse, or Maas as the Dutch called it, told of the real reason. Someone in the War Office had been hedging their bets, keeping 5th Commando Brigade close at hand in case they were needed again.

They had first been put on standby in October, when Operation Market-Garden had failed to capture Arnhem Bridge.[1] Carter was unsurprised at the failure of the operation. Twice he had experienced the intelligence failures and incorrect assumptions that had caused 15 Cdo to be left out on a limb behind enemy lines waiting for troops that were too slow to reach their positions and relieve them.

On both occasions it had cost the commando a lot of men. Now it had happened for a third time, on a much larger scale and at a much higher cost. But this time the final objective hadn't been achieved, so instead of being a close-run thing, as the operations in Sicily and Italy had been, Market-Garden had been an abject failure. Of course, it wasn't portrayed as such in the newspapers and cinema newsreels, but the withdrawal back to the line of the Maas told its own story. The extended front line that led all the way to Arnhem, couldn't be defended, so the combined British and American forces had to withdraw to a front line they could defend.

But that wasn't why Carter was sat shivering in the cellar of the ruined house that was his HQ. No, that was the surprise attack by the Germans in the Ardennes, where they were trying to drive a wedge through a bulge in the Allied line, intent in splitting the Americans from the British and trapping the British in northern Belgium, where they could be surrounded and forced to surrender, along with their supplies of much needed fuel.

But it hadn't worked. The Americans had held out and eventually driven the Germans back. But the British were forced to move troops away from the north of Belgium to support the American defence further south, as their own forces there had been moved to counter the German attack in the Ardennes. Montgomery had been given command of that sector, including all the American troops there, while Patton had charged up from the south to form the other half of a pincer movement that stopped the Germans in their tracks.

But that had stretched the line, so 5th Cdo Bde had been rushed across the English Channel. By the time they arrived the battle was all but won, so instead they marched northwest to take part in operation Blackcock.

This had been an attack into an area of The Netherlands known as South Limburg, a finger shaped piece of land pointing south between Belgium and Germany. The western side of it was marked by the River Maas, or Meuse if you preferred, which wound its way northwards through Maastricht and Venlo before turning west at Nijmegen and joining the Waal, or Lower Rhein as it was sometimes known.

They had joined the operation in company with 6th Airborne Division once again, capturing Sittard and moving on to Maasbracht, driving the Germans in front of them along both side of the river. There they had rested for a couple of days at a convent, where some of the cheekier commandos had persuaded the nuns to do their laundry, in exchange for tins of British bully beef and sardines. It had probably been a fair swap, as the Dutch were short of food.

Then had come the assault on Linne.

They had done it "Russian style", or so Carter had been told, riding on the backs of American tanks, while 3 Troop had advanced on foot to make a flanking attack from the left. The tanks helped them smash through the outer defences of the town, but they'd then had to fight house by house, street by street. The Germans had put up a stiff resistance, leaving much of the town a smoking ruin. What they hadn't stolen they'd smashed to prevent its use by the victors.

The commandos had tried to fight the fires, but the frozen water mains meant that they were unable to stop the destruction. Now they hunkered down in the cellars of what remained. Any movement in the upper portions of the buildings attracted the attentions of German snipers who were now to the east of the town, their backs to the German border and fighting for every inch of ground. They were no longer defending the Nazi ideology, now they were defending their homes.

In travelling north, they had by-passed Saint-Joost and Montford, where the Germans had held out for several more weeks.

The front line here was what the Brigadier called "fluid", which meant that the Allies held the towns along the river while the Germans still controlled the open countryside and some of the smaller towns and villages.

Another country for Carter to check off his list of those visited since he had joined the commandos in 1941. But not the country he had expected it to be.

The experts said it was the coldest winter in a decade and Carter, for one, believed them. The river behind their positions was frozen solid, the ice so thick that you could drive a Jeep across. Carter knew it to be true because he had done it frequently, using it as a short cut to Brigade HQ.

As they had done in France, the commandos gave the Germans no respite, forcing them to move more troops into the area to defend against them, which weakened their lines elsewhere. But it didn't diminish their determination to keep the commandos out of Germany. The ancient city of Aachen had fallen to the Americans before the start of the Battle of the Bulge, and no German wanted to give up any more of their country. At least, not without a fight.

The men were constantly cold. So unexpected had been the move to Belgium that they hadn't been able to draw any clothing suitable for this weather. The QM had scrounged up a supply of short sleeved leather jackets that the men wore under their battledress to stop the wind and they had raided every shop in Belgium and Holland that they passed to try to find gloves. They'd paid, of course; Monty took a very dim view of looting, but you can't fire a rifle while wearing mittens, so holes had to be cut in them and that allowed the cold in. The worst was when the men got wet. Hypothermia was sure to follow.

Of course, it wasn't just them that had suffered. 'The war will be over by Christmas' everyone had been saying. Planning for a longer war, therefore, had neglected the rigours of fighting in winter. All the Allies were short of winter clothing, unlike the Germans who had learnt their lessons in Russia the hard way. They even had snow camouflaged uniforms.

Rumour had it that half of the hospitalisations during the recent battle in the Ardennes had been 'non-combat injuries', a euphemism for frostbite and trench foot[2]. As a precaution, Carter had reinstated one of the lessons his father had taught him about life in the trenches: daily foot inspections to make sure the men weren't going to suffer from the latter injury, at least. Although it was somewhat demeaning it had worked, with several cases caught in the early stages and treated before they could impair the soldier's fighting ability.

They had been equipped with sleeping bags, by some fluke. They found the best way to use them was to sleep naked. Something to do with the body heating up the air inside the bag, which it couldn't do if they were wearing clothes. But that meant having to scramble into a lot of clothing if the alarm was raised because of an enemy incursion. Fortunately, that didn't happen very often. The Germans preferred to keep their distance and let their mortars and artillery do the hard work.

Carter heard a noise behind him and turned to see Gordon, his batman, holding a mug in one hand and a mess tin in the other. "Lunch, Sir." He announced.

"What have we today, Gordon? And if you say bully beef, I'll probably rip off your leg and beat you to death with it."

"No, Sir. No bully beef today. The ration party ran into an American unit near the supply depot and managed to swap some bully beef for some spam."

Carter grunted. Spam wasn't his favourite, but it made a change from bully beef. One day some big-wig in Whitehall would realise that the variety of rations he enjoyed would be appreciated by the troops in the front line and he'd earn the gratitude of all by commissioning supplies of food that provided a variation of diet.

"I've fried up a couple of slices and served it with some baked beans."

"Thank you Gordon. Have you eaten?"

"I had mine while I was cooking yours, Sir. They also managed to get some decent coffee, so I've bagged a tin of it for you. It should last a couple of weeks, with luck."

"I don't suppose they swapped any C-Rations as well?" The American field ration packs were much preferred by the British, being considered superior to their own compo[3] rations.

"You've got to be kidding, Sir. The Yanks may be a bit gullible, but they aren't stupid."

Compared to the Dutch civilians, his men were eating well, so Carter knew he shouldn't grumble. The British were trying to get food to the population, but it was well known that in the German held territories to the west and north, civilians were dying of hunger.[4]

"Visitor for you, Sir." Ecclestone, Carter's clerk, announced from the cellar's doorway.

"Show him in."

"Morning, Sir." A Major stepped over the threshold vacated by Ecclestone and saluted. Carter noted the Royal Artillery badge on his battered peaked cap.

"Please don't salute. It makes German snipers happy and I'd rather not do that."

"Sorry, Sir." The officer had the decency to look abashed. "Poulter, Jeremy Poulter, C Battery, 1st Mountain Regiment."

Carter took a moment to take in some of the detail of the man's introduction.

"Erm …"

"I know, Sir. What's a mountain regiment doing in the flattest part of Europe? It could be worse, we could be the 85th; they're from East Anglia, which is also a bit short on mountains."

"So what is a mountain regiment doing in Holland?"

"It's because of our guns, Sir. We use pack howitzers[5]. They're specially designed to be taken apart and put back together quickly, so they can be carried by mules. We're actually using Jeeps at the moment though. But our guns make us useful for things like river crossings, because you can carry the bits of the gun in a rowing boat, pretty much. We were sent over to support the commandos when they had to cross the Scheldt estuary to capture Walcheren island[6]. We were actually cooling our heels waiting to be sent home again when a staff officer spotted us and thought we might be useful to your brigade. So my battery has been assigned to your sector of the line."

"I'm sorry if we prevented you being sent home." Carter felt some sympathy for the man.

"Actually, it's a bit of a lucky break for us. We were almost certain to be sent to Burma, like the other mountain regiments, where we would be foot slogging it through the jungle with mules. It may be cold here, but at least we're spared the flies and the disease."

"So, what can you do for me and my unit?"

"As you know, a howitzer is an indirect fire weapon, much like a mortar, so we can fire from behind cover such as buildings. That makes us much harder to locate and target. And because we can take the weapons apart, we can set them up pretty much anywhere that has a solid floor. If you wanted, I could set one up in this cellar." He looked skywards through the ruined building, where the clouds were visible through the holes in the ceiling.

Interesting, thought Carter. With that sort of additional firepower, he could carry out more effective raids, deeper into the German positions.

"What are you like for counter-mortar fire?" The German mortars were a constant irritant to the commandos.

"Our speciality, Sir. It was what we were doing most of the time on Walcheren. Because we've got double the range of an 81 mm mortar, we can fire on them, but they can't retaliate against us. And our shells carry a much bigger punch. I think we can guarantee your men getting a better night's sleep."

"Good. Set yourself up on the western side of the town, along the river and I'll send fire orders through when we need you."

"We've got our own artillery spotters, Sir. We can position them with your forward OPs if you like. They have their own radios, so we can cut out the middle-man, so to speak."

"Good idea. Come along to my evening briefing this evening, eighteen hundred hours, and I'll introduce you to my officers and you can explain what you have to offer.

[1] Operation Market-Garden was the plan to drop paratroops into Holland to capture key bridges across the Maas, Waal and Rheine Rivers, to be relieved by ground troops advancing from the Belgian border. The airborne troops were the 82nd and 101st airborne divisions of the US Army and the 1st Airborne Division from Britain and the Polish 1st Independent Parachute Brigade. The British

division's objective was Arnhem Bridge itself. The ground troops were provided by the British XXX Corps, led by the highly experienced Lieutenant General Brian Horrocks. It was Montgomery's plan to pave the way for the invasion of northern Germany from the west. Intelligence reports of a German armoured division resting near Arnhem were ignored (they would later also fight at the Battle of the Bulge) and the time taken for the ground troops to reach Arnhem was massively underestimated, with delays caused by heavy German opposition on the single road along which the British had to advance, and some bridges being destroyed and having to be replaced. The ground advance was supposed to take three days but actually took seven, by which time the Germans had retaken Arnhem Bridge, leaving it impractical for the advance to continue. An estimated 17,000 Allied soldiers were killed, wounded or taken prisoner. For a reasonably accurate record of the operation read Cornelius Ryan's "A Bridge Too Far" or watch the film of the same name. As suggested in the story above, Montgomery had attempted two similar, though smaller scale, operations in Sicily and Italy in 1943 and had been lucky to get away without them becoming failures. Had he been using troops less tenacious than the commandos those potential failures might have been a reality.

[2] Frostbite is caused when the skin and the flesh just beneath it freezes, usually as a result of extensive exposure to cold. However, it can also result from direct contact with frozen objects, such as metal surfaces. This then causes the flesh to die. Fingers, toes and even whole limbs can be lost to frostbite. Trench foot is caused by feet being constantly cold and wet simultaneously. It is dissimilar to frostbite, in that it causes flesh to swell and become painful, though extreme cases can also result in feet having to be amputated. The American soldiers in World War II were particularly prone to trench foot because their boots weren't as watertight as was necessary for the muddy conditions of the Ardennes. Having experienced the problems in World War I, the British were better prepared, though cases still occur to this day and there was a big re-occurrence during

the Falkland's War of 1982 that led to a new type of combat boot being issued to the British Army. Ironically it was based on the design of the American combat boot which had to be hurriedly introduced to help eradicate trench foot during World War II.

[3] Compo (composite) ration packs were introduced at the end of the First World War and were largely unchanged for the Second World War. They were made up of bully beef (corned beef) or sardines in tins, hard tack biscuits and the makings for tea – tea leaves, powdered milk and sugar. They also included boiled sweets. Later in the war more variety was added into the packs in the form of tins of "M & V" stew: meat and vegetables. The modern equivalents offer far more variety with better quality contents and now come in Halal, Kosher and vegan options. The author lived on the 1960s/70s versions of compo rations for periods while serving in the RAF and quite liked them, though it wasn't unusual for catering staff to issue one type of pack to a unit for several days consumption, so limiting variety to whatever that type of pack contained. Fortunately, the author likes 'bully beef'.

[4] From September 1944 until the end of the war, rations for Dutch civilians were cut several times. Even then, actual stocks of food were scarce, especially in western Holland, which became isolated under German control when the British finally crossed the border into Germany. About 4.5 million people were affected and about 18,000 civilian deaths were attributed directly to malnutrition and it was a contributory factor in thousands more deaths. The winter of 1944/45 became known as the Hongerwinter (hungry winter). Both the RAF (Operation Manna) and USAAC (Operation Chowhound) flew mercy missions to drop food to the Dutch, with the Germans agreeing not to fire on the aircraft. However, the German soldiers were also hungry and not all of the food got to its intended recipients.

[5] The QF 3.7 inch pack howitzer was introduced into the British army in 1917 for use on the Western Front. It was designed to be carried in 8 mule loads, with additional mules required to carry the ammunition. It's 20 lb shell had a maximum range of just under 6,000 yards, more than double that of a 3 inch/81 mm mortar, but it packed a considerably heavier punch. It remained in the British army inventory until 1960 but hadn't been used since 1945. It continued in service with the Indian and Pakistani armies until the 1970s and is still in use with the Nepalese army.

[6] Operation Infatuate (1 – 8 Nov 1944), carried out by 4th Commando Brigade and troops from 10 (IA) Cdo.

* * *

The mountain guns were soon put to good use. There was an enemy mortar position that had been bothering the commandos for some time. Although the commandos had replied with their own mortars, they hadn't been able to silence it. The mortar OPs just couldn't get a clear enough line of sight on the weapon to get any bombs close enough and the town's buildings prevented the brigades field artillery from getting a clear enough line of sight to permit a blanket bombardment.

Under cover of darkness the gunners, with the help of willing commando hands, dismantled one of their guns and moved it up onto the top floor of a burnt out house close to the edge of town, not far from the river.

The first German bomb fell just as the thin winter Sun rose. OPs positioned along the bank reported the sound of the tube's discharge, providing a compass bearing which Carter and Poulter plotted onto their maps. After comparing their results, the artillery officer gave his orders and the howitzer fired.

The whole house shook as the gun blasted its first shell westwards. Masonry fell somewhere behind them and Carter suspected it was the house's chimney stack.

They heard the fall of shell and saw a pillar of smoke rise behind the bank of trees that obscured the German position.

The OPs reported in again, providing minor adjustments to the gun's range and bearing, based on the sounds they had heard earlier. Three more rounds were blasted off in quick succession, then the gun was dismantled and carried back downstairs, leaving the house deserted. If the Germans had managed to do the same as the British and locate the howitzer's position, it would bring down an artillery barrage on their heads.

But there was no retaliation and the German mortars didn't fire again that day. Whenever they did fire, the howitzers were employed again and within a few days the German mortaring ceased completely. They'd had enough.

* * *

A sombre looking Capt Marchant stuck his head into Carter's cellar. He had come a long way, both figuratively and actually, since Carter had met him at Worthing station a year before. Now he was the commander of 6 Troop, his predecessors having either been killed on D-Day or in the fighting since.

"You're looking very serious, Dennis."

"I'm afraid I've got a bit of bad news. We lost a man this morning."

"I didn't hear any firing. Besides, your troop is in reserve."

"Yes, Sir. That's what makes it more tragic. A forward OP from 5 Troop had thought they'd heard the noise of tanks along the Roermond Road. They didn't know if they were friendly or Jerry's, so I was asked to send a couple of blokes out in the Jeep." The commando had been allocated another Jeep since arriving in Holland and Carter had assigned it to whichever troop was in reserve, so they could use it for ammunition and ration resupply trips to the rear areas. "Anyway, I sent Patterdale and Trainor out along the road. On the way back they took a wrong turn and ran into a Jerry mine."

Mines were a constant problem. The Germans would sneak forward at night and bury them in the snow. The standard operating procedure now was for no road to be used if the snow was fresh until after a mine detector had been along it. But that was no use to a driver who was trying to navigate in a snow bound area where the road signs had been removed and every feature looked the same.

"Did you lose both men?"

"No. Thankfully Trainor made it back, but there's no sign of Patterdale. Trainor said that he was alive the last time he saw him, but wounded. He didn't know how badly though. They split up to make it more difficult for the Jerries to follow them both."

That was also standard procedure and had been since Normandy.

"And what of the tanks?"

"A couple of Shermans. It wasn't clear what they were up to."

It never was. They could have been mounting a forward reconnaissance, or they could have just fancied a drive in the countryside. Or, like the commandos in the Jeep, they could have been lost.

"OK, let me know if he turns up."

Missing in Action, that's how Patterdale would be reported. It was the worst possible news for relatives. It gave them hope but at the same time it left them in limbo, not sure if they would ever see their loved one again. If he was a prisoner, it might take weeks for the notification to arrive via the Red Cross. On the other hand, Patterdale might already have died from loss of blood and the next snow could hide his body until the commando had long gone.

* * *

As soon as darkness fell, Carter led an eight man patrol out to locate the Jeep and hunt for Tpr Patterdale. His mate, Tpr Trainor, went with them to guide them to where the Jeep had been abandoned. It was a good job he was available because the brisk north easterly wind had started to fill in his footprints. They found the Jeep, already half buried in snow on the windward side.

"There's nothing can be done with that." Carter could see from the damage that it couldn't be moved without a recovery vehicle. "Strip it of anything of use and we'll let REME know where to find it." The most important thing still on board the vehicle was the Browning M2 heavy machine gun and its ammunition, which would have made a nice present for the Germans if it had been left behind.

"I've got a trail here." Danny Glass told him, pointing towards the east, the route that led towards the German lines; the opposite route to that taken by Trainor.

There were blood stains in the snow, evidence of Patterdale's injury. It was a lot of blood, or at least it seemed that way to Carter's eyes. On the one side was a normal footprint, its outline already starting to blur as snow blew across it. On the other side was more of an elongated drag mark, blood staining the snow in and around it. They started to follow, Glass in the lead.

They had gone barely a hundred yards when Glass raised his arm to signal they should halt. Lowering himself gently to one knee, he tapped his left hand against right forearm, then patted his head: leader, close on me. Carter crept forward in response to the signal.

Sound carried a long way at night and even further over snow, they had discovered. Glass continued to use hand signals. People think sound is muffled by snow, but what actually happens is that all traces of echo are removed by it, so it sounds muted when it isn't. As Carter drew level with him, he held his left fist up, the thumb pointing downward: enemy detected. Then he pointed to where he thought they might be. It was right on their line of advance. Carter could hear voices now. They were quiet, the Germans trying not to attract attention, but loud enough to reach him and Glass. Twenty, maybe thirty yards, Carter guessed. If Glass hadn't such sharp hearing, they might have blundered into them.

A mine laying party perhaps, or a patrol resting up before moving again. Either way Carter couldn't risk continuing the search. He had no idea how many men there might be in front of them, or in which direction they might move. To stay where they were would risk detection if the patrol came their way.

The Germans were good at camouflage and many wore white smocks to allow them to blend in with the snow. It was a lesson they had learned during the winter war in Finland back in 1940, when they had been supporting the Finns in their fight against the Russians. If he sent a scout ahead he might see one or two, while an entire company could remain invisible. Carter made a circling motion: Turn around, then pointed back the way they had come.

Glass obediently followed Carter's lead and they made it back to the rest of the patrol, before heading back the way they had come. Carter toyed with the idea of waiting at the jeep in the hope that they could resume the search, but eventually dismissed the idea. The trail would almost certainly have been obscured by the boots of the Germans. They might spend half the night searching for the one set of prints that would allow them to follow Patterdale. And then they might find that he had already been taken prisoner by the Germans anyway.

Much as he hated to do it, Carter couldn't risk the lives of eight men in what was probably going to be a fruitless search anyway. If Patterdale was still out there, he'd be dead from the cold by morning, if he hadn't bled to death already.

* * *

"Got an odd one here, Sir." Tpr James, Carter's radio operator called from the neighbouring room.

Carter laid aside his pen, grateful for the distraction from the report on the previous night's patrols that he had been writing.

"What is it, James?"

"A sniper on the north side of town is reporting movement in front of him."

"So, what's odd about that? What's odd is that he shouldn't be chatting on the radio about it, he should be shooting at whatever it is."

"He isn't the one on the radio. It's an OP close by. He called to them to see what they made of it and now they're reporting back to the Troop commander."

"Still not much odd about that that, James. Are you feeling alright?" It was unusual for the radio operator to interrupt him unless he considered the matter to be important.

"What's odd is that the sniper thinks it's Arnold Patterdale."

"No! That's impossible. He went missing three days go. He can't still be alive."

"That's what the OP said, but the sniper said he'd seen him through his 'scope and he was positive it's Patterdale.

Carter went back to his desk and checked the map to identify the location of that day's OPs. "What's the call sign for the OP, James?

"Garden 6 Bravo, Sir". So, they were from 6 Troop and the sniper would be too. And Patterdale was from 6 Troop, which made a mistaken identity much less likely. Carter started to put on his webbing. "Find O'Driscoll and get him to bring my Jeep around to 6 Troop's positions on Rijksweg." Carter instructed, buckling his belt and reaching for his Tommy gun. As James went to find the driver, Carter jammed his steel helmet on his head and was halfway up the stairs out of the cellar.

An officer running anywhere always attracts attention and when it's the CO it attracts everyone's attention, so Carter got some odd looks from his men as he sprinted through the street of Linne to Rijksweg. A couple of commandos lounged in the doorway of a house. "Where's the OP? Carter asked, as he hurried past.

"Up here. Sir." One of them pointed upwards through the doorway.

"Is that Garden 6 Bravo?" Carter asked, wanting to be sure before he expended more energy.

"Yeah, that's them."

Carter was just about to push past them when he stopped. He might be able to save himself and unnecessary trip. It would be unusual for a sniper to be in the same location as an OP, but he might be close by. "Is there a sniper somewhere round here too?"

"Four houses down, Sir." The trooper pointed along the street. "He's in the attic."

From where he was, Carter could see that the 'attic' was no more than a collection of burnt-out rafters.

"Thanks. Find me a stretcher, or an old door we can use as a stretcher." He said as he left. "And when my Jeep arrives tell him to wait here for me."

Carter had to take care climbing the stairs. Some were intact, others were burnt out while others were halfway between. They might bear his weight, or they might crumble under him and send him straight down to the cellar level to break bones. But at last he made it safely to the attic level. Keeping his head low, barely able to see over the top step, he hissed a call to the sniper, hidden somewhere within.

"It's the CO. Can I come in?"

"Keep low and crawl forward. Where you see my track marks, the floor will take your weight." The whispered reply came back. Although they were some distance from the enemy, snipers always operated as if there was a German right outside the door.

Carter saw the scuffs and scratches that the trooper meant, crossing the fire damaged floorboards towards one corner of the attic. A jumble of roof tiles and broken bricks filled one corner, where a chimney stack had collapsed. Carter could just about make out the shape of a body lying there.

Crawling forward, he made his way towards the man. Any sight of him from outside would give the sniper's position away, so he had to hug the floorboards and move slowly. It took him several minutes to cover a distance of less than ten yards.

He recognised the sniper, an old hand. "OK, Aston, where's this ghost you think is Patterdale?"

"'Ee ain;t no ghost, Sir. I'd know 'im anywhere." He eased his way back, leaving his rifle where it lay propped up on a sandbag behind the bricks he was using for cover, so Carter could take his place. "You'll need to use the scope."

"What am I looking for?"

"Just raise the rifle, don't change the angle or you'll lose him. He hasn't moved for a few minutes now."

Carter did as he was told but could see nothing but the trees in the distance. He raised the rifle's butt slowly, to lower the barrel. Even then he almost missed it. There, in the snow, some dark smudges that might be blood; or they might be engine oil. If he had crawled all the way from the Jeep, it meant he was moving left to right. Carter adjusted the rifle's angle carefully. There. Definitely a body of some sort. The magnification of the scope still didn't make the object large enough for a clear identification.

"I were just about to send 'im to meet is maker when I recognised 'im. We wuz at Achnacarry together. Been together ever since." Aston whispered.

"He's not showing his face right now, that's the problem." Carter replied.

"Well, if you ain't going to take my word for it …"

"No, you're right." Carter interjected. The man wouldn't be a sniper if he didn't have good eyesight. If he said it was Patterdale, then it must surely be Patterdale. "OK, I'm going to take my Jeep out and bring him in. If there's any sign of activity from the Jerries, you know what to do."

"It will be my pleasure, Sir."

Carter suspected it would be, too. The snipers were a strange breed. For a start they were quite happy to keep themselves to themselves. They didn't actually shun company, but they didn't seek it out either. It was probably because they spent so much time on their own in the first place.

Carter heard the sound of his Jeep approaching, so he made his way back across the room to the top of the stairs and slithered over the edge. Only when he was sure he wouldn't betray the sniper's position did he dare to stand up.

The two troopers he had sent to look for a stretcher stood there. Lying on the ground was a long canvass roll with wooden handles projecting from the end. The Jeep sat by the roadside, its exhaust burbling away, O'Driscoll behind the wheel.

"Right, you two. Are you mates with Patterdale?" Carter asked.

"He was alright." One of them said.

"He was dating my sister." The other replied. Carter was unsure if the trooper approved of that relationship.

"Well, you're just about to save his life, I hope. There's a man out there in the snow and I think its him. We're going out in the Jeep to fetch him. O'Driscoll will drive and I'll be in the front seat. You two in the back. When we get to him, no messing around. Just grab him, sling him on the stretcher and hang on for your lives. Better have the stretcher set up and ready.

The two men unrolled it and opened it up, the metal braces locking into place to create a flat surface twenty four inches wide; just about enough to accommodate a man's shoulders. They laid it across the rear of the Jeep, behind the upright of the machine gun mount and just in front of the spare wheel. They clambered in on either side between the stretcher and the front seats. Carter climbed in next to O'Driscoll.

"OK, Paddy. At the end of the road turn right and head straight out across the field. I'll point you in the right direction. Don't stop for anything, going or coming back."

"I've got you, Sorr. Don't stop for anything."

"Other than picking up the casualty of course. And make sure this thing's in 4 wheel drive."

O'Driscoll gave him a look that suggested he didn't need telling that, but kept quiet. Putting the vehicle in gear he drove them down to the end of the street and swung around the corner.

There was a short lane, then they were through a gate and bouncing across snow covered fields. The wind had the effect of forming the snow into waves. Every so often they would hit a deeper patch of snow and the Jeep would slow down as O'Driscoll tried to force the vehicle through it.

Searching the tree line, Carter tried to pick out the landmarks he had seen from the attic. It all looked different from this level. There had been a tall, thin tree flanked by two broader ones. Something like an ash flanked by oaks, he thought. There! He had them.

"That way!" Carter yelled above the roar of the wind in his ears as he pointed out the direction. O'Driscoll made a slight course direction, causing the Jeep to fishtail, then they were heading for the trees Carter had picked out. "Slightly left of the tall thin one." He shouted.

The vehicle must have hit some sort of obstruction hidden by the snow, because it launched itself into the air to crash down heavily once more. The wheels span as they tried to gain traction.

"Steady on, Paddy, you lunatic." One of the men in the back shouted.

"Ach, it's nothing to fret about." O'Driscoll shouted. He changed gear, swung the vehicle in a long curve and got them back on course again.

"There!" Carter pointed to the right, where a body lay in the snow. As they approached at a slower speed, Carter thought he saw it move. From the uniform, there was no doubt about the nationality of whoever it was. The man wore no webbing, but his rifle lay gripped in his hand. Definitely a commando then.

O'Driscoll brought the Jeep to s skidding halt. The man on the ground tried to lift himself, dragging his weapon upwards as though to defend himself.

"Take it easy, Patterdale. You're in safe hands."

"Lucky? Sorry, Colonel Carter, is that you? Or am I seeing things. Is this heaven?"

"Only if heaven is under three feet of fuckin' snow." One of the commandos said as they dropped the stretcher onto the ground beside Patterdale. One of them grabbed him under the shoulders, the other under the hips and Carter slung his Tommy gun behind him so he could lift his knees. Below his right knee, the trooper's trouser leg was a bloody mess of rags. His boot was barely recognisable as footwear.

A spurt of snow gouted up close to Carter and they heard the crack of a rifle. Someone had spotted them at last and they weren't friendly. A little belatedly, Carter thought it might have been a good idea to arrange a truce while they recovered the injured man. Hindsight, he thought. It was such a wonderful thing.

The three men heaved the body onto the stretcher, then manhandled it onto the back of the Jeep. Another bullet spanged off the Jeep's bonnet.

O'Driscoll had vacated his driving seat and was now holding onto the spade grips of the Browning. He let rip a long salvo of bullets. It might have been in the right direction, but it equally might not have been. But it was eastwards, so close enough.

"Get back in the driver's seat, Paddy." Carter commanded. There was no room for the stretcher, two commandos and someone firing the gun.

Running around to the far side of the vehicle, Carter threw himself in just as O'Driscoll let the clutch out, sending the jeep careening back across the fields once more. Mortar bombs crumped close by and smoke started to spill over the frozen landscape. Good, thought Carter. Someone was thinking for themselves. If they could stay behind the smoke's cover, they might even make it back to their own side in safety.

Carter watched the field ambulance until it had disappeared along the road, hoping that the bright red cross symbols would protect it from enemy mortars. While the Germans normally respected such niceties, mainly out of self-interest, it wasn't unknown for fanatical officers or NCOs to give the order to open fire despite the fact that it would constitute a war crime.

He shook his head in wonderment. He had witnessed some amazing things from his men since joining the commandos; acts of heroism and self-sacrifice that went far beyond the call of duty, but what Patterdale had done must rank amongst the most incredible.

As they had waited for the field ambulance to arrive and the Medical Officer had done his best to dress Patterdale' wounds, his story had emerged through the man's chattering teeth.

When the Jeep had hit the mine, the flat metal plate that was the accelerator pedal had been blown upwards, shattering the bones in his right foot and splitting the gap between his tibia and fibia. Shock had prevented him from feeling the injury until he had separated from Trainor and suddenly found himself collapsing in a heap beside the road. He had crawled as far as he could to put distance between himself and the Jeep. It wasn't unknown for the Germans to machine gun or mortar wrecked vehicles in the hope of finishing off any survivors.

As a native of the Yorkshire Dales he had often seen sheep emerge unharmed from burial within snow drifts, so he had dug his way inside one to hide from enemy patrols. It had been a wise precaution as several passed close to him during that day and the following night. It seemed that the heat of his own breath had kept his snow hole warm enough to prevent hypothermia setting in.

With the arrival of the next day, his leg was so painful that he decided he had to try to crawl to the British positions. After quenching his thirst with some melted snow, he had started. His webbing had proved too much of a weight for him to manage, dragging along the ground and slowing his progress, so he had abandoned it, burying it to avoid detection, but he had filled his pockets with ammunition and did his best to bind his wounds with a field dressing before doing so. Then he had crawled some more, dragging only his rifle with him.

That night he had dug himself another snow hole, but he must have become disoriented at some point because he was surprised to find himself far to the east of Linne. He had been trying to get back to the town when the sharp-eyed Aston had spotted him.

The cold had helped, the Medical Officer said. It had thickened Patterdales blood and made it easier for the blood vessels to clot and prevent further blood loss. But frost bite was now the worst worry. While there hadn't been any evidence on his fingers or the toes of his other foot, the lack of covering on the injured foot could result in them being lost. That was if the leg could be saved at all, which the MO had confided only after Patterdale had been dispatched to the field hospital.

Since they had arrived in Belgium in the middle of winter, the commandos had been granted an issue of rum each day to help keep out the cold.[1] Carter made sure that Aston was given a double ration for his part in the rescue, along with O'Driscoll and the other two troopers who had gone with him to rescue Patterdale

[1] It has now been discovered that giving people alcohol to "keep out the cold" is not a good idea. It has the opposite effect to the that desired. The effect of the alcohol is to send blood to the surface vessels of the skin, away from the body's core, where it cools more rapidly. So, instead of warming the body it cools it down. The feeling of heat is purely psychological and is caused by the skin flushing because of the increased blood flow. The best thing to keep out the cold is hot food and drink, which release energy into the bloodstream to provide heat.

* * *

The bodies lying on the floor in their sleeping bags were snoring loudly, as was the sentry outside the house, next to the white painted halftrack, who was supposed to be keeping watch. A troop of Girl Guides could have taken this village, Carter thought, as he kicked the foot of the nearest sleeping bag.

The occupant stirred. "What's up buddy? I'm not due on sentry. Wake Hillstrom." He turned over and tried to go back to sleep."

"Carter, 15 Cdo and you'll call me Sir." Carter barked.

"Wh ... Yes, Sir." The American struggled to get upright and salute but trapped inside the confines of his sleeping bag all he did was collapse back into a heap, landing on his neighbour.

"Hey, whatya doin?"" the man protested as the rest of the section started to wake.

Carter had been told to send a troop to take over from a company of American mechanised infantry who had been occupying the village of Montfort, hallway between Linne and Maasbracht. It stood some distance back from the river, in ground that was still contested by both sides. It had finally been liberated by the Durham Light Infantry, but they had moved on while a company of Americans had been assigned as a temporary garrison. The Americans could count themselves lucky that the Germans hadn't sent a patrol into the town or all seven of them and, probably, the rest of the company would now be either dead or prisoners of war.

"Cheese it." The first soldier said. "We got a Lim ... I mean British officer here."

The men pulled themselves upright and started to roll up their sleeping bags and gather their kit together. Carter shook his head in disbelief. The Americans appeared to be unaware of the danger they had put themselves in.

"You must be our relief, Sir." The senior man, a Corporal, said.

"I am. I think the rest of your company may already have left. There doesn't seem to be anyone else in the village."

"Yeah, we were left behind to tell you the layout."

"And you thought it would be OK to sleep on the job?"

The man found a great deal of interest in the toes of his boots all of a sudden. "My men scouted the German positions on the way in, so we probably know more about the whereabouts of the Germans than you do right now. Go on, get out." Carter snapped.

The men hurriedly left the house and a few moments later Carter heard the sound of the halftrack's engine starting, then the squeal of its tracks as it headed out of town.

Back in the street, Carter was greeted by the grinning faces of Able section. "They didn't look happy, Lucky." One of them ventured.

"And neither will you if you don't wipe those smirks off your faces. Let's go."

He led them through the streets towards the centre of the small town. His presence wasn't necessary; the troop commander was more than capable of taking care of defending the place if it was needed. Truth to tell he was bored. The commando had been in Linne for nearly a fortnight, with no sign of any further advance. Operation Blackcock was almost finished. Roermond, the primary objective, was under British control and the final enemy defenders of the line between the Maas and the German border were being mopped up.

The village was a mess. It had been repeatedly bombed[1] by the Allies in an attempt to shift the defenders. The commandos had both seen and heard the raids coming in over a four day period; British and Canadian fighter-bombers swooping low to drop their loads within the village's perimeter. A lot of civilians had been killed, according to the daily intelligence brief.

Entering the village's central square, Carter could hear voices raised in argument. A small van sat there, the initials USO[2] painted on the side. A group of commandos were arguing with what Carter presumed to be the vehicle's occupants, though they were all stood beside it. What was quite apparent was that the three occupants were all female.

A smell of fresh coffee drifted across to Carter and he knew that the van would be filled with luxuries such as donuts, chewing gum, chocolate bars and cigarettes none of which, with the exception of cigarettes, the commandos had seen since leaving England.

"Sgt Major Green." Carter summoned the figure he recognised most easily.

"Sir?" Green said as he arrived in front of his CO.

"What's the row about?"

"These USO girls won't let the men have anything from their van. We were just trying to persuade them."

"Perhaps I need to have a chat with them." He walked the short distance to where the two groups still stood in a state of belligerence.

"Excuse me, Madam." Carter addressed the oldest, a middle aged and grey haired, quite formidable looking woman he assumed to be in charge. "My Sergeant Major tells me you won't let my men have any of the food or drink you have in your van."

"That's right. It's for Our Boys only." She spoke with the clipped New England accents that Carter associated with actresses such as Katherine Hepburn. Carter could clearly hear the capital letters when she said 'Our Boys'. "I've been given very strict instructions about that."

"I have some dollars, can I buy some of it?"

The woman looked thoughtful for a moment, trying to work out if that would constitute disobedience to her orders.

"No, I'm sorry, but if I let you have it, then some of Our Boys will go without."

There was little point in arguing with that sort of logic, Carter knew, even though the nearest American troops would now be several miles distant and getting further away by the minute. It was the sort of thing he had heard from stores clerks since the day he joined the Army: 'If I give it to you, I won't have one to give to anyone else if they want it.' But if the women and their van stayed here, his men might take matters into their own hands and that might cause some sort of international incident.

Carter decided a change of tactic might be necessary. "What are you ladies doing so far forward? I though the USO stayed well behind the lines."

"We are behind the lines." The women said, stating something she knew, with absolute certainty, to be a fact.

"No, you aren't. The nearest German positions are less than four hundred yards away. They could start dropping mortar bombs on our heads at any time."

"But I was told …"

"It doesn't matter what you were told, Madame. I'd be happy to take you to my forward positions and show you the Germans, if you don't believe me."

The way the woman's face went very pale told Carter that she did believe him. The two younger women looked terrified at the news. Carter was sure one of them was about to break down in tears.

"I think it would be best if you went back to the nearest American positions." Carter suggested as gently as he could.

"You're right. Come on girls." She turned her attention to her two younger companions. "Get in the van."

"I didn't mean right now, Madame. It's far too dangerous to use the roads during daylight hours. I'll find you somewhere safe and you can leave after dark."

"It was driving in the dark got us here in the first place. I'm not even too sure where 'here' is. No, we're going. And if we can't use the van, we'll walk."

She started pulling heavy coats and hats out of the front of the van, handing them to her companions.

"Really, ladies, that's not a good idea."

"We're going and you can't stop us." She pulled herself up to her full, quite intimidating, height.

Carter knew when a battle wasn't worth fighting. "Very well. As you wish." Carter conceded defeat. "I'll assign a couple of my men to take you by the safest route and hand you over to the next unit along the road." That would be in Saint-Joost. Carter nodded at Green, who turned to address a couple of the men who were still standing around listening to the exchange.

"I want you to assure me that you will take good care of our vehicle, until we can send for it." The woman said, as she started to follow the two troopers who had been assigned as her escort.

"I will, Madame. Your vehicle will be quite safe with us." He watched them as they disappeared from the square and into a side street.

"So, you're not going to allow the men to have anything, even though the women have gone." Green said, a tone of censure in his voice.

"Sgt Major Green, I gave that woman my word as an officer that her van would be looked after." Carter used his sternest tone, but he couldn't prevent a smile twitching his lips. "But she didn't mention anything about the van's contents. Just make sure that some of it gets back to Linne. Fair shares for all."

He turned to leave the square himself, going to find O'Driscoll and his armed escort, then he thought of something and turned back again. "Grab me a cup of coffee and a Hershey Bar, will you?"

The van, emptied of its contents, was still sitting in the village square several days later when Carter's men were replaced by a platoon of infantry who were to garrison the village until the Dutch civilian authorities could be re-established.

[1] 19th to 23rd January 1945. 186 Dutch civilians were killed.

[2] United Services Organization. Established in 1941 to provide canteen facilities for American troops at home and overseas. As well as providing mobile canteens like the one encountered by Carter's men, they also ran static clubs in American cities and some overseas locations such as London and, later, Paris. They laid on dances and concert parties. Some big Hollywood names performed at those, the best-known being comedian and actor Bob Hope. Many of the USO's staff were volunteers, but the majority who served overseas were employees. Many marriages came out of meetings in USO clubs.

6 - Operation Widgeon

There was a splash and a surge of water and the first Buffalo[1] started to make its way across the Maas once again.

The commando had been doing this for a fortnight now, clambering into the vehicles, entering the Maas on the one side, crossing over and then disembarking and advancing for an assault. The men were fed up with it, but Carter wasn't yet satisfied. Some men were still hesitating before jumping to the ground and that meant they left themselves open to sniper or machinegun fire.

"Faster Cunningham!" Carter yelled at a man perched on the rear of a vehicle. He heard the shout, looked up to see who was shouting and immediately launched himself off once he recognised the CO.

Carter was frustrated as well. Half the brigade were advancing along the line of the Maas towards Venlo as part of Operation Grenade, the main thrust of which was headed east towards Monchengladbach and then onwards to the Rhine.

That was what they were training for, Carter had worked that much out. The river was several hundred yards wide in parts, so it wasn't possible to cross it any other way than in these infernal machines or in boats, if the enemy blew the bridges, which they almost certainly would.

"It's no good, Howard." Carter stood next to his 2IC, the man responsible for the training. "They're going to have to be much slicker if I'm to report us ready for whatever we're training for."

"It's the rocking motion, Sir. It upsets the men's balance."

Carter had noticed how the vehicles rocked on their suspension for several seconds after they had been brought to a halt. It was a feature of the vehicles that couldn't be overcome. Even at walking pace they seemed to do it.

"Well, the men are going to have to learn to deal with it. This is how we're going to go into combat." He avoided any reference to their likely target, though he doubted that there was a man in the commando who hadn't worked it out. They were on the German side of the Maas already, so the next watery obstacle to be crossed was the Rhine; it was a simple deduction.

They only had half a dozen of the Buffaloes at the moment, which meant that only two troops could practice at a time, Ramsey had tried to vary the training by sending the troops out on other types of exercise if it wasn't their turn in the vehicles, but after two months of almost non-stop combat, the commandos didn't feel they needed to train much.

But they couldn't be left idle, either. The Dutch in Maasbracht had started to re-open their bars and cafes and if the men wandered in there, trouble was bound to follow. The Dutch were a friendly lot and keen to show their gratitude for their liberation from the Germans, but the commandos were interested in making the acquaintance of the Dutch women as much as they were interested in the Dutch beer. That was bound to cause friction, just as it had everywhere else they had been, including back home in England.

At least the weather was better. At the end of February, a general thaw had set in, opening up the river and giving the troops some relief from the constant cold. It still wasn't spring, but at least it was no longer arctic conditions. Most of the men had experienced worse at Achnacarry or in Norway, but that was no consolation for the ones who could still remember the heat of Africa, Sicily and Italy. They had complained about that, as well, but there wasn't a man in the commando that wouldn't swap right now if given a chance.

"I noticed yesterday that 3 Tp were a lot faster than the others." Carter remarked.

"Yes, well they have been parachute trained[2], so they know how to land properly." Ramsey pointed out.

Of course, why hadn't Carter thought of that? Sometimes the most obvious solutions to a problem escape notice.

"Ah, yes. OK, Howard, get 3 Tp to teach the others how to land and roll the way they do. I want all the troops down to less than 5 seconds to get out of these contraptions by the end of the week."

[1] Landing Vehicle Tracked (aka LVT, Buffalo or Amtrack (amphibious tractor)). Essentially a large metal container, similar in shape to a rubbish skip, fitted with a radial aircraft engine which powered caterpillar tracks like those of a tank. Over 18,000 were built by the Americans for landing operations. They were used extensively by the Americans in the Pacific theatre and on a smaller scale by the British and Australians. In Northwest Europe they were the main mode of transport for river crossings, first used by the commandos at Walcheren (Operation Infatuate). They had a crew of 2 or 3 (depending on whether it had a one or two machine guns fitted) and could carry between 18 and 23 personnel and their equipment, depending on which mark was in use. The Mk 4 had a ramp installed at the rear so it could carry a light vehicle, such as a Jeep but the ones used by the commandos were earlier marks, so the troops had to clamber in and out over the sides or rear. They were 8 ft 2 high, which made for a daunting jump as the men's heads would be around 14 feet above ground if they stood upright – the height of a 1st floor window. Top speed was 20mph on land or just over 7 mph in the water. They were notoriously hard to steer when in a strong current.

[2] The original concept for the commandos was that they should be dual role, both surface raiders and paratroops. 2 Cdo became the designated paratroop commando and were based at Ringway (now Manchester Airport) to do their training. They would go on to form 1st Btn The Parachute Regiment in 1942. The intention to have a paratroop capability amongst the other commandos was maintained, with one troop in each commando being trained in the role, though most of the trainees only underwent ground training. Because of aircraft shortages, very few made the live parachute jump that would qualify them in the role.

* * *

Operation Plunder, they were calling it; the plan to cross the River Rhine on a broad front, all the way from Emmerich on the Dutch border to Wesel in the centre and then on to Walsum, just north of Duisburg, where the Ruhr joined the Rhine. To the west of Wesel were the British and to the right was the American 9th Army, but Wesel itself was a British target.

That had been given its own codename, Operation Widgeon and it would be led by 5th Cdo Brigade.

Carter and his men had arrived on the southern bank of the Rhine the previous week and preparations were now well advanced. The artillery maintained a constant barrage of smoke shells to conceal their activity, but Carter knew that would fool no one. If the British were using smoke, the Germans would conclude, then they must be hiding something and the most obvious thing to hide would be preparations for an assault across the river.

They were positioned in the broad, flat, low lying area behind the dykes that kept the river within its banks. Carter had used the cover of the smoke to work his way forward and view the task in prospect. They had been briefed by now, of course, but seeing the lie of the land in daylight, in advance, would be of considerable help.

To his right lay the two bridges that crossed the river to enter the town that lay on the northern bank. The Germans had blown gaping holes in the spans of the stone-built railway bridge and the RAF had bombed the metal spans of the road bridge so heavily that it looked like Meccano set that had been trampled on by army boots. Several spans lay in the river and the others were canted at angles. Engineers would be able to use the solid foundations to anchor sections of Bailey bridge, but not until the Germans had been cleared from the northern end. Which meant not until after the commandos had done their job and taken the town.

As a ruse to convince the enemy that the commandos were only raiding, there would be no re-supply across the river. That wouldn't come until there was a bridge open. The memory of earlier operations involving being cut off from the bulk of the army still haunted Carter's dreams. But at least this time the army would be in full view and it would be possible for supplies to reach them across the river if the engineers were slow to repair the bridges. So long as the Buffaloes were still present, that was. The thought of paddling across in open boats to re-supply them was too hideous for Carter to contemplate, even though it might come to that.

The far side of the river, four hundred yards away, was similar to the southern bank, dykes protecting flatter ground. The Buffaloes were capable of climbing the steep banks, Carter knew that. Even if they weren't the commandos could do it on foot anyway.

Four hundred yards under the constant view of the enemy. It was a good thing they were going at night.

The commandos would cross in three waves. On the left flank would go 49 Cdo, with the brigade tactical HQ to direct operations once the rest of the force was across. 16 Cdo would cross and advance towards the town, laying white tape so that the rest of the force could follow. Once there they would start to move to the right, to the northern end of the bridge. Both commandos would paddle across in boats, so as not to alert the enemy of their presence.

At least, that was the hope. Then would follow 15 Cdo in the Buffaloes, landing then following the white tape until they reached the outskirts of the town. There they would pause, because the RAF were supposed to be keeping the Germans below ground level with a bombing raid and the commandos couldn't proceed so long as that was in progress.

With the Buffaloes having returned to the south bank, they would collect 17 Cdo, who would sweep around to the west of the town to enter from that side. Across on the right of the bridge American troops from their 30th Infantry Division would be mounting a similar attack from the east.

The encirclement of the town was to be completed in the morning with Operation Varsity, the arrival of the American 17th Airborne Division and the British 6th Airborne Division, flying in from England.

As a plan it sounded fine, but Carter was still not happy about not having proper re-supply. With just one hundred rounds of ammunition per man, plus whatever Bren gun and Vickers ammunition, mortar bombs and PIAT missiles could be carried along with them, they would need to conserve their resources. If the Germans counter attacked in force the commandos could run out of ammunition within a few minutes.

While the commandos were taking the town, the pack howitzers would be moved up to the riverbank to provide some artillery support. That would be helpful when it came to countering any German resistance. Once the town was in Allied hands the guns would be moved across the river and into the town to bolster the defences.

When he returned to their forward positions, Carter ordered extra of everything to be loaded into the Buffaloes. If the enemy weren't firing on them when they landed, they could unload it and leave it behind the dykes to be collected later. It would help and it would give the men confidence that he had thought that far ahead. At the final briefing that evening he would let the COs of the other commandos know what he had done so they could consider doing the same. Though knowing them, they had probably already thought of it.

* * *

The drone of heavy bombers helped to drown out the splash of paddles as the first two commandos started across the river. It could take up to ten minutes to complete the journey, so the engines of the Buffaloes remained turned off to reduce the noise from the south bank that might alert the enemy to the impending crossing.

Bombs started falling. It was just the first wave, designed to provide cover for the initial crossing. But any Germans troops guarding the far bank would remain unaffected. To keep them occupied the artillery were providing a steady bombardment. It was a something that had been happening for days, so it wouldn't give the game away any more than it had on the previous nights..

There was the sound of machine guns, but they were distant. Carter placed them no closer than the bridges. Perhaps the Germans had spotted something on the American side, or perhaps they were firing into the night sky in the hope of hitting an aircraft.

Anti-Aircraft rounds burst high above and the pencil beams of searchlights tried to locate the bombers and illuminate them for the gunners. Carter was surprised at how much gunfire there was. It suggested that the Germans were intent on putting up a stout defence of the town.

The minutes ticked by, but all Carter could do was sit on the lightly armoured roof of the driver's cab of the Buffalo and stare into the darkness in front of them. The dykes blocked out any view across the river, as well as suppressing any sound, so if there was a fight going on he would hardly know about it.

"Sir," Tpr James tapped him on the arm.

"Yes James."

"Codeword Mountjoy received."

Carter breathed a sigh of relief. It meant the brigade's tactical HQ was safely across and there was little enough resistance to allow the Buffaloes to start their crossing. Carter rapped the butt of his Tommy gun on the roof of the cab. Inside the driver, a trooper from 4th Regiment Royal Armoured Corps, started the engine. All along the line of waiting vehicles the sound of starters coughing and engines revving broke the tension. The waiting, always the worst part of an operation from a psychological point of view, was over.

The vehicle didn't have much armour, but what it had was better than nothing and he made a good target for a machine gunner if he stayed on the roof. As the Buffalo lurched forward, Carter dropped into the passenger compartment to join his men.

They could only tell where they were by the attitude of the vehicle. After a few minutes it tilted upwards, which meant they had reached the dyke on the southern shore of the Rhine. The revs dropped as the engine struggled with the slope, then they increased in both volume and pitch as the driver put the vehicle into a lower gear. Theoretically, the tracked vehicle should be able to cope with anything short of a vertical wall, but Carter wouldn't like to put that to the test. But it was coping with the dyke,

The vehicle tilted forward again, rocking wildly on its suspension as it crossed the flat upper surface, then titled down towards the water. Gravity would do more of the work than the tracks. They were applying more of a braking force than they were moving the Buffalo forward.

There was a splash and sheets of water shot skywards as the vehicle nose dived into the water. A wave surged over the cab, sloshing water into the passenger compartment, then the Buffalo steadied. The wind blew spray inboard and soldiers cursed as they were given a soaking. Carter felt some cold river water on his face, but his position on the downwind side of the vehicle meant he didn't get too much of it.

Above his head another tankie manned the port side machine gun.

"Any sign of opposition?" Carter called to him.

"Flares and some tracer fire, but nothing major." The man reported.

Probably forward listening posts. Carter concluded. They'd be radioing back to the units to raise the alarm. It was a race against time now.

"We're being pushed downstream." The tankie reported, unbidden.

It was a problem they had experienced while training on the Maas, but the current of the Rhine, fed by the melting snow in the mountains of Switzerland, meant that the river was flowing considerably faster.

The only counter to it was to point the nose of the craft upstream a little and try to fight the current, but it would slow them down. He had a choice to make. They could continue to let the river carry them downstream and make a longer journey back on foot, or they could fight the current but take longer to make the crossing. Given the likelihood of the Germans moving against them as soon as the air raid was over, the risk of a slow crossing was too great.

"Tell the driver to keep going forward as best he can, but don't fight the river." Carter instructed. There was a hatch in front of the gunner that could be raised to shout instructions inside to the driver. It was a crude method of communication, but it worked – most of the time.

"James." Carter attracted the attention of his radio operator. "Tell the troop commanders not to fight the river. Keep going forward as best they can."

"Roger, Lucky."

The crossing seemed to take forever, but Carter knew that at 7 mph, it couldn't take more than a couple of minutes, even with the Buffalo being pushed downstream. He fell forward, banging the rim of his steel helmet against the bulkhead in front of him, as the Buffalo seemed to come to a stop. But it was only the tracks getting a grip of the bank. Once more the vehicle's nose titled upwards and it started the climb to the top of the northern dyke.

"Stand by." Carter warned his men. They would drop to the bottom on the other side, carry on for a bit before the driver would stop the vehicle to allow the commandos to disembark.

As the Buffalo reached the top, bullets started to ping against the sides and crack overhead. The machine gunner traversed the barrel of his weapon to the right and opened fire, sending a long burst of point five inch bullets towards an unseen target.

"The natives aren't very friendly." He shouted down to Carter.

"How many?"

"No idea, Sir. One machine gun firing at us and a couple more further along trying to engage the Buffaloes on the right flank. Nothing to our left."

It seemed that the Germans had expected them to come out of the water closer to Wesel, which they would have, had it not been for the current. So they hadn't anticipated the river playing its unplanned part in the operation either. That was good. It meant he could send the troops to his left forward, then around the back of the defences, while the vehicles to his front engaged them with heavy calibre fire.

Flares started to soar upwards as the enemy tried to illuminate the commandos, but they were also too far to the right, which left the majority of the force still hidden in the darkness.

Carter was thrown off balance once again as the Buffalo tilted downwards for the final time. It slid to the bottom, then levelled off. The order was to advance for a hundred yards beyond the dyke before stopping, so that vehicles that had lagged behind didn't run into the ones that were already ashore.

When the vehicle finally lurched to a halt, the men poured over the sides. Carter was pleased that he had spent so much time on the drill, as the machine guns sought them out. More opened up on them, a second line of defence hidden beyond the dykes, creating a crossfire. The heavy machine guns barked a reply from the Buffaloes, but they were already withdrawing, one track going forward, the other in reverse, to turn them in their own length; this was not their fight.

Being so far out of position meant that Carter had to rethink how he manoeuvred the commando. They had expected to arrive at the end of some strips of white tape and then advance inland in columns until they reached the edge of the town. But now they would first have to find the white tape and the enemy machine gunners stood in the way of that. Oh well, every soldier knew that no plan survived first contact with the enemy. It required a new plan and he was the man responsible for coming up with it at a moment's notice. It was why he had a crown and pip on his shoulder.

"James, radio the troop commanders! Skirmish line by troops, 6 Tp to anchor their right flank on the river." If Carter was correct and they hadn't drifted out of position, they would be the nearest troop to the machine guns. When they had assembled in preparation for the assault he had lined them up in troop order, 1 Tp on the left and 6 Tp on the right. If they had maintained their positions during the crossing then 6 Tp would now be the closest to the Germans defences. 1 and 3 Tps would march diagonally inland to straighten the line, while 4 and 5 Tp would form up to his right, leaving him on the centre to assess progress and try to direct his men as best he could. In the dark it wouldn't be easy. 2 Tp would lag behind, burdened by their heavy weapons, waiting for orders to deploy them where they would have most impact.

The defences didn't appear to be strong, probably not more than half a dozen machine guns with some rifles in support. But that would be enough to pin a couple of troops down if he let his men go to ground. He had to keep them moving.

"All acknowledged." The radio operator told Carter, letting him know that the troop commanders were doing as he had ordered.

Star shells exploded above their heads and the men instinctively dived for cover. "Radio C battery. Tell them to lay smoke across our front." Carter started to issue new instructions, trying to read his map while holding a shielded torch in one hand and his Tommy gun in the other. He read off a grid reference. It didn't have to be particularly accurate so long as it was far enough ahead of the commando not to risk injuring his men. Half a dozen shells would do the job. Laying smoke was the only counter to the light being provided by the flares.

The first shell exploded a few seconds later. "Radio the battery again. Adjust five degrees to the east and switch to HE."

High explosive shells would help to keep the Germans' heads down while his men fought their way forward. "Cease firing on my red flare." Carter concluded the order.

James started to report the troops arriving in position, having made contact with the men on either side of them. The left flank would be open and undefended, but Carter didn't think there would be a serious threat from that side. Ramsey would be on that end of the line, so he would have to make sure that the Germans didn't get around behind them in the darkness.

"All troops advance." Carter issued the order. Steadily they fought their way forward, using the smoke as cover. Bren teams sprinted ahead to either side of each troop, firing diagonally into the drifting fog. The troop commanders used different tactics, depending on how they saw the threat in front of them. 1 Tp, out on the left, just marched forward in line abreast, the men pointing their rifles ahead of them, bayonets at the ready. On the top and sides of the dyke, 6 Tp advanced by sections, half of the men providing covering fire while the other half sprinted forward, then taking cover while the others caught up and passed them.

Grenades cracked as defensive positions were attacked and overcome. 4 Tp, immediately to Carter's right, rushed the nearest machine gun position, then were passed it and halfway to the next one before the enemy realised that their flank had been turned and they were firing in the wrong direction, still aiming at the troops nearest to the river.

A gout of mud and fire flew up to Carter's front and he felt the blast of an artillery shell. Too close for comfort. He pulled his Very pistol from his belt and fired it skywards, hoping he had remembered to load it with a red flare, then breathing a sigh of relief as the night sky took on a crimson tinge.

Carter tried to estimate his position, consulting the map again. In their boats, 16 Cdo would have been able to keep a straighter course, so they should have arrived pretty much where they had expected. There had been some fighting, but nothing serious. It seemed that the defences closer to the town hadn't been manned. That made sense, those defences were closer to the where the RAF had been dropping their bombs. But Carter now had to make sure they didn't overrun 16 Cdo's line of advance or they'd miss the tapes they were supposed to be following to the town's outskirts.

If they kept going on this course for too long they would enter the town too close to the river, which would put 16 Cdo on their wrong side. The potential for them and his own men to mistake each other for the enemy was considerable. Besides, they had to pause to let the RAF chase the defenders back into their air raid shelters, so that the commandos could take control above ground. The German garrison commander would know they were there now and if he was given time to organise a defence of the town it would make the brigade's job a lot harder.

"Message from 6 Tp, Lucky." James reported. "They've found the white tape."

"OK. New orders. All troops to angle towards the river and follow 6 Tp." Most of the firing to their front had ceased, which suggested there were no more defences ahead of them. At least, none that had Germans in them. The RAF seemed to have achieved their aim of keeping the defenders heads down during the initial crossings. But they would be flooding out of their shelters now, intent on getting to their positions. Carter had to expect to encounter some heading for the riverbank.

"Message to 1 Tp, James. Watch out for enemy troops, secure the left flank. Then message to 2 Tp: deploy Vickers guns as directed by 1 Tp's commander."

When James had received the acknowledgement from the troop commanders, Carter led him towards the river at a slow jog. It was as much as his heavily laden radio operator could manage. Carter wanted to be up front when they approached the town, so he could assess the situation. His troop commanders could be relied upon to make progress, but undirected progress wasn't what was needed. They had objectives to be taken if their defences were to form an unbroken perimeter, to prevent the Germans counter attacking and it was Carter's job to keep each troop moving not just forward, but forward in the right direction.

He found the tape, stretched between pegs as 16 Cdo had left it. Turning to follow it, he passed his men as they made their way forward, bent almost double under their burdens. Carter wished he could let them drop some of it for collection later, but there was too much risk of them becoming cut off from the river by a flanking attack. It was what he would do if he was commanding the defences.

He found Dennis Marchant at the head of 6 Tp, identifying him by a white rag tied around his upper arm.

"Have you got scouts out?" Carter asked.

"Yes, three men, one following the tape and one either side looking for enemy on the flanks."

"Good man. They know where to stop?"

"We covered it in the briefing." Keeping his eyes forward, Marchant did his best to keep the impatience out of his voice.

"It's always worth repeating." Carter was glad the darkness hid his wry smile. He knew his junior officers thought he laboured his points sometimes. But experience told Carter that no matter how many times you repeated a briefing, there was always a trooper who forgot some vital point in the heat of the moment.

Marchant pulled them up short, raising his hand to shoulder height to signal to the men behind him.

Out of the darkness appeared Marchant's scout. "Marker's up ahead, Sir. Thirty yards." He reported.

Marchant signalled the men to get down, then followed his own order. Carter also knelt, peering into the darkness. He checked his watch. By some miracle they were still on schedule, despite the earlier fighting and the increased distance they'd had to cover.

Silence is sometimes comparative. The commandos were quiet, as they should be, just the occasional rattle of equipment to indicate there was anyone within a hundred yards. But at the same time there were plenty of other sounds. The distant bark of machine guns told Carter that the Americans were having to fight their way across the river on the far side of the town. There was also the thump of anti-aircraft guns, the slower rate indicating the presence of 88 mm heavy guns, counterpointed by faster firing twin barrelled weapons. The night sky was pierced by searchlight beams. Carter could hear no sound of aircraft, but the gunners would have been given warnings by radar stations and listening posts.

Once again, the waiting gnawed at Carter's nerves. The men would be fretting as well, but there was nothing to be done. If they went in now they would be on the receiving end of three hundred tons of bombs. Carter had no idea how many individual missiles that was, but it sounded a lot.[1]

Carter's ears pricked up. There it was, the sound of aircraft engines, just at the limit of his hearing. Even as he listened, the sound grew louder. More anti-aircraft fire sounded, the shells bursting directly above the town and to the west of it, the line of approach for the bombers.

Flares started to drop from above, creating strings of light pointing down towards the ground. That would be the Pathfinder force, crewed by specially trained navigators guiding the heavy bomber squadrons behind them to the target and illuminating it so that there was no excuse for the bombs dropping short, as they had in so many raids earlier in the war. Surrounded by the explosions of guns and with the possibility of being intercepted by night fighters on the way home, it was understandable that crews might be tempted to drop their bomb loads early so they could start the turn for home.

Carter saw one aircraft pinned by the beam of a searchlight. Instinct would have made Carter take avoiding action, but the bomber maintained its course, flak bursting all around it. It was too high for him to identify the type, but he suspected it would be a Lancaster. They seemed to be the workhorses of the RAF these days.[2]

The first bombs started to fall and Carter had to cover his ears to protect them. Blast waves swept past him, buffeting him and dragging at his steel helmet, trying to pull it from his head. They had been assured they would have a two hundred yard minimum clearance from the target area, but that seemed optimistic.

That view was confirmed a few moments later when a stick of bombs stitched their way across the countryside not far in front of them. This time the blast knocked Carter onto his backside. He swore that if he ever got his hands on the bomb aimer who dropped that lot, he'd make him wish he'd never joined the RAF.

Smoke from the blast and the fires the bombs started roiled around them, catching in their throats and making it hard to breath, It was hard to imagine anyone surviving such a bombardment.

The sound of aero engines started to fade as the air raid came to an end, so Carter checked his watch. The briefing from the RAF liaison officer attached to XXX Corps had been very specific. "I know you commando types are keen, but don't try to enter the town before the designated time. Stragglers may be arriving right up to the cut-off time and you don't want to get caught in the open by a stray thousand pounder going off in your face."

The second hand ticked around to the appointed minute and Carter put his whistle to his lips. While the raid had been going on the troops behind had been spreading out into line abreast so that they would enter the town in a single line. That wouldn't last, of course. It was a city, so the way would be blocked by houses and factories, forcing the commandos to change direction to get around the obstructions. They would have to watch out for snipers as they made their way forward. They knew from bitter experience how dedicated some of them were to their job and not even an RAF bombing raid would force the most steadfast to abandon his chosen position.

The silence after the raid ended was almost eerie. In truth it wasn't silence, it was just an absence of noise after the cacophony of destruction that had preceded it. The crackle of flames and rumble of collapsing masonry soon filtered through Carter's numbed ears to register in his brain.

The sound of crackling flames could be clearly heard, punctuated by crashes as masonry fell to the ground as walls gave up the fight with gravity to stay upright. The men would have to take care. It was one thing to be killed by an enemy sniper, but another matter entirely to be crushed under a collapsing building.

Before D-Day they had spent a fortnight in Limehouse, in the East End of London, training for street fighting, but many of the men had joined the commando since then, so wouldn't understand the dangers and the techniques of urban warfare. The 'mouse-holing', knocking holes in partition walls so that men could progress along from house to house to avoid exposing themselves in the street. Then there was the rat run, breaking through the tiles of the roof to sprint along the ridge of a row of houses and be waiting for the enemy at the end, as he exited the last house expecting to make a getaway.

They had experienced a little of it in the fight for Linne, but Wesel was a much larger town and would likely need them to fight that way again.

4 Tp, who Carter had elected to join, started to close up as they headed towards a gap between two buildings. The street would be on the far side.

"Stop bunching!" Carter heard Percy Lisle bark as he saw the danger. The men spread out again in response to the shout, slowing down to let others move ahead of them. So far so good, there was no sign of the enemy.

They edged between the two buildings, factories of some sort, Carter thought, and started to spread sideways along the street. They were greeted by scenes of utter devastation. Fires burnt out of control in some buildings, while others lay in heaps of rubble, not enough fuel available to catch fire.

At the far end of the street a fire tender was being operated by half a dozen men, trying to quench the flames in a house they thought might saveable; or perhaps to prevent the fire from spreading to a less damaged building. Seeing the commandos arrive, they dropped their hoses and ran. The water gushed along the street, hissing and steaming where it made contact with the flames.

Street maps had been put together from a combination of aerial reconnaissance photographs and pre-war maps, but they were scant on detail, especially street names. Carter would navigate by compass mainly, to reach his destination. Their objective was a wire factory on the northwest side of town, where he would set up his HQ, his troops spread out in the buildings, what was left of them, to form defences. Four-nine would take up positions to his left and 17 Cdo would move to the right. 16 Cdo would catch up with them once the bridge was secure and XXX Corps and the American started to cross the river.

They found a police officer frantically trying to dig into the rubble of a house, convinced there was someone still alive inside. Seeing the commandos arrive he raised his hands in surrender. Carter ordered that he be disarmed, but he was allowed to carry on with his self-appointed task. Seeing what the commandos had done, a couple of civilians crawled out of their hiding places and went to help him.

The first proper resistance was encountered at a crossroads where a main road passed across their front, while the minor road they were using continued ahead of them. Carter checked his map. That would be the road from the west that followed the line of the river, though at some distance from it. Sandbags had been put in place, with machine guns zeroed in on the crossing to prevent any sort of progress. Scouts were sent to see if any way could be found to get around the position's flanks. They were in an older part of the town now, with buildings that stood close together, at least they had until the RAF reduced them to rubble.

Mountains of rubble provided obstacles, but they also provided cover for anyone bold enough to attempt to move forward. There were plenty of commandos who were that bold. Lisle sent a section out to the right, which then split into pairs to navigate the moonscape like terrain. Another section was sent to the left. The two Germans machine guns fired on anyone who was unwise enough to get close to the junction, but Carter knew that it was just his men keeping them distracted so that the flanking parties would escape notice.

The defence must have been put together hastily, because the machine gun nests should have been protected by riflemen to prevent just such a manoeuvre.

The lack of defenders up until that point told Carter that the garrison hadn't had a chance to get into position when the bombing raid had ended. So, they had traded ground for time and were now going to protect the northern part of the town, hoping to slow the advance for long enough to organise a counterattack. That might take minutes, or it might take hours, depending on how many Germans soldiers had been in the town. Intelligence reports suggested at least a Brigade, which meant anything up to two thousand men.

Brick dust flew up and spattered Carter's face. He jerked back, throwing himself down behind a mound of rubble. So, not just a couple of machine guns; there was at least one sniper out there and Carter had very nearly become his first victim of the attack.

"Did anyone see his muzzle flash?" Carter looked at the men to his left and right.

"What muzzle flash?" Someone chuckled, taking pleasure in his CO's discomfort.

"Yes, I've got him, Lucky." A trooper replied form further along the line of prone bodies. "The buildings to the right of the right-hand machine gun. There's a window. He's there; or he was when he fired. He may have moved now."

It was common for a sniper to move after firing, so as not to fall victim to a counter-snipe. They were lucky in a way. With so many upper floors of houses no longer being available, the sniper had to fire from much lower down, which made it harder for him to find a target.

"Would you like to see if me and Danny Boy can move him for yez, Sorr?" Carter heard Paddy O'Driscoll call. He and Glass formed a Bren gun team now that they had been released from HQ duties and were back with 4 Tp.

"Give it ago." Carter replied.

More shots rang out along the street, from both sides of the opposite junction. Either the enemy was getting more troops into position using unseen routes, or they had remained concealed up to that point. Judging by the number of rounds being fired, the Germans must be at least platoon strength.

"James, message to 2 Tp. I want mortar fire on the houses on the far side of that junction." Carter read off the grid reference from his map. It wasn't the most accurate document, but he deliberately aimed long so that he could make adjustments later without risking his own men by providing a reference that might turn out to be too short.

A bomb dropped in the middle of the street that ran perpendicular to the main road. About fifty yards too long, Carter estimated. He sent the adjustment and a second bomb fell, this time only a few yards too long. A final adjustment had mortar bombs peppering the crossing and the houses on either side.

Carter ducked and crawled sideways until he found 4 Tp's commander. "Do you fancy trying a frontal assault, Percy?"

"If we can get about thirty yards further forward." Lisle replied.

"We've got half the troop that far forward already." Carter nodded towards the backs of steel helmets that were visible behind cover.

"I'll get the others moving. Can you tell 2 Tp when to stop mortaring?"

"I'll do that, then give two blasts on my whistle. Don't worry, I'll be right alongside you."

"I'm not worried, Lucky." Lisle grinned. "I'm just concerned you might get yourself killed and leave me in command of the advance."

Carter laughed, easing the tension of the situation.

One machine gun had fallen silent, too long an interval having passed for it just to be re-loading. But if the crew had been injured, it wouldn't take the Germans long to replace them. It was a window of opportunity not to be missed.

"Send Baker and Charlie sections across now." Carter urged. If they could get into the machine gun nest it would provide them cover while they lobbed grenades to take out the supporting riflemen. It would also give them control over three sides of the crossroads instead of just two.

Lisle shouted orders and the men stood up and charged across the road. One fell and lay still, but the others kept going. The machine gun stayed mercifully silent, but rifles sought out the attackers, sparks striking form the ground to show how close they were getting. The first grenades exploded, but they were thrown by the Germans. They weren't very accurate, the throwers having misjudged the speed at which the commandos were running.

But that wasn't going to be the main attack and if Carter didn't move, he'd be left behind. He crawled forward on his hands and knees, Tpr James right on his heels. Masonry chips flew as rifle shots sought him out and he felt something thump into his pack, but he didn't stop until he reached the cover of the front walls of the ruined house that made up what had become the front line of the attack.

"Message to 2 Tp, three rounds smoke then cease firing."

As soon as the smoke bombs started to land, Carter blew his whistle. The line rose as one and sprinted for the far side of the junction, between the dark, the smoke from the mortar bombs, the smoke from the fires and flickering shadows caused by the flames, it look like a scene from Dante's inferno, painted by an artist with far too much fondness for red and orange paint.

Sheer weight of numbers and aggression carried the commandos through the defences and into the bombed-out buildings beyond. Individual skirmishes broke out as the defenders tried to flee and the commandos hunted them down.

With the first line of defences breached, the commandos moved on, mainly in section strength, clearing one building or heap of rubble after another. The Germans fell back; they had no option. If they stood and fought, the commandos worked around behind them to threaten them from behind. They had little alternative but to surrender, die or withdraw even further.

A larger structure loomed out of the darkness. Bombs had taken their toll, but it size meant that some of it still stood upright. A shattered gate held one half of a painted sign. Though the paint was blistered, Carter could just make out the word *Drahtfabrik*; wire factory.

They had reached their objective. All they had to do now was hold it until the rest of the army arrived.

[1] XXX Corps had requested a bombardment of 300 tons of bombs split across two waves, but someone in the RAF chain of command has increased that to 1,000 tons. It devastated the town, leaving hardly a building undamaged.

[2] Carter was right to assume they were Lancasters, but for the wrong reason. In all 195 Avro Lancasters made up the two waves, with 23 Mosquito aircraft from the Pathfinder force used to mark the

targets. The real workhorse of Bomber Command was actually the Vickers Wellington, with over 11,000 built. The Lancaster was in a poor second place with only 7,000 built, not many more than the Handley Page Halifax at 6,000. The fourth aircraft type of the heavy bomber fleet was the Shorts Stirling, with just over 2,000 built. The big difference between the Wellington and the Lancaster was that the latter carried more than 3 times the payload: 14,000 lbs (6¼ tons) compared to 4,000 lbs (2 tons) (approx weights).

***

The following morning Carter witnessed the single largest loss of life he would ever see. What made it more tragic, in his eyes at least, was that it was avoidable.

It started at ten hundred hours and was called Operation Varsity. Carter hadn't liked the sound of it when he had attended the briefing over a week earlier. A daylight drop by paratroops was always fraught with danger. He had seen that in Normandy when 1st Airborne Division had been dropped in during daylight hours on D Day, to bolster the British attack. The slow-moving gliders made a juicy target for anti-aircraft guns and paratroops were more vulnerable to ground fire than pheasants on a Boxing Day shoot.

And here was history repeating itself. This time it was 6th Airborne doing the daylight drop, accompanied by the US 17th Airborne Division.

The British guns had been ordered to cease fire because of the risk of a glider being hit by a flying shell, or the paratroops drifting away from the drop zones and finding themselves under British artillery fire. But that allowed the German artillery to move back towards Wesel once more and open fire on the aircraft and troops.

From where they were on the edge of Wesel, Carter's men could do little to intervene. Where enemy guns came within range, his Brens and Vickers could open fire, but the action was concentrated on the Diersfordter Forest, a couple of miles to the north west of the town and too far away for any commandos to intervene. Even

Carter's heavy mortars were prohibited from use until the landing was over and the howitzers of the Mountain Regiment definitely couldn't fire.

Over seventeen thousand airborne troops were due to land from the two divisions and Carter would find out later that they suffered over two thousand five hundred casualties.

And they needn't have suffered a single one.

By ten hundred hours the British and Americans assault force were firmly in control of Wesel and infantry units were already crossing the Rhine, some in boats, some in Buffaloes and some picking their way across the superstructure of the damaged road bridge. Engineers were already surveying the two bridges to see what needed to be done to create a road crossing. A pontoon bridge would have been the quickest solution, but the speed of the river's current ruled that out. But the engineers were adept at constructing spans of Bailey Bridge and it wouldn't take long for them to get tanks across.

The air landing could have been stopped, there had been plenty of time to get a message through and turn the aircraft back. Or it could have been diverted to drop south of the river in the wide-open fields that were under Allied control. Carter wondered if anyone had thought of it. Or maybe they had thought of it, but the officers in command of the airborne operation went ahead anyway.

The operation would be counted as a victory because the airborne troops succeeded in capturing their objectives, but they were objectives that could have waited for XXX Corps to cross the river in strength. Well, that was Carter's opinion and that of many of the men who witnessed the helpless airborne infantry and paratroops being shot out of the sky.

But the lack of British artillery wasn't just a problem for the airborne troops, it was also a problem for him. The mainstay of the German anti-aircraft artillery was the 88 mm gun and it made an excellent piece of field artillery as well. They started to open up on Carter's positions, allowing German infantry to start encroaching on the British lines.

But the commandos dug in with their typical dogged determination. They had taken this bit of the town and no Nazi was going to take it back off them. As soon as the last of the paratroops had landed Carter started issuing fire orders for C battery, who were now across the river and well positioned to provide him with artillery support. His own mortars would also have targets within range.

Advance units from the Cheshire Regiment started to arrive, filling gaps in the perimeter line and adding their weight of numbers. By nightfall all meaningful resistance was over and the town was declared to be in Allied hands.

7 – From the Aller to the Baltic

12th April 1945

The Aller River, though only a tributary of the Weser, was going to prove to be a difficult crossing for the commando, Carter knew. Probably more difficult than the Rhine.

The opposite bank was steep, too steep for Buffaloes to climb and topped with dense pine forest. It was also infested with German marines, rushed south from their barracks on the Baltic coast to join the defence of the river alongside SS Troops. This was the strongest defence of any river crossing that the Germans had mounted since Wesel, which made Carter wonder why.

Was this some desperate last-ditch stand? Or was there something on the other side of the river that the Germans needed to protect? There had been no mention of any high value targets in the intelligence briefing. But, then again, the intelligence briefing didn't tell the troops on the ground everything.

This one would also be different. There were two bridges, about a mile apart. 16 Cdo would take the road bridge while 15 were allocated the railway bridge.

An attempt had been made to demolish it, but it hadn't worked properly. The track bed had dropped into the river, but the supporting steel work was still in place. If all went well, the commandos would be able to work their way across the skeleton and seize the far end of the bridge before the defenders realised what was happening.

The problem with being part of 11th Armoured Division, Carter had discovered, was that they were heavy on armour and light on infantry. They only had 159th Infantry Brigade to support two brigades of tanks and armoured reconnaissance units. The infantry had to stay close to the tanks to support them, so once across the river the commandos would be on their own until the engineers could get new bridges in place to allow the armour to cross – again.

As commandos they were used to getting the tough jobs; it was expected and was also a matter of pride. But being left high and dry and at the mercy of bridge builders wasn't something they welcomed. Not after their experiences in Italy, anyway.

And the Germans would want to regain control of the bridges in order to prevent the armour from crossing. A couple of well sited anti-tank guns could halt the attack, quite literally, in its tracks.

On either side, the pine forests stretched out. They would have to be cleared the hard way. 17 and 49 commandos would follow 15 across, using boats for speed, and fan out to the right of the bridge, while his men would move left to link up with 16 Cdo after they captured the road bridge. The intelligence reports suggested that the German marines were a full division strong and then there was the SS to take into account. That was a significant numerical advantage over a brigade of commandos.

But what was worrying the men right then, as they rested in the small town of Essel, was the smell. They had noticed it as they advanced northwards and it had become stronger by the hour. They were used to the smell of death by now. Sicily, Italy and Normandy had provided them with that experience as bodies had lain on the battlefields for days before being buried. But this was more than just the stench of rotting corpses. It was a rank smell, like an abattoir that hadn't been cleaned out for months; the smell of blood, shit and corruption, but on a massive scale.

It was a mystery that wouldn't be resolved until they got across the river and that wouldn't happen until that night.

After Wesel they had marched north, back under the command of 6th Airborne Division, hitching rides whenever they could, but mainly foot slogging. The Germans put up only token resistance most of the way, firing a few rounds to slow the advance then retreating to the next town, village or natural line of defence, such as a river. For the most part they seemed to leave the fighting to the Hitler Youth, who they had armed with *Panzerfuaste*, single shot weapons that fired an armour piercing missile. They were an effective weapon against tanks, but useless against commandos unless they exploded close by. The tally of prisoners taken rose rapidly. Over eight hundred had been captured at Wesel alone, almost two hundred by Carter's men.

The ancient city of Munster wasn't heavily defended and the commandos captured it in a day. There they encountered large numbers of German civilians for the first time, especially women. Despite Carter making sure his men were on their best behaviour, the women seemed overly scared of the victors.

A chatty prisoner solved the puzzle for Carter. News had arrived from the east about the way the Russian army was behaving in the towns and cities they captured. The well-disciplined front-line combat troops were quickly withdrawn, to be replaced by an ill-disciplined rabble from the eastern lands. Stories of rape and murder were rife. No doubt Goebbels was using those stories to stoke up fear of the British, Canadians and Americans as well, trying to inspire the German army to fight harder.

While in Munster, Carter had found a trooper standing outside a house as though on guard.

"What are you doing here, Murray?" The soldier should have been with his section, not hanging around outside a house like a lovelorn teenager waiting for the sight of a pretty girl.

"Just waiting for my mate." The soldier had replied, looking a little shifty. Carter grew suspicious.

"What's inside?"

"Nuffin', Sir." The soldier looked even more sheepish.

"I'm going inside, so you may as well tell me."

"Well, It's Harry, you know, Harry Hedges. He's in there with a woman, like."

Carter's heart sank. Firstly, Montgomery had issued a strict 'no fraternisation' order. Until it could be established who the Nazis were and weren't, Monty didn't want British soldiers getting into compromising situations with German women and perhaps having to marry them. There was also the issue of the soldiers' behaviour in general. Carter didn't want one of his men to be accused of the sort of atrocities that the Russians seemed to be committing.

"Wait there. I'll deal with you when I come out."

The trooper stepped to one side and Carter turned the door handle, pushing it open. There was only one room habitable, as far as he could see. That is to say it still had four walls and a ceiling. It was to one side of what had been a hallway, but now the outer wall was a heap of rubble that no longer separated it from a neighbouring ruin. Carter stood in the doorway, not sure if he was seeing what he was seeing.

Sitting in a battered armchair was a young woman, no more than twenty by Carter's estimation, though in need of a good meal like most German civilians. She seemed calm. Sitting on a hardback chair next to a table was Tpr Henry Hedges, a baby cradled in his arm as he fed the child from a bottle. Carter wasn't good with guessing the ages of babies, but this one looked no more than a few months old.

"What's going on here, Hedges?" Carter kept his voice calm, not wishing to alarm the child or its mother.

"This lady saw us in the street, Sir. She begged us for milk. She pretty much dragged me inside to show me the baby."

"You still had milk?" Fresh milk was a luxury rarely seen these days, though they had recently been given some, along with some fresh eggs.

"Only the powdered stuff in my rations, Sir. So I mixed up some of that and crushed a bit of tooth breaker[1] into it and the little chap seems to be loving it."

"You could have left the mother to feed it." Carter admonished.

"I know, but I'm missing me own kids back home. I'm sorry, Sir. I meant no harm." He made to stand up and hand the baby back to its mother.

"That's OK. Carry on now you've started. But why was Murray looking so shifty outside."

"Because the little twat has a filthy mind, I 'spect, Sir. He thinks I'm doing the nasty with this poor *Fraulein*. But I wouldn't harm a woman and I'd batter any man that did."

Carter nodded a farewell to the young woman, who had watched the exchange with an air of incomprehension, then returned outside.

"Your pal Hedges is feeding a baby" Carter poked him in the chest with his finger. "Shame on you for thinking he might be doing anything else. When he comes out, you make sure you catch up with your section." He was just about to leave, when he thought of something. "Give the young woman the rest of your dried milk. She's going to need it."

"But what about my tea?" The soldier protested.

"Your contribution to the reputation of the British army and your punishment for having a mind like a sewer, Murray."

Carter chuckled at the memory. Back in Normandy, at the battle for Amfreville, Carter had seen Hedges strangle a German soldier with his bare hands, but here he was bottle feeding a German baby from his own rations. The commandos were a peculiar type of killer, he realised.

From Munster they had moved north to Osnabruck, where the fighting had been a bit more intense. The ancient town stood at the crossroads between Holland to the west and Hanover further east, and on the direct line of march to the port city of Hamburg, which was Montgomery's major objective in northern Germany.

It was in Osnabruck that Carter found the Padre returning to camp with his injured driver and two German soldiers he had taken prisoner, while being unarmed himself.

Following behind the commando, the driver had taken a wrong turning and driven the Padre's Jeep into a German ambush on the outskirts of the town. The driver was injured and the two of them were captured while the pastor of a local church had been dressing the driver's wounds and feeding them with some of his own meagre lunch. The German patrol intervened and took the two men prisoner, while the pastor was lucky not to have been executed on the spot for aiding an enemy. If the soldiers had been SS, he probably would have been killed.

The Germans started to escort the two prisoners towards the centre of the town, crossing a railway embankment and making their way through the gardens of houses for about a mile. But the wounded driver slowed them down too much. In the end the NCO in charge of the men had left the two British in the custody of two of his soldiers while the rest of the patrol continued on its way.

"Are we your prisoners still?" The Padre had asked. "Or are you now our prisoners?"

Whether the Germans had understood the question or not the Padre didn't know, but the two men put down their rifles, took off their helmets and equipment harnesses and raised their hands.

Knowing the commandos would be at the forefront of the fighting, they then headed for where the most noise was being made until they stumbled into a section of commandos clearing a house of its defenders.

"That's the rest of them." The Padre had pointed towards a larger group of German soldiers, sitting against a wall under guard. "That's the ones who captured us."

The commandos also had beer for the first time since leaving England in late December. In the part of town that they captured stood a brewery, almost intact. One of Carter's officers had once been a manager in a brewery and swore he could get it operating again.

"There's a brew ready, still in its vats. All it needs is filtering and bottling." He said.

Carter decided he didn't want to know any more. He suspected that it would be classed as looting if they drank it, but the officer said it would be a pity to waste the brew as it would go off quickly if it wasn't bottled. Time for him to imitate Nelson, Carter thought, and turn a blind eye.

Suddenly the commando became very popular with visitors as word got around the division that there was beer on offer. But they were on the move again the following morning, complete with a few hangovers.

It was also in Osnabruck that Carter received a visit from an irate American Brigadier, claiming that the lunch laid on for him and his HQ staff had gone missing. Commandos had been seen in the area and were the prime suspects. Carter denied all knowledge of the theft, blamed it on the Royal Marine commandos who were safely distant on the far side of the town and pacified the Brigadier with a bottle of Scotch he had been saving.

He was glad he had taken the precaution of disposing of the dinner plate and cutlery that had been brought to him by his batman, Gordon. "A gift from 3 Tp, Sir." He laid the plate down and Carter was greeted by the sight of the first pork chop he had seen since his last leave in Scotland, nestling on a bed of mashed potatoes and gravy.

Gordon had reluctantly told him the story after the Brigadier had departed. 3 Tp had come across a house that was just behind the American brigade HQ and seemed to be in use as some sort of officers' mess. Looking inside they had seen the table laid out with white linen and gleaming silver. Hearing voices, they had hidden in a neighbouring room, emerging after the voices had fallen silent. Now, sitting on the table, were plates of steaming, delicious food, just waiting for someone to come along and eat it.

Thirty seconds later the table was bare but for its tablecloth.

Carter had initially been touched by the generosity of his men in feeding him, assuming the food had been discovered in a shop somewhere and legally purchased. But now he realised the gift was only to make him an accessory after the fact of the theft. He would have been angry, were it not for the fact that he had pulled a similar stunt with a deer that he and Angus Fraser had poached during a training exercise at Achnacarry, implicating the training school's CO by having it served up for dinner in the officers' mess.

Then they had crossed the Weser, north of Osnabruck. The other three commandos had been tasked with capturing the village of Leese, while his own had been assigned what they later discovered was a V weapons factory.

They had seen the V1s, of course, flying over their heads in Normandy, heading for England. Strange things they were, with stubby wings and an engine that sounded like someone blowing a very elongated raspberry. But that threat no longer existed. Once the

British had got this far north, the Germans no longer had anywhere within range of the British mainland from where they could fire those weapons. There were still Germans in western Holland, of course, cut off from Germany and left to their own devices while the British concentrated their efforts further inland. While they may still have been in range, there was no way for the German High Command to get the weapons to them.

But now the Germans had launched their new secret weapon, the V2. This was more sinister. It shot directly upwards into the atmosphere before falling back to earth in an arc that would send it crashing into London. Or Antwerp. The Germans were using a lot of them against the port, trying to disrupt the main Allied supply route.

They had found partially assembled rockets, but none intact. If there were any more, the Germans had moved them further north, out of harm's way.

At Leese Carter had also seen another strange sight, another of the Nazis secret weapons. It was an aircraft, in the conventional sense, but lacked propellers. As a budding engineer Carter wondered how it was powered. Beneath either wing was what appeared to be an engine, but that was where the similarity ended. Carter had heard of theoretical devices called jet engines but assumed that they were no more than the primitive devices that the Germans had used on their V1 missiles. This was something far more advanced.[2]

In the aircraft's nose were four machine guns, which it was using to strafe the troops on the ground, before flying off when the RAF appeared. Not that the RAF had a chance of catching it, not at the speed it was flying.

They had said farewell to 6th Airborne Division after Osnabruck and now came under the command of 11th Armoured Division. That at least gave them the advantage of armoured support for their more recent operations. They were also able to hitch rides on the backs of the tanks as they advanced.

After crossing the Weser, Carter had ridden on the back of a Sherman tank, directing its fire to make sure the enemy stayed put while his men had advanced towards them. It turned out that the V weapons factory was being defended by *Volksturm*, the German equivalent of the Home Guard; old men, young boys and men considered unfit for full military service. By this stage of the war that meant they had at least one limb missing. After disarming the prisoners, Carter had sent them home to their families. Most of them had come from the area around Leese, so they didn't have far to go and it was safely in the brigade's hands.

Some of the troops that had opposed them were *Volksgrenadiers*. These were made up of a hotch-potch of personnel that Himmler had cobbled together to provide the infantry needed to mount Operation *Herbstnebel*, or Autumn Mist in English[3], what had become known by the Allies as the Battle of the Bulge. They were made up of *Kriegsmarine* sailors who no longer had any ships, *Luftwaffe* personnel with no aircraft to maintain, soldiers recalled from medical discharge and civilians dragged from their factories and offices and put into uniform. Although hastily assembled in late 1944, many of them had seen a lot of action since and their hard-won experience made them a bitter opponent.

Realising that his mind was wandering, Carter dragged himself back to the present and what he would say to his men that evening. Back in the early days he had spoken spontaneously before an operation, but he had found it harder to do since moving up the chain of command. Perhaps it was the burden of responsibility, making him choose his words with more caution. The cheery 'let's get stuck into them' approach wasn't so befitting of his rank. It was his plan that the men would be attempting to deliver and for which they were risking their lives. They deserved to hear more than just cheerful optimism before they committed themselves to battle.

[1] Tooth breaker – slang for the hard tack biscuits which came in ration packs.

[2] This aircraft was the Messerschmidt Me 262 which was the first operational jet fighter. It went into service in April 1944. The first one was shot down by a Bofors anti-aircraft gun of the RAF

Regiment in November 1944, the first ever confirmed ground to air kill of a jet aircraft. Initially the Me 262 was used against Allied bombers (which is why Carter wouldn't have seen them before, as they flew too high), where it was very effective. Several were seen over northern Germany in the closing weeks of the war, being used mainly in a ground attack role. Had it been introduced earlier in the war or in greater numbers, it would have had considerably more impact than it did. The only British fighters capable of catching it were the Gloster Meteor, which it never met in combat, or the Hawker Tempest and de Havilland Mosquito, but they would have needed to intercept from the front or side to get only the merest snapshot at the Me 262. Most Me 262s that were destroyed was the result of them being caught while taking off or landing, or while on the ground. The first British jet fighter, the Gloster Meteor, didn't enter operational service until July 1944 and wasn't used over Germany. The first operational American jet fighter was the P-80 Shooting Star and didn't enter service until 1945, though the Americans can claim the first jet powered aircraft with the Bell P-59, which had beaten both the Me 262 and the meteor into the air – but using an engine based on a British design that had been gifted to their ally

[3] The German name for the Battle of the Bulge is usually given as Operation *Wacht am Rhein*, Operation Watch on the Rhine in English. This was its original name, given by Hitler, but it was changed to Operation *Herbstnebel* in October 1944.

* * *

The steel cut into Carter's feet, so he had to try to ignore the pain as he moved to the next steel strut to carefully find a foothold. There were four troopers in front of him, working their way across the bridge as silently as possible, with more on the far side of the gap that had once been filled by the railway track.

Carter's boots bumped against his chest, suspended around his neck by their knotted laces. It made less noise to try to cross in stockinged feet, but it was a torment at the same time. The edges of the steel angles were corroded and shards of rust stabbed into his soles and snagged on his thick woollen socks. There would be nothing left of them to darn by the time he reached the other side, he felt sure. He'd have to write and ask Fiona to send him some more, as soon as the fight for the river was over. Assuming he was still alive by then, of course.

He shouldn't be at the front, his troop commanders had reminded him, but Carter wasn't one to sit at the rear waiting for news. While he surrendered to their pleas not to lead from the very front, he had insisted on being right behind the first half of Able section of 3 Tp, who were to cross first. Behind him were the other half of the section. Strung out along the bridge on his side were three more sections, with the other four on the far side. The rest of the commando were waiting patiently on the southern bank. If 3 Tp were successful in capturing the northern end of the bridge, they would follow, protected by the covering fire from the leading troop. If they weren't, then they would be taking to Goatley boats to attempt an assault across the river. It would be a hellish task under fire, so Carter was counting on this attempt to save as many commando lives as possible.

So far they had attracted no attention and Carter wondered if the Germans had withdrawn from the bridge's end for the night. He had sent patrols across on the two previous nights and they had taken prisoners and killed several defenders, so it was possible that the German commander was no longer willing to risk men defending the top of the banks at night. The Marines had never fought commandos before and might not understand that their preferred time for an attack was the middle of the night. If the Germans had withdrawn, it would be a costly mistake for them.

Looking upwards, Carter could still make out the blackness of the steel structure against the slightly lighter sky, but beyond that he could now see the tops of the trees on the northern bank. It meant they were almost across.

The man in front of him stopped and waited for Carter to reach him. "Twenty feet to go, Lucky." The trooper whispered, then moved off again.

Th leading man must have his feet on the ground by now, Carter thought, but still no alarm had been raised. Surely the Germans wouldn't leave the bridge entirely unguarded. They may not know much about commando tactics, but the ability cross a bridge by clambering along the sides was something that most armies understood.

"*Scheiße, Tommies! Sie sind gegenüber.*" A voice shouted in the darkness.

"*Lauf*!" Carter heard a second voice, instantly followed by the sound of pounding feet which faded rapidly. So, there had been sentries, but they had either been asleep or looking the wrong way. What had alerted them Carter would never find out, but he had heard nothing. But they were probably half way to Berlin by now. When they reached someone they could report to, it would set the cat amongst the pigeons.

Carter moved his left foot forward and felt it touch solid ground. Even though it was rough concrete, it was a blessed relief after the cutting edges of the girders. He moved his right foot to place it next to his left, then let go of the upright he had been holding. Grabbing the barrel of his Tommy gun he swung it around to his front and pointed it along the railway line; or where the gap in the trees showed where the railway line ran.

He moved away from the bridge to give room for the soldiers behind him. No doubt they had heard the panicked shouts and speeded up now that discovery was no longer an issue.

Once 3 Tp were across and the NCOs were deploying them around the bridge to protect their prize, Carter started to direct the new arrivals along the left hand bank. Once they had reached the point midway between the road and rail bridges, the troop would turn right and start to make their way into the thickly packed pine trees, clearing them of any defenders. That was the plan anyway.

All except for 2 Tp with their heavy weapons. The mortars couldn't fire through the thickly interwoven branches, so they had to stay in the open. He might even have to send them back across the river to find firing locations on the southern bank if their support was needed at the western end of the line. No armour could penetrate the forest, so that meant the PIATs could stay at the end of the bridge. If any tank attempted to approach along the railway line, they would be able to engage from there. Finally, the Vickers guns also needed a clear field of fire. Their job would be to tackle any infantry that came in support of armour, or which tried to re-take the bridge by frontal assault.

The men in the trees would feel more vulnerable without the support of the Vickers, but that couldn't be helped. They had to fight over the terrain that was, not the terrain they wished for.

When the last troop was across and moving into the trees, Carter took a section from 3 Tp and started to reconnoitre along the railway line. The sky was getting lighter as daylight approached. There was no sound of the alarm having been raised by the two fleeing sentries, so perhaps they had just hidden in the forest.

They had discovered the bodies of Germans soldiers hanging from streetlamps in both Munster and Osnabruck, signs around their necks saying *"Die Strafe für Deserteure"*, which Spencer had told him meant 'the punishment for deserters'. Perhaps the two Germans were just as afraid of their own side as they were of the British. Prisoners taken in recent weeks had mentioned NSFOs[1], commited Nazis attached to Wermacht units to indoctrinate them and, when necessary, shoot any soldier who wavered in battle.

They had gone about two hundred yards when Carter heard the sound of feet crunching on the track bed of the railway line. It was rhythmic and evenly paced, which meant troops marching.

Yes, that made sense. With dawn approaching, the Germans would be moving into their forward defensive positions ready to repel an attack. Whoever was in command here really should have studied the commando doctrine of fighting at night, because his lack of knowledge was going to cost him dearly; he just didn't know it yet. Carter waved half the section into cover in the fringes of the pine trees to the right, while he led the other half to the left, making sure the Bren gun was with him.

The sound of voices started to be heard above the crunch of feet and the sound of a laugh as someone made a joke. The enemy seemed to be relaxed, which must mean that they hadn't run into the two sentries. Either that or they were totally incompetent. Carter doubted it was the latter.

The silhouettes of heads bobbed against the lightening sky as the marching men drew closer. The colours of uniforms could start to be seen. Carter did a quick count. Platoon strength, by his reckoning. He couldn't believe his luck.

He tapped the Bren gunner on the shoulder and nodded towards the target, raising his Tommy gun to indicate that he would use it to give the signal to open fire. The gunner nodded back.

The paler shade of a face emerged beneath the shadow of a steel helmet. That was close enough, Carter decided. Raising his weapon to his shoulder, he fired a long burst at the middle soldier in the front rank. His target fell, just as the Bren gun opened up beside him.

Panic engulfed the marching formation. Some tried to unsling their rifles to retaliate, others turned and ran while some just stood there, not knowing what to do. As soldiers around them were hit, one or two had the sense to raise their arms above their heads in surrender.

"Cease fire" Carter's voice echoed along the railway line as he saw there was no further threat from the German platoon; or what was left of the platoon. Half a dozen bodies lay still with others clutching at wounds or rolling on the ground in agony. They wouldn't be as badly hurt as they made out. If you could roll around, you weren't badly enough injured to die.

"*Hände hoch! Ihr seid Gefangene!* " The section's corporal shouted. 'Hands up! You are prisoners!' Several weeks earlier Carter had asked Tpr Spencer to hold some classes in basic German so that orders such as that could be shouted. Many an enemy soldier owed his life to Carter's foresight.

There were half a dozen of them standing, uninjured. Carter's men hurried forward to disarm them, before herding them back towards the bridge. The dead and wounded would have to be left where they were until the Germans recovered them. Carter had only one doctor available and he would be needed to look after his own men.

Carter forced the pace. With the sound of shooting on that side of the bridge, any element of surprise had finally gone.

[1] *Nationalsozialistische Führungsoffiziere* (NSFO; "National Socialist Leadership Officers". Created in 1943 to bolster the political indoctrination of the Wehrmacht. By the end of 1944 there were more than 1,100 full time officers and up to 47,000 part time holders of the title. They had carte blanche to deal with deserters and waverers.

* * *

The pine trees were so closely packed together that it was almost impossible to decide where one tree ended and another started. The branches grew low to the ground, forcing the commandos to move on hands and knees a lot of the time. Wicked spikes of dead branch stuck out from the trunks at angles and weren't seen until they had poked into a face and even an eye. Beneath their knees the thick blanket of pine needles concealed dropped cones, raised roots and dead branches. There wasn't a man in the commando that hadn't stifled an 'ouch' or a curse as they struggled forward.

A crashing sound was followed by the crack of rifles, then laughter as a wild boar went onto the menu for that evening's meal – if they could find some way of cooking it without setting fire to the forest around them. It didn't occur to any of the men that the wicked tusks on the boars were dangerous weapons. And it was spring, when the new litters were being protected by mothers who were capable of disembowelling a man with one swipe of their snout. That wasn't something they would find out until they were well clear of the forest. Perhaps ignorance was bliss, Carter reflected later.

Progress was laboured as the line had to move at the pace of the slowest to avoid gaps appearing into which Germans might sneak. If there were any there, they could escape detection just by lying still and letting the Tommy's pass them by. The blessing was that it would be impossible for snipers to work. With straight line visibility limited to the next tree on their route, no sniper would be able to get a clear shot.

As they progressed through the forest it began to thin at last, but all that allowed was a fall of mortar bombs, like a sudden hailstorm. They fell well short, suggesting they were at the limit of the range for the tubes, or perhaps just fired speculatively rather than in a targeted attack.

Carter decided to call a halt. "Dig in, lads." He ordered. "We'll let them come to us."

After a few minutes the bombs stopped falling, except for the occasional one sent their way as a discouragement to proceed.

"Can you get brigade on the radio?" Carter asked his radio operator, who was sweating visibly under his burden. The close air within the forest prevented them from getting cool. It was only April, but it felt more like August to the men right then.

As Carter set to with a trenching tool, James started twiddling with the knobs on his radio set.

"Nothing much, Sir. Nothing from Brigade and I can barely hear the troops on either side of us. It's the trees. They trap the signals."[1]

The digging was tough. The intertwined roots of the trees formed a barrier and the ground was stony. It explained why there were no broad-leaved trees. They needed better soil if they were to take root. Every foot dug soaked the men in sweat. They piled the earth into walls around them, so they didn't have to dig so deep, but it was almost midday before Carter was satisfied that he had a defensive line that was capable of repelling an attack.

The men settled down to wait. Without good radio communications Carter established a system of runners to keep the troops in contact with each other. He sent a radio and operator back to the river to set up a communications link with the brigade HQ, who were still on the other side. Without being able to communicate it would be a waste of their time crossing, because they would, in turn, lose contact with divisional HQ.

To keep the men occupied while they waited for the enemy to decide what they were going to do, Carter set them the task of clearing routes back to the river for ammunition parties to use. A determined attack would use up all they had very quickly, so if he wasn't careful they'd end up having to fight the enemy with bayonets, trenching tools and fists. It might come to that anyway, even with ammunition. Even though the trees were thinner, it would still be possible for the enemy to creep close, if they were skilful enough.

They didn't have any axes with which to chop down trees, but trenching tools were good enough to hack the lower branches down, allowing men easier passage without risk of losing an eye. Carter sent back to the river for white tape and that was looped from tree to tree to mark the routes.

Use the ground, he thought to himself; patrols would be able to move quite freely using the forest as cover. Fighting patrols were needed to prevent incursions.

 He also sent reconnaissance patrols forward to see what was happening and he also established listening posts, just as he would at night, to alert them to enemy movements.

Eventually the German commander would make a decision about what he wanted to do. He would either fight or he'd withdraw. Whichever it was, Carter had to be ready. The one blessing of this location, as far as Carter was concerned, was that the lack of air penetrating the forest meant that the infernal smell, whatever it was, no longer reached them.

The first enemy probes came as the commandos were eating a late lunch. Along the line groups of up to a dozen German marines crept through the packed trees, searching the commandos out. As soon as one was spotted a commando would take a pot shot, sending them back behind cover, which was plentiful. These weren't concerted attacks. They were assessments of their strength and Carter wasn't anxious for them to discover how thinly spread the commandos were. The numbers counted in the Germans' favour and if they worked that out, Carter and his men would soon be under pressure.

Ronnie Pickering, 1 Tp's CO, came to report to him.

"I led a patrol forward myself. We're about two hundred yards short of the forest edge. It doesn't stop, as such, it sort of breaks up into clearings, which then merge together to form scrubby ground, then open fields. The Germans are dug in beyond that, perhaps five hundred yards in front of us.

"What sort of strength?"

"It's not clear. I couldn't see any armour, but that doesn't mean there's none there."

"Armour's no use to them here. They can have a hundred tanks out there and not be able to reach us."

"No, but they'd be able to shell us. But that applies to artillery as well, so I take your point. If they do have armour, they'll send it down the road and the railway line, trying to get to the river and cut us off. We'll have to rely on Division's artillery to stop them doing that."

"We've got OPs out along the road, both ours and the artillery's, to give warning. We'll let division deal with that threat. Any idea of numbers of troops?"

"Judging by the extent of the earthworks, I'd say at least a regiment directly opposite us, with a layered defence, so if we managed to break through the front line, we'd just be between two lots of trenches."

So, thought Carter, a frontal attack isn't viable. At the same time the Germans seemed to be reluctant to come into the woods. A stand-off then. That suited Carter. If they could hold where they were, the armoured regiments would be across the river by the next day and they'd power through and around the back to roll the enemy up from the flanks. At the same time, any enemy armour would have to leave the commandos behind them if they didn't clear the forest first. No tank commander could risk that. With no visibility to the side of the tanks, the commandos could do all sorts of damage and the narrow approaches through the forest meant they were limited to single file, or two abreast at best.

Good, thought Carter. The tactical situation favoured the commandos overall. All they had to do was prevent the Germans from forcing them back to the river. If they stopped the lead tanks, assuming any were sent, they'd be putting a cork in a bottle.

[1] This may sound unlikely, but trees do affect radio signals. The sap absorbs them, reducing their power. Add to that the fact that there is no straight line for a radio signal to take and both transmission and reception can be severely restricted. This also affects modern day devices such as mobile phones. If your signal is breaking up, look around to see if you are near any trees and move away from them.

* * *

At dawn the enemy come in force and Carter and his men were hard put to keep them at bay. Only the terrain itself prevented them from being overrun by the first assault.

The Germans flitted from tree to tree, minimising the time they spent in the open and only offering the commandos the opportunity to take snap shots. The forest crackled with the sound of rifle fire and the bark of Bren guns. But still the terrain offered the commandos a slight advantage. The Germans favoured the use of machine guns to support their attacks and the trees prevented any effective use of them. They were more of a burden than an asset, as far as Carter could judge.

But the defenders were also hampered in terms of their weapons. They were unable to use grenades. To throw a grenade it requires overhead clearance so the bomb can arc towards its target and that clearance wasn't available. Neither could the commandos make flat throws, like a fielder aiming a cricket ball at the stumps, because there were too many trees in the way.

But the commandos were great improvisers and they had tied grenades to tree trunks and used fishing line to act as trip wires, which pulled the grenade's pin. But they were one shot weapons and once used, that was it, the enemy could advance knowing there was little chance of another grenade being present. But the ones that were triggered caused casualties and encouraged caution and everything that slowed the German attacks was to be welcomed.

As each attack petered out, there was a short respite, then the next wave was launched. They were getting through ammunition at an incredible rate and the ammunition parties were struggling to keep up with the rate of re-supply. Troop commanders were hamstrung by the need to keep enough men in the defences to prevent gaps opening up, while at the same time removing men from the line to send back to carry ammunition.

As the morning progressed, Carter realised his position was untenable. He had just emptied his Tommy gun once more, only to find that he had no more full magazines. He drew his Webley, ready to use it if necessary, but that wouldn't help the riflemen and Bren gunners. The next German advance could see them out of ammunition and being overwhelmed.

As the most recent attack withdrew to catch its breath, Carter pulled out his notebook and started scribbling orders. He called men forward from his team of runners, taking cover immediately behind him, and gave them their instructions.

"Get back to the radio operators at the river. Tell them to send code word 'Shelldrake'. Then give him the longer message and tell him to send that."

As the man scuttled away between the trees, Carter called the next man forward, handing him two notes. "3 Tp, then 1 Tp. When you've delivered the messages, stay with 1 Tp."

The same instruction was given to a third runner, the only variation being that the recipients were 5 and 6 Troops. Finally he called the last man forward."

"OK, Faversham. You know what to do?"

"As soon as you give the order, Sir."

"Good man. Just keep your head down until then." He crawled his way across to 4 Tp's CO, Jeremy Villiers. He told him the plan and they settled down to wait.

The seconds ticked by, turning into minutes. Those dragged by with leaden feet. Carter hoped that the orders he had given would be acted upon before the next attack started. If it didn't, they'd be in trouble.

The ground shook as though and earthquake had just started. The sound of explosions ripped through the forest. The blast waves shook pine cones and dead wood loose to fall around the commandos, forcing them to cover their heads, but there was nothing they could do to protect the rest of their bodies.

It sounded as though the whole forest was being bludgeoned to death. It was what Carter had been waiting for. The codeword Sheldrake had been a 'vector fire' order, commanding every gun in 11the Armoured Division that was in range to start shelling the woodland in front of Carter's positions. They were only required to fire three rounds, but the combined force was devastating.

Carter rose and stepped over the parapet of his position and started to walk forward, crouching to pass under the branches of the trees on his line. To his right and left Carter saw 4 Tp following and the other four troops would react to seeing them.

Silence fell after they had walked no more than fifty yards, but smoke and the smell of burning drifted through the trees. Above the crackle of burning pines, Carter could hear the shrieks of badly injured men. At last, gaps in the trees started to widen as the forest thinned. Carter caught glimpses of the devastation he had called down on the Germans.

But this was no time for sympathy. The Germans would have done as much, and more, to his men.

"Now Faversham"

The trooper raised a battered bugle to his lips and blew a short series of rising notes.

"Again, man. Twice more." Carter ordered, but his men were already responding. He heard Lisle's shout of "charge" and the men started to sprint forward, breaking through the final lines of trees and into the enemy's assembly area.

Bodies lay scattered around like broken toys while the ground was littered with shell craters. At the sight of Carter's men appearing, a wounded man started to crawl away. Carter ran past him, the man was no threat. Other Germans staggered around, clearly shell shocked and unable to recover their wits quickly enough. Only when they had sprinted another hundred yards did the first of the enemy show any resistance.

On the way Carter scooped up an abandoned German weapon, which already had a bayonet fitted. He holstered his Webley and joined his men in their bayonet charge, screaming their defiance as they ran.

They stopped for no man. Anyone who showed the least sign of resistance was killed. A marine appeared in Carter's path, thrusting with his rifle. Carter stabbed but the enemy's rifle got in the way and his bayonet skidded off the man's side. But it didn't matter. The commando to Carter's right took the man in the centre of his chest. Carter turned to thank the man for his intervention and wasn't surprised to see the grinning face of Prof Green. No doubt Glass and O'Driscoll weren't far away.

On they ran, Carter's lungs bursting with the effort, until they were into the first line of the Germans' prepared positions. Carter leapt a low sandbag wall, discovered a man cowering in the bottom of the trench and stabbed down, ending the man's life. The trench was otherwise empty, vacated when the Germans had started to make their latest advance, so Carter scrambled over the rear parapet and moved on. All along the line he could see Germans clambering out of their positions and fleeing. Some were turning and firing on the commandos defiantly, but many were just running pell-mell.

An officer was gesticulating, trying to rally some sort of defence, but he was wasting his time. His men just sprinted past him, intent only in escaping the fury of the commandos. Carter saw the man make his own decision and he turned and followed his men northwards.

Two commandos had grabbed an abandoned MG 42 and were attempting to turn it to fire on the fleeing enemy. But Carter had other ideas.

Having left the woods behind, they had exposed their flanks, but at the same time he had also exposed the enemy's flanks. If he acted quickly he could capitalise on that and relieve the pressure on the commandos on either side of his own.

He grabbed men at random. "Find 5 Tp." He ordered. "They're to face front." To the next he issued different orders. "My compliments to 6 Tp, they're to attack the enemy flank, using whatever weapons they can find." He issued similar orders for 1 and 3 troops, before ordering Jeremy Lisle to get his men facing forward as well. It was a thin line of defence, but the enemy showed no signs of being organised enough for a counterattack.

He felt a tug on his arm. "Yes James." His radio operator was breathing heavily, having had to run to keep up with the charging commandos.

"From Brigade, Sir. Codeword Colt Forty Five".

Carter tried not to let the relief show on his face. It meant that the engineers had finished constructing one of the bridges and the tanks were starting to cross. With them would come more infantry. If they moved at the pace of the infantry, he'd be seeing the first Comet[1] tanks arriving in around twenty minutes.

All around him commandos were salvaging abandoned German weapons and bringing them into use; mortars, MG-42s, MP-40s and even rifles, if they had run out of ammunition for their own.

The distraction caused by the firing was making the Germans commit troops to face them. It was also making the ones already committed to the attack on the forest more nervous. They had a fear of getting cut off and some started to withdraw from the fringes of the pines. NCOs and officers berated them, but still some sneaked past while backs were turned. It relieved the pressure on 16 Cdo and allowed them to move forward and take the initiative.

The growl of heavy engines intruded above the noise of firing, counterpointed by the squeal of tank tracks. The cavalry had finally arrived, quite literally. Carter looked over his shoulder towards the railway line and saw the barrel of a tank gun appear from behind the curtain of pine trees. Flanking it was infantry, looking clean and well rested compared to Carter's own men. He knew that a company strength had crossed the river the previous evening to bolster the defence of the bridge, but these probably weren't the same men. They looked as though they had just come off a parade ground.

The tank swerved away from his side of the bridge, towards 17 Cdo's positions on the far side of the railway. No doubt some pre-planned manoeuvre. But the tanks had been seen by the enemy on Carter's side and it was clear that the enemy no longer wanted to continue the fight without armour of their own to support them. The enemy still had tanks aplenty, but they had no fuel for them. At least, that was what the brigade intelligence officer had told them during their briefing.

Newly arriving tanks were turning towards Carter's positions now, four of them, infantry advancing alongside them with bayonets at the ready. The tanks machine guns stuttered as they saw groups of German soldiers and their main armament thundered from time to time as they located suitable targets.

It was enough for the enemy troops in front of 16 Cdo's positions. They turned and started to clamber out of their positions and head north. The machine guns and mortar bombs followed them, but Carter held his men back from pursuing. It would be too easy to be lured into a poor position from which to fight.

The German marines had met the commandos and learnt a salutary lesson. The next time they met, Carter felt sure, his men would have an easier fight.

Carter started to issue orders for James to relay over the radio. His men were tired and needed rest, but there was still so much to do.

The wounded had to be treated and moved back to the dressing station on the far side of the bridge; the dead had to be gathered up and they would be moved back too, so that they could be given a decent burial. He could do with some help to get things organised.

"James, ask the troop commanders to locate the 2IC and send him to me." Carter instructed.

It was a few minutes later that the RSM, Fred Chalk, arrived. "You're looking for the 2IC, Sir?"

"I am, RSM. Where is he? Off somewhere trimming his moustache, no doubt." The 2IC's pencil thin moustache was something of a standing joke within the commando. Since their arrival back in Europe in December he'd been unable to trim it properly and it now made him look more like a child with a particularly shaky hand had drawn it on his face.

"I'm afraid the 2IC didn't make it, Sir." Fred Chalk's tone was sombre. "He caught a bayonet in the guts. He died just a few minutes ago."

At once Carter regretted his choice of words. It was true that he had never quite taken to the 2IC. The man always had a slightly superior look, as though he had a bad smell under his nose and his manner often suggested that he thought that he could do a better job than Carter at leading the commando. But they had rubbed along together somehow and if Carter wanted something complicated organising, it was to Howard Ramsey that he always turned. The man was a born administrator.

"Show me." Carter ordered, then followed the RSM back towards the edge of the forest. They found Ramsey propped against the trunk of a tree. Someone had tried to dress his wound and he had a blood-stained field dressing wrapped around his exposed stomach.

Belly wounds were always killers. All the men knew that. Some might linger for days in extreme agony. At least Ramsey had been spared that.

"He was leading 5 and 6 troops in the charge Sir. Right at the front." Fred Chalk seemed to think that might make some difference for Carter but, after his first raid into France the year before, Carter had never doubted his deputy's bravery. It was only ever his manner that had irked and that now seemed so insignificant a matter.

"Find O'Driscoll and send him back across the bridge for my Jeep." Carter straightened up to address the RSM. "He's to collect the Major's body and drive it to the casualty area himself."

"Understood, Sir. What about the rest of the commando?"

"The troop commanders have been given their orders. Once the rest of the division has secured the forward area, the men are to withdraw back to the bridge and rest. When O'Driscoll gets back from delivering Major Ramsey's body, I'll get him to take me to Brigade HQ to find out what they want us to do next. I'm guessing we'll spend the rest of the day consolidating the front line, while we wait for the other bridge to be completed, then we'll advance to the next objective. Have you seen the QM?"

"He was over with 6 Tp, last time I saw him."

"Send him my compliments and ask him to start organising ammunition replenishment. Second priority is rations for the men. They must have eaten just about everything they were carrying when we crossed the bridge. Make sure he gets whatever men he needs to do the lifting and carrying."

Carter looked down at Ramsey's body once again. Such a waste. He'd have made a good staff officer one day, Carter knew. He would have relished it as well. It would be a hard letter for him to write to his next of kin.

He headed back to where the men were still holding the front line, waiting for the infantry to arrive in large enough numbers to take over. Tanks sat with their engines idling, their commanders sitting on the edges of the hatches, binoculars to their eyes as they sought out targets. But what targets there had been were now some way distant and getting further away by the minute.

The smoke of battle had drifted away and the terrible smell that had tormented them since their arrival, several days earlier, made its presence known once more.

What in the dickens was that? Carter asked himself. He fished around in his pack for his binoculars. "Mind if I join you?" Carter called up to the sergeant sitting in the turret of the nearest tank.

"Certainly, Sir." The man stiffened, as though trying to come to attention.

"As you were, Sgt." Carter smiled at him, using the footholds welded to the rear of the tank's hull to climb up. "I just wanted to see if I could identify the source of that smell." Carter explained.

"Yeah, horrible, ain't it? I think it's coming from over there, judging by the breeze." The NCO pointed to the north and slightly eastwards.

There was something there, but Carter couldn't quite make out what it was. He adjusted the focus of his binoculars and the shapes became more distinctive. Huts, hundreds of them, arranged in rows. And towers of some sort. Squat shapes elevated on stilts to make them higher. It looked too big to be a military barracks, unless it housed a whole division. But if that was the case the intelligence bods would have mentioned it, surely? So what …

A prison. It had to be. He examined one of the towers in more detail. The roof sloped downwards on one side. If it were a barracks, the guards would be looking outwards, so the higher side of the roof would be facing outwards, while the rain ran down the slope to fall on the inner side. But the roofs sloped the other way, which meant the guards were looking inwards; which made it a prison. The guards wouldn't be looking for anyone trying to break in, only for the inmates trying to break out.

Carter had never been in a prison, but he had passed one when he had been at university, so he knew that prisons didn't smell like that. They were kept spotlessly clean by the free labour available from the inmates. If anything, they smelt of disinfectant. But this place smelt of death and corruption.

Carter's mind went back to North Africa and the lengthy conversation he'd had with a captured German officer. The man had told him about death camps the Nazis had set up in Poland. Was that what this place was? All the evidence supported the notion.[2]

"What's there, Sir?" The Sergeant asked, levelling his own binoculars in the same direction.

"Germany's shame." Carter replied, before jumping down from the back of the tank.

[1] The Comet was a British tank built by Leyland Motors (in the days when they only built trucks and busses) and introduced into the Army in December 1944. It was fitted with a 17 Pdr (76.2 mm) gun. It benefited from many of the lessons learnt about tank design during the North African campaigns, particularly the shortcomings of the Churchill and Cromwell tanks. Because of its late introduction (further delayed by the Battle of the Bulge), 11th Armoured Division were the only one to be fully re-equipped with the tank by the end of the war. It remained in British army service until 1958.

[2] This was Belsen concentration camp. See the Historical Notes for more information.

*　*　*

"On no account are the men to go near the camp." Brigadier Vernon had ordered when Carter reported to him later in the day. "It will be secured by designated troops from the division, so there is no need for the commandos to have anything to do with it. There are reports of a typhus outbreak amongst the prisoners and we don't want any of our men coming down with it. We can't afford to quarantine a whole commando."

The brigadier had paused to take a breath. "To be honest with you, Stephen," he continued in a more moderate tone, "I suspect that Army HQ are also worried about how your men might react to seeing what has happened in there. We can't afford any rough justice being administered. That would just make us look as bad as the Nazis. So, for you men's own good, don't let them approach within a mile of the camp."

It hadn't made a jot of difference, of course. Carter had suspected it wouldn't. All the prohibition did was excite more curiosity amongst the men.

They didn't dare ignore a direct order and enter the camp, but several patrols did get 'lost' and stray within range to see what the conditions were like inside. Rumours spread quickly throughout the day and night.

The brigadier had been right. It did get a rection from the men. As they advanced northwards the next day, Carter soon realised that Germans taken prisoner were being brought back with abrasions and bruises that didn't look as though they had anything to do with combat. He also noticed that the men were less friendly towards the civilians as well, directing dark looks in their direction and shouting insults.

The latter Carter was able to do something about and he had a few of the worst offenders brought in front of him to be given dire warnings of what would happen if they behaved like that again. But in terms of roughing up of prisoners, there was little he could do. When he asked questions, he was met with a united front of denial or stubborn silence. The prisoners didn't make any direct complaints. Perhaps they would save their breath until they had a more sympathetic audience, such as the Red Cross.

Their next objective was the River Elbe and Montgomery was in a hurry to get there. It was pretty obvious that the war would be over soon, perhaps within days, certainly weeks, and Montgomery wanted a final feather in his cap: the capture of Hamburg, Germany's second largest city. He was denied any involvement in the battle for Berlin by the simple fact of the Americans advancing through the centre of the country in a race with the Russians, but he could take Hamburg.

* * *

They had lost a lot of good men at the Aller, Carter reflected. Experienced men who had come all the way through from Normandy and earlier. Some of replacements that came in were good men, arriving from commandos that had been withdrawn from combat. Others, though, were direct from the depot at Achnacarry. The latter were raw, untested, but Carter hoped they wouldn't have too much fighting to do. He certainly didn't have time to train them himself.

They were transferred to the 15th (Scottish) Infantry Division. Monty needed the 11th Armoured for the attack on Hamburg, but he didn't need the commandos as well, not for that operation. So the commando brigade was re-assigned and would link up with the American 9th Army to advance to the Baltic Sea. 15th Division had a good reputation, arriving in Normandy not long after D-Day and being at the heart of the battle for Caen. They had then fought their way north through Belgium, Holland and Germany. Now they were to lead what was probably going to be the last set piece river crossing of the war, which is why the commandos were attached to them. As with the other major rivers that had been crossed, it would be the commandos leading the way.

The proportion of the northern part of Germany that was no longer under Nazi control was getting smaller by the day and their arrival on the Baltic would reduce it down to the state of Schleswig-Holstein, which joined Germany to Denmark.

But first they had to cross the Elbe

The reconnaissance that Carter had carried out told him it would be another tough nut to crack. The main objective was the town of Lauenburg, which the division was to capture before they could link up with the Americans. The river was wide at that point, fast flowing and with steep dykes on the southern side and high cliffs on the other side; at least one hundred and fifty feet in places. The Buffaloes would take them across and deposit them at the foot of the cliffs, but there was only one way to capture them and that that was to climb.

16 Cdo was to turn left to attempt to capture a road bridge on that flank. If they succeeded it would be big help in getting the infantry across, but Carter held out little hope of that. The Germans had got into the habit of blowing even the smallest bridges to slow the Allied advance. 17 Cdo had been withdraw because they had suffered so

many casualties since crossing the Rhine and had been replaced by another Royal Marine commando, 39. They and 49 would cross the river on 15 Cdo's right flank and the three units would advance north, then west to enter the town.

Danny Glass had been wounded at the Aller, a shrapnel injury to the head, bad enough to need hospitalisation, but he couldn't be kept in a hospital bed. Told that he was to be sent back to England, on the second morning he had risen before dawn, gathered his kit together and walked out, then hitched a ride back to the commando. His head was still heavily bandaged, which brought a lot of comments about turbans and the Indian Army, which made it hard for Carter to avoid seeing him.

But he did avoid it, officially at least.

If he or the medical officer were officially notified that Glass was absent without leave from the field hospital he would have to be arrested and Carter didn't want to have to do that.

Prof Green made sure that Glass was kept as far from the HQ tent as was possible and if Carter was seen heading in his direction, Glass was quickly moved out of his line of sight. It didn't remove the possibility of the Redcaps[1] turning up to look for Glass, but that was Glass's risk, not Carter's.

The crossing was planned for the night of 27th/28th April. There was no element of surprise other than keeping the Buffaloes concealed behind the dykes and using smoke to hide troop movements. They might as well have held a sign up saying 'we're on our way'.

[1] Redcaps – slang for the Royal Military Police, taken from the red covering for their peaked caps. For similar reasons the Royal Airforce Police are called 'snowdrops'.

* * *

Once more the current was strong, but Carter had learnt from their previous experiences. He started the Buffaloes further upstream this time and let the river push them down towards their selected landing places.

The vehicles had barely slid into the water before the machine guns started firing on them from the heights above the river. Smoke had been laid, but it was drifting too low to conceal them from the defensive positions on the heights. Flares lit up the night, hanging in the sky one their small parachutes and exposing the assault craft. Carter was grateful that Germans didn't seem to have much artillery, not enough to target the whole assault force. The occasional blast of a shell or, perhaps, a mortar bomb, could be heard but it was the machine guns that were most dangerous.

Bullets zipped around like angry wasps, pinging off the Buffaloes armour. The angle of fire allowed bullets to intrude into the body of the vehicles, forcing the commandos to crouch lower and lower and to bunch up around the front of the vehicle. The machine gunner above Carter's head returned fire with his heavy machine gun, then he was gone as a bullet hit him and he crashed to the bottom of the vehicle. A commando pressed forward, scrambled into his place and took up the challenge again. A Bren gun team also stuck its head above the vehicle's side and started to return fire, using the originating point of the enemy's tracer rounds to give them an aiming point.

As the Buffaloes neared the northern bank the angle necessary for the enemy to fire was such that they had to stand up in their positions to aim. On the opposite banks snipers and machine gunners took the opportunity to lay down covering fire.

Artillery shells had been falling on the heights, trying to keep the enemy's heads down, but it ceased abruptly as the forward observers saw the Buffaloes angle upwards as they gained the opposite bank. There was the narrowest portion of foreshore where they could discharge their passengers.

The commandos leapt over the side, the rearmost splashing into the water then wading ashore. Grenades bumped and rolled down the steep slopes to explode amongst the first to attempt the climb.

Men fell.

If Carter delayed for even a second, the men would start to retreat behind the Buffaloes, seeking cover. The attack would stall. Besides, he needed the Buffaloes to go back and start ferrying ammunition across. They would also be needed to evacuate the wounded.

"Come on men!" Carter bawled as loudly as he could to make himself heard. "Let's get these Nazi bastards."

He dashed forward and upwards, grabbing whatever he could to haul himself higher: roots, branches of scrubby bushes, clumps of grass; anything that could give him a hand hold. The firing from the far side of the river was keeping the worst of the enemy fire at bay, but grenades still tumbled down on them. The higher they got, the better their chances as the delay on the fuses would eventually mean the bombs would explode behind them, not amongst them. There was only a limited time the Germans could hang onto them once they had pulled the detonation chord, or they'd risk blowing themselves up.

The only counter to the grenades at the moment was for the men to throw themselves flat when one came near and hope for the best that the blast and the shrapnel was deflected upwards rather than sideways. The number of wounded was increasing through, Carter could see that. It would be touch and go as to whether any of them would make it to the top of the cliffs.

But the commandos still crawled upwards, scrambling for hand holds and toe holds. Working in pairs, one would raise his rifle and fire on the enemy grenadiers while his pal moved another few feet, then they reversed roles so the other could catch up.

Carter had two men with him. He didn't have to look to know it was Glass and O'Driscoll, the Bren gun team. Green wouldn't be far away, Carter knew. Glass's helmet sat on top of his thick bandages like a book balanced on a head, but Carter had insisted to Green that Glass wasn't going to be allowed to take part if he didn't have any head protection. Another sliver of shrapnel in his head could undo the work of the surgeon and would probably prove to be terminal.

Raising his Tommy gun, Carter loosed a stream of rapid fire rounds. Glass and O'Driscoll dashed upwards another few feet before throwing themselves down and planting the bipod of the gun into the ground and sending a stream of point three-of-three rounds upwards. Carter pushed hard with his feet against some tussocky grass and levered himself past them, gaining a few more precious yards.

A grenade bounced by without exploding, while rifle shots cracked above his head. The angle wasn't good for the enemy on the top of the cliffs, they were having to lean further and further over the edge to select targets and that was making it easier for the infantry snipers and machine gunners of the far bank to target them.

Glancing to his right Carter could see that the first commandos were nearing the summit. If enough could gain the higher ground they'd be able to force the grenadiers back into their defensive positions to take cover, which would allow the rest of the men to reach the summit. But it was desperate stuff.

They knew that the enemy on the cliffs were the German marines once again, supported by a battalion of *Volksgrenadiers*. Carter had to admire their bravery. They weren't going to give up their positions easily.

Rushing forward once more, Carter came almost face to face with a German soldier, his arm raised to throw yet another grenade. Without really thinking about it, Carter fired his gun and the man fell backwards, dead.

Carter threw himself flat just in case the German had already pulled the det chord on his grenade, but nothing happened. Raising his head, he realised that he could see some of the \Germans on the left. The cliffs were levelling out near their summit, providing a broader field of fire. Carter aimed at the ones he could see and pulled his trigger until he heard the sound of the flat click that signified he'd exhausted his ammunition. He quickly changed the magazine as Glass and O'Driscoll threw themselves down next to him and brought their Bren gun into action with practised ease.

Caught in the open, the Germans started to retreat, still firing their weapons and throwing grenades, but more and more commandos were reaching the top of the cliffs. They were in no mood to stand for any defiance from their enemy and rushed forward to kill before the Germans could reach the safety of their pre-prepared positions.

It took several minutes to neutralise the Germans defences and continue the advance. Four-nine commando, to his immediate right, had carried the hill alongside his own men, but three-nine, beyond them, had struggled more, so the whole brigade had to wait for them to prevent their right flank becoming exposed. It gave the German marines time to regroup in the broken farmland between the cliffs and the town's suburbs. They seemed intent on making a stand, rather than just abandoning the town to its fate.

Once again Carter had to admire his enemy's determination, but it meant his own commando taking more casualties in the fighting.

The fighting went on for most of the rest of the night, with the commandos skirmishing their way forward and the German marines falling back towards the town.

It ended suddenly. News reached Carter that 16 Cdo had taken the road bridge intact and infantry were now flooding over and into the town by a route that was almost undefended. The same news must have reached the Germans, because they started to surrender in larger and larger numbers, until there was no one left for Carter's men to fight. 39 and 49 Cdos rushed around to the northern side of the town and any hope of retreat ended for the defenders. Moving forward, Carter prepared his positions for a counterattack that would never come.

In the morning he received an unexpected gift. A lorry arrived carrying forty eight bottles of champagne, sent by the Brigadier to be shared with Carter's men. Apparently, it was part payment for a bet on a horse race, a vice that gave Vernon a great deal of pleasure and more than a little pain. It seemed like a fitting end to the battle for the men to be able to drink a mug of it each. Carter found out later, from Vernon, that the champagne was valued at a thousand pounds; a generous gift, but one typical of the man.

Carter took an unopened bottle for himself and stored it in his big pack. He had a feeling that he might have a use for it in the near future.

As the commando rested on Luneburg Heath, they heard of the suicide of Adolf Hitler and his mistress Eva Braun. The men cheered and shouted abuse towards Berlin. The same day, not far away across the heath, General Dempsey, commander of the British 2nd Army Group, received the surrender of four German Generals, which effectively ended the resistance in Northern Germany. The meeting didn't go well for the Germans and they left the meeting thoroughly humiliated.

* * *

Once the garrison troops arrived to take control of the town, Carter's men were ordered back on the road for their final objective: Lubeck. The ancient port city was just forty miles to their north. Once there, they could go no further without getting their feet wet.

The US 9th Army provided the transport, in the form of tanks and armoured troop carriers, on the back of which the commandos were able to ride.

After all that had gone before, 15 Cdo's arrival in Lubeck was something of an anti-climax. Halting outside the town, the commandos prepared to advance. Carter went forward with the commander of the leading tank unit to carry out a reconnaissance, but in terms of the city's defences, nothing seemed to be manned. Patrols sent into the suburbs reported that there were no soldiers visible and white bed sheets were flying from the windows of houses.

The streets in the centre of the city were too narrow to risk tanks, made even more narrow by the bomb damage caused by several raids over the years of conflict. Lubeck had been the first German city to be targeted by the RAF's heavy bombers, back in 1940. Carter went forward in his Jeep, carrying a flag of truce and flanked by commandos on foot. He was met on the *Rathaus* steps by a German Major, who informed him that the city was his to occupy at his leisure.

After that it turned into a tourist's day out for the commandos. One of them even managed to find a second-hand camera for sale in a shop and used the film that was still inside it to take pictures of his mates posing in front of the most prominent buildings and landmarks, though many of them were little more than ruins.

They were given little time to rest or enjoy themselves, however. The rest of the division arrived and started to occupy the city and the commando was sent thirty miles eastwards to the smaller town of Wismar.

As at Lubeck, a reconnaissance found no evidence of defenders. Carter left most of his men on the outskirts of the town while he led a single troop into the centre.

They soon had to get into defensive positions as they heard the sound of tank tracks. Carter knew they weren't British or American, because none of their armour was closer than Lubeck. To Carter it seemed like a cruel trick of fate to have to fight German tanks when the war was all but over. They had seen no sign of German armour in weeks yet here, in this insignificant little town, the Germans had chosen to defend with whatever they had left.

His men gripped their weapons and waited around the perimeter of the town's central square, ready to do what they could to defend their prize. There was a crash of falling masonry, followed by the grinding of gears as the tank hit something solid and had to extricate itself, but the sound of its engine and its clattering tracks grew louder.

Infantry appeared, ducking in and out of the cover of buildings. Seeing the commandos, they threw themselves flat and prepared to fire. Then the tank appeared.

It was a big one, but Carter could see at once that it wasn't German. For a start it had a large red star emblazoned on the turret. The Russians had arrived.

Carter stood and waved his helmet, pushing his Tommy gun behind his back to show he wasn't going to be aggressive. He shouted at his men not to fire on the new arrivals. A Russian soldier rose nervously, half crouching, half standing. When no one shot at him he stood up straight and shouted something of his own. Carter's German was poor, but his Russian was non-existent.

An officer appeared from behind the tank and strode forward, summoned by the shouting. Carter strode forward to meet him and they exchanged salutes.

"Lt Col Carter. 15 Cdo, British Army." Carter said.

The Russian said something in return, then there was a general relaxation as both sides exchanged tokens of friendship. No one could understand anyone else but, somehow, they made themselves understood. The Russians went away with packets of British cigarettes and cans of bully beef and the British got vodka in exchange. Carter had heard stories of the fiery liquid and gave orders for it not to be drunk until they were safely out of the line and into a rest area.

Neither side seemed to want to leave the town, so Carter radioed back to brigade for orders. While the impromptu barter market continued, Brigade consulted Division, Division consulted Corps and, for all Carter knew, the King himself may have become involved. In the end it was decided that the commandos should withdraw to the outskirts of the town and leave the centre to the Russians.

It was only hours later that they were given fresh orders. The commandos were surprised to be loaded onto trucks and sent twenty miles to the other side of Lubeck, to the town of Neustadt. Here they had a grisly task to carry out.

On 3rd May, as the commandos had been leaving Lubeck to travel east, the RAF had attacked three ships anchored in Lubeck Bay, not far from Neustadt. The ships were the Cap Arcona, Thielbek and an ocean liner, the Deutschland. All three were sunk. But they held a secret cargo.

Concealed in the holds of the three ships were hundreds of concentration camp victims, slave labourers working in the factories of Hamburg who had been rushed north when the city came under threat from the advancing British. Held initially in a barracks in Neustadt that had been used by marines, they had then been loaded onto to the three ships. But, being invisible to the pilots of the attacking aircraft, they had perished when the ships were sunk.

The crews of the ships had been rescued by local craft that went to their aid, but no one even considered the prisoners held beneath the decks.

Now their bodies littered the shoreline and bobbed, lifeless, in the bay.

The commandos were ordered to collect them up and bring them ashore for identification and burial. The Cap Arcona was only half sunk and the bodies still inside it also had to be recovered.

Using Goatley boats, Buffaloes and whatever else could be found in the local harbour, they started the job without complaint, though most of them said it was the worst thing they had done since they had joined the army. Considering that many of them had faced their own possible death several times over, that was a significant statement.

* * *

Carter replaced the handset of the field telephone into its cradle and sat back in his camp chair. After a lot of energy expended in cleaning, they had made some parts of the barracks habitable and he had allowed himself the luxury of setting up an office in what was once the guard room.

"Sgt Maj Green." Carter called.

"Sir!" Green responded, stepping into the room and coming to attention.

"Are Glass and O'Driscoll around?"

"O'Driscoll's outside with your Jeep, in case you want to go anywhere. Glass is …"

"Never mind trying to tell me he's still in the field hospital, because we both know that isn't true." Carter chuckled. "Tell them to get in here. And bring their mugs with them."

While Green went to do as he had been ordered, Carter went to his big pack, which was sitting alongside a camp bed in the corner of the small room. Compared to what Carter had endured over the previous four months, it was as good as a suite at the Ritz as far as he was concerned. He pulled his bottle of champagne from the pack and started to strip away the foil from the cork.

The three men who had accompanied him around Europe and Africa for the previous four years now filed in and came to attention in front of his desk. Glass's head was till bound in bandages, but they weren't as thick as they had been, though he couldn't yet wear his green beret.

Twisting the cork from the bottle, it came free with a gentle pop. The warm wine fizzed upwards and Green rushed forward to get his mug underneath the bottom to prevent any of the precious wine being wasted.

Filling the other men's mugs, then his own, Carter looked at the three of them as they looked back with a puzzled expression.

"Gentlemen, we have been through a lot together, so I have decided that you should be the first to hear the news. The war in Europe is officially over."

The three men yelled with delight, hugged each other, slapped each other on the back, shook hands and then went round doing it all again. Even Carter, despite his rank, was dragged into the celebration.

"I think this calls for a toast." Green said, when they had calmed down a little.

"I agree." Carter replied. "Let's make it the Scottish toast[1]."

The men formed a loose square facing inwards. Carter raised his mug in front of his face. "Here's to us." He intoned.

"There's none like us." Green took up the baton.

"There's some like us." Said Glass.

"But they're all dead." O'Driscoll finished off.

They drank their champagne down in one long gulp.

"I think I've got some of that Rooskie vodka in my pack." Glass said.

"And it can stay there." Carter replied. "There may not be a war on anymore, but you've still got a job to do and if you're fit enough to drink champagne, you're fit enough to join the men out in the bay. Sgt Major Green, please pass my compliments to the RSM and ask him to parade the commando at sixteen hundred hours today. I shall make the formal announcement."

He watched the backs of the three men as they left his office, grumbling good humouredly about not being allowed a proper celebration.

Then he sat down to continue with what he had been doing before taking the telephone call. Picking up his pen once more, he carried on writing the letter of condolence he had been composing, to the mother of one of his men who had died crossing the Elbe.

[1] Attributed to Robert Burns and learnt by the commandos when they were based in Ayrshire, Burns' home county.

Epilogue

19th November 1945

Victoria Station, London

The train pulled into the platform and doors slammed open, disgorging its cargo of commandos. Commuters leaving another train surged around, colliding with some of the soldiers and contrasting with the khaki of the men who struggled with their large sausage shaped kitbags and heavy webbing. They carried no weapons, those having be handed in to the armory before they left the barracks in Worthing.

That didn't mean none of them were armed, of course. Many carried 'souvenirs' of their travels and combat experience. There wasn't a chest that didn't bear at least one medal ribbon and they would all have more once the bureaucracy caught up and issued them with the war service medals that all military personnel were entitled to receive. But a keen-eyed observer would notice that the number of ribbons for awards for gallantry was higher than might be expected on a body of men of this size.

Regimental Sergeant Major Chalk started shouting orders, the other NCO's picking up the commands and relaying them to their own sections and troops. The men were chivvied into three ranks, their backs to the train, the commuters eddying around them, muttering words of protest at the platform being so obstructed.

How times had changed, thought Carter. A year earlier and those same commuters would have stood aside out of respect for Britain's fighting men, but today they were just an impediment to progress towards the daily grind of work. Carter was reminded of the Kipling poem, 'Tommy', that laments the way that soldiers are treated in peacetime.

Most troops were routed away from London these days. Those arriving back from overseas were loaded onto troop trains that would take them from the docks direct to whatever garrison town they were destined to reside in until their discharge papers came through. The only soldiers who travelled via London were those destined for the barracks in the nation's capital city, or they were travelling independently and had to make connections to other parts of the country. With the ending of hostilities, soldiers were no longer required to wear uniform while visiting the capital on leave.

But these commandos were being scattered to the four corners of the country, so it was decided that the best place for them to disperse was right here.

Carter stood with his officers, to one side of the men forming into their ranks. They would 'take post' when Fred Chalk signalled that order had been restored. The last man to take up his position would be Carter himself.

It had been a busy time for the first few weeks after the commando's return from Germany in early June. After a spell of leave they had thrown themselves into training for Burma once again. Taking up where they had left off in December the previous year; when they had been rushed back into the fighting in Europe. But that training had ended in August, when two incredible new weapons had been exploded above two cities in Japan, forcing that country's capitulation and bringing a final end to the war.

Since then, 15 Cdo had been in limbo, with no one knowing what was to happen with them. Carter had kept them busy, of course, but the men's hearts were no longer in it, he could tell.

Then their own bombshell dropped. The Army commandos were to be disbanded. Combined Operations headquarters had always been dominated by the Royal Navy, who considered that raiding from the sea was their remit, not that of the Army. Now they had got their way. The Royal Marines would now form the backbone of the commandos. The Army was no longer needed, except in specialist roles. The soldiers hadn't even been offered the opportunity to transfer across to the Royal Marines to continue to serve their country in the best way they knew how.

Appeals had been made to the former Prime Minister, Winston Churchill; after all, the commandos had been his brainchild. But he no longer wielded as much influence as he once had. There were new men in power now. As for the new government, they were too busy trying to rebuild the country. The internal politicking of the Armed Forces wasn't going to be allowed to distract them from the job at hand.

Carter looked at the faces of the men, picking out some in particular. So few of them had been with the commando as long as himself. Fewer still had survived from the beginning, when they had first been established in June 1940. There was Green, O'Driscoll and Glass of course, who had arrived from Achnacarry with him in the summer of '41. Andrew Frazer had left them to go to Brigade HQ and was now back with his regiment in Scotland. Molly Brown, who had been with the commando longer than Carter, was now in Burma, waiting to come home. Then there was the indomitable Fred Chalk. He had been in the very first intake. Carter thought that if the world were to end tomorrow, Fred Chalk would emerge from the rubble, dust himself off and start ordering the insects to get things cleaned up.

They would now all disperse, going back to the regiments and corps where they had been serving before they had volunteered for this dangerous life. Those who had been conscripted or had volunteered for the Army on 'hostilities only' terms would soon be discharged. The Territorial Army units would be stood down and their members, including those who had joined the commandos, would return to their civilian jobs, their weekly parades in the Drill Hall and their annual summer camps. The regulars, like Fred, would serve out their time until discharge. Unless, of course, another war started. If Tommy was needed again, it would be soldiers like Fred who would be first to defend the beaches or to board the troop ships.

Carter's future was mapped out. Officially he was posted to his regiment's depot in Huntingdonshire, but the Colonel had telephoned him to say that two Lieutenant Colonels in the barracks, Carter and the CO of the training battalion, was one Lieutenant Colonel too many. Perhaps he was best to sit and wait for his discharge papers at home. Carter had accepted the offer with alacrity. He would work on the farm until the new academic year started in 1946, then take up the place he had been offered at Glasgow University, to finish his undergraduate degree in engineering.

After that? Well, he'd wait and see. There were exciting things happening in aeronautics and rocketry. There was also a sizeable proportion of the world that needed rebuilding and that was the job of engineers as well. And if he didn't fancy that, there was always life on the farm, which he rather enjoyed.

There was a stamping of feet close by and Carter was roused from his reverie by the arrival of Fred Chalk to announce that the commando was ready.

"Officer's take post." The 2IC ordered. He was new, posted in after the end of the European war, to go to Burma, but had been disappointed like the rest of them when it was cancelled. The officers marched away to take their positions in front of their troops, exchanging salutes with the Troop Sergeant Majors.

Finally, Carter was able to take his place in front of his command, facing them.

"Parade ready for your orders, Sir." The 2IC gave a smart salute.

"Thank you, Major Hemmings." Carter returned the salute. He paused to give time for the 2IC to turn around and take his position between 3 and 4 troops and ten paces in front of them. For fifty yards in each direction, he could see the three lines of green berets, the proud symbol of the commandos. Their cap badges were still different, a matter of deep frustration for one and all, but that green head covering still united them and still marked them out as part of Britain's military elite.

The platform was empty of civilians now, the trains standing vacant, waiting for passengers to take back to the south coast.

There would be no speeches today. The hubbub of the station, the hissing steam, the shrieks of whistles and the clatter of couplings, would render him almost inaudible. He had made his speeches when General Laycock had come down to Worthing to take the salute at the farewell parade the previous week.

The night before last he had been hosted to dinner in the Sergeants' Mess, where he had said his farewells to his NCOs, then the previous night there had been a formal dinner for the officers, the table glittering with borrowed silver. The commandos hadn't existed long enough to accumulate any ornaments of their own. It had been a late night, with memories being shared and stories told and the officers doing their best to drink the remains of the mess bar's stocks of alcohol. Before he had made his apologies and left, allowing his officers the freedom to carouse a little without his inhibiting presence, he had asked them to drink a toast to the fallen. It had been the saddest moment of his life.

Carter drew in his breath in preparation. A train whistle screamed and he had to let the breath out until the noise diminished. He tried again to give his final order.

"15 Cdo!" He gave the warning call. "15 Cdo, Dis….miss."

THE END

Historical Notes

By the point in the war's progress at which this book starts, the commandos had been organised into four Special Service brigades. As with their earlier titles of Special Service battalions, the commandos hated the name because of the initials and many senior officers refused to use it, referring to themselves as Commando Brigades instead. My 5th and 6th Brigades were, in fact, 1st and 4th commando brigades. 1st Commando Brigade consisted of 3, 4 and 6 Cdos and 45 (RM) Cdo, while 4th Commando Brigade was made up 41, 46, 47 and 48 (RM) Cdos. Some swaps were made later in the war as combat depleted commandos were returned home to re-fit. 2nd Commando Brigade served in Italy and 3rd Commando Brigade were in Burma. A full list of all the wartime commandos and their potted histories may be found after these notes.

D-Day was the biggest single military operation ever mounted in the history of warfare. The number of men, ships, tanks and aircraft involved was staggering and it is difficult to imagine such an operation even being contemplated today, let alone being achieved. It was evidence of what nations can do when they put their mind to it and focus all their resources on the task. I have already had my fictitious Brigadier Vernon explain the high-level plan, who landed on which beach, so I won't repeat that.

On Sword Beach, 3rd Infantry Division failed to meet its objective for the first day, which was the capture of the town of Caen, which was a strategic crossroads for the area. They were stopped 5 km (about 3 miles) short of the town. Caen wasn't finally liberated until 4th August, almost two months after the landings. Montgomery was not best pleased, as the ability of the British army to break out of its beachhead depended on the successful capture of Caen.

As a consequence, the Germans were able to reinforce the area in front of the British beachhead and halt further progress. I Corps, which had command of both Sword and Juno beaches, was commanded by Lt Gen John Crocker. He was replaced after D-Day because of the lack of success of both the British and Canadians and was replaced by a Canadian, General Crerar

Their greatest achievement was perhaps the capture of the island of Walcheren (Operation Infatuate, 1 – 8 November 1944) on the Scheldt estuary, essential for the re-opening of the port of Antwerp and the shortening of the Allied supply lines, which stretched all the way back to Cherbourg in Normandy. However, it could only be achieved with the aid of 4th Cdo Bde, who crossed the Scheldt in amphibious vehicles to assault the island after attempts to cross the causeway connecting it to the mainland had failed. By the end of the war the Corps had barely entered Germany, halting to the south of Bremerhaven.

With the battle to take Caen concentrating the minds of the Corps commander, it is unsurprising that 6th Airborne Division, with 1st Commando Brigade attached, spent so long in the front line. It was the normal practice to rotate troops at regular intervals, each unit usually not spending more than one week in three in direct contact with the enemy (a pattern that had been established during the First World War). Troops not in the line spent a week 'resting', which usually meant moving supplies or helping with construction projects, before spending a week in reserve prior to their return to the front line.

With replacement troops all being committed to the battle for Caen and the Battle of the Falaise Gap, it was felt that the paratroops and commandos were vital to hold the British left flank and so were kept in the field for eighty-four days without a break. There may have been a psychological factor in that deployment as well. The Germans would have expected the British to use their best troops for the breakout, who were undoubtedly the commandos and the paratroops. By keeping 6th Airborne where they were, they were saying to the Germans 'this is the direction we intended taking'. It wasn't and if it was intended to fool the Germans, it didn't.

I have fictionalised very little with regard to the prelude to D-Day, operations on D-Day itself and its aftermath. Most of the actions I have described were taken from first-hand accounts (see

Further Reading) and the only details of importance that have been changed are the identities of those who participated. If you found some incidents hard to believe, well, that was the commandos for you. They did some pretty unbelievable things throughout the war.

I have been asked about Steven Carter's age, as some readers feel he seems unfeasibly young for the rank he holds. In the fictional biography I created for Carter, he was born in February 1920, making him 24 on D-Day. First of all, promotion came quickly in the commandos because of combat casualties and they preferred to promote from within, because that was where the commandos' experience lay. Where an infantry battalion might have an older officer posted in from another battalion to take command, that was considered to be inappropriate when such specialist training was required.

Having young commanding officers wasn't that unusual elsewhere in the Armed forces. Wing Commander Guy Gibson, former CO of 617 (Dambusters) Sqn, was just 26 when he died in 1944 and his rank was the RAF's equivalent of Carter's. Gibson was just 24 when he commanded the operation that gained him his fame. So, I feel that Carter's age for his rank is justified, considering the amount of leadership and combat experience I have given him over this series of books. There were certainly real-life officers in the commandos who could match him.

Ramsey's involvement in a raid at Hardelot is fictitious. While Hardelot was raided by commandos on more than one occasion, this wasn't one of them.

The folding bicycles with which the commandos were issued weren't popular. The butterfly nuts that secured the frame were prone to coming loose, causing the bike to fold in half at random intervals. As the troops started off cycling in ranks of three, much as they would march, this not only caused the crash of the unfortunate cyclist, it usually took out the other two cyclists in that rank and any others behind that were unable to take avoiding action. Readers who watch the Tour de France and other cycle racing will be familiar with the scene of accidents within the peloton, but imagine the same thing with rifles, heavy backpacks, radio sets etc. Even when the commandos switched to single file to reduce the risk, troops behind an unfortunate cyclist were still prone to being brought down.

The cycles were heavy to carry along with the rest of the commando's burden. Not only was each commando expected to carry his own kit, he was also expected to carry additional weaponry or stores. A member of the 3 inch mortar team would carry one of the three components that made up the weapon (tube, base plate or bipod), for example, but all the commandos carried something extra: spare magazines for the Bren guns, belts of ammunition for the Vickers guns, mortar bombs (typically two per man strung on a rope around the neck or hung over the handlebars of the bike. Each bomb weighed 10lbs (4.5 kg)). Then there were spare batteries for the radios, climbing ropes etc. The wonder wasn't that so many men 'lost' their bikes, it was that so many clung on to them.

Several landing craft did hit "false" beaches, my father's being one of them. As he was only 5 ft 8 in tall, he struggled in the deep water and was lucky to make it ashore at all. He did let go of his bike – it was either that or let go of the spare radio battery he was also carrying (by then he had been trained as a signaller with the Heavy Weapons Troop). He walked all the way to the bridge, in the company of others like him, but still made good time, arriving at about midday.

Much of the action immediately following the beach landings on D-Day has been fictionalised but conforms to contemporary accounts in terms of the tactics used. The landing craft carrying 6 Tp, 3 Cdo, was hit by an artillery shell, causing heavy casualties. I don't wish to denigrate the combat performance of the 2nd Btn, East Yorkshire Regiment, but they hadn't made the progress expected of them and their advance had stalled, meaning the commandos had to move forward with their flanks dangerously exposed.

The flooding of the fields across the road from the beach was real. The depth of water varied from almost dry to waste deep and even deeper in the ditches that criss-crossed the fields, which meant that some of the commandos crossed almost dry-shod while others struggled through mud and water. As described, many of the mortar bombs fired at the commandos failed to detonate in the mud, otherwise the advance would have been considerably slower and would have caused more casualties. This part of Sword Beach has now been developed, so it isn't possible to see it as 3 Cdo would have experienced it.

The scene depicting the first commandos crossing the bridge was taken directly from the memoirs of Tpr Stan Scott (see Further Reading). He briefly took shelter in a dugout with a Bren gun team from the Ox and Bucks Light Infantry, one of whom, "Bill" Bailey, he met many years later in exactly the same spot, while visiting what is now known as Pegasus Bridge. It was this quirk of history that prompted me to write a reunion for Carter.

Stan Scott identifies the commando killed on the bridge as Tpr Campbell, but the 3 Cdo Roll of Honour doesn't list any Campbell as having been killed. There are four men of that name listed in the 3 Cdo nominal roll, so it must be assumed that it was a case of faulty memory.

The men named as being the first commandos to cross the bridge are Scott himself, Tprs Jimmy Synnott, Ossie Osbourne and Campbell (probably with a first name having the initial A, but this isn't certain) and one unnamed trooper. As none of those names appear in the Roll of Honour, it may have been the unnamed man who was the one who was killed. Peter Young details the conversation that took place (which I have copied almost verbatim) and also records a man being killed crossing the bridge but doesn't provide a name.

The film "The Longest Day" depicts the arrival of the 1st Cdo Bde as a formation of men marching behind Brigadier Lord Lovat (played by Peter Lawford) with his piper, Bill Millin (Leslie de Laspee), playing a jaunty tune as the paratroops stood and cheered, waving their red berets in greeting. All the contemporary accounts show this to be a complete Hollywood fabrication.

The commandos arrived in fragmented groups, much as I have described. Their first arrival was, as I have Carter suggest, a few minutes behind schedule at around 11 am. The whole commando didn't complete the crossing until around 3 pm. Lord Lovat (he was 25th chief (or 'Laird') of the Clan Fraser of Lovat) didn't arrive with his Brigade HQ until around 2 pm.

3 Cdo were given the task of capturing the Merville Battery for the second time on D-Day and it was their 4 and 5 tps that made the attack. The casualty rate was high, with Maj John Pooley the most senior death amongst the commandos. They succeeded in capturing the battery but were unable to fully disable the guns. Once they withdrew, in the face of a heavy counterattack, the battery was brought back into action at various times and became a bit of a thorn in the side of the invasion force, until it was finally captured by the Ox and Bucks Light Infantry on 17th August 1944, as part of Operation Paddle, the eastwards breakout from the beachhead.

The attack by 3 Cdo on the Merville Battery was always a bone of contention for the veterans of the commando. In their opinion the battery could have been silenced by gunfire from ships offshore, thereby preventing a considerable loss of life. This was all the more aggravated by the fact that the commando always knew they wouldn't be able to hold the battery against the Germans because of its isolated position. Their view was that fire from offshore should at least have been attempted before committing ground troops.

The Merville Battery itself is now a museum and there is another museum where the original Pegasus Bridge is displayed.

The 84 days between D-Day and the departure of 3 Cdo from Normandy was taken up with the sort of aggressive patrolling I have described. Many of the incidents I have incorporated into my story really happened, including the destruction of a valuable collection of wine. The attack on the "goulash cannon" was also taken from real life, but I have relocated it for this book. The attack actually took place close to the Merville Battery. The commandos really did stroll around behind the German lines as though they owned the place and were hardly ever recognised. The raid on the cottages, to capture officers, was fictional but similar raids were common during the 84 day period.

Tpr Fred Rabbetts was killed when his patrol encountered a minefield laid by friendly forces in neighbouring positions. He was a good friend of my father's and had been with the commando since before Operation Archery (my Operation Absolom) in 1941.

Peter Young identified the B-26 Martin Marauder bombers that bombed the commando's positions as belonging to the RAF, but they must have been American. Although the RAF used that type of aircraft, it was only in the Mediterranean theatre.

LCpl Ernest Langley was loosely based on Tpr Richard Lawrence, real name Ernst Lenel, who was killed in action om 23rd June 1944 while trying to persuade Germans to desert and cross over to the British lines.

3 Cdo were finally withdrawn from combat when they reached the River Seine, just south of Honfleur, at the end of August 1944. After a few days they left Normandy completely. My father's service records show him arriving back in England officially on 7th September 1944.

In total 1st Commando Brigade suffered the loss of twenty seven officers (18%) and eight hundred and ninety ORs (40%). An infantry officer reading this would probably be shocked by those numbers, but the commandos thought them nothing out of the ordinary.

The majority of the commandos killed on D-Day and in the weeks afterwards, are buried in the Commonwealth War Graves Commission cemetery at Ranville, not far from the Orne bridges. The gravestones of the men of the Parachute Regiment are easy to identify from their cap badge, but those of the commandos aren't so easy to find, because they bear the cap badges of their original regiments. Only the graves of the Royal Marine commandos share a common cap badge.

From December 1944 onwards the only real fiction is the inclusion of Steven Carter and 15 Cdo at the heart of the action, rather than the real people and units. The events described actually happened (though not necessarily in the same units or in the same order) and can be found in the books referenced under "Further Reading". I am particularly grateful for the memories of Tpr Stan

Scott and my own father. On the commando's return to England, Peter Young had been posted to Burma where his adventures continued but aren't relevant to this book. John Durnford-Slater was part of Montgomery's staff and still in close contact with 1st Cdo Bde, but more as an observer than an active participant. I draw on him for strategy, but for action it is my other sources whose stories are recounted here.

After returning to England to undergo "jungle warfare" training, 1st Cdo Bde was rushed back across the English Channel at the end of December 1944 to bolster the northern flank of the British positions during and after what became known as "The Battle of the Bulge". Please don't refer to the film of that name for anything approaching an accurate account of the battle. I would recommend "Snow and Steel" by Peter Caddick-Adams as a far more accurate account.

The 1st Mountain Regiment, Royal Artillery, really were attached to 1st Cdo Brigade, having originally been sent to Europe to support 4th Cdo Bde in the operation to capture Flushing (Vlissingen) on the island of Walcheren in November 1944, in southwestern Holland (Operation Infatuate). They remained with 1st Cdo Bde until after the crossing of the Aller, where they contributed to the artillery barrage that is incorporated into my story.

The trooper who was injured when his Jeep hit a mine, spending three days crawling through the snow to reach the British lines, was Tpr Walter Selby. He survived his injuries, though he was invalided out of the Army.

Why Operation Varsity was allowed to go ahead remains a mystery to this day. There was time to cancel it. While mention is made of the airborne achievements of D Day and the famous debacle at Arnhem, the operation at Wesel gets barely a mention. Even on-line sources report it as a great victory, when it should more properly be regarded as a tragedy. As with Dieppe, I suspect that reputations were at stake and it was allowed to drift into obscurity rather than cause embarrassment. The British parachute and airborne infantry regiments involved in the operation weren't accorded a battle honour for it and that speaks volumes in an army that likes to celebrate its victories. Instead, Operation Varsity was subsumed under the heading of "The Rhine" which was a generic award for all the units that took part in Operation Plunder, including those units who saw little actual fighting.

The padre who took the two German soldiers prisoner at Osnabruck was actually the brigade's RC chaplain, Father Thomas Quinlan, not 3 Cdo's own. The story appeared in the Illustrated London News published on 25th May 1945.

It was 6 Cdo that actually carried out the bayonet charge through the forest on the northern bank of the Aller. It is believed to be the last time a bugle call was used to commence such an attack in the British army.

The commandos were ordered not to approach Belsen (Bergen-Belsen to give it its full title) concentration camp as it was thought that they might exact summary justice on the guards who were still inside the camp. There was also a typhus outbreak which could have infected the British troops. The first troops to actually enter the camp were artillerymen from the US Army, who were attached to 11th Armoured Division. They had been chosen because they had been vaccinated against a wide range of infectious diseases prior to their leaving the USA, unlike their British allies who were less well protected. They were relieved by British and American medical units who provided medical assistance to the prisoners.

By agreement with the Camp Commandant, who had crossed the Allied lines of 12th April 1945 to negotiate the camp's surrender, the guards were put under arrest as PoWs, not as war criminals. However, many later faced war crimes tribunals for their offences.

The camp authorities had tried to bury some of the dead in an attempt to conceal their treatment of them, but that task was too great to be completed because of the speed of the British advance. It was thought to be the reason why the fighting for the river crossing was so fierce, to allow time for that. 60,000 starving prisoners were discovered along with 13,000 unburied dead. 45 former camp personnel stood trial for war crimes. The former commandant, Josef

Kramer, 16 male SS guards and 16 female guards were convicted of committing war crimes at the camp. 11, including Kramer, were sentenced to death, the remainder were either acquitted or given prison sentences.

During its existence as a concentration camp (it had previously been a PoW camp) over 120,000 prisoners had passed through its gates, mainly Jews, Poles, Russians, Dutch, Czechs, Germans and Austrians. Most of the Jews were later sent to extermination camps such as Auschwitz, though there were still some present in the camp when it was liberated. Their omission from the transports to the death camps was probably related to their usefulness to the Nazis in the running of the camp.

My father and other sources recall that German soldiers taken prisoner in the weeks after the liberation of Belsen were subjected to "rough handling", though no one elaborates on what that term might mean. I think it is safe to assume that some degree of physical violence was involved, though there is no record of prisoners dying as a result of their treatment.

The gift to the commando of champagne was real. The winning horse was "Court Martial" owned by Lord Astor and it won the 2,000 Guineas. He went on to win the Champion Stakes and came third in The Derby. The winner of the bet and real donor of the champagne was Brigadier John Durnford-Slater. He also won £1,000 in cash, worth around £43,000 today, giving the champagne the same approximate value. The high price of the champagne is related to the production difficulties caused by the war, making the wine a very expensive luxury.

The bombing of the Cap Arcona and the other two prison ships anchored in Lubeck Bay was the result of faulty intelligence. The Allies had received information that the three ships were going to be used to smuggle high ranking Nazis out of Germany, which is why the attack was ordered. With the concentration camp victims concealed below deck there was no visible sign that the intelligence was wrong, so the attack went ahead.

The bombing took place on 3rd May 1945, the day before the hostilities formally ceased in the area. VE Day followed on 8th May.

2,000 prisoners on board the Deutschland were rescued by the trawler Athena. Only 50 out of 2,800 on board the Thielbek survived, all by their own efforts and 200 out of 5,000 survived from the Cap Arcona, also through their own efforts. The victims came from at least 30 countries, including some Americans. They were buried in a number of mass graves in the local area. Bones from those whose bodies weren't recovered continued to be washed ashore for years afterwards. There are several monuments to the victims in the local area.

The final scene, told in the Epilogue, was lifted straight from the Daily Mirror newspaper, which ran a picture and a short piece on the disbandment ceremony for 3 Cdo held at Victoria Station. It is also referred to by Stan Scott. 3 Cdo were sufficiently famous for their final parade to attract the attention of the daily newspapers. The background to the end of the Army commandos was as I described it. They were no longer needed in such large numbers and the role would be carried forward by the Royal Marines, who still carry the commando legacy to this day.

The personnel of 3 Cdo earned 6 Distinguished Service Orders (DSOs), 23 Military Crosses (MCs), another 33 Military Medals (MMs) and 5 Distinguished Conduct Medals (DCMs). A further 18 Mentioned-in-Dispatches (MiDs) are recorded and one George Cross. It may seem surprising that there were no Victoria Crosses awarded to the commando, but in a unit where bravery is commonplace it was probably hard to appear brave enough to receive such a high award. 8 Victoria Crosses were awarded to commandos in other units.

The 3 Cdo Roll of Honour on the Commando Veterans' Archive website records the names of 188 men who died while serving with the unit in its 5 years in existence. This does not include those men who served with 3 Cdo for a period but who died while serving with other commando units.

The 3 Commando Nominal Roll, from the same source, records the names of 1,413 soldiers who served with the commando at some point – and the list isn't complete. Given that a commando unit was never more than 400 strong, even allowing for sizeable numbers of men being posted to other units at various times and having to be replaced, the commando was effectively completely re-formed 3 times because of casualties. That would be like every player in a football team being substituted because of injuries, then all of the substitutes being substituted and then most of them being substituted as well. If you were to suggest such a possibility to the CO of an infantry battalion, he would think you insane. Even during the First World War, bad as it was, no unit suffered casualty levels on that scale.

It might be expected that such well-trained, highly motivated men would be welcomed back into their units with open arms. Sadly, this wasn't the case for many. They had committed the cardinal sin of disloyalty to the regiment by volunteering for other duties.

The number of NCOs in a battalion is fixed, so many highly decorated individuals suddenly appearing through the barrack gates was a cause of friction, rivalry and more than a little jealousy. Most of the men who had earned promotions to NCO rank in the commandos had to take demotions if their service was continuing. Stan Scott found that he had 'volunteered' to join the Royal Military Police, his new CO having decided that his commando service made him suited to the roll. Stan disagreed but had no say in the matter. He wasn't the only former commando to suffer such indignities. I don't mean that as a slur on the Royal Military Police, or any other unit, only as an indication of how little respect was accorded to the returning commandos.

My father had joined the Middlesex Regiment in 1938. They were one of four specialist machine gun regiments, so he was posted to the Machine Gun Training School at Chester, who had no idea what to do with him. For the next 7 months he was given "make work" tasks to carry out (peeling spuds, washing dishes, sweeping floors, etc) or he performed sentry duty. Eventually he was posted to a battalion in Germany to resume his military career with his regiment but, again, he wasn't exactly treated like the prodigal son.

My father hadn't been given any promotions while in the commandos. I have no idea why but, perhaps, in an elite unit he just hadn't stood out enough. He earned promotions quickly in his battalion though – and promptly lost them again. Alcohol seems to have played a part and, I think, with 21st century hindsight it is possible to conclude that he was suffering from post-traumatic stress disorder (PTSD). That was not something that the Army recognised back in the 1940s and 50s and so it would not have been diagnosed or even suspected. However, he did eventually hold onto his stripes and my father concluded his military service in 1962 with the rank of Company Sergeant Major. Unfortunately, the decoration that is missing from his collection is the Long Service and Good Conduct Medal, because bis past misdemeanours had rendered him ineligible to receive it.

Of all his military service, it was the commandos that gave my father the greatest pride. He rarely spoke to his family about what he had done or seen, but he never missed the reunions where he could share his memories with his former comrades in arms - probably the only people who could understand what they had all been through.

As I write the closing sections of this book, my father's medals hang in their frame on the wall, within touching distance. Needless to say, they are one of my most prized possessions.

* * *

The Army commandos were established in June 1940 on the direct orders of Winston Churchill. The original concept, a force that could raid across the channel into occupied France, was the brainchild of Col (later Brigadier) Dudley Clarke, a Royal Artillery officer who was a genius at devising deception operations. His suggestion found its way to Churchill's ear and he was taken by it.

It was Churchill who recognised that to maintain the war effort until victory could be achieved, he needed to maintain the morale of the British people following the disaster that had been the evacuation from Dunkirk. The skilful use of propaganda had turned that defeat into a sort of victory, the 'miracle of Dunkirk', but genuine victories, however small, would be needed if he was to convince the British people that the war could be won.

It would be the commandos that would provide those small victories. Often the targets of their raids were insignificant in military terms but, on occasions, they had a far greater impact than could ever have been imagined. For example, following successive raids on Norway, Adolf Hitler became convinced that they were the prelude to an invasion of that country as a steppingstone for invading Denmark and then Germany itself. No such plan existed, but Hitler ordered 300,000 additional troops to be sent to Norway, where they remained for the rest of the war, along with additional Luftwaffe and naval units. The fact that the invasion of Norway never came about was proof to Hitler that his counter-strategy had worked. Had those troops been available at Stalingrad, El Alamein or in Normandy in 1944, who knows how the outcomes of those battles might have been affected.

15 Commando is a fictitious unit. The Army commandos were numbered 1 to 14 (excluding 13). 50, 51 and 52 commandos were formed in North Africa.

The Parachute Regiment were formed from No 2 Commando, who had originally been set up to take on the role of paratroops. Even after the establishment of the Parachute Regiment in 1942, the commandos still trained some of their troops in parachuting, though there is no record of them ever having undertaken that role.

No 10 (Inter Allied) Commando was made up of members of the armed forces from occupied countries in Europe who had escaped. There were two French troops, one Norwegian, one Dutch, one Belgian, one Polish, one Yugoslavian and a troop of German speakers, many of whom were Jewish. They often accompanied other commandos on raids to act as guides and interpreters, as well as carrying out raids of their own.

Achnacarry House is the ancestral home of Clan Cameron and it was taken over by the War Office to become the Commando Training Centre. The original occupants of the house moved into cottages in the grounds. During the course of World War II over 25,000 commandos were trained there, plus some of their American counterparts, the Rangers, who were modelled on the commandos. Originally each commando was responsible for providing their own training, before the first training centres were set up at Inveraray and Lochailort, in late 1940, before moving to Achnacarry.

The first Royal Marine commandos didn't come into being until 19th February 1942. 40 (RM) Cdo was, like the army commandos, made up of volunteers, but subsequent units (41- 48) were RM battalions who were ordered to convert. For this reason the army commandos tended to look down on their RM counterparts. However, the RM commandos fought bravely and in all theatres of the war. They carried the commando legacy onwards at the end of the war and continue to do so to this day.

If you wish to find out more about the Army commandos there are a number of books on the subject, including my own, which details my father's wartime service; it's called "A Commando's Story". I have provided the titles of some of these books at the end of these notes. These also provided the sources for much of my research for this book and the others in the series.

This final volume in the Carter's Commandos' series concentrates on operation is North West Europe before, during and after D-Day. Once the war was over there was a review of commando operations to decide their future. Commodore Louis Mountbatten had been Head of Combined Operations prior to his departure to India to become Viceroy and he had stamped the Royal Navy's imprint on that organisation. As such, it was decided that the future of commando operations lay in the hands of the Royal Marines.

As for Carter, is his story over?

Well, to quote a Winston Churchill speech made at Westminster College, Fulton, Missouri on 5th March 1946. "From Stettin in the Baltic to Trieste in the Adriatic, an iron curtain has descended across the Continent [...] The Communist parties, which were very small in all these Eastern States of Europe, have been raised to pre-eminence and power far beyond their numbers and are seeking everywhere to obtain totalitarian control."

Elsewhere in the world there are other communists struggling to gain power and in China they will succeed under the leadership of Mao Tse Tung. Such success provides encouragement for others o continue the fight. Also, many former colonies of European nations are reluctant to accept the return of the authority of the colonial powers and are willing to take up arms to stake their claims to becoming independent nations.

Surely, against that backdrop, there must be new challenges ahead for someone with carter's skill sets.

We shall have to wait and see.

A Brief Account of the World War II Commandos and Their Operations

Having stolen, or at least borrowed, so many of their stories, it would be wrong of me to end this book without recounting something of the doings of the real Army Commandos. It would also be churlish of me not to include the Royal Marine Commandos. Late in the war as they were formed, they also did some pretty amazing things. So below, commando by commando, is a short history of their World War II operations.

1 Cdo: They should have been the first commando to go into action, but that honour went to 3 Cdo. After a stuttering start, caused mainly by political interference and reorganisations, 1 Cdo carried out its first raid on France in August 1941. 1 Cdo later provided a small detachment alongside 2 Cdo at St Nazaire. Sgt Thomas Franck Durrant was awarded a posthumous VC for his part in the raid. The next combat for 1 Cdo wasn't until their participation in the invasion of North Africa (Operation Torch) alongside American forces in November 1942. After returning to the UK the commando were sent to the Far East to join 14th Army. They were very much a part of the Burma campaign, but their most notable action was during the Battle of Hill 170, in the Kangaw region. Lt George Arthur Knowland of 1 Cdo was awarded a posthumous VC for his part in the battle.

2 Cdo: Designated as the "parachute" commando, this set them on a course that resulted in them becoming the 1st Battalion the Parachute Regiment. A new 2 Cdo was raised in February 1941. Their most famous operation was Chariot, a daring raid which crashed the destroyer HMS Campbelltown into the gates of the large dry dock at St Nazaire. It cost them nearly half their men killed or captured, but it put the dock out of use for the remainder of the war, preventing the large German surface raiders from putting to sea because they had no safe harbour to which they could return for repairs, without running the gauntlet of British naval patrols north of Scotland. Lt Col Augustus Charles Newman, CO of 2 Cdo, was awarded a VC for his leadership of the operation. After that they were sent to take part in the operations to capture Sicily and Italy. While in Italy they carried out additional raids on the coasts of Yugoslavia and Albania.

3 Cdo: Of the 38 battle honours displayed on the Commando Standard, 3 Cdo were involved in the actions that resulted in the award of 7 of them, not including the more general awards for campaigns in which the commando took part, such as the Italy campaign and the D Day landings. 3 Cdo were the most active of all the commandos and, thanks to press coverage and newsreels, probably one of the most famous units in the British Army during World War II, for a while at least. They carried out the first recognised commando raid, on Guernsey, in July 1940. It didn't go well but they learnt a lot from it. After that they conducted raids on the Lofoten Islands and Vaagso in Norway in 1941 (Book 1 of the Carter's Commandos series is loosely based on that) and then Dieppe in 1942 (Book 3) when only 80 men of the commando made it ashore in France, having encountered a German E Boat flotilla while crossing the English Channel. After spells in Gibraltar, Algeria and Egypt, 3 Cdo took part in the invasion of Sicily in July 1943 before conducting an abortive attempt to capture a bridge on the River Leonardo (Book 5), ahead of the British advance towards Catania. Because of delays at the town of Lentini, that raid might have caused the loss of the entire commando but didn't result in the award of a battle honour. Thankfully, most of the commando were able to make their way back to the safety of the British lines. In Italy 3 Cdo landed behind German lines on several occasions to force the withdrawal of German forces. As part of a Brigade strength force they captured the town of Termoli (Book 6) during Operation Devon and held out for 3 days, waiting for the 8th Army to repair a bridge and relieve them. They then returned to the UK to train for D Day. On 6th June 1944 they were the commando that raced to Pegasus Bridge to relieve the 6th Airborne Division, before helping to anchor the left flank of the British beachhead for 84 days without relief. Returning to the UK in September, they had to be rushed into Belgium in December 1944 to reinforce the British line during the so-called Battle of the Bulge. As part of 1st Commando Brigade they spearheaded Montgomery's advance into Germany, crossing the Rhine, Weser, Aller and Elbe rivers and capturing the key towns of Wesel, Munster and Osnabruck, before ending the war in Europe on the Baltic coast. In May 1945 they were withdrawn back to the UK to prepare to go to the Far East, but the war ended before they could depart. This was my father's unit, which he joined in time for the Vaagso raid. He remained with them for the rest of the war.*

* Operations described in books 2 and 4 were entirely fictional.

4 Cdo: This commando joined 3 Cdo in their raid on the Lofoten Islands before conducting a raid on Hardelot in France in April 1941. Their next major raid was Dieppe where, unlike 3 Cdo, they got ashore unscathed to attack and destroy a German artillery battery. Lt Patrick Anthony Porteous was awarded a VC for his part in the raid. On D Day they went ashore on Sword beach to capture objectives in the town of Ouistreham before joining the rest of 1st Commando Brigade on the left flank of the beachhead for 84 days, then participating in the breakout and advance along the northern French and Belgian coasts. Their last operation in Europe saw them transferred to 4th Commando Brigade, replacing the combat depleted 46 (RM) Cdo, for the capture of the town of Flushing in the Netherlands as part of the attack on heavily defended Walcheren island, necessary to open the River Scheldt to allow Allied access to the port of Antwerp. Afterwards they remained in the western Netherlands. At the end of the war in Europe, 4 Cdo were billeted at Recklinghausen, Germany, and most of them were posted to 3 and 6 commandos in preparation for departure for the Far East, but the war ended before they could embark.

5 Cdo: This commando's first operation was an unopposed raid by two troops on Hardelot and Merlimot near Boulogne. They also provided demolition parties for 2 Cdo's raid on St Nazaire. In March 1942 the commando was chosen to carry out an operation on Madagascar which was intended to deny the Germans the use of the Vichy French colony as a naval or U Boat base. Following their transfer to India, 5 Cdo carried out several operations in the Arakan, Burma, including landings at Akyab and Mybon and involvement in the battle for Kangaw. They were earmarked as part of the force to invade Malaya, but the war came to an end before the plan could be carried out.

6 Cdo: The commando's first action was Operation Kitbag (December 1941), a raid on Floro in Norway. The raid was aborted before landing when several casualties were caused by a grenade exploding below decks on their landing ship. The Captain of the landing ship was also unsure of their position and thought it better to withdraw than risk running aground. 6 Cdo joined 1 Cdo on Operation Torch, the invasion of North Africa before being withdrawn back to the UK in preparation for D Day. On 6th June, 6 Cdo were part of the force that advanced to Pegasus Bridge to relieve the paratroops. They remained part of 1st Commando Brigade, sharing in the succession of river crossings and the advances into Germany. Like 3 Cdo, they were withdrawn to UK with the intention of transferring to the Far East, but the war ended before they could depart.

7 Cdo: This commando didn't see any action before departing for the Middle East in 1941. Arriving at Alexandria they were designated A Battalion of Layforce (see note on Layforce, below). They saw action in Bardia (Libya) and Crete. Most of the commando was captured on Crete and the remnant of the commando was disbanded.

8 Cdo: This commando was formed from volunteers from the Brigade of Guards and, like 7 Cdo, didn't see action until they joined Layforce as B Battalion. They also took part in the action at Bardia and also provided a force of 80 men during the siege of Tobruk and participated in the defence of Crete. They were eventually disbanded, with many of their members going to units such as the Long Range Desert Group. One of their most famous officers was Major David Sterling, who founded the Special Air Service (SAS), though it wouldn't be known by that name for some time.

9 Cdo: After a raid on Houlgate, France in November 1941 and providing a contingent for the St Nazaire raid, the commando was sent to Gibraltar. After returning to the UK for refitting they returned to the Mediterranean to carry out raids on the islands of Tremiti and Pianosa, off the east coast of Italy. In December 1943 the commando carried out a raid on the Garigliano area, north of Naples. Further operations were carried out in Italy before the commando transferred to Greece, before returning to Italy to end the war in Commachio, south of Ravenna.

10 (IA) Cdo: This was a multi-national commando made up of troops and refugees who had escaped from occupied Europe. There were 2 troops of French, one of Norwegians, one Belgian, one Dutch, one Polish and one Yugoslavian. The final troop was made up of German speaking refugees, many of whom were Jewish. It would be impossible to name all the operations in which this commando took part. Suffice to say, if their country was being raided, the relevant troop would be present in some form or other. They acted as guides or translators on many occasions. The Norwegian and French troops also carried out independent operations against their homelands. On D Day the French troops went ashore at both Ouistreham (Sword Beach) and Arromanches

(Gold Beach) before taking part in the liberation of Paris. The Norwegian, Dutch, Belgian, Polish and German speaking troops also took part in the invasion of Normandy and other operations in France, Belgium, Holland and Germany. The German speaking troop were spread around all the commandos to act as interpreters. One of things they were good at was sneaking close to the enemy front line and persuading the German sentries to desert. The Yugoslav troop went to Italy to participate in raids against Yugoslavia and Albania.

11 Cdo: Called "The Scottish Commando", because of where it was raised. In January 1941 the commando joined Layforce as C Battalion and went to Syria as part of the operation to prevent the Vichy French from giving access to the country to Germany. They attacked the Litani river area of Syria. From their garrison in Cyprus, 11 Cdo provided a small force to carry out a raid to try to capture General Erwin Rommel from his residence in Libya in November 1941. The operation was unsuccessful, mainly because Rommel had left the area several weeks earlier. Maj Geoffrey Charles Tasker Keyes was awarded a posthumous VC for his part in the raid. Suffering from shortages of troops, the commando was disbanded along with the rest of Layforce.

12 Cdo: This commando was formed in Northern Ireland and initially carried out operations against the Norwegian coast. The commando became spilt in two, with one half in Scotland still operating against Norway and the other half based in the south of England for operations against France. Here they provided a recovery party for Operation Biting, a Parachute Regiment operation to capture a German radar station at Bruneval, France and bring back components from it. They also carried out raids against the Channel Islands. The commando was disbanded in 1943 as the focus of the war shifted to the Mediterranean. The personnel transferred to other commandos, mainly 1, 5 and 6.

14 Cdo (not that the commandos were superstitious or anything): This was a short-lived commando, raised in December 1942 specifically for operations against the Norwegian coast. They were involved in two small raids before being disbanded in August 1943.

The Middle East commandos: 50, 51 and 52 commandos were raised in the Middle East from volunteers from the 8th Army. They saw little action until they became part of Layforce, as D Battalion, but were disbanded along with the rest of Layforce.

Layforce: The aim of Layforce, under the command of Col Robert Laycock, was to carry out harassing and disruptive actions against the Italian and German forces in the eastern Mediterranean. The force was made up of 7, 8 and 11 commandos and the three Middle East commandos: 50,51 and 52. Following their actions at Bardia, Litani River, Crete and Tobruk the force was severely depleted and Laycock was unable to obtain replacements. Pressure was mounting from Middle East HQ in Cairo to re-assign the remnants as ordinary infantry soldiers. Thanks to Churchill's intervention, orders were given to form a Middle East Commando, pulling together the remaining elements of Layforce. However, there still weren't enough men to allow the commando to be an effective force in the Mediterranean. While the title "Middle East Commando" remained in place for a while the men were quietly transferred to other commando units operating in the Mediterranean theatre. Laycock was later promoted to Brigadier and given command of 2nd Special Service Brigade, which would become 2nd Commando Brigade (2 and 9 commandos and 40 and 43 (RM) commandos). Their area of operation was Sicily, Italy and the Yugoslav/Albanian coast.

40 (RM) Cdo: The first Royal Marine commando to form in 1942, taking volunteers from the Corps. Because of the attachment of the Argyle and Sutherland Highlanders to the Corps, soldiers from that regiment were also allowed to volunteer for the new commando. 40 (RM) Cdo's first action was a baptism of fire during the Dieppe raid in August 1942. After that a group was selected for special missions and sent aboard HMS Fidelity, a former French merchant ship (La Rhin) converted for Royal Navy service. It was used to drop agents off the south coast of France and the coasts of Portugal and Spain. It was destined to go to the Far East but, unfortunately, on 30th December 1942 the ship was torpedoed close to the Azores while sailing as part of convoy ON154, with the loss of 53 commandos, 274 crew and 55 survivors from the SS Empire Shackleton, which had been torpedoed two days before. In 1943 the commando was transferred to Italy where they were brigaded with 3 Cdo for a while. They then served with distinction, carrying out several raids on the Italian and Yugoslav coasts.

41 (RM) Cdo. Formed from a disbanded Royal Marine Battalion. After serving at Salerno, the battalion participated in D Day as part of 4th Commando Brigade. Like 1st Commando brigade, 41 Cdo landed on Sword beach, but at the western end rather than the eastern end. They later joined 4 Cdo in the assault on Walcheren.

42 (RM) Cdo: Formed from a disbanded Royal Marine Battalion. This commando went straight to the Far East, but not without delays as their ship was bombed in the Mediterranean Sea and they had to wait in Egypt while repairs were carried out. On arrival they served alongside 1 and 5 Cdos in Burma, being involved in many of the same actions.

43 (RM) Cdo: Formed from a disbanded Royal Marine Battalion. Served in Italy, carrying out raiding operations against the Yugoslav coast. Cpl Thomas Peck Hunter was awarded a posthumous VC for actions that took place in Italy on 3rd April 1945.

44 (RM) Cdo): Formed from a disbanded Royal Marine Battalion. Served in the Far East alongside 1 and 5 Cdos, being involved in many of the same actions.

45 (RM) Cdo: Formed from a disbanded Royal Marine Battalion. Formed specifically for the invasion of Normandy, they were part of 1st Commando Brigade, alongside 3, 4 and 6 commandos. LCpl Henry Eric Varden was awarded a posthumous VC for actions that took place in Germany on 23rd January 1945.

46 (RM) Cdo: Formed from a disbanded Royal Marine Battalion. As part of 4th Commando Brigade they went ashore on D Day on Gold Beach. Having suffered heavy casualties, 46 (RM) Cdo was withdrawn to the Isle of Wight in September 1944. They returned to Europe for operations in Germany in 1945 as part of 1st Commando Brigade, replacing 4 Cdo.

47 (RM) Cdo: Formed from a disbanded Royal Marine Battalion. They were also part of 4th Commando Brigade and served in France, Holland and Germany and participated in the attack on Walcheren.

48 (RM) Cdo: Formed from a disbanded Royal Marine Battalion. Part of 4th Commando Brigade, this was the only commando to join the Canadians on Juno beach on D Day. Along with other commandos they formed part of the assault on Walcheren in Holland, where they remained until the end of the war, before moving to barracks in Germany.

RM Engineer Commando: Formed specifically to go ashore ahead of the Normandy landings to demolish or dismantle beach defences. After the landings they carried out other engineering tasks, such as bridge building and the construction of strong points. A section also travelled to the Far East to carry out a similar roll in Burma.

RN Beach Commando: Formed in 1942 after confusion during landings at Diego Suarez, Madagascar, disrupted landing operations. They were specifically formed to take control of beach operations and guide troops to their assigned sections of beach, keep vehicles moving and marshalling the arrival and departure of landing craft.

Their first action was Operation Jubilee, the raid on Dieppe in August 1942. They took part in all the landing operations in North Africa, Italy and Sicily. Their presence was very much in demand for D-Day and their last action was at Walcheren in the Netherlands. They were also present in the Far East and took part in landings at Kangaw.

30 Commando: Formed in 1942 as a specialist intelligence gathering unit, their job was to land and capture material of intelligence value before the enemy had a chance to destroy it. They were made up of specialists drawn from all three branches of the Armed Forces. They first saw action at Dieppe, where it is thought that their objective was to capture a new type of Enigma machine. In 1943 they were renamed 30 Assault Unit and later changed their name back to 30 Cdo (such are the vagaries (at times) of military decision making). They also operated in North Africa, Sicily, Italy and then in North West Europe. They disbanded in 1946, but in 2010 the Royal Marines established 30 Commando Information Exploitation Group, which carries the legacy of the original 30 Cdo.

Small Scale Raiding Force (SSRF). Also known as 62 Cdo. Formed in 1942 as a unit specialising in the handling of small boats for raiding purposes. A typical raiding party would be between 8 and 10 men. About half their numbers were officers. They carried out a number of raids on the coast of northern France and the Channel Islands until they were disbanded at the end of 1943.

Present-day Commandos: At the time of writing, the present-day commandos are all provided by the Royal Marines, with some support provided by Army personnel. They are 40 Cdo, 42 Cdo, 43 Cdo, 45 Cdo, 47 Cdo (Raiding Group), the aforementioned 30 Cdo IX Group, The Commando Logistics Regiment, Commando Engineers and 29 Commando Royal Artillery.*

* The absence of the Special Boat Service from this list might be considered an omission but, technically at least, they are not commandos, they are "Special Forces". They are administered by the Royal Navy, not by the Royal Marines, and are under the operational command of the Director of Special Forces, who also exercises operational command over the SAS.

Further Reading.

For first-hand accounts of Commando operations and training at Achnacarry, try the following:

Cubitt, Robert; A Commando's Story; Selfishgenie Publishing; 2018.
Durnford-Slater, John, Brigadier: Commando: Memoirs of a Fighting Commando in World War II; Greenhill Books; new edition 2002.
Gilchrist, Donald; Castle Commando; The Highland Council; 3rd revised edition, 1993.
Scott, Stan and Barber, Neil; Fighting With The Commandos; Pen and Sword Military; 2008.
Young, Peter, Brigadier; Storm from the Sea; Greenhill Books; new edition 2002.

For a more general overview of the commandos and their operations:

Saunders, Hilary St George; The Green Beret; YBS The Book Service Ltd; new edition 1972.

A wealth of information, photographs and personal accounts can be found on the Commando Veterans Archive website:
http://www.commandoveterans.org/

And Now

Both the author Robert Cubitt and Selfishgenie Publishing hope that you have enjoyed reading this story.

Please tell people about this eBook, write a review on Amazon or mention it on your favourite social networking site. Word of mouth is an author's best friend and is much appreciated. Thank you.

Find Robert Cubitt on Facebook at https://www.facebook.com/robertocubitt and 'like' his page; follow him on Twitter @**Robert_Cubitt**

For further titles that may be of interest to you please visit our website at **selfishgenie.com** where you can sign up for our newsletter.

Printed in Great Britain
by Amazon